Strikers

Ann Christy

Also by Ann Christy

For Jordan
From tiny baby
to princess under a cloud of white hair
to brilliant student and actress
to working mother and wife,
you have always been the first,
and brightest, star in my sky.
I Love You

Chapter One

The streets are busy, streams of people joining the flow of bodies from every corner and alley, all of them moving toward the town center. Dust rises from the sun-baked streets in a low cloud from so many feet and the chatter is loud in the morning air.

I jump up on a bench and scan the moving crowd for familiar faces. Cassi's bright hair draws my attention from across the narrow dirt road. Her red-gold curls stand out in a veritable sea of brown. I raise my arm in a wave, hoping she'll see me. When that doesn't work, I cup my hands around my mouth and call out her name. It's loud enough to earn me a few looks from people passing by, but it does the trick because she looks around, searching for me. When she finally sees me, she gives me a wide, happy grin and beckons me over with impatient swoops of her hand.

I hop down from the bench, raising another small cloud of dust and weave through the moving crowd with a minimum of bumps and apologies on the way.

"Where's Connor?" I ask once I gain the relative safety of the strip of paving stones that make up the sidewalk.

Before Cassi can answer, we see him bobbing his way through the crowd with ease, on his way to join us. He pushes back the light brown hair that perpetually falls into his eyes and gives us both a cocky grin.

"Hello, ladies. Did I miss the parade?" he asks.

Out of habit, I look him over. The two dark lines on his neck are still only two in number, which is good, but he has that strained look behind his grin that tells me there is trouble brewing.

He notes my look and whispers, "Later, Karas." The emphasis on my name lets me know that what he has to say is for me alone. Cassi is sweet and loves us both, but that's the problem with Cassi. She *is* sweet and doesn't like to hear about the bad things in life. Everyone shields her, and that includes Connor and me.

"Noooo," Cassi says, drawing out the word to note her impatience. "But we will if we don't get moving."

We set out together, keeping to the sidewalk in a tight huddle as we make our way toward the main street and the town square that waits there. I shove my hands into the pockets of my jacket against the cool spring morning and kick my favorite boots together to knock the dust off. They're Texas Army issue, bought because they last and are cheap, but they're comfortable. I've dimmed down the military part by adding something of my own to them, a pair of sky blue laces. I traded a half pound of my better quality slingshot stones for them. Not a great trade, but worth it.

"It's probably just more people from the wild lands. There are always more of those," Cassi says with a sigh.

"I doubt it's just Wilders. They don't cross the borders just to cross them. They come for a reason. Smuggling or raiding, maybe," Connor counters and pushes back his hair once more.

He needs a haircut but I know he won't get one at home. To be more precise, he won't get one unless whatever scheme his parents are cooking up requires a clean cut boy to make it work. I make a mental note to bring some scissors to school when Monday rolls around and corner him after classes.

"Well, then it's probably some Strikers," Cassi says and then stops, realizing what she said. She gives Connor a sidelong glance full of apology and adds, "Probably not though, and I'm sure it's nobody we know if it is."

I drop one hand from my pocket and let it find Connor's as we walk side by side. While Cassi keeps her eyes forward in embarrassment at her thoughtless comment, I give his hand a quick, reassuring squeeze and then let go. It's enough. He knows I'm here for him.

Both of Connor's older brothers were Strikers, meaning they attempted to leave Texas, an illegal act. His oldest brother waited too long to make a break for the border and had four strikes on his neck when he finally did. He got caught, earning his fifth and final strike. Declared a Habitual Offender, he was put down less than twenty-four hours after being returned to the Bailar jurisdiction. He faced his justice without ever getting a chance to see his family since they were off on the venture that had earned Connor his first strike.

His next older brother was smarter, going Striker and making for the Texas border before the tattoo of his third strike had fully scabbed over. Had Connor been able to, I think he might have gone with him. The two strikes on his neck—one for selling some cure-all elixir of his parents' and the other for collecting plants for their concoction from private property—gave him ample reason to try. He didn't though. So far, Maddix hasn't been caught and he's been gone six months. He has to be beyond the northern border and well into the wild lands by now. All I can do is hope, along with Connor, that he isn't among the unfortunate people we'll see paraded past today.

To break the mood and get them talking again, I say, "It could be anything, but it's probably not pirates breaking the blockade sailing ships here in our desert and it's probably not Climbers that came over the wall hundreds of miles south of here. It's probably smugglers. It's almost always smugglers."

Cassi has decided views about the romantic nature of pirates and the sea in general, mostly informed by romantic tales rather than our history lessons at school. We live in North Texas so it's odd that she loves the sea, a sea we've never seen and aren't likely to, at that.

It works because she says, "Pirates are probably nothing like they tell us in civics class. I think they're probably just trying to break the blockade—maybe even disarm the mines in the Gulf—so we can get to the sea again."

Connor laughs and I'm relieved because it's a genuine laugh. He's had a crush on Cassi since before I can remember and does his best to burst any bubbles she might have on the noble nature of pirates. Not to mention that there are probably more mines than fish in the Gulf and all of them have been searching those waters for a ship to detonate under for over a century. And every time a boat does try to leave the coast, the mines find it.

"And they're probably all handsome and carry maidens with curly hair away to their beautiful ships, sailing away into the sunset," he teases.

The sudden somber mood is well and truly broken and they chat about whatever ridiculous thing Cassi has imagined lately as we cross the last block to the square. Several hundred people line the two-block-long square and we have to jostle our way through to find a good space to watch from. Rather than try for the furthest corner, nearest the area where the prisoners will come from, we settle for a spot near the middle.

The winter brown grass is beginning to show signs of greening and signs posted around the square advise us to keep off the grass in emphatic red script. They even have exclamation points in case the red doesn't get our attention. Everyone is very careful to remain on the narrow sidewalk surrounding the square, me included. Little violations like that won't earn anyone a strike, but they cost money and most people don't have much of that rattling around in their pockets.

Once we're settled, the cold seeps in. We huddle closer to share a bit of warmth while we wait for what Bailar cleverly calls a "Parade." It isn't mandatory to come to every parade, but it is one of those things that everyone knows they should come to. It's one of those things that if you don't show up often enough, it will be noted down somewhere and your loyalty might come into question.

My ears start to sting from the cold, so I pull my hair out of its standard ponytail and wrap it around my neck instead. It's weird looking, but it works. I'm going to miss this handy scarf when I finally do sell my hair. It won't stay in place if I move, but so long as I'm standing here, I might as well be a little warmer. Connor gives me a look and shakes his head.

With school out and many people off work for the weekend, there's quite a crowd for today's event. And more than half the faces I see around me wear those carefully neutral expressions that don't completely hide the fact that they'd rather be somewhere else. A good number of them probably have a Striker somewhere in their family line, or a smuggler, or both. Seeing prisoners paraded past is a special sort of pain for them, not knowing what day will be the day they see their loved one on their way to die.

"I hope they get here soon," Cassi complains as she bounces on her toes in the cool air, hands shoved deeply into her jacket pockets. Her jacket is thin, thinner even than mine, and has likely been worn by every one of her older siblings before her. Bright floral patches reinforce the elbows and collar and it makes the old denim look fashionable and purposeful.

She has the kind of mother who will go to the trouble of choosing just the right fabric, saving up for whatever small piece might be needed, and then sewing it so her daughter can be proud in her hand-me-downs. Neither Connor nor I have that and it shows.

My jacket is old and too tight around the shoulders and chest. I've been saving up what I can to buy a new one for next winter, but it's hard when the only jobs I can get are the crap ones available to a sixteen-year-old who already has a strike. Mostly, I muck out stalls or haul soiled hay out to the composting operation just outside of town. It's nasty work, but reliable, and I usually have Connor for company.

Connor's jacket is huge on his wiry frame, almost swallowing him from neck to knee. It belonged to his older brother, a much bigger boy than Connor will ever be. I'm not short for a girl, or particularly tall for that matter, but at the same height as me, he is decidedly short for a guy. He starts to shrug out of the oversized coat at her complaint, but Cassi stops him with a wave of her hand and gives him a smile.

Cassi's wish for the soldiers to hurry comes true, because the piping toot of a horn from the escort vehicle sounds from somewhere beyond the square. A moment later, the tiny electric vehicle comes into view and crawls along at a walking pace toward the square.

Like everyone else, I try to look behind it to see what I can see, but the car has created a cloud of thick dust behind it at least twice the size of the car. It obscures anything I might see, and just looking at it raises a tickle in my throat.

It was a dry winter, only a few paltry dustings of snow and far too few good rains. The amount of dirt that flies into the air with every movement tells me, and everyone else, exactly how dry it was. We're all hoping for a wet spring. We need the grasslands around Bailar to green so the cattle will prosper. Without a generous spring, we won't have enough grazing land to support the calving season and the long summer of the calves' growth. So far, we're not getting our wishes and it's already mid-March.

The car speeds up to a running pace, then stops abruptly as it comes even with the first people watching. A youngish soldier pops up out of the open top and says something to someone in the crowd. They don't normally do that. Instead, they generally pace the lines of prisoners behind them. That he's gossiping means there's something—or someone—of note in his line. I can't hear what he's saying but I can see a ripple of agitation move through the crowd as I squeeze out of the crowd to peer down the block.

The ripple fades quickly and the car start-stops its way toward us, the soldier calling out to friends every so often as they move along the street. I don't know the soldier, though I've seen him around. He doesn't stop near us, but I hear him anyway and my heart sinks.

A group of Strikers and smugglers has been caught. That isn't good. I was holding out hope that they were just people from the wild lands that no one knew. I look at Connor and see lines of anticipatory pain on his face. There aren't that many people who try to go Striker, percentage wise, in the population and he's already lost one brother. He stares toward the approaching cloud of dust behind the car as if he might see through it if he looks hard enough.

I hope with everything I've got that his brother isn't in that group. *Please, please*, I think, *he can't take more loss.*

A lot of Strikers turn to smuggling, so getting caught during their initial escape from Texas isn't the only risk they run. They know the territory inside the border and they can make a good living being hired out for smuggling runs if they manage to avoid getting caught. But they *are* caught often enough for it to be foolish in my eyes. I don't think any potential profit would be enough to make me try my luck at smuggling if worse comes to worst and I have to escape as a Striker.

The soldier and his car pass us by. He's young and I know his face. From a good family without a strike between them, he wouldn't have associated with me or my ilk, but I remember him well enough. He graduated last year and, like most members of the better families in the Bailar territory, joined the Texas Army for his short—and safe—stint of service.

The car jerks to a stop just past us and the soldier pops out and waves at someone in the crowd with a grin. I turn to see who it is and feel my face flush immediately. Not twenty feet from me, just the distance of the dozen people crammed together between us, stands Jovan Foley.

Almost a head taller than anyone else around him, he waves a hand at the soldier and returns the teased greeting, assuring him that it will be him doing the capturing of Strikers next year. His smile is genuine and wide, his perfect teeth flashing from between equally perfect lips. He's so obscenely perfect I can't even keep looking at him.

I look away and try to focus on Connor because he'll need my support if his brother is in this group. As tense as he is, with his shoulders bunched up, he'll need the support of a friend even if his brother *isn't* in that line.

I reach down and clasp his hand in mine. It's cold and sweaty, which is a surprisingly unpleasant combination, but I don't let go. I see Cassi has his other hand folded between both of hers at his other side. He gives my hand a quick return squeeze and flashes a look of gratitude my way. It makes me glad that he can take comfort from us being here with him. I'm not sure it would comfort me if our positions were reversed. If it were me, I'd probably want to be alone and seethe in frustration with no one to interrupt me.

As the dust settles back to the ground, vague shapes come into view, visible enough so that I can see the prisoners are in a single column. At about the point they come even with the square, perhaps a block away in terms of distance, the figures become clear enough that I can start to make out details.

The line of people walks toward us in jerky forward movements, the chains that bind them neck to neck making it difficult for them to stay in step. It's always like this, but at least there's only a single line of prisoners today. When there are a lot captured, they string them along in multiple lines and they fall all over each other. Fewer prisoners means less chance that Connor's brother is among them, too.

There are an even dozen, eleven men and a person I think might be a woman trapped in the center of the line. I scan the faces but Connor's small gasp next to me makes me follow his gaze. And there he is.

Chapter Two

Maddix Blake is fourth in the line and his face bears the marks of his capture. I'm surprised I even recognize him. Both his eyes are blackened and the nose between them is swollen to twice its normal size. Dried brown blood cakes his nose, chin and shirt. The only clear spot on his face is around his lips, where he's clearly been licking them in the dry air. He's searching faces in the crowd, no doubt looking for his family, but he has yet to see Connor.

Connor seems frozen where he stands and just stares at Maddix, even after I give him a shake. His lips are parted and his brows are drawn together. It's his way. He shuts down when he's hurt. He's not like me. My anger boils up so high that I can't feel the hurt anymore. If this were a brother of mine, I'd be screaming my head off and doing something stupid. Instead, it's like he's waiting for a blow to fall, going inside himself so the part of him that has to live each day misses all the pain.

I lean in and whisper into his ear, "He only has three strikes. Escape will give him a fourth but he's over eighteen now. He can get a job in the fields away from your parents and start earning them off. He'll come through this."

For a moment I don't think Connor has heard a word I said because his eyes don't shift, or even blink. Then he turns to me and says, "Escape is a fourth strike, but he should have been long gone by now. He must have been caught smuggling." He looks at me and his eyes are so sad I want to cry. Then he says what I've just figured out: "That will be a fifth strike. Habitual."

There's nothing we can do and we both know it. Like everyone else, we'll just have to wait and see what's decided. It's a helpless feeling. Maddix is still searching the crowd. It's drawing the ire of the others in the line as his movements jerk the chain they all must contend with. I can't do much, but I can ease his mind.

I raise my arm and wave to draw Maddix's attention until he finally sees us. I point at Connor and see the conflicting emotions spread across Maddix's battered face. There's sadness and fear but also something very close to relief at seeing his brother safe.

The bulky coat obscures any view of Connor's neck and I can see Maddix doing his best to look, no doubt checking to see if Connor has earned another strike. I hold up two fingers and Maddix gives me a nod and a smile. It's grotesque on his battered face and the movement has caused blood to flow from his nose again.

He loses his footing as a jerk ripples through the chain from some misstep behind him. He struggles to stay upright as the metal collar around his neck digs in and pulls. When he gets his feet back under him, his eyes meet mine again. His gaze is steady and he points with his chin toward the front of the line.

I don't see what he's looking at. I don't know the three ahead of him so I give him a shrug. He jerks his chin again and mouths the word "first" at me.

I scan the first man in line again. They're all caked in so much dust from walking however many miles behind the car I can't even tell what color their clothes might be. Only small glimpses of black or blue interrupt the nearly uniform coating of brown. Even their faces and hair are an almost even tan color.

The first man in line is just another brown and dusty figure, though he looks older somehow to my eyes. Dark creases in the dust on his face near his eyes show where crow's feet have spread. He's looking around at the crowd with the same intensity Maddix had, studying faces and then jerking his head on to the next.

A glance back at Maddix earns me a quick, imperative nod so I figure there must be something here I should know. I raise an arm to draw the man's attention. It's apparently too tentative a gesture to stand out in this crowd so I buck up some nerve and shout, "Hey!"

He sees me, gives me a once-over and then studies my face for a moment. The way he's looking at me makes me feel strange. I start to back up a step to hide in the crowd again.

Suddenly, he smiles at me and shouts, "Karas!"

The soldier walking along the line hurries forward and hits the man in the back with his stick so hard that he staggers. He looks away from me long enough to shuffle awkwardly and regain his precarious balance. The blow he takes makes me flinch for him. I know how it must have hurt. But it also stops me from moving backward and into the safety of the anonymous crowd. How does he know my name?

The joy in his face when he saw me was impossible to miss. He looked at me like I was the most important sight in his world. It was familiar and strange all at once. I try to see past the dust and dirt, but it has dulled his features and made him seem just like all the others in the line. Just another body headed for justice and then gone forever. I have no clue who he might be.

He seems to understand that I don't recognize him. He leans to the side a little and strains his neck above the metal collar to reveal something underneath. After a few tries, I can see it's a word, boldly tattooed in big letters on the side of his neck: *Free*.

I can feel myself stumbling back and I grab the arm of a stranger to keep from stepping on the street and getting a fine. It's the shock of that particular word tattooed in that particular style that does it. It can't be who I think it is.

He's moving past me now, further down the long square, but I search his face once more, trying to match it with the few tattered photos I've managed to save over the years. He's much older than in the photos so there's really no way to tell. If it really is him, he's the last person in the world I expected to see today and I forget about Maddix and Connor and everything else.

I have to see him again, so I push through the crowd and leave Connor and Cassi behind. I know it's rude, but I shove my way through the tightly packed people, not really hearing the muttered curses or shouts that follow me. My hand contacts something that doesn't move away. It's hard yet yielding at the same time. Then that something grabs my arm. I look up to see Jovan, his face intent on mine and his long fingers completely encircling my arm.

"What's wrong, Karas?" he asks. His gaze is solemn and concerned. I think it is the first time he's spoken to me in almost two years except for the standard "Hey" when we meet in the hall at school.

"That man. I...I...it's important," I stumble for words but there just aren't any. Everything wants to come out in a jumble. Instead, I try to pull my arm from his and move away. I know I look frantic, panicked even, but I just need to go. I yank my arm again.

Jovan doesn't let go. He looks at the line of prisoners and then back at me. He gives me one quick nod as if my incredibly incomplete answer made perfect sense and settles the matter.

His grip on my arm doesn't loosen as he half drags, half leads me through the crush of people. I feel like I'm about four years old but at least I'm making progress. People move aside for him and when they don't, he makes a path by saying, "Coming through. Make a hole!"

His tone couldn't possibly be mistaken for a request and people melt away in front of him. It's just another way in which being a Foley pays off.

During a parade no one is supposed to be on the street itself anywhere along the path of the parade. A child might get away with letting a foot fall next to the sidewalk, but nothing more. It's a firm rule meant to ensure that no one tries to make contact with the prisoners by darting out into the street.

At some point he gets impatient and I feel his arm circle my back and lift me entirely from the ground. It's uncomfortable, his arm squeezing my ribs and my feet dangling above the pavement. Even my hair is trapped between his arm and my back, but it gets us moving faster so I tuck my chin in and suffer the ride.

Jovan manages to maneuver me to the front row of people at the end of the town square, well ahead of the line of prisoners. He jerks me up and out of the street when we're shoved forward by the disgruntled mass of people behind us. He takes a stance behind me, one hand firmly on each of my shoulders, and seems to plant himself like a tree, shielding me from any further pushes.

My toes are pressed right to the edge of the sidewalk and I wave at the man, who has tried to follow my progress but lost me in the crowd. When he sees me, we smile at each other and I glance back at Jovan. I know I should explain and thank him, to somehow let him know how much this means to me, but all I can think of right now is the man at the front of the line.

He risks getting tangled in the chains or receiving another blow from the soldier, but he turns a little and exposes the front and other side of his neck. He wants to be sure I know who he is. The full line of text is there and it's something I've seen in every picture of him except the one of him as a small boy. The words *Free is Free* run in an almost unbroken circle around his neck. The only gap is where three strike marks have been tattooed into the skin.

Yes, I know him even though I have absolutely no memory of him. Even in those hazy memories of early childhood that never make sense, he isn't present. I've tried to have them, studied pictures of him and tried, but there's nothing. This man disappeared as a Striker when I was barely a year old, so it's no surprise I don't remember. But I still know who he is. He is my father, Jordan Quick.

Chapter Three

Just like that, he's gone. The Courthouse stands on the opposite corner of the town square and I watch as they prod the line of prisoners into a side door for processing. Even if they do decide to administer a "final adjudication," as they euphemistically call it when they put a criminal to death, they won't do it right now.

I have a little time to sort out what I should do, both about my father and Maddix. There must be something that can be done, though it may only be to see him and speak with him. While justice is implacable and has no mercy, nor does it allow exceptions, it is also very thorough. They won't kill anyone until their identity is confirmed and their charge count is double-checked.

The hands on my shoulder are warm and heavy, so I know I'm going to need to do some explaining when I turn around. The disappearance of the prisoners is the signal that we're free to go and people spill out into the street, releasing the pressure from so many bodies on the sidewalk. A few people shove past me roughly and I step back, closer to Jovan, out of reflex.

The pressure of him against my back startles me and I step off the curb and out from under his hands in one move. When I turn, his hands have dropped to his sides. He doesn't say anything to me, which just makes this entire situation more awkward, if that's possible.

What can I say to him that won't sound incredibly pathetic? "Oh, hey, thanks for carrying me around, but that was my habitual criminal father who left me with a drunk who likes to use me for a punching bag"? While I stand there searching for words, he just looks at me with those crazy beautiful eyes of his.

"Thanks," I say, settling for simplicity.

"Someone you know?" he asks, stepping off the curb to stand in front of me again.

I can't help the laugh that comes out, or the bitter sound in it, but I can shut it off as soon as it happens. His eyes aren't judging and he doesn't look like he wants to get away from me as quickly as he can, so I decide there's no harm in telling something like the truth.

"It was my father. He's been gone a while," I say and let that hang in the air between us.

He knows my father is a Striker. We've gone to the same schools since I started going to school, though he's a year ahead of me. Before the full force of parental influence came down on him, we were playground chums for a while, teaming up in games. Anything that involved speed or knocking things—or other people—down, we excelled at. We were more than that, really. I'd rather not think about that. That was then.

Jovan nods slowly, working it all out in his head. He was always like that. Slow to answer, but usually coming up with the right one. He says, "He wouldn't have come unless it was important."

That's as far as he gets before his father appears out of the remaining crowd. He gives me a sour look, like he just saw someone pull down their pants and pee on the street. His eyes slide away from my face, effectively dismissing me, and he says to Jovan, "Come on, your mother is waiting. We've got a lot to do today."

Jovan has the smarts not to try to keep talking to me, and the good grace to turn back and give me a little nod, as he follows his father toward the hospital on the other side of the square. I do notice that even they don't walk on the grass, taking the long way around like all the rest of us.

Cassi and Connor are still halfway down the block and I can see bright flashes of Cassi's hair as she jumps up and looks for me. It's almost comical, the way it bounces up like someone spent hours trying to make it that way. She hates it. I wish it were mine.

She gives me an aggrieved look and lets out a loud sigh when I return. Connor looks like someone hit him with a hammer, dazed. I don't say anything because I'm not sure what to say. Instead, I wrap an arm around each of them and pull them in close for a hug. I'm not sure if I'm comforting Connor or taking comfort myself. Maybe it's both.

We stand there for a moment until it gets weird and then break the embrace to stand with our more customary distances between us.

"What do you think, Connor?" I ask. It's better to ask him something mental than emotional. He focuses better on those things and gets less lost. He's a thinker.

Connor tugs at his jacket and says, flatly, "I think I'm going to lose another brother."

It's a very final statement and said with absolute certainty. And, truthfully, he's probably right. Unless his brother was somehow caught only as a Striker rather than with smugglers, he will earn two strikes, which makes five for Maddix. You can earn off strikes with time and good citizenship, but only if you've got less than five. People with five no longer have time. Judgment is followed within a single day by the injection that will end a life.

I do understand that society in general can't afford the danger and disorder that habitual criminals bring. I understand it intellectually, that is. But I can't help thinking that there's something very different between a thief who won't stop, an arsonist who can't stop, and kids who live under rules that seem designed to weed them out.

Cassi and I know Maddix well, and we both know he doesn't deserve the strikes he's already got. His parents deserve them. But now that Connor has brought the subject up in the most direct way possible, we have to deal with it. Right now, Cassi looks like she's going to start to cry and that would be bad. Once she gets going, she's like a loud faucet.

"I saw my father," I say, without preamble. I can't think of any other way to say it.

It does the trick. Cassi's pucker disappears like it was never there and her face smooths, her impending tears forgotten. Connor looks up at me sharply, his eyes keen and his thoughts switching gears.

"How do you know? I mean, how do you know it's him?" he asks.

"Maddix pointed him out and I saw him. It was him, I'm sure of it."

"Maddix?" he asks, as confused as I am.

I shrug because I don't know what else to do. How do I express the many possibilities this opens up?

"They must have been together. That has to mean something," Cassi says.

Connor nods but keeps looking at me, waiting for me to chime in and offer more than I already have.

All I can do is sigh and guess, so I do. "Maddix knew who he was, so they must have been together at some point. They knew each other somehow." I catch my mistake and correct it, saying, "Know each other."

"Your dad's been gone your whole life. Why would he come back? Smuggler?" Cassi asks.

Again, I shrug because I have no idea what's going on or why he would return. Or why Maddix would be with him. It's possible he was a smuggler whose number finally came up and he got caught. That would be the most logical answer, but anyone who could hop the border as a smuggler without getting caught for fifteen years should be good at it by now. Certainly, good enough to know not to bring a young newbie out with them and get picked up by a patrol.

"I have to get in to see him," I say.

Connor nods again, like he was expecting me to say that. Under the age of eighteen, anyone declared habitual gets the privilege of time with their family before justice is served. Over that age and it's just done. Connor won't get a visit with Maddix either if the worst happens.

"And I want to see Maddix," he says.

We stand there in the street as the people clear out around us, going back to their homes or run errands or whatever else they had planned for their Saturday. The day is beginning to warm a little and it isn't quite as frigid. The dry air won't hold the cold night temperatures long past sunrise. It's still cool, but not cold, and the day is promising to be a fine one. The weather being nice is wrong in every possible way it could be. It should be storming to match my mood. With lightning.

Cassi rubs at her strike-free neck, perhaps considering whether or not hatching some plot with us is worth the mark it might earn her. Connor notes it too and I see he's about to let Cassi off the hook when she says, "Breaking into the Courthouse isn't exactly easy but it's probably easier than breaking out of it."

I laugh because it's such a perfectly logical statement but also perfectly ridiculous. Breaking into the Courthouse is just about the last thing anyone would want to do. And that's the subject we're all dancing around here, finding some way to break into the Courthouse so that we can get to the prisoners. Even Connor gives a sideways smile.

We're drawing looks from the few people who remain as well as a pair of patrol soldiers making their way down the street. They move with lazy confident strides, like they own the place. Which they do, in a way.

Bailar has a small population but a surprisingly large number of soldiers. They patrol the dry lands to the west and the borders to the north. Bailar is the last bit of civilization before those places, so we get to host all of those not out on patrol. I'm not a fan.

"Let's go," I say and we turn to walk back the way we came. We can't go to my house because my Mom is home and probably already dipping into her bottle for the day. Cassi's place is out because there are always people around. Connor lives too far out and I'm not letting him anywhere near his parents until we have this sorted anyway. Who knows what they'll do if they find out about Maddix? Connor can sleep in our shed tonight if need be.

We stay quiet until we reach the canal, the strip of water that comes all the way from the lake and provides water to the town. It looks brown and dirty from up here, but it comes out of the faucets clean and clear. At least it looks clear if the container isn't too deep.

Settling down on a patch of concrete next to the canal—our favorite spot when the weather is good—makes me feel a little more normal. For a moment, it's like any other day. But only for a moment.

Cassi starts us out and suggests, "We could just ask to see them."

Connor tosses back, "True, but they'll say no and then we'll need to figure out a plan anyway, so why not do it now?"

"I swore I'd never go back after getting this," I say and gesture toward my neck. "And outside of getting myself busted again so they'll bring me in for a strike, I have no idea how to get beyond the foyer."

Connor's expression goes serious and he says, "No, don't even think of doing that. It won't get you back by the prisoners anyway. It would be a waste of a strike."

He's right and I know it. "Then how do we get in there? What we need is someone who belongs there to let us in."

Connor and I shrug at each other because neither of us has anyone like that. As far as I know, Cassi also lacks inside contacts. But instead of looking as lost as we are, she squirms on the concrete.

"What?" I ask. "You know someone?"

"Well, yeah. You do, too. I saw you disappear with him during the parade. Jovan Foley."

Chapter Four

It takes ten minutes of tossing yes and no back and forth between us, along with some arguments about why it would be stupid even to tell Jovan about what we're planning, before we settle down.

"She's right, Karas," Connor says as if the matter were decided.

Cassi seems equally convinced and adds, "He would do it. Even better, he could do it."

I tune them out while I roll this idea around in my head for a minute. It's better than anything I can think of. We do need someone who belongs inside the Courthouse and he's an ideal choice. He's not officially in the Army yet, but he might as well be.

He's already doing Cadet Patrols, earning time against future promotions, and he has a uniform. His father is a member of the Civil Authority and is in the Courthouse every day, which means Jovan is known there. In truth, he's our only shot.

"You think you know him well enough to ask him for something like this?" I ask Cassi.

I almost don't want to know the answer to that. While Jovan is, at least as far as I can tell, perfect in every way, so is Cassi. With her curly red hair, skin as white as new milk and covered in freckles, she's a picture of what every girl wants to look like. Even her eyes are a shade of brown prettier than the average brown. It would be natural for something more to happen between them. But if anything has happened between them, I really don't want to know. Plus, Cassi knows all about the mutual crush Jovan and I

21

had going as kids. I don't think she'd do that, even if I do insist that I'm long over it.

She must have noticed my expression because she laughs at me and says, "Not like *that*. His parents would have a conniption!"

"Not for you, they wouldn't," I say.

She cocks her head to the side and looks up as she thinks. "Well, maybe not but I'm pretty sure they don't want a dummy as the mother of their grandchildren."

That's more than Connor can take. He won't stand for anyone making fun of Cassi, even when she's picking on herself. "You are not stupid. Dyslexia has nothing to do with intelligence." He points to his head and adds, "It's just a crossed wire."

She waves it away. We've heard it many times, but it doesn't erase the fact that most people think she's stupid because she struggles to read. She even has issues with numbers when she looks at them too long. "Anyway, he's been helping my brother. He did so well on his Army Aptitude test that they've assigned Jovan to help him make the decision. He's been taking him on patrols, helping him study for placement and all that stuff."

"Your brother's going into the Army?" I ask, aghast.

No matter what, Cassi isn't stupid, and we both know that no matter how well her brother does on any placement test, he'll be a grunt working in the dry lands or fighting off Climbers at the southern border. He'll be doing the most dangerous work because he's not a Foley or a Sampson or a member of any family with clout.

Again, she waves it all away and says, "He's got to do something and he's too smart for anything he can get around here." She pauses and pulls something out of her inner coat pocket. It's a pair of glasses. Glasses with rose-colored lenses. She holds them up and says, "He gave me these."

Connor and I both laugh at that. It has to be a joke. Rose-colored glasses and Cassi make a perfect match for a joke.

She glares at us, knowing exactly what we're laughing about. "It's for my dyslexia. He actually took the time to look it up for me at the hospital. He even brought a bunch of colored plastic bits over and had me try them until

I found a color that worked. It was pink. It works," she says and finishes by slipping the small lenses onto her face.

It actually looks really good on her.

She slips them back off and into her pocket, her face serious again when she looks at us. "He's been really nice to my whole family and I think he would at least listen to us."

"You were friends once. What do you think?" Connor asks me.

Do I think Jovan is trustworthy? Do I think he would listen and not tell, maybe even find a way to help us? He helped me today even when he had no clue what I needed. But helping us break into the Courthouse, possibly earning a strike, is a very different thing than carrying me along through a reluctant crowd.

I can't help but think of the way he picked me up so effortlessly and the way his shirt smelled of clean laundry and warmth. When I tucked my head into his shoulder, it fit so perfectly. Then I remember the boy he was. Remembering the way we exchanged kisses on the playground long before we understood the importance of kisses almost makes me smile. I shake my head and push those thoughts away. This is no time for daydreaming about Jovan.

"He's trustworthy to a point," I say, then add, "but only to a point."

We're in agreement by the time the sun is warm enough that we loosen our jackets. I don't want to go home and Connor really shouldn't, but if we descend on Cassi's house her mother will go all maternal on us and make things difficult.

Connor and I settle for waiting where we are. We'll leave only long enough to grab some food if the wait grows long, but Cassi is confident that Jovan will be there early in the day. Either way, we'll wait for her, no matter the outcome.

She flounces off, happy and seemingly unaware of the seriousness of what we're contemplating. Connor and I lie back on the warming cement slab and look at the endless blue sky above us. We talk a while, but it isn't long before I hear his breathing become steady during one of the long pauses in our conversation. I turn to see his eyes have closed.

I sigh and my stomach rumbles in hunger. I've got nothing stashed in my pockets and I'm too tired to move. My thoughts keep turning back to my father. The entire concept of him showing up just doesn't seem to want to settle into my mind.

There has to be something more to it than just getting caught. He was dirty and dusty and certainly older, but he looked good all the same. His clothes looked nice and his coat was thick and warm, made in a style I've never seen around Bailar. His hair was cut neatly and he had no beard, just a few days stubble, so he was clearly able to take care of himself. He didn't look like a ratty old smuggler or someone who eked out his survival in the wild lands to the north.

I'd like to keep thinking, keep awake, but the sun is warming the cement and the air is shifting from cool to almost warm. It's definitely rolling toward spring. It feels good to lie here and Connor's breathing is calming. I feel sleep coming over me but rather than fight it, I decide it will pass the time and let it take me.

*****

Someone shakes me roughly from behind and I groan at the pain in my hip where it meets the cement. I've turned to my side, like I do in bed, and tucked myself up into a ball. I roll over to see Cassi squatting between Connor and me. This time she's shaking him, at least.

I groan again as I sit up. My body feels as stiff as a board and I'm foggy from sleep. Rubbing my eyes, I say, "I was out like a light."

Connor is waking up, confused like he usually is when he sleeps deeply. I look around and am startled to see Jovan standing a few feet away. He's off the concrete, like he doesn't want to intrude, and has his arms crossed against his chest like he's embarrassed to find us sleeping like we're homeless.

That makes two of us, because I'm embarrassed he found us like this. Still, I can't control the huge yawn that comes out and the shiver that follows directly after. I shrug in his direction and he surprises me with a smile. It's a small smile, one that barely turns up his lips, but a real one.

It takes a few moments of stomping to get my blood moving while Cassi soothes Connor as he wakes up completely, but eventually we're all awake and ready to find out how Jovan can help us. That he's here means Cassi has achieved at least a partial success, and I clap her on the back to let her know it's appreciated.

Rather than sit back down, we walk along the canal away from town. The other side of the road has a line of small houses. The exact same kind of small houses go several rows back, mine included. Half of them aren't occupied and the other half are quiet so there's no one to question our actions. Four teens walking along the canal isn't unusual enough to raise any questions anyway.

Jovan doesn't waste any time. Almost as soon as our feet get moving he says, "You guys shouldn't do this. Really."

"Yeah, I figured that part out already," I say, not quite keeping the sarcasm out of my voice. He shoots me a look that I ignore.

Connor must sense the tension because he adopts his reasonable tone and says, "We're well aware of the risks, but this is her father we're talking about. And my brother."

Jovan is taller than any of us by at least several inches, so when he looks at us, he is looking down at us. Normally, that would make me uncomfortable, but his look is searching and concerned. There's nothing superior about it.

"I can probably get you in. I might even be able to get you out. But it's a risk. It's a crime."

All of us give him a nod. We know this and two of us already have strikes on our necks to prove we understand what that means. Jovan looks at Cassi and says, "You don't need to go inside, so you're going to help us on the outside where I need it. Can you do that?"

She looks relieved and I cringe inside. I hadn't even considered that she had no reason other than her friendship with us for going inside the Courthouse. Jovan is apparently a better friend than I am. And he gave her pink glasses.

"Sometime around midnight the soldiers on duty get a meal. It's called midrats," he says, then shakes his head at our lost looks. "It doesn't matter. What matters is that it's always a cadet that goes to get the meal and bring it to them before going on patrol duty. Always."

I can see where this is going. I can also see that he's doing more than just telling us how we might weasel our way in for a visit. He's talking about actually getting us in himself.

"Why are you doing this?" I break in before he can go on. "I mean, you don't actually have to go in with us. So why do it?"

The look he gives me isn't one I can easily interpret. It's steady, but distant, like I've hurt him somehow just by asking. It feels uncomfortable enough to make me look away and I cover by looking to Connor for support. He looks just as skeptical as I am.

"It's a good question," Connor says. "Why would you do this?"

"Because it's for a good reason," Jovan answers. The way he cuts the sentence off makes it clear that's the only answer we'll get.

I see Cassi giving me a sidelong grin out of the corner of my eye. I ignore it.

"On most nights the cadet who brings the food will take the place of the soldier on duty at the desk so they can all go back and eat. That leaves no one but the cadet watching the entrance to the cells for at least fifteen minutes, maybe longer if things are relaxed inside. Given the load that came in, I wouldn't bank on more than ten minutes tonight."

As he speaks, I can see it in my mind. I've been in there and know the layout pretty well. Offices and courts are upstairs, the jail is on the ground floor. No one stays in the jail for long so it's a fairly straightforward arrangement and doesn't use up the entire ground floor. I can vaguely remember a couple of doors that led further into the building but not where they led to.

"That will give us what, eight minutes, if we move fast?" Connor asks, his face grim at the short time span we'll get for all our trouble.

Jovan looks sorry when he nods, as if he wishes he could offer more. "And that will be only if you get in fast. Less if there are any snags. It's all I can do."

Cassi is looking at us with hopeful eyes. I can see she wants very badly for this to work for us, for those minutes to be enough. It has to be enough because short of magically spiriting them out of there, I can't see any other solution.

"It'll have to be enough," I say and nod to Connor. "Right?"

"We'll make do with what we can get," he answers.

"Right," Jovan says and rubs his hands together. "Let's get our plan together so we don't wind up in the cells along with them."

Chapter Five

Sneaking out of the house is going to be easy tonight. My mom wasn't even awake when I came home in the afternoon. She didn't even stir when I made dinner for Connor and me. The smell of alcohol seeping out of her pores was so strong I could smell it when I leaned close to her on the couch to see if she was breathing.

It's a habit to check for that now. She's not old and she still manages to keep away from the booze when she's working, but the minute she comes home she starts making up for lost time. It has to be doing terrible things to her body and I'm not yet ready to lose the only parent I have. I dislike her, fear her even, but I still love her deep down inside.

Except that now, at least for the moment, I have two parents. It's a situation that's likely to change in the very near future. Once they confirm his identity so they know they're killing the right person, he'll be dead.

I slip out of my room and down the stairs of our little house right on time for our midnight rendezvous. Each creak or wobbly stair is as familiar as my hand, so I don't make any noise. Peeking around the wall to the living room, I see my mother still on the couch, out like a light. The blanket my grandma knitted, now so soaked in alcohol fumes I can hardly bear to touch it, is draped across the cushions in haphazard disarray. Normally, I'd tuck it around her but I can't afford for her to wake up tonight.

The front door is creaky beyond help, so I sneak out the back door. It's cold again now that it's been dark for a while, and I can see my breath. The weeds that pass for a lawn are still dead or only greening in patches. The ground crunches under my boots as I tiptoe over to the rickety shed in the back corner of the yard. A feeble bit of light comes through the dirt-encrusted window, so I don't bother to knock before I pull open the door.

Connor is sitting in a pool of light from his flashlight, his eyes mere inches from the pages of a book.

"You'll go blind reading like that," I say, and then grin when he starts and drops the book.

"Cheese and crackers, Karas!" he exclaims.

Connor says that cursing is a sign of low intelligence. I say a good cuss word used judiciously is like pepper on top of a fried egg. Absolutely necessary and it adds a little spice where it's needed most. We've agreed to disagree on that matter.

"You ready?" I ask.

He picks up the book and dusts it off. I do feel a bit bad about that and I hope I haven't caused it any damage. They are expensive and hard to come by, especially the wordy kind that Connor prefers, filled with tales of dragons and such.

Tucking the book away, he grabs his flashlight and slips that into another of his voluminous pockets. He's always got them filled with everything from food to spare clothes. If I had his family—the only family in town I can think of that's worse than mine—I'd probably do the same. They make their dubious living with a constant stream of schemes but use their children to carry out anything that might earn a strike, saving themselves from paying for their actions. It's disgusting.

It doesn't take long to make our way to the place where we're supposed to meet Cassi and Jovan. The streets are dark and quiet, and the loudest sound I can hear is the barking of a dog in some distant yard.

We reach the dark corner and, for a moment, I think we're the only ones there. Before I even have a chance to complain that the others are late, Jovan seems to melt out of the darkness behind us. I try not to jump when he appears like that. I'm all nerves and it feels like almost anything could make me fly right out of my skin.

"Cassi's already in place," he says, not taking the time for small talk. He's wearing his Cadet uniform, which is just like a regular Army uniform save for the lack of rank patches. I don't like it on him. It makes him look too much like all the rest of them.

He's got a box in his hands. The scents of meatloaf and gravy wafting out of it make my mouth water. Connor and I made do with whatever I could find and get out of the house without my mom waking up. We definitely didn't eat meatloaf.

"You're sure about this?" I ask him. It's only fair to offer him a chance to back out.

He nods but I can't see his face well enough to read the expression there. Only the barest suggestion of light reaches us from a single bulb outside the Courthouse. It carves his face into stark patches of light and shadow, devoid of expression.

"Go back around the building and stay out of sight of the cameras. Come up just like we talked about and stay behind the loading platform. It will hide you. Be ready," he says and hefts the box. His voice sounds sure, but there's a thready note in there that gives away his nervousness. He should be nervous. I'm so terrified I want to puke all over his perfectly polished boots.

I don't though and the urge passes. Just as I'm about to ask him if he's sure again, he walks away toward the front of the Courthouse. I grab Connor's hand and we take off in a quiet walk-run around the other corner, heading toward the back door.

It seems to take forever to get around the block. The Courthouse is huge and covers the entire block, corner to corner. I've lived here my entire life, but I never really noticed that until tonight. Now that I'm running around, hunched over and silent, it seems quite unreasonably large. And in the dark, the pale stone seems to glow as well as loom over us.

With the darkness so complete and the night so quiet, everything seems stretched to its breaking point. My nerves, the silent night, and quite possibly our luck.

Before we turn the corner into the field of view of the cameras, we stop and take stock. Neither of us has a watch, but Jovan made sure we knew there was usually a minute or two of chatting or jokes before the soldiers took their food back to the break room. Once we round this corner, we'll need to be careful like we've never been before.

The camera should be pointed so that it covers the side entrance and the stairs leading to the loading dock, but not as far back as the corner where we are. Jovan told me we should keep low, get to the concrete lip under the loading dock and then stay put.

A quick look around the corner confirms what he said. Our only real worry is being seen by anyone who happens to be looking this way from another building or the street. And I see nothing. It's completely still outside. Late-night activity is not a common thing around Bailar. I take Connor's hand again and we shuffle, almost bent double, until we reach the safety of the loading dock overhang.

It's rather nice under here, cozy even, which is absurd and makes me smile. At a questioning grunt from Connor, I say, "Nothing. It's a bit like a playhouse under here."

He smiles back at me and pats my shoulder. "You're such an idiot," he says and I hold back a laugh. I know it's just tension making us do this, but it's still funny for a few seconds.

We shuffle along under the overhang till we're closer to the door side of it, but not so far that the camera will see us. Once there, we've got nothing to do but crouch and wait. It seems to take forever and my thighs start to burn from the crouch. Somehow, it doesn't seem right to sit down so I stick it out. The burn tells me it's been more than a minute or two, more like five.

I worry at a hangnail until it tears free with a sharp burst of pain, then clench my fist to prevent me from biting my fingernails. It's probably just stress, but it seems like the air is getting thicker. Pulling in each breath feels like work. It feels exactly the same as when I pull the covers up over my head in winter and the air immediately gets stale and stuffy.

I'm just to the point of convincing myself I've got to go back to the corner where I can stand up and get a full breath when the door opens and a wedge of light spills out. Jovan leans out and motions us forward impatiently.

Connor follows me out from under the overhang and flips a rude gesture at the sign above the door that reads "Total Freedom Total Responsibility." I can breathe again, but my heart is pounding and I could swear that my stomach is doing flips inside me.

Jovan eyes me, a question in his expression, and I answer, "I'm fine."

He ushers us inside and pulls the door closed so carefully it doesn't make even a whisper of noise. He holds a finger to his lips and leads us through the area where prisoners are processed. I remember it well from my own strike.

There's the sound of a loud laugh beyond the closed door on the other side of the space. At the sound, my heart hammers in my chest. They are too close. The distance of a single room lies between us and them. The same distance lies between us being illicit visitors and us becoming prisoners in those cells.

I shake the thought away, and we all unfreeze as the laughter fades. Jovan's sigh is louder than any noise we've made so far. I tap him on the back, and then hold a finger to my lips when he turns.

Only a few lights are burning. Even here there are economies to be made and power doesn't grow on trees. Even if it did, this part of Texas isn't exactly covered in those either. The patches of light on the walls and floor are unsettling and make me more nervous. I can hear Connor breathing heavily behind me so I know it's not just me.

Jovan opens the door to the cells but stops me with a hand before I can walk past him. He bends so close I can feel his breath on my cheek when he whispers, "Five minutes, Karas. No more. They're on edge tonight."

The seriousness of his expression stalls any smart comment I might be otherwise tempted to make. Really, on edge? Like we're not. Still, five minutes with the father I've never known, but always dreamed of, seems a paltry amount of time. Then again, no amount of time would really be enough.

Connor gives a tight nod at that. I don't look at Jovan again but enter the dim cell block, eyes searching. I'm not sure what I expected, maybe for him to shut the door and call to his soldier friends or, at best, take a spot at the doorway and watch our backs. I know for sure that I didn't expect him to say what he does.

"I'm sorry I can't give you longer," he whispers far too loudly.

Maybe it's the tone of his voice, or the kindness of his words, but a lump forms in my throat. If I turn back, I'll start to cry and I don't want to do that. Instead, I turn my head just enough for him to know I've heard him and nod. There's no time for more.

Chapter Six

Every second I waste is one less second I get to spend with my father. Jovan didn't say which cells they were in, but there aren't that many. There are a few dim light fixtures along the walkway between the cells. They provide just enough light to see inside each of them. It makes sense since the soldiers must have to make rounds. I've never spent a full night in here so I don't know what their procedure is.

Most of the prisoners are asleep, two to a cell. With most of them under blankets and facing away from me, I can't figure out who is who. Connor has moved ahead of me and I hear him hiss his brother's name into one of the cells. The noise wakes the man I'm looking at and he rolls over in his bunk so I can see his face. Not my father. He's a hard-looking man with two scars running across his face. They pucker one side of his face into a parody of a grin.

I back away and move on to the next cell, hoping that man keeps quiet and doesn't wake the rest of them. If they make noise, I won't even get my precious few minutes.

There's a man's hand reaching out of the last cell on my side, but he's not making noise. Somehow, I know that's him and I hurry to the end, keeping my footsteps as light as I can.

And there he is.

His face is clean now and there's no mistaking that he's the man in every photo I've managed to save from my mother's rages. He's the man holding the baby version of me in the light of a window, smiling down while a fat baby fist reaches for his face. He's the one carrying that same baby on his chest and laughing while he harvests in our garden. All the images I have of him collapse into this older, but still smiling, man I see between the bars of his cell.

"Karas," he says. His voice is soft, like he's testing a new word instead of saying my name. His eyes are shiny with tears and the hand that he reaches out of the bars tries to touch my hair.

That movement breaks me out of my spell and I step back, out of his reach. My father he may be, but I don't know him and I don't like to be touched by strangers—or even most people I know.

"You're my father. Why are you here?" I ask, coldly. I can't help that my voice is hard. I didn't do it on purpose. It just came out that way.

He pulls his hand back and grips the bars. He looks like I just slapped him. He nods across to the cell where Connor stands talking to Maddix and says, "He made it to the border and they sent him on to me. I heard about your mom." He stops and his hand opens like he's offering me something. He swallows so hard I can hear it and says, "I'm so sorry."

The lump in my throat from before is back, but this time it's not a little one. It's so big it's choking me and I can't breathe past it. It feels like it will never let me go and I bend over, trying to stifle a sob squeezing past the lump. When I heave in a breath it feels like I'm breathing in fire.

Both of his arms reach out as far as they can go and even though I see them coming, I don't step backward. My feet seem to have a mind of their own and before I know it, I'm pressed up against the bars, choking while my father smooths my hair and tells me everything will be okay.

Even though everything in me just wants to cry, to hit something and just break down, I can feel the seconds ticking away. I can also hear the other men waking and beginning to stir. There is no time for this.

The breath I heave in sounds asthmatic and whistles its way inside me, but it doesn't come back out a sob, even though it still burns inside my chest. When I face my father again, tears have run down his cheeks and into the lines beside his mouth. They're real tears.

"We've only got a few minutes," I say, though it sounds garbled.

Those words seem to hit home and he tries to peer down the hallway and see who's there. He nods and lets my arm go. When he draws his hand away from my hair, he does so reluctantly, running the long ponytail through his fingers. Then he pulls a chain from around his neck and holds it out to me through the bars.

I take it and ask, "What's this for?"

Two little medallions clink together on the chain. One is plain gold. The other looks like a charm, maybe a memento he wants to pass on before he's put down. There are a few leaves, a nut of some kind and a design that looks like flowing water. It's beautifully rendered in gold and so detailed I'm almost afraid to handle it.

"If we only have a minute, then I need to tell you things," he says and plucks one of the medallions from my hand. When he holds it up, I see my name etched into the back.

"This is yours. The other is mine," he says and then turns it so I can see what he does. "Watch carefully how I open it."

He squeezes the edges with two fingers where there are tiny indentations in the metal and then taps a raised dot on the back. When he does, a small wafer of metal loosens enough for him to pull it up. He holds it up and inside of the medallion is a circle of blue that looks a bit like glass, but the medallion itself seems too thin to contain both metal and glass.

He holds it up and says, "Pay attention. This is you. It's coded with your DNA, but most people don't have a way to check that. It's got enough money loaded onto it to get you set up. With this, you can start a whole new life."

I'm confused and it shows. How do you put money on a slip of shiny blue whatever? How did he even get my DNA? I know what DNA is. We learned about it in school and I know they can identify criminals with it because of some super fancy machine they have down south. I shake my head and ask, "DNA? Mine?"

He slips the little wafer back in, snaps it closed and says, "I used to carry one of your baby booties when I went on a run. It doesn't matter. What matters is that this is important and can't be replaced. Don't lose it."

He lets the medallion go and it slithers down the chain in my hand to clink against the other one. Before I can even ask the million questions I have, he says, "The other one is mine. I left my main one at home, but that one has a good bit on it, too. Use it."

I shake my head again, completely confused. Home? Use the medallions? Money is made of silver. How can I use jewelry for money other than by selling it? There's some noise behind me and I turn to see Connor moving with purpose back down the hallway toward Jovan. Maddix is pressed up against the bars and whispering for him to come back. I turn back to my father because all I have is this moment and I want it with him.

"I don't understand. I can't use this? What would I use it for?"

He grips my hand through the bars and I see that his fingernails are shaped just like mine. It's just another shock to take in. I have fingernails like my father's.

"Listen, Karas," he says and I look into his eyes. "Go north over the border and then east. There's a border wall. When you get to it, show your medallion and give your name. Tell them you're already a citizen and let them verify it. The territory I live in, Silver Lake, is registered so they'll give you directions or a map. It's a long way but it's a big area, so they'll be able to tell you at any border gate. The address and everything else is on the chip, just in case."

He stops and licks his lips, eyes moving toward the end of the hall where we can both hear something going on between Connor and Jovan. He looks back at me and continues, his words coming faster. "When you get to Silver Lake, just ask for my farm. It's called River Oaks. The design on the pendant means River Oaks in case you forget. You'll get all the rest you need to know there. Do you have that? Tell me."

The whispers are rising toward speech and I'm worried something is going wrong but I do as he asks and say, "North over the border, east to the border fence, Silver Lake and then your farm, River Oaks."

He nods while I talk and then reaches out to stroke my hair and cup my face. He smiles like he's happy, which is odd since he'll probably be dead in twenty-four hours. Maybe less. But the smile is warm and contagious and I can't help but return it.

"It's a long way. Don't give up," he says. Tears well up in his eyes again and he grips the back of my head and runs his thumb across my cheek. His voice is hoarse when he says, "I never would have left you had I known what would happen. I had no choice at the time. You were a baby."

This explanation is not enough for the younger version of me that hid on the roof in the rain while my mother rampaged around the house beneath me looking to break a bottle on my head. It's not enough for the part of me that sleeps lightly or not at all even now when she gets mean or has to clean up the house because it would never get done otherwise.

But for the part of me that's starting to realize that life is complicated and generally sucky, it's almost understandable. I can't imagine trying to go Striker with a baby in tow. Getting through the dry lands, the wild lands and every person that lies between the border and Bailar is hard for a person who's fit and well prepared.

Striking with a baby would be an invitation for the baby to die. Probably for both people to die and if not, then most certainly get caught. Only the most desperate would try it. Someone who thought their baby would be loved and cared for by its mother wouldn't risk it. I guess I never thought about whether or not my father would have taken me with him when he went Striker. I just sort of assumed he abandoned my mom and me. That he didn't makes me want to cry again.

I nod at him because that thickness is building up in my chest again. He has such kind eyes, though they are pulled down with sadness. He doesn't look like a bad man. He looks like a farmer or a cattle worker or any other sort of hard-working man. Rough hands, sun-worn skin and a lean body from working more than he eats is what I see in front of me. I wonder what he sees.

"I love you, Karas," he says. "I never went a single day without thinking of you and wishing I could see you. I came as soon as I knew."

"You came back for me," I answer. It's all I can say, but it means so much. Only real love would make him do this, risk this.

Before we say anything more, Jovan and Connor barge down the hallway and Jovan grabs my arm roughly. I sense my father stiffen at the move but I don't have time to deal with it.

"Talk sense into him, Karas," Jovan hisses into my face.

"I'm not leaving without Maddix," Connor says.

Chapter Seven

Connor looks adamant and he's not even bothering to whisper. This is not good. More of the men are awake and they are certainly paying close attention to what's going on in their midst. I gape at the two of them like a fish out of water for a moment, then yank my arm out of Jovan's grasp.

"We can't do that, Connor," I say, then jerk my thumb at Jovan. "They'll know it was him."

"So," Connor says, crossing his arms across his chest, a mulish look spreading across his face. "It's one strike for him. But it's my brother's life. And your father's."

He's not thinking clearly. I never should have tried this. Or if I did, I should have left Connor out of it. Now it's my turn to grab an arm and I do, gripping so hard I know it will leave a mark. He winces but I have his attention.

"No, it's not a strike," I say and count off for him, raising a finger for each strike I can think of. "He came in with intent to commit a crime, he broke me in, broke you in. That's three."

I can see Connor is getting it so I keep on counting. "And if he breaks out your brother and my father..." I let the sentence hang and allow the handful of fingers I'm holding up do the rest of the talking.

Connor looks back at his brother. Maddix shakes his head no. Jovan lets out a sigh of relief but that just stokes my anger.

I turn on him and say, "You could do us the favor of not looking quite so happy they'll die and you won't get into trouble."

We've been in here too long and I know it. I'm taking my pain out on him and he doesn't deserve it. He's risked quite a lot, including his entire future, to get us these precious minutes and I should be thanking him, not berating him. I blow out a breath and say, "I'm sorry. That wasn't fair."

It seems Connor isn't done yet. The two dark lines on his neck almost throb with his pulse when he says, "He's a Foley and all the offenses happened at the same time. He'll get one strike. At most, two. You know I'm right, Karas."

The look I give Connor is so cold even I get frostbite from it and he has the good grace to look away. The problem is he's not entirely wrong. Justice is written clearly, but it's a puddle of muddy water in the way it gets practiced.

The rules for Immediate Final Adjudication are clear. Murder, rape, sexual offenses against children and anything like that gets you the needle the minute a guilty verdict is read. No problem. Everyone understands that.

For lesser crimes, the ones worthy of a strike, things are not so clear-cut. A single event can wind up costing all five strikes if there were many crimes committed during that event. But that would defeat the purpose of strikes—distinguishing who is a habitual offender versus someone having one really bad day—so they aren't judged that way. Instead, it's up to the judge and a simple majority of jurors to decide which, if any, offenses can be combined.

They might take a strict view and say that each element required thought and offered an opportunity to stop, giving more strikes. Some might take a looser view and decide that once begun, all offenses were part of the same crime. The simple truth is that coming from a good family with money and connections means fewer—or no—strikes, while families like Connor's and mine can expect to get more.

He's right. If I had to make a bet, I'd bet Jovan will walk out with two at most. None if he says we made him do it.

But I'm not willing to bet on anyone's life. That's where I differ from my mother, Connor's parents and all the others who think this system is the right way to do things.

"No," I say and hope it sounds like it's a final decision that brooks no argument.

It's too bad all the men now standing at the bars of their cells don't like my answer.

The man with the scar and the pulled up lip presses his face to the bars and says, "You try to leave and I'll bring them all in here." He grins and it makes his face look even worse, if that's possible. His grin widens and he adds, "All it'll take is a yell. And I've got some good lungs on me."

This is bad. Mostly because he's right. I can tell that Jovan is just this side of panicking. He's been looking behind him like he expects someone to march in for the past two minutes. We are way past his five minute mark. We're probably inching toward ten.

I have no idea what comes over me, or even how I might describe it. It's some automatic reaction that makes me take two steps toward Jovan, reach out and snatch the gun from his holster, then hold it up a few inches from the forehead of the man in the cell.

For the span of a long breath no one says anything. I look at him and he looks at the barrel of the gun. Then he backs away and holds his hands up.

"Hey, now. I didn't mean it," he says.

That's a lie and we both know it. The gun stays steady when I turn to Jovan, his mouth hanging open and eyes on the gun.

"We've got to go. Now," I say.

Jovan seems to shake out of it and holds out his hand for the gun. "Right, give me the gun."

"Once we're gone," I say and give the man in the cell a level look. "Just in case I need to use it."

Connor is looking at me just like Jovan, his mouth hanging open and something like fear in his eyes. This is his fault and he knows it. I have no idea if I could really shoot someone. If the need arises, I'm hoping I can. Possibly, I'll squeal and run away as quickly as possible. There's no way to tell which way it will go at this point.

My father has been quiet this whole time, watching it all play out without adding more confusion to our situation. Now he whispers, "Go, Karas."

We move backward, Connor telling Maddix how sorry he is the whole way and for one relief-filled moment, I think we'll make it.

Then the door to the break room opens behind us and I hear voices.

Chapter Eight

Time comes to a stop as we face each other across the reception area. I'm not even sure my heart beats in the short time it takes for us to take in the presence of the others. In that flash, I see two duty belts with guns on hooks behind the duty desk that stands between us. I also see that neither of the two soldiers is wearing one. Lastly, I see our way out of this.

The eyes of one of the soldiers slide toward the duty desk and he telegraphs his intentions. He's tensing to go for the gun belts. I swing the gun toward him and take two steps out into the big open space. He freezes and there we stand for an endless moment.

I have no idea what I'm doing, but I know I have to do it.

"Don't even think about it. Put up your hands," I say and then look at Jovan. "You too, soldier boy."

Jovan looks at me in confusion. He doesn't understand what I'm doing. That I'm trying to save him as well as us.

I wave my hand for him to comply and he does, raising his hands from his sides slowly. When I point him over towards the soldiers, he goes, dragging his feet a little but without any words that might make this incredibly stupid plan impossible to carry off.

Connor rushes past me, grabs the two duty belts from their hooks, and drops them at my feet. He plucks one of the guns from a belt and stands next to me. He looks a lot more confident than I feel holding a weapon, but I know he's faking. We are equally clueless. Aside from a butchering knife, the most dangerous weapon either of us has held is a slingshot.

My thoughts are a little jumbled and it's hard to decide which thing to do in what order. We're holding guns so this is now a situation where we either get away or we die. If they get hold of weapons, or if they have any more on them, we're toast.

"Connor, leave the gun here and go get the keys. Let my Dad and Maddix out and have them come up here to help me a minute," I say. I'm surprised my voice is so calm and steady. The rest of me feels like it might shake to pieces.

He gives me a look, but I must appear confident because he carefully places the gun on the floor next to my feet. He's cautious when he approaches them and I can see the two soldiers measuring their chances. I can also see Jovan positioning himself to intervene.

"The first one who tries anything gets the first bullet. The next gets one, too."

Both of them freeze again and the shorter soldier, the one who looked like he was game for taking a chance, glares at me, but holds his hands up higher. Connor pulls the keys off another hook and scoots past me without a word. I hear clanking and the squeak of rusty metal hinges. Seconds later my father slides up next to me.

I risk a glance and see disappointment in his eyes. Not directed at me, but at what has happened. He's calm, though, and steady as far as I can see. I hear more clanking but also more noise from the other men in the cells. They aren't going to let us take two and leave the rest of them to face punishment.

Maddix rushes up and he's not the picture of calm my father is. He utters a profanity and pushes his hands through his hair like he doesn't know what to do. My father puts a hand on his shoulder and whispers for him to be calm.

They must know each other pretty well, because Maddix responds like he's used to following his lead, taking a deep breath and shaking his hands out like he's flinging away the stress. It's strange to think that he knows my father and I don't.

"Dad, you and Maddix go pat those guys down. Take everything." I kick the duty belts at my feet and say, "Get the handcuffs and get them secure. Take care of soldier boy last. He's a cadet."

Clearly, my father is quicker on the uptake than Jovan was, because he gives me a nod and stoops to retrieve the cuffs, his eyes only leaving the soldiers for the barest minimum required to unsnap the handcuff holster.

We all stand in silence while he and Maddix pat the soldiers down. He's surprisingly good at it, my father. His pats are quick and professional, very thorough. Maddix is less so and my father reaches down to pull a knife from the soldier's boot that Maddix missed. He even takes their belts.

When they are cuffed, he pushes them to the floor, but it isn't ungentle. It's like he's done it a million times before. He even puts them against the wall so they'll be comfortable.

For Jovan it's more awkward. His pat-down is less thorough and even I can see the shape of a pocketknife in his pocket from all the way across the room. My father takes his duty belt and the rest, cuffs him with his own cuffs and then moves to seat him against the wall with the others.

"No," I say. "Soldier boy, to me." I say it like I'm just another soldier because that's the way they talk when they stop you on the street. Like a dog. It's necessary, though. I want no question in these soldiers minds that there are only two people in charge here. My father and me.

He shuffles forward with hesitant steps and when he nears, I shove him around to face away from me and say, "Knees." He kneels and it's a relief not to see his face anymore. I can't stand seeing the betrayal there. Even the back of his bowed neck looks vulnerable. How can a bared neck look hurt and sad? I don't know, but it does.

My father walks toward me when I shoot a glance his way. When he comes close, I bend to grab the gun next to my feet and hand it to him. He takes it and gives me a wink when he clicks off the safety and racks the slide. I make a note to remember that next time. My own gun has had neither of those things done to it. I'm clearly an amateur.

All of us look at each other then—Maddix, Connor, my father and me. Whether they understand completely what I'm up to, I can't know, but they're willing to follow my lead at the moment. The two soldiers are watching us, trying to figure out what's going to happen to them. I'd certainly be worried if I were them.

I coil a fist into the back of Jovan's shirt and jerk so he'll stand up. It feels incredibly wrong to do it, but I put the barrel of the gun right up against his spine and look back at the two soldiers.

"He's a Foley. If you do anything, I'll shoot him first. You're not worth spit, but he is. If he dies, you'll wind up in those cells, too. Behave and you might make it out of this."

With that, I push Jovan forward and go in to talk to our new friends in the cells. We have a problem that still isn't solved.

Chapter Nine

I pull the door to the cell block closed behind me, though I'm careful to be sure it doesn't lock. I don't need that complication on top of everything else.

In the walkway between the cell rows, I feel like I have an audience. A hostile audience, at that. The nine men and one woman—at least I think she's a woman, though I'm still having doubts—wear a mixed bag of expressions on their faces. Hope, anger, fear and everything else a person can feel is on display and the air is thick with tension. Most disturbingly, on a few faces I see a mean sort of victory that I don't like at all.

Jovan is still looking at me like he doesn't know me at all. Or maybe like he's just figured out who I am and doesn't like it a single bit. I lower the gun and say, "We have a problem."

One of the younger cell inhabitants, four strikes plain on his neck, says, "Are you going to let us out or what?"

I consider him for a moment, then ask, "What are your strikes for?"

If he blushes, I can't tell, but he glances away and licks his lips, which is almost the same thing. He gives me a measured look and answers, "One for stealing, two for assault and one for destruction of private property."

The way he says it is straightforward and emotionless, like someone reading a list, and he keeps his gaze steady on mine. Instead of launching into a list of reasons why the strikes were undeserved, he just waits and lets me decide how to interpret the information. That's how I know there's more to his story and he's probably not as bad as his list of offenses might make me think.

"Let's see what we see, okay?" I ask.

He nods once and looks at Jovan, rightly guessing that it somehow hinges on him.

"What are you playing at?" Jovan asks and rattles the handcuffs still binding his wrists behind his back. "Why did you lock me up? Did you think I would turn on you?"

He's angry that I would think that. I can tell by the way his voice changes and gets tight. Does he really think so poorly of me that this is what he assumes first? And I guess it's even worse that he assumes I think so poorly of him.

"Uh, in case you didn't notice, now they think we forced you to do this. You're not involved. Get it?" I ask, but I can't stop the bitter tone that creeps in.

He winces. It's real and unpracticed, so now I know he gets it and feels like a turd for thinking I would turn on him. It gives me a small measure of satisfaction and that isn't nice of me at all.

"Listen up. We can't leave them out there for long. You said you're on watch for the rest of the night. How long until someone else comes here?" I ask, talking fast.

When he doesn't answer me fast enough—he looks like a confused new calf—I wave my hand at him to hurry.

"Uh, it would depend."

Through my teeth, I say, "Please do not make me drag every bit of information out of you, Jovan. Just work with me here." I'm frustrated with how long this is taking.

I've never been one of those people who somehow stay all calm and collected under stress. If I'm stressed for too long or too severely, I get snippy with people and eventually, angry and plain short-tempered. It's a flaw.

"Sorry. Well, it depends…" At my loud sigh he gives me a pleading look and I grit my teeth. I close my eyes and take a breath. When I open them again, he says, "If anyone calls for a soldier, like if a crime happens or something like that, then they'll notice if no one answers. But if nothing happens, then we should be good until five. That's when my patrol is supposed to end and I go home."

That's good and bad. There's nothing I can do to prevent anyone calling for soldiers so I can't waste precious time worrying about that. Since it's the weekend, cadets will do the morning patrol, which is just a nice way of saying they'll do gopher duty, fetching things and answering easy calls. With cadets, I can be reasonably sure the morning shift will not be showing up early. All in all, it's as good as it can get.

Except for the people in the cells. That's the bad.

"Jovan, I can put you in a cell with the other two, but that won't stop anyone from finding out you were involved as it stands now."

My pointed glance at the cells tells the rest of the story and he seems to sag a little. All these prisoners are going to race over each other to barter their freedom for information about what went on in here tonight. I think Jovan had begun to hope he might be able to get away with his ill-advised impulse to help us. Alas, no good deed goes unpunished.

"But," I say and then stop. I can't believe I'm about to suggest what I'm going to, but it *is* an option. My mouth is dry so I swallow. There's not a drop of moisture in my mouth or throat so all that happens is that it hurts and my throat clicks. It's so horrible I can barely work up the spit to speak the words. "We can either let them go or we can kill them."

The options lay between us like a bad smell. Those in the cells aren't going to sit idly by while I discuss ending their very short lives. Most of them will get final adjudication tomorrow and be dead by nightfall, but every hour of life a person can get is all the more precious when they know there are only a few such hours left. They start working themselves up for a loud round of making their preferences known.

I can't simply hush them so I raise the gun instead and say, "The first one to raise their voice will make my decision for me. I'll be left with only one option."

It's like a soundproof door closes on them it gets quiet so fast. The only sounds are Jovan's hard breaths and those of the young man with four strikes. And young he is. Cleaned up and without a layer of fine Texas dust marring his features, he's not much older than I am.

"We...you can't do that," Jovan says. His face is flushed. He's scared and he wants to distance himself from this decision.

"Which one?" I ask.

"Either!" he hisses back at me. "You don't know *what* any of these guys did, Karas. We don't even have them identified yet."

I nod, giving in on that point. He's right that I don't know what all they did to earn their strikes and go Striker. For all I know they could be really bad criminals, the dangerous kind. I start walking down the line of cells, looking at the occupants to either side.

They are mostly young, but not all. The woman—and I'm still not completely sure she is one—and the grinning man are the only ones aside from my father who seem to have any real age behind them. What I do see is strikes. Three and four strikes on every single neck. Except the grinning man. He doesn't have even one.

I stop at his cell and ask, "Where are you from?"

He grins at me, making his creepy scar even creepier, but he answers. "North."

"Wild lands?"

He nods but doesn't specify where. It wouldn't make any difference anyway since all I know of the north is that it is wild and that very bad people live there.

"Smuggler?" I ask.

He nods again but this time he adds, "Mostly medical supplies. I also do regulated trade of some of the electronics overflow for the Tribes."

This does surprise me. The Tribes inhabit the vast desert west of Texas, over the border, and are the primary conduit for any official trade we have. Not many places outside of Texas will trade with us, but those who do have only one decent path to get it to us—through the Tribe lands. They work those routes for us and extract a pretty percentage for themselves in the bargain. That would mean this ugly man has an official trade business as well as a smuggling route. It seems ludicrous to risk a good living by smuggling when you can do it officially with an assurance of safety.

"Then why smuggle?" I ask, genuinely curious.

"Are you kidding? How much trade do you think you've been getting here lately? What do you think you have left to trade with? I'll tell you in case you don't know. Not much," he says, emphasizing the last bit with a shake of his head.

I'm not sure what he means about not having much. We have lots that people want here in Texas. Or, at least I think we do. He seems surprised that I don't know this for myself when he notes my admittedly blank look. I turn away and shrug. There's no time to waste. It does explain a lot, though, about the lack of necessary things in the market during the last few years.

"What do you say, Jovan?"

He shakes his head at me, pushing back any attempt I might make to force him to share in this decision.

"Okay, let's try this," I say and turn to the other cells. "Is there anyone in this group who thinks there is any other person in this group that they wouldn't want with them if I let them out."

The cells are silent and that says volumes. If they're willing to go out into the dark with each other, with no possibility of help and a long way to travel, then none of them can really be that bad.

"Well, Jovan. This is what we're going to do. I'm going to let these fine people out and they are going to leave without letting on that you're in on this." I turn to the cells and ask them, "Am I right about none of you making a peep?"

Murmurs of assent and nods all around are no less than I expected. Their other choices aren't grand: death now or death in a day or less. Jovan doesn't say a word either, so I decide to take that as assent to this very quick plan.

"After that, I'm going to make a big fuss dragging you out there and use you to get those other two in these cells. Then I'm going to make an even bigger fuss by hitting you in the head and locking you in the cell. After that, you will lay there like you are out for the count until the next watch comes in. You can do the rest, can't you?"

He nods, but tentatively, so I ask him again," You can do that, right?"

"Yeah, I can figure it out," he says, sullenly. "Do you really have to hit me? Can't you just lock me up?"

"It will give you a good reason not to talk. Since we're good, let's get started."

Chapter Ten

There's no clock in the cell block so that's the first thing I look at when I go back out into the reception area. I can hardly believe that less than thirty minutes have passed since the midnight meet-up behind the Justice building. That's good, but the truth is that even if we get till five in the morning before the alarm is raised, it's not enough time.

I shove Jovan ahead of me and put him on his knees again, my gun very elaborately on his neck so the soldiers see me do it. Now that he's playing along, I have to fight the urge to laugh at how badly Jovan plays prisoner. The taller of the two soldiers blanches, his eyes round, so his acting can't be as bad as it looks to me. The shorter one glares at me like he wouldn't object to knocking me around a little. I don't blame him.

I jerk my head to bring my father over and he sidesteps over to me, a steady eye on the two soldiers looking miserable and defiant on the floor. They're probably wondering how many strikes they'll get for getting into this mess. I hope they'll get none.

When he leans in I tell him what I've got planned and ask if he thinks all those brought in with him are safe to let go. He considers a second or two and I can see he's really weighing everything.

"Maybe," he says but his frown and furrowed brow tell me his answer isn't as certain as I would like it to be.

He must see my uncertainty because he takes one hand from his gun, shoots a look at the two soldiers to let them know he hasn't forgotten them, and then squeezes me on the shoulder. It's a quick gesture, finished almost before I can enjoy it, but no less warm for having been so brief in duration. There's no way he can know what that simple touch means to me.

"Let's do it. It's the best option we have," he says quietly, and looks back at the soldiers, making ready for the next part of our increasingly elaborate act.

We both know that the danger of being outnumbered by all those in the cells once they're free is probably the most significant we'll face in this building at this point. My father moves to the other side of the room, where he can keep the soldiers and the entire path from the cell block to the door in view.

Connor clearly has no idea what's going on and he still has the keys. I wave him over once I know my Dad is in position and ready, Maddix at his side. I give him the short version and I can feel the arguments welling up inside him, ready to come out. Connor is a thinker and he's probably found about a million reasons why this won't work. I'm pretty sure he's about to list them all for me.

We don't have time to argue and I tell him so before he has a chance to launch into anything that will give us away. Connor doesn't feel good about it, I can tell that, but he trusts me. He jingles the keys and then goes, his feet light on the tile floor in typical Connor fashion.

The first to come out are the maybe-woman and the young four-striker I spoke with first.

"Where's our stuff?" asks the person I'm now positive is a woman. Her voice was rough and harsh in the cell block when she spoke in whispers. Now that she's speaking in a regular tone it's clear and low, but very feminine. She has the voice of a singer.

Her question throws me and I look at my father.

"We need it," she urges. She's right. It's cold at night and there's a whole lot of dry, nearly barren, land between them and freedom.

My father waves the barrel of his gun at the two soldiers and demands, "Well? Where is it?"

The taller soldier, the one who's been most compliant, answers. "It's in the property vault." He looks at us, realizing what we'll ask next and adds,

"We can't get in there and unless you've got a whole slew of keys for the doors between here and there, you won't get in either. Only supervisors have access."

We can't set them loose to steal or bring attention to themselves, but I'm not sure anyone can actually survive out there without a coat and some water at the very least. Then I see the two coats on the hooks by the door and jerk my chin that direction, "Take those and go. Fast. There aren't enough for everyone."

They don't waste time after that. One quick grim smile of thanks from the boy and they're out the door.

The next two are mad they can't get their stuff, but leave quickly enough. I go in and make the announcement before the next round, hoping we can get a move on if they don't waste time deciding if they're going to strip the soldiers naked for their clothes. Before the minute hand on the clock has moved from one number to the next, the last six prisoners are gone and the room is chilly from the constantly opening door.

Connor comes out, keys in hand, and says, "We're ready for them."

The soldiers get marched into two opposing cells and I step back while my father and Maddix strip the soldiers of their boots and trousers. Even their socks come off and fly out of the cells like little bats.

When it comes time for the shirts, they are careful, unlocking one handcuff, ripping off the shirt, and then cuffing the soldier to the bars of his cell. It takes mere moments before they are finished and the cell doors locked. While I have no real need of their clothes, at least not that I know of, Maddix made the excellent point that we don't have a lot extra and it's cold outside. So, down to the underclothes they go. Except Jovan. I just can't go there.

Now comes the hard part. Jovan is the last person I'd want to hit but if I don't, his life is going to change for the worse. Depending on how things go, it might even end. I have no choice in the matter. It's one of the most unlikely things I could ever have imagined doing.

But I have to. Just the way his eyes search mine, full of encouragement, is making me hate myself just a little. I wish he'd close those eyes and just let me get to it.

I push him into a cell well away from the others and tell him to get back to his knees. He obliges, turning his back to me. Even the little hairs near the top of his neck, where his closely cropped hair fades into his tan skin, seem to want to stay my hand and invite me instead to brush my hand along them instead of hit him.

Just as I raise my arm, my father says, "Karas, try this instead." He slides a nightstick he's taken from the soldiers my way and it rattles across the floor toward my feet.

"Less chance of breaking the gun," he adds and it takes me a moment to decide if he's actually joking with me at a time like this. I want to ask him to do it for me. But this is Jovan, and I don't think I could bear watching anyone else do him harm. Plus, I've got to pull the blow so as not to hurt him too badly.

I shake my head at the bad joke and grab the stick. It's more comfortable to me, less alien than the gun. I know better how to heft and control the simple piece of hard wood. When I look at my father, he quirks one of his eyebrows up as if to tell me he understands, but wants me to get on with it.

One of the soldiers pipes up and says, "Don't do it. You'll kill him. Please."

His plea is more for himself because he's just a regular soldier and worth less than nothing if Jovan dies. They can't see us well in the dim light, but their imaginations are probably more than making up for that.

I pull back the stick exactly as I do when I'm going after a raccoon running loose in the garden. When I let the stick come down, I realize I'm not holding back enough a fraction of a second after it's too late to fix it. I meant for it to be a tap, something he could point to and show a nice lump but not really hurt him. Him pretending to be out—maybe taking an actual nap—was the goal. The sound of the impact, dull but wrong, is loud in the room and the soldier who spoke lets out a groan.

Jovan folds as gracefully as a bird onto the hard floor but his head impacts the cement floor anyway. That sound is even worse than the one my stick made, if that's possible. I cringe.

Then the worst thing that could happen for Jovan happens. Worst aside from death, that is. He groans, rolls over and starts making incomprehensible noises that are probably meant to be words. He's not out, but not coherent enough to play like he is.

While I want to help him and apologize till the sun comes up, I step backward and out of the cell instead. Connor and Maddix grab all the soldiers' gear and make for the reception area, eager to put distance between us and this place. My father is probably no less eager. Every line of his body seems taut with suppressed energy. Even so, he seems to sense that I'm in a little over my head and having difficulty processing the sudden change in my existence.

His steps are quiet. He puts a gentle hand on my shoulder and whispers, "We should go."

The soldiers are quiet, perhaps thinking that we'll hit them too if they make noise. Jovan, on the other hand, rears up even as I turn to go and looks around with unfocused eyes. They slide over me, then back like he's having difficulty nailing down exactly where I'm at. He says, "Sorry, Karas. Thought this would work. Just wanted you to see your father." He snuffles a little, his eyes wandering back toward me and adds, "You have such pretty eyes, like the sky."

His words are a little slurred, but unfortunately clear enough for anyone who can hear them to understand. That last bit proves he has no clue what he's saying, but it doesn't matter because the first part is logical enough.

The taller soldier gasps but the short one laughs. It's a bark of a laugh, bitter and victorious all at once. His voice is low and mean when he says, "Nice try."

I really don't like the look on his face. There's no question now what will happen when we leave. Jovan will be found out and this soldier will be only too happy to let the information flow. Whether Jovan can deflect it or deny it and do a good enough job is something I doubt. He may have dropped our friendship, but he has always been an honest soul. He'll crack.

My fist clenches around the night-stick and the soldier's eyes dart toward it, then back to my face. The victory slides off and uncertainty comes back. He knows what I'm thinking and what I'm thinking is that I'll have to bash his brains in.

My father grabs the nightstick and says, "No. That's not someplace you want to go. Let's get him up."

Chapter Eleven

The choice is made and I can do nothing except make sure he doesn't die in the process of moving him around. Jovan isn't a small person. He towers over me when he's standing and he's like a long floppy burden right now. We grab him, my father at Jovan's shoulders and I at his feet, and do a clumsy job of maneuvering him out of the cell and into reception.

Maddix and Connor are going through the duty desks and the shelves behind the big counter that splits the room. There are growing piles of stuff on the counter and the floor. They stop and gape at us when we huff our way out of the cell block with a groaning Jovan between us. This isn't what we had planned out, so clearly something has gone wrong. My father gets Jovan's head onto the pile of uniforms and eases him down as I settle his feet.

Jovan immediately tries to get up, uncoordinated and confused. My father presses him gently back down and tells me, "Keep him still, Karas. We have to get moving."

Inside, I feel like a thousand bees are boiling out of a hive that's inexplicably become lodged in my stomach. Panic is building and I know what will happen when it gets to be too much. I'll make a mess of things by running or fighting or just creating general havoc. We can't afford for that to happen now so I stroke Jovan's forehead to keep him still, close my eyes and count slowly. It helps to bring me out of my frantic emotions and puts me back in the moment. I feel better by the time I get to twenty.

Around me, the steady activity continues. My father is like the calm center of a storm, comfortable despite the fact that time is passing dangerously quickly. He even seems to know where everything would logically be, opening and closing drawers or calling out something that should be searched for.

When I hear the sound of a successful find, I open my eyes to see him bouncing a handful of keys in his hand and smiling. He's got a nice smile, very genuine, not at all the smile of a hardened criminal. Not that I would know what that looks like, really.

Maddix stops cramming things into bags as my father dangles several sets of keys in his hand. "Yes!" he exclaims. "That will get us out of here."

That's when I realize the keys must be for the Army vehicles here at the Courthouse. They're probably all charging in the garage we passed less than an hour ago.

My father tosses the keys and Maddix snatches them out of the air. He says, "Go find out what kinds of vehicles they have and check the charges on every vehicle. Hurry."

Maddix dashes through the door and is gone like a shot into the dark night. My father goes back to his searching, disappearing into the break room that the soldiers came out of.

Under my hand Jovan moves differently, his movements with less aimless agitation and more purpose. His eyes are open and steady now, no longer roaming around and unable to focus. He winces when I touch the side of his head but smiles to take the sting out of it.

He grabs my hand when I pull away and asks, "This didn't go exactly as planned, did it?"

I shake my head, not sure how I'm going to break the news to him that his privileged life as a Foley has probably just ended. Unless he wants to go in and kill a couple of soldiers and blame it on the escapees, that is.

"I'm sorry," I say and rest my free hand in my lap, letting him keep the other. I'm not sure why he has my hand since he's not really doing anything with it. He's simply holding it like he might hold a pencil or a piece of chalk, absently. Even so, I can feel how hot his hand is against my stress-cold skin.

He sighs and says, "It was bound to happen, one way or another." He tucks in his chin, puts on a deep and very cultured voice and says, "There is the right way to do things, the wrong way to do things, and then there is the Jovan way of doing things."

He rolls his eyes and I can tell this is something he's heard many times. The voice is clearly an imitation of his father's, who I've heard speak a good many times, even though the last time he directly spoke to me I was just a kid. Perfect though the Foley life may appear from the outside, it clearly isn't perfect in Jovan's view.

Maddix comes rushing back in and breaks the moment, for which I'll be eternally grateful. "Most of them are about half-charged, four or five lights, except the little one they used to bring us in. That one's got three lights. There are the two little cars, one prairie jumper and a four-door. I put the right key on top of each one."

My father asks Jovan, "Is that all of them?"

Jovan nods gingerly and adds, "Except for the patrol that's out now in the other prairie jumper. They're scheduled to go to the lake area tonight. Nowhere close to us."

My father hands a packed bag to Connor, who stacks it with several others by the door, clearly thinking hard. He says, "Okay, Connor, we're taking the prairie jumper so load up everything in the back of it but don't start it. We'll need all the juice."

Connor looks like he might balk at this strange man telling him what to do, but an encouraging nod from Maddix settles the matter and he sets to the task.

"Maddix, we need to drain the other vehicles of charge. Unhook them, cut the charging cables and then reverse the leads. That will drain them fast."

A quick nod of understanding and Maddix is gone again, leaving just the three of us in the room. I still don't understand how he is so calm and matter-of-fact about the situation we're in. It's a dire one and I'm having a hard time wrapping my mind around it.

All those little details are in my brain but I can't let them come forward right now or they'll paralyze me. Details like me not living in this town anymore after this night, like my mom not having anyone to take care of her, like leaving everyone I know other than the people with me behind forever.

Even the idea of never seeing Mr. Carpenter, the man who runs the compost operation, who always has a smile and a cup of milk for me, is hard to take in. I've not had a chance to prepare for it, so all of the consequences keep bouncing off my thoughts like moths against a porch light.

Not my father, though. He's as cool as a spring morning and doesn't seem at all ruffled by the idea of his daughter, who he left fifteen years ago, helping him to rob a Courthouse. That, and a bunch of other crimes too numerous to count at this point.

Jovan levers himself into a sitting position, letting my hand go so he can use both of his to brace himself. I back away and stand, not really wanting to be near him given what I've just done to his life. He'll figure that out soon and I can't see him holding my hand for comfort once he does.

He shakes his head and probes the back of it with careful fingers, sucking in a hissing breath when he finds the spot where I hit him. He looks up at me from under his brow and says, "Not bad. But it wasn't hard enough."

He winces when he pushes on it with a finger so I say, "Stop messing with it."

"I just wanted to make sure it was just a lump and not a soft spot," he explains, but I'm relieved to see his hand drop away without any blood on it.

Just then my father interrupts us by tossing a sack my way. It's just a rough burlap sack like the ones used by everyone for almost everything: food, supplies, clothes and anything else that needs toting. This one isn't patched all over like the ones I have, and it has the dark green stripe that identifies it as Army issue.

"Pack those uniforms and then get him to the garage. We need to move out," he says.

"What about food? What about Mom?" I ask. Where before it felt like we were moving far too slowly, now it feels like everything is going too fast. I'm leaving too much, too soon.

He sighs, gives a little shake of his head and says, "We can't risk you seeing her, Karas. I hope you understand."

I nod, because he's right even though he doesn't understand what it's really like at home with her. But that isn't why I need to go home. "My garden has stuff we can take, plus I have water carriers. There's plenty of early spring stuff like carrots, beets…" I let the sentence trail off.

The dry lands stand between us and the border and water may be hard to find. Food will be even scarcer. And I saw him come out of the break room with just three small canteens, the kind the soldiers carry on their belts. Those won't last us half a day.

It startles me to see him chew the inside of his cheek because it is exactly what I do when I'm indecisive or in a bind. It's a terrible habit but one I've never been able to break entirely. For some reason, seeing him do the same makes me smile. It's like a link between us, even though we are strangers.

"Water's not that hard to find. You'd be surprised how quickly the dry lands end once we head east. But food, that can be hard when you can't stop to hunt." He looks at me with a measuring gaze and asks, "How quickly can you get what you need?"

"Fast enough," I say. "Faster if I take Connor."

He sighs again, but not in a way that signals impatience or anything. It's more like the sigh of someone who has to deal with an inevitable delay, so I know what he's about to say.

Connor comes back for another load by the time I've extricated myself and helped Jovan to his feet. Jovan sways for a moment, but quickly steadies and offers me a smile to let me know he's fine. He takes Connor's place at the pile of bags and says nothing as he loads himself up with all the remaining bags. For good or ill, he's with us.

Chapter Twelve

The streets are dark and quiet. It feels like days instead of a scant hour since I set out with Connor for a final visit with my father. Everything has changed since then and it shows in how I see the dark buildings around us.

I see them through eyes that are saying goodbye. Now the buildings seem shabbier, their fading paint gray in the darkness, the windows old, dusty and dark. As we jog the few blocks between the Courthouse and my home, the sounds of water in the canal across the street accompany us.

The houses are all the same here, varying only in their color. Like everything else, the paint is old and faded to lackluster versions of the original shade. Pale blue that's nearing gray, lilac where it was once purple and even a faded yellow so pale it glows white in the faint moonlight.

At my house, we dip around to the back. Connor doesn't need me to tell him what we need. We head straight for my garden shed and he heaves up the pile of sacks on my workbench, lifting a cloud of dust along with the rough burlap. I grab the snips and a small trowel for the garden.

"I need some light," I whisper. No one will hear us out here, but I find it difficult to speak normally while we're being so stealthy.

My only flashlight is in the house, but Connor pulls his out of one of his voluminous pockets and starts to wind it while we're in the slight protection of the shed. It whines terribly and the sound makes me wince.

"Let's go," he says when he's done winding.

"Wait," I say and start pulling old containers and general junk off a pile in the back corner. When I get to my buckets, I fill up a couple of small bags with the best of my tumbled stones. Connor and I have spent days on end turning the handle on my tumbler to create each batch. These buckets represent years of intermittent labor. I've been hiding them here in the shed as a sort of savings account, meaning to sell them when I finally reached my eighteenth birthday and can get away from this house.

I hand one bag to Connor and tuck the other into my coat pocket along with my handful of steel balls and my slingshot. It's a weak weapon, but useful against rats, and it's the most common one around, given how costly gun ammunition is.

"You've got yours, right?" I ask. He knows I mean his slingshot and nods.

Most of the yard is just weeds struggling to find purchase after our dry winter and spring, but the far corner holds the neat rows of my garden. We depend on that food and I feel bad for taking it, but the truth is that my mother will simply let it die. Not because she's lazy, because she's not, but because she won't think of it before a lack of water takes its toll.

Between the two of us we harvest all the beets, radishes and most of the carrots. They aren't large but they're big enough to be worth it. We snip greens until I have an entire sack of kale and chard. Not much else is ready for harvest, and I regret that we've got to leave the rest.

"Is this it?" Connor asks, and I can see he's calculating how long this will last five full-grown people.

"I have dried food inside," I offer.

"We need it," he says and lets the implication hang. I risk waking my mom if I go inside and start rummaging around in the cabinets.

I pluck up an empty sack before running to the back door. This door doesn't creak. I've been careful to grease the hinges since I'm the only one who uses this door. The front door is the opposite. It squeaks terribly so that I'll always know when my mother enters or leaves the house.

The kitchen seems like something from another life. It's the same, but different. The dishes from dinner are still in the sink but otherwise it's neat and clean. I sniff and find the distinct scent of grain alcohol lingering in the air. There's no time to muck about with things, so I grab two tin canisters of grain from the cupboard along with two of dried fruit.

I'm tempted to grab more, but I can't leave my mother without anything. It will take her days to figure out how to take care of things for herself as it is. If I weren't so sure there will be soldiers here demanding to know where I am within hours, I'd be inclined to say that it might take her days to realize that I'm well and truly gone.

Something won't let me leave yet. I need to see her again, make sure she isn't lying on her back so she won't choke if she gets sick, make sure there's nothing amiss and that she hasn't kicked her covers off.

I tiptoe on careful feet into the living room, avoiding the boards I know will creak. There's just one light on—a dim one that doesn't use a great deal of energy—powered by the small turbine on the roof. It doesn't stay lit all the time, because there must be at least some wind for it to work, but tonight it casts shadows around the room.

One of those shadows is my mother and it doesn't look like she's moved much since I left. Lying on the couch with a blanket drawn up tight around her chin, she's quiet. On the floor is a half-empty bottle of grain spirits. It's a small bottle, but the alcohol inside is very strong and it doesn't take much. She had nothing but empty bottles when I left for the parade, so this one must have been newly filled. Based on the level remaining, I figure she's out for the night. Her heavy breathing bears this out.

Slipping past her, I duck up the stairs and into my room to grab my pack. In it go the necessities of a new life. Mostly, that includes underwear, socks and my two best shirts. My room is almost bare of things I can take and that suddenly seems sad to me.

I never really noticed it before. I think of this house as the place I'll escape from when the time comes to start a new life, rather than the place I call home. The walls are water-stained where the increasingly uncommon rain leaks in around the windows. There's a straw-filled mattress on a bed of creaky springs, and an old dresser missing two of its four drawers. That's all I have to show for my life to date.

Everything important I own is hidden from view to keep it safe. My three big buckets of laboriously tumbled stones, the ones I was saving to sell when I turned eighteen and could leave. I have so little else.

That's it aside from my memory box, and that's such a small thing. My few photos and valueless odds and ends are all it contains. I pull out the floorboard under my bed and take it, the last thing I need from my childhood home.

Back in the living room, I check to be sure she hasn't stirred but all seems the same. I creep forward and look down at her. Like this, with her face softened in sleep, she looks younger and far less angry than when she's awake. The lines on her face are smoothed by the dim light and lack of expression.

I've always liked looking at her when she's like this, though I know she would be angry if she knew I did it. Sometimes, when I know she's deeply passed out, I talk to her. Then, when I know it's safe, I talk to her about my day or my worries or just tell her that I love her.

I do none of that now. I dare not chance waking her by touching her or smoothing back the lock of dark blond hair that has fallen over her eyes. Instead, I walk back the way I came and leave my house for the last time.

Connor and I make it back to the Courthouse without any fuss, each of us doing our best not to let the bulky bags slap against our legs and bruise the contents within. The small door to the garage, next to the big bay doors for the vehicles, is cracked open and leaking weak light into the street. We step in and find them all waiting for us, even Cassi. Her face is drawn and pale in the light, full of trepidation.

"Cassi! Why are you here? No one saw you. Go home!" I exclaim, handing my bags off to Maddix.

Her curls shake along with her head as she says, "I can't. They'll come asking and then what will I do?"

She's right. Cassi is sweet and kind and never thinks poorly of anyone. I can almost see it. Soldiers with grim faces, maybe even an officer, will come and bang on her family's door, asking what she knows about her two closest friends. They'll ask her about yesterday's meeting with all of us on the side of the canal, in full view of the world. No, Cassi can't go home.

"Oh, Cassi," I say. It's all I can say.

The tears run down her freckled face and her chin shakes, but even so, she is resolute. She hugs me tightly and whispers, "It's worth it. We saved all of them, right?"

My father comes around the side of the vehicle. His tiny nod says it's time to go. We pile in except for Maddix, who tries to lift the garage door as silently as possible. Jovan slides in with my father in the front, the rest of us climb into the rear seat.

The cargo area in back behind us is roomy, as it must be for a prairie jumper meant to take patrols and all the supplies they will need at remote outposts. Right now it's depressingly empty, our paltry number of sacks barely making a dent in the available space.

We are utterly silent when my father starts the big vehicle. The only sign that it's running is the panel of tiny lights populating the dash. That's one good thing about the electric vehicles. My father eases the jumper out of the garage and Maddix closes the garage door as quietly as he can. Then he jumps in, squeezing Jovan to the middle of the front seat.

We start along the dark main street, the reverse of the path the prisoners walked just the day before. Everyone is silent, doubtless wrapped up in their own thoughts about what they are leaving behind, what they're going toward and how things are about to change. Cassi takes my hand and we twine our fingers together, her grip tight and desperate for comfort.

On my other side, Connor sits still and silent, looking out of the window at the darkened buildings as we sail past and out into the night. I find his hand lying limply on his leg, and grip it in mine.

He turns from the window and says, "I guess we're Strikers now, too." Then he smiles, but his smile doesn't reach his eyes.

Chapter Thirteen

The tires whine beneath us on the road and we leave the town behind us. It disappears into a smudge of light and then into nothing quite quickly. Our town isn't large but it's all I've ever known.

I've never been more than a day's walk from it in my life. To the west, a few hours' hike has brought me past the last of anything truly green and into the dry lands. I've camped out there many times with Connor and Cassi, watching the stars and listening to the wind through the scrubby brush. The ruins of Carolton, a place that always seems to be crawling with soldiers for reasons I can't determine, is the furthest I've ever gone west. Connor and I collect stones for our tumblers there.

To the east, the grazing lands stretch endlessly, as flat as a piece of paper. In spring and summer it's beautiful, with endless grasses waving in the constant breezes. Out there, there's only the shriek of a hawk or the lowing of cattle to break the wind's mellow song. South of Bailar, I've been limited to a couple of trips to the lake. Beyond that are the bigger cities and only the very wealthy can get permits to go there. Even for them, a permit like that is a rare thing.

But north is a direction I've not gone before at all. Bailar territory is close to the Texas border. Beyond are the contentious areas where the wild lands begin, and the places where the wars were fought generations ago. There is one additional smaller town, more of an outpost really, to the north. I've met those that live there because they come to Bailar to trade and shop for food.

Perhaps it's because I've always wondered what lies beyond Bailar that my curiosity is warring with my terror at leaving everything I've ever known behind. There is a certain excitement to it all that I can't deny, but I feel guilty for it when Cassi squeezes my hand again.

"How far will we get on this much charge?" Maddix asks.

Both Jovan and my father start to answer, but my father stops and gestures for Jovan to go on.

"This one is little over half-charged so we'll get about sixty miles, no more."

"We should have taken one of the smaller vehicles," Connor complains.

Jovan turns as much as he can in his seat to look back at us. He looks well enough to me. His color is normal as far as I can see in the glow of the dashboard, and his eyes are tracking fine.

"All the batteries are sized according to the size of the vehicle. All of them get about the same number of miles per charge," he answers.

Connor grumps and then leans on his arm against the window, looking outside like he didn't hear what Jovan said. I've no idea why he's so upset. He got his brother back and a ready escape from his parents and the future strikes they would surely earn for him. And he gets to escape with friends and family to support him, rather than running for his life alone. He should be happy, or at least not angry. But Connor is not a fan of change in general, so I put it down to that.

"That will get us to Wicha but from there we'll be on foot," my father says.

I'd like to answer that with more questions but I'm hesitant. Not because I don't want to ask or am shy, but because I don't know what to call him. I know I called him "Dad" before, when I wasn't thinking about it, but that was an accident.

When speaking of him or thinking of him, I've always thought of him as Dad. "Father" is a pretentious word that is purposefully distant. "Dad" is a familiar word full of affection, but can that possibly be the right name to call someone who has never been more than a name and an image in a few fading photographs? What do I call him? Jordan? Perhaps that's safer. No matter if he did come back for me, as it seems he has—he's still a stranger.

"Jordan," I say tentatively and wait for a clue as to how this will be received. His eyes flick up in the rearview mirror but nothing in his quick glance tells me one way or another.

"You got a question?" he asks, when I say nothing more.

"Isn't Wicha dangerous?" I ask.

Wicha is the source of many stories and none of them are good. It's very close to the border and took a great deal of damage in the war for freedom. Supposedly, it isn't inhabited, at least officially. Unofficially, it is said that people who come near it are often not heard from again. Even patrols are careful in the ruins of Wicha.

"It is, but mostly from the falling buildings and such. There are people there, and they're technically Texans, but who really knows? They could be Wilders who came over and settled there," he says and shrugs like it's irrelevant.

Jovan tries to turn again, but he's squeezed between the other two and can't really manage it, so he turns to the side and speaks upward, like he's chatting with the roof of the prairie jumper. "We just need to be sure we're in shelter by daylight and we don't go into any claimed territory. It's pretty straightforward. They don't like soldiers, but don't mind Strikers or anyone else not in a position to arrest them. So I'll need to be sure I'm not wearing these."

He means his cadet uniform. He's lucky because one of the bags in the back is from his locker at the Courthouse and has a change of clothes in it. Otherwise, he'd be limited to wearing burlap sacks if uniforms are a problem. Jordan is nodding in agreement while he watches the dark road ahead of us.

The road is so bumpy it feels like we're driving over a giant washboard. The bounces are coming so fast it makes all our speech sound funny. From my perch in the middle, I can see the dashboard lights over Jovan's shoulder. One of the lights on the charge meter has just gone out and we're down to four already. Half a charge doesn't last long.

I have so many questions but all of them lead back to a single focus: my father. How did he hook up with Maddix? Why did they both come back? The questions are endless.

"Maddix, why did you come back?" I ask, after we've been quiet a while.

He twists in his seat like an eel till he's facing us. Maddix is tall and lanky, but not awkward. He was always the one who could clamber up a drainpipe and jump off a roof with a flip as a flourish. He has the same board-straight hair as Connor, but his is longer and that softens the angles somehow. Maddix would have been one of those boys all the girls in school crushed on if he had come from a different family. To me, he's more like a brother, though I'm not blind to his good looks. The bruises and swollen nose hide those looks for now, but he'll heal soon enough.

Maddix grins and reaches out a long arm to flick Connor on the top of his head, not hard, but as a tease. "I had to come back for my brother here. After I met up with Jordan, we talked and—well, here we are."

That is possibly the most incomplete answer I've ever heard and I scowl at him until he laughs and says, "There's a lot more to it, but that's for when we stop and have some time to talk. I'm not the only one with a story." He jabs a thumb toward my father, still intent on the road ahead, and twists back around to sit facing forward again.

Silence settles over us again like a blanket, each of us wrapped up in our own thoughts. Cassi's eyes have closed in sleep, her head shifting against the window. The marks of her tears are still on her cheeks, faint streaks of lighter skin on her dusty face. Her freckles stand out along those streaks and it makes her seem so young, rather than a year older than me.

Connor is still staring out of the window too, but he keeps glancing toward his brother in the front seat, as if reassuring himself that he's still there. Our hands are still entwined on the small bit of seat between us and I'm not about to let go.

Out of all us, it's only Connor whose life might be said to have improved by this turn of events. His two strikes would surely not have been his last and now, he will finally be free from his parents and their never-ending schemes. Even I can't be sure my life will change for the better by striking, only that it will be different.

Outside, the land is dark and formless as it passes by, the only illumination from the headlights directly ahead of us. All those lights serve up is a quickly passing series of potholes my father swerves to avoid. While I watch, another light goes out on the charge indicator.

Chapter Fourteen

I startle awake when the nature of the road changes. Instead of the washboard shaking, it's become a slow, violent lurching. When I rub my eyes and the world comes back into focus, I see all three in the front seat peering forward and to the sides intently. Cassi and Connor both have hold of the straps above the windows and Connor has his other arm stretched protectively across my chest. I tap his arm to let him know I'm awake and grip the front seats to keep myself in place.

The world outside has changed in the brief time I was asleep. There's just rubble and the shells of half-fallen buildings, all of it eerily lit in flashes by the moving headlights. I can't make heads or tails of what I'm seeing, but everyone else seems to be looking for something specific.

Maddix breaks the silence by pointing at something to the right and yelling, "There!"

My father jerks the wheel and illuminates what Maddix pointed to. Its looks just like another pile of rubble to me, but with a big black hole in it. He stops the vehicle, leaving it pointed toward the black recess, and says, "Go check it out. It looks good from here."

Maddix climbs out of the jumper and runs toward the hole, a flashlight in his hand. When he gets close to it I can see it's much larger than it looked. He's dwarfed inside it and his light flickers around the ragged walls. He disappears inside, only the glow of his light telling me which way he went.

He comes out and waves the flashlight for Jordan to drive forward. The vehicle jerks and I look at the dash. It has one light remaining on the charge panel and it's flickering between yellow and red, a sign I take to mean we're about out of juice.

When we pull even with Maddix, he leans in to say, "It's tighter further inside so everyone needs to get out now." To my father he says, "You can climb out the back once you pull in."

We scramble out and wait while my father drives into the maw of what was once a building. When the lights go out, the darkness is oppressive. I must not be the only one who feels it because Maddix turns the flashlight back on and starts winding the crank.

Inside the cave of rubble, my father pops out of the rear hatch of the jumper with a grin and waves us forward to collect our bags and such. It doesn't take long to get all of our stuff, which is depressing because we've got a long way to go if we're going to get away.

"Let's start grabbing stuff to close this up," my father says and drops his parcels to look around.

I dig out my flashlight and examine the area. I've never seen anything like this place. The remains of buildings are everywhere, jumbled in heaps. Small gaps here and there show where streets must have once divided them. Twisted spires of rusted metal stick up out of broken masonry, and the glitter of long broken glass reflects from the piles.

My father, Jovan and Maddix are stacking junk at the opening of the cave in a deceptively haphazard pile. I grab an old board and it makes a sharp snap as the rotted wood breaks free.

Soon enough, it will be hard to tell that there was ever a gap there instead of this disordered pile of broken concrete, brick and wood. I have no idea what it might look like later, when full daylight comes, but by the light of all our flashlights, it's pretty convincing.

"That'll have to do. Let's go," my father says, slinging a couple of our sacks over one shoulder. I notice he keeps his hand free on the side he carries the gun in case he needs to grab the weapon quickly.

We load up and head into the rubble in single file, my father taking the lead and Maddix pulling up the rear. It's not easy going without my hands free to help balance or pull myself up on the shaky piles of rocks, but the short window of time we have to get hidden for the day urges me onward.

I marvel at the size of the city while we walk. Block after block of destruction in what was once a place where people lived and commerce was done. It's hard to believe so many people could have lived in one place. How could they ever grow enough food for themselves with no space between the buildings for crops?

I've heard about Dallas and Houston but never been to either place. I always hoped I'd earn enough someday to merit a permit, even if only to go and see for a little while. The way those cities are described sounds a little like this, only without the destruction. We send crops and meat there because they can't grow enough for themselves. It's a part of the general tax. I wonder if this place was the same and needed support from dozens of communities like our cities do.

Purple and pink are beginning to show on the horizon when my father finally calls a halt. We're all sweaty and grimy and I'm so thirsty my tongue feels like it's swelling inside my mouth. It's not yet true dawn, but that's only a few minutes away. Even so, its light enough that I can see our surroundings beyond the circle of my flashlight in shades of gray.

Apparently, my father can too because he and Maddix examine the rubble and the few standing walls nearby with care, as if they're looking for something. They nod at each other in some unspoken agreement while the rest of us stand there and try to catch our breath.

"In here," my father says and jumps lightly down from a giant wedge of concrete that has lifted up under some enormous pressure to create a good vantage point.

We follow him into a building made of pale stone that's still in pretty good shape, all things considered. The windows are all gone but the walls are mostly intact. I count as we enter and see nine more rows of holes where windows used to be above the ground floor. I can't tell if the roof is intact, but with so many floors above us, we at least have a shot at a dry place if the longed-for spring rain finally comes.

He leads us further into the interior until the last of the brightening dawn behind us disappears and the darkness is broken only by our wavering flashlights. Finally, he grunts and drops his burdens.

"This will do," he says.

The room is pretty big and has just one door. A large wooden table lies canted to the side in the center, one of its supports having collapsed sometime in the past. A few old chairs on wheels in the corner are thickly covered in dust. It's as good a place as any.

We set about pushing all the debris to one side of the room, leaving us a clear space to gather. We turn the long table up on its side to block the doorway, and it makes me feel safer, more hidden, almost immediately. I'm so tired I feel like I could sleep for days, but I want information even more than sleep. I need to know what we're planning, where we're going and most importantly, I need to know why he came back.

There's no fire possible in the closed room so a cold supper and the blessed relief of water is what we're allowed. One of my water containers is emptied almost immediately. A gallon of water between the six of us only lasts a few rounds. We've got two more and the little canteens, but at this rate, they won't last long. My father sprinkles some of the water inside the bag that I put the greens in, perhaps hoping they won't wilt as badly if there's moisture.

While we munch on carrots brushed relatively free of dirt and some spinach, we talk.

"I know you've got questions, but the bottom line up front is that Maddix let me know what was going on with you and I came to get you. He came back for Connor," my father says.

The way he says it is very matter-of-fact, like it's the most reasonable thing in the world to come back for a daughter he left behind without a word when she was an infant barely taking her first steps. But there is a message behind his words and I think I understand them. My mother wasn't always like this. She hadn't always been a drunk. He didn't know she'd become the way she is. How could he?

I glance at my father and he gives me a half-smile, letting me know that I'm right.

"I made it to the border," Maddix says, taking over the story. "They take all your information there, like your name and all of that, and when I told them I was from Bailar Territory and from the town of Bailar, they let me come in. Before I knew it, they had me talking with Jordan on a radio. I told him everything I knew and, well, the rest is history."

"And you came back with him?" I ask Maddix.

"Honestly, I never thought I'd come back, but once I met Jordan and I had a chance to see what was out there, I had to come back for my little brother. You wouldn't believe what the world is really like."

Cassi yawns loudly and I take it as a hint, even though I'm sure she doesn't mean it that way.

"So how long are we staying here?" I ask, indicating the room around us.

Jordan sighs and says, "I hate to burn the time but I think we should stay here and get some rest while it's light out and then head out tonight. If we hid the jumper as well as I think we did, then we should be safe. There's a lot to search here and if we're lucky, they won't even try."

"How likely is that?" I ask.

"Pretty likely, I'd say. Wicha is big and spread out over a large area. This building wasn't marked and I didn't see any marks anywhere near it, so I don't think this is claimed territory. Those marks aren't easy to read or find, so mostly the soldiers just avoid this area. It's too easy to lose your vehicle and everything else in Wicha if you come up on a bad group."

Jovan has settled down, his head nestled on his arm and his long legs stretched out behind me, but he stirs and says, "That's true. But this time they might make an exception."

"Which is exactly why laying low in here for a while is a good idea. It's much easier to get past any guards in the dark," my father answers.

That seems to be the end of it because he settles down as well, using one of our sacks for a pillow. Everyone else does the same so I do, too. I can't help but look at Jordan one last time before turning off my flashlight. There's more to him than I can guess at, but if we make it out of this, it looks like I'll have lots of time to find out.

Chapter Fifteen

Jovan wakes me with a gentle push on my shoulder. When I open my eyes he smiles and says, "You were snoring."

I just grunt at him and push his hand away. Waking up isn't my best skill and I'm usually a little grumpy and confused for a minute or two. When I sit up my entire body feels like someone beat on it with a bag of sand. Stiff and sore is really not a strong enough description. Between scrambling over rubble in the dark and sleeping on a hard floor, I'm a moody mess.

Weak light is leaking around the big table we used for a door and it's enough to see everyone else is either awake or getting there. Jordan turns on a flashlight and sets it so that the light reflects off the stained ceiling, instantly brightening the room enough to make me squint.

"How long were we asleep?" I ask, nodding towards Jovan's watch.

He glances down and says, "It's about an hour before dark. You've been snoring all day." He grins at me to show he's joking, but I'm not in any mood to be teased and it shows. At my sour expression, he pulls a face and drawls, "Oookay."

We pass around another water carrier, Jordan cautioning us to take only what we need to break our immediate thirst. It's hard to resist gulping down as much as I can hold, but I do. It tastes clean and delicious, and it washes away the dry, dirty feeling in my throat and mouth.

I'm hungry and I feel grimy on top of being thirsty. When I run my fingers through my hair to pull out the snarls, dust flies out in a cloud. It's hopeless so I put it back into its ponytail and leave it alone.

Jordan motions us over to the opposite corner of the room. He squats and smooths out the thick layer of dirt on the floor. We surround his work area and he draws a picture for us while he speaks.

"Wicha is laid out along this road here," he says, and points to a long snaking line he's drawn. "But it's spread pretty widely out from there. We want to avoid going through here or here, and especially here."

He emphasizes the locations by poking his finger into the dirt. To me it looks like he's making a line of dots along both sides of the road he's drawn, leaving us with very little space to maneuver. He makes a new line well away from the others and says, "We've got a better shot at getting through if we take the small streets around to the north. No vehicles could make it through there and it's not a likely place for patrols to make camp. There are too many places for people to hide or sneak up on them."

Jovan nods, obviously following this line of reasoning, while the rest of us just look on. I have no idea what would be best, but I can figure out that if we're going through places that vehicles can't get through, then there's more rubble. I'm not looking forward to it. My thighs are burning just thinking about more hours of rubble-climbing.

Jordan tells us he's going to scout, so we help move the heavy table away from the door. The light is golden, the kind that comes right before sunset. I wish I were at home, sitting on the roof with Connor and watching the sun disappear, knowing a good dinner and a warm bed awaited me below.

Before he slips out, Jordan turns to me and runs a rough palm across my cheek. He smiles and says, "I'm so happy you're here, Karas. Things will get better, you'll see."

It's an odd thing to say given our situation, but I return the smile with a tentative one of my own. Then he disappears into the street and I'm left hoping he'll return safe and sound.

Before we've even finished packing up, he slips back in and tells us we're clear to go. He leads once more and we trail along behind him like ducklings. The rubble is less intense as we leave the area where the tall buildings dominate. As we move north and the moon rises to break the darkness, the buildings grow squatter, with more space between them. I can see the faded remains of lines on some of the broken asphalt between buildings, and Jordan tells me those are parking lots, places where people parked their cars while they went inside the stores to shop.

I find it hard to believe. The lot we're crossing is huge and just the few lines I can make out with my flashlight tell me the individual spaces were small. That means there's room for a hundred cars at least. The low line of a one-story building lies to the side of the lot, all the windows broken out, some of the gaps filled with old wood while others yawn black and empty. Just from the number of them and the shapes of old door openings, I can tell there were a dozen stores. It seems impossible that so many people had cars and there were so many places to shop.

In Bailar we've got exactly one store. Any number of stalls might be set up in the town market, but we've just got the one store. As for cars, the soldiers have them and the regular people have the town transport. That consists of two open-sided buses that can seat a dozen people, with hanging-on room for a few more if they don't mind being jerked around. Only one is in use at a time, but you can be sure that every half hour during the day it will come around and get you to the other side of our small town in less than fifteen minutes. I can't imagine a need for so many cars.

Jordan hurries us along in these open spaces and we make good time. The moon is high in the sky when he stops us for a much-needed break. My legs have loosened up and they feel better than they did when I first woke up. My feet, on the other hand, are dog-tired. The way Cassi drops to the ground and groans when she loosens her bootlaces tells me I'm not the only one feeling it.

She and Connor have been talking quietly for most of the night. Behind me, I heard the low back-and-forth between Jovan and Maddix every once in a while, too. Jordan has been quiet and intent, scanning ahead of us and figuring out our path. It's only me who has been both alone and unoccupied, simply following along. I know it's not intentional, but I feel a little left out.

I drop next to Cassi and nudge her shoulder. "How are you holding up?"

She grimaces and flexes her feet. "Okay, I guess. Sore," she answers.

"No, I mean the whole thing."

"Oh," she says softly.

We're silent for so long that I figure she doesn't want to answer me, or maybe that she's mad at me for what's happened. I would deserve it, so I say, "I got you into this and I'm so sorry. I'll do my best to make it up to you."

I have absolutely no idea how you make up to someone the loss of a happy family home but I know I'll give it a try.

When she looks at me, I don't see any anger there. What I do see is the same girl who looks for the positive no matter what's going on. She cocks her head to the side, draws her brows together and says, "This isn't your fault. No one here is to blame. We're here because things in Texas are jacked up and the situation forced our hand. People shouldn't die because of stupid things."

She's right about that part. People shouldn't be declared habitual criminals, and suffer the death penalty that comes with such a declaration, when they don't always even get to control whether or not they break a law. Who can keep track of them given how fast they change? And a law against leaving the Texas Republic is just stupid. I squeeze her shoulder, hoping she'll know how much she means to me.

Jordan tells us we have five minutes and there are moans all around. I lean back and let myself collapse onto the cold ground. After I close my eyes, I hear a whoof of noise as someone drops next to me. Slitting one eye open, I see Jovan beside me, arms and legs outstretched like he's exhausted. Now I'm surrounded on both sides by people whose lives I am at least partially responsible for ruining.

Jovan rolls his head to face me and grins when he see me peering at him. His grin is like an infectious disease, spreading whenever it comes in range.

I return it. He touches his head and gives a dramatic wince, which functions to peel the smile right off my face.

"Hey," he says. "I didn't mean it like that. I was only teasing."

"How is your head, really?" I ask. I do feel bad about it.

The uncertain way he looks at me almost looks like it's he who has reason to feel guilty. "I'm fine. Honest."

The awkward silence that falls between us is almost unendurable, so I close my eyes and pretend I'm resting. I'm so relieved when Jordan calls for us to get moving, I almost jump up and grab my stuff, doing my best not to meet Jovan's gaze. Connor and Maddix head out, heads together in conversation and this time I'm the one left to bring up the rear with Jovan.

I'm apparently never going to get over my inherent inability to simply be normal around him. As we walk, I glance at him now and then. He's paying attention to everything around us, peering out into the darkness to either side of our track and occasionally turning around to watch behind us.

It eliminates the need to chat with him or else be rude, but not forever. He and Maddix were speaking while they walked before. I glance up again and this time, instead of seeing him looking somewhere else, I catch him watching me. He looks away and if the sliver of moon were giving us a little more light, I'm pretty sure I would have seen him blush. It's just something about the way he jerked his head that screamed "blush".

I'd like to launch into random talk and break the ice that's built up between us. He and I have a complicated past. We were close as children but then, suddenly and without explanation, he stopped talking to me. Not the kind of drifting apart that has happened with other friends as we grew up. It was from one day to the next. And it was the day after our kiss behind the school. That makes it doubly uncomfortable and hard to simply gloss over.

If I had just had the nerve to ask him why back then, we might not be this tense around each other all the time. But I didn't. Instead, I was confused and hurt and then there was this giant wall between us. It was easier to pretend I didn't miss him. Of course, I had lost more than my friend when that happened. He was my first boyfriend, my first bad kiss and then, my first heartbreak.

Eventually, I found out the reason behind it, and that should have made me feel better. It didn't. The wound had scarred over and it was there to stay. But it did help me understand.

When that teacher saw us kissing, she reported us to his father. His demand that we not see each other had been followed with the threat of having my mother fired and us turned out of housing. Really, what choice did Jovan have? I only wish he'd shared the reason with me.

Cassi breaks away from the trio and saves me from yet more uncomfortable silence by joining us. "Jordan says we're going to rest as soon as the moon goes down. Maybe build a fire and get some food," she says, clearly excited by the idea of being warm.

To tell the truth, I'm pretty excited by that thought too. I'm hungrier than I've been in a long time and my feet are already getting sore again.

"Good," I say. "Any idea what we're doing after that?"

She shakes her head and hunches down further into her thin jacket to conserve some warmth. "Not really. He says we'll be clear of the main part of Wicha soon and can spend the day in the outskirts. By the end of tomorrow night, we should be close to the Benton outpost."

Jovan starts at the mention of Benton. "Benton is manned. We have to steer clear of that."

Cassi just shrugs as if to say that we should talk to Jordan about it.

By the time the moon starts to sink in the sky and the dawn is just an hour or so away, we're walking through areas less cluttered with rubble, the buildings more intact. There's still not an undamaged pane of glass to be found, but the rooftops look fairly straight and we passed whole rows of homes where the walls show no signs of collapse. It's abandoned. I can feel that without bothering to look inside any of the houses or buildings. There's a desolate feeling to the place and our footsteps are the only purposeful sounds around us.

Jordan calls a halt and walks around while we wait in the street. He peers into gaps and examines the walls of nearby buildings with care. He even examines the ground, looking for something, though I don't know what.

Standing still is letting the cold seep in and I'm shivering by the time he waves us over to one of the empty houses. He clears away some shards of glass still managing to cling to the sill of a broken window, then helps each of us through before following. The way he jumps down, lightly and with perfect ease, makes me wish I'd inherited a little of that grace and confidence. I'm a klutz.

There's a lot of broken furniture in the house. I touch a fabric covered couch and when I do, the fabric crumbles away under my fingers. The smell is dry, but also somehow rotten. It's all mixed in with the rank earthiness of ancient mouse droppings.

"We could break some of this up for a fire," I suggest, indicating the couch and the other broken furnishings.

Jordan drops his packs, puts his hands to the small of his back and groans as he stretches his muscles. He takes in our surroundings and shakes his head. "I'd rather not use this stuff. All this was chemically treated when it was new. Let me see what I can get outside."

With that, he's out of the window again and I hear his footsteps as he walks to the back of the house. Within a minute, he's back at the window and calls in, "I need some help out here bringing in wood."

Everyone else is sitting and stretching out, so I wave off their half-hearted volunteering and follow Jordan out the window. The moon is almost gone and the night is growing darker by the minute. I follow the sound of a winding flashlight and then squint against the light when he clicks it back on.

"We can use this," he says and points to a dead tree. It's still standing but the ground around it is littered with fallen limbs.

We gather armfuls of the branches and I'm surprised at how light they are. They've been dead a long time but the air out here is so dry and rainfall so meager that they haven't rotted, merely seasoned. We've been passing many of these dead trees, more than I've ever seen alive in one spot if I were to add them all together, except at the lake.

Trees aren't common out here on the borders of the dry lands. Some exist, but generally they are short things that tolerate drought. Even then, they're found only on the margins of the waterways or where there is a spring under the ground to supply them. And almost never have I seen a tended tree that didn't pay for itself by producing something of value.

"Why are there so many trees here?" I ask. What I'd really like to do is talk to him, find out about him, understand this person who is also my father. It's safer to ask about trees.

Jordan stands, his arms laden with a pile of branches taller than his head. I can't even see his whole face, just the shine of his eyes between the limbs.

"It wasn't always this dry out here, plus people watered them and their lawns and such," he answers.

There must be more to it than that so I ask, "Were these fruit trees or something?"

He chuckles and says, "Nope. People just liked trees in their yards. It was a different time."

He leads me to a broken concrete area behind the house. A door I hadn't seen while we were inside is now open and hanging askew from a single hinge. A light flares and I see Jovan, already squatting and looking at the broken chunks of concrete. He waves with his light at a spot where we should drop our wood but barely spares us another glance. I watch while he and my father create a sort of wall out of broken masonry behind which they build a small fire.

At the first crackle, the others join us and we gather around the rapidly warming spot. With the house shielding us from the wind and the little wall reflecting back the heat—and hiding the light—it's almost cozy. We don't often have heat this luxuriously intense in our homes and I intend to enjoy it, even if we are running for our lives. Natural gas wells provide fuel for heating, but the cost means we use it as little as possible, mostly for cooking. Heating is reserved for the coldest days. This fire is something different altogether.

Jordan surprises me again when he pulls out two camp pots from the assortment of bags. Soon enough, we're all sharing a pot of greens boiled with a little jerky. I feel better almost the moment it reaches my stomach. We eat all of the greens because they won't keep well for too much longer. For now, we're full and warm and safe. I know it won't last.

Chapter Sixteen

Jordan wakes me with a finger pressed to my lips. Outside the window the sky is clear and bright, the sun high. I rub my eyes, groggy from too little sleep, and he hands me a canteen. It's filled with cold tea we brewed before the rising sun made it necessary to put out the fire so the smoke wouldn't give us away. The tea is like a jolt to my system it's so good and he smiles at my moan, beckoning for me to follow him outside. It must be our turn on watch, so I pull on my boots and follow.

Between two of the houses, there's a wall made of concrete blocks that's still in pretty good shape. That's where we've decided to keep our watch from. A roof would be better, but they are as brittle as last fall's leaves and not even remotely safe to stand on.

Connor and Maddix meet us halfway, not waiting for us to make it all the way to the wall. During their watch, they sighted a single plume of dust, moving fast in the direction of the old highway but it didn't pause or turn around. That's good.

I look them both over to see how things are between them, but they seem the same as they did before Maddix left. If there were any hard feelings or any emotional stuff, they've worked it out of their systems. They go back to the house for some sleep and we toward our perch. After a few steps, I hear Connor say my name.

When I turn back, a hand shading my eyes against the glare of the sun, he shifts his feet like he's not sure what he wants to say. Then he jogs the dozen steps between us and surprises me by wrapping me in a hug. Not the one-armed half-hug we like to call a "man hug" but a full-on arms-wrapped-as-tight-as-they-can type of hug.

To say that I'm surprised would be an understatement. Connor is affectionate, but not touchy in that way. He's not the one to initiate the physical comfort he needs. It's always Cassi or I that reaches for his hand when we know he needs it. Not today, though. After a beat, I wrap my arms around him as well. He smells of dust and sweat, which is probably what I smell like, too.

"Thank you," he whispers in my ear.

"Thank *you*," I whisper back.

It's all we need to say. We each know what we're saying to the other. He's thanking me for going for broke inside the jail and I'm thanking him for giving me the courage to even go inside the jail in the first place. We're a team.

When we break our embrace he turns and runs to the house without looking back. I can see from the stiff posture that he's a little embarrassed. I look at Jordan, who is already atop the wall and looking around, but he doesn't acknowledge my little emotional moment with Connor. At the wall, he reaches down a hand for me and I barely have a chance to touch the wall with my toes before he pulls me up with apparent ease.

There's nothing to see, for which I'm grateful. No plumes of dust to indicate searching vehicles, no smoke from a patrol's campfire. The only sounds are the wind through the remains of the houses and the slither of sand rubbing against itself.

Now's my chance to talk to him, really talk to him. I've haven't had a single moment alone with him and after what he told me in his cell, when he thought he had only a few minutes in this life left to say anything at all to me, I've got a lot of questions.

He seems to sense how hard it is for me to get started, because he stops a few paces from me on the wall and asks, "How ya doing, Karas?"

"Well, I've lost my home, my mom and any hope of a normal life. I'm also guaranteed a hot shot and a grave if I don't run for my life fast enough. Other than that, I'm good," I say, my voice flat with sarcasm.

I have no idea why I answered like that. It's true, but it isn't what I wanted to say at all. It's a curse. When I'm hurt or confused or anything other than asleep, I strike out. It's my defensive offense, according to Cassi.

His face is calm, no hint of anger to be found in the lines of his face.

"I'm sorry," I say. "I have a mean mouth."

His sudden laugh surprises me. Apparently, this is my day for surprises. Or rather, another day for surprises.

"What?" I ask, turning my palms up to emphasize my question.

He shakes his head and takes the few steps between us with light, confident footfalls on the narrow wall. But he's smiling and that's probably the biggest surprise of all. If I had said that to my mother, I'd be holding my hands over my head to protect it from a blow.

"I missed so much that I can't get back. You're a pistol," he says and his eyes seem to drink in my features, memorizing them all.

I don't say anything to that. I can tell he has more to say so I just wait and let the sun warm me.

"You've turned out so beautiful," he says. He reaches out to run my ponytail through his fingers, and then drops it against my shoulder. "And you have a whole lot more hair. You were a very bald baby."

It's a funny thing to say so I laugh. I tell him about my genius plan to sell it. The big truck that collects it comes a few times a year and they pay well. The sides of the truck are bright with pictures of people with bald heads next to pictures of them with full heads of hair.

I've never heard of a disease that makes hair fall out, though there are certainly bald people, but the truck and the nicely dressed people inside it pay good money and they say it will help out the sick. Brown doesn't fetch the premium of a true blond, but it's enough to make me want it handy.

He frowns and says, "Karas, they don't buy it for ill people to have hair. They buy it for rich people to make into wigs so they can have prettier hair."

"What? No," I say, thinking of some rich person walking around with my hair on their head. "Really?"

He nods and says, "It's just another lie."

97

I'd like to ask him what he means by another lie but I've got more important things I want to know first. He takes one more look around us, searching the horizon, then sits down on the wall, patting it for me to join him.

"Go ahead, Karas. Ask me what you want," he says.

"Why did you leave?"

He points to the three strikes on his neck and says, "Three strikes. I had no choice."

"You could have just stopped getting strikes," I counter. "You know, stop living a life of crime." There goes my mouth again, so I clamp it shut.

He nods toward the strike on my neck and says, "I suppose you got that living a life of crime."

I can feel my face redden and I shake my head. "Did Maddix tell you?"

He nods, but says, "I'd like to hear it from you."

This isn't a story I want to tell him. It embarrasses me that my mother is like she is and telling this story just reinforces the reality.

"It's okay. Just tell me," he urges. His voice is gentle in the quiet that surrounds us.

So I tell him. I tell him about a night not much different from any other, her drunk, me closed up in my room trying to avoid her. Only this time she wasn't satisfied with just banging on my door a few times and yelling. This time she kept pounding and then she started really working on the door, kicking it with increasing force as her anger spiraled out of control.

I made it out of the window and onto the roof just in time to hear the door crack. It wasn't until much later, after I got convicted and a strike inked onto my neck, that I came home and saw the heavy garden spade on the floor of my room amongst the shards of wood that remained of my door.

"I heard the crash and knew she was really worked up so I had to clear out. I usually just go to Cassi's when that happens. Normally, I just hop a few roofs, come down where I know she won't see me and then hoof it over. No problem." I pull up my pant leg and show him the long scar on my shin. It's healed into a shiny pink line. "Only this time, I fell through someone's roof. Destruction of state property."

He shakes his head and says, "This isn't how things were supposed to be."

"Maybe not, but it's the way things are," I say. There's no point in debating history because it doesn't change the present. The present is controlled by those who win in this life and we're not them.

"I don't have your good excuse, but I did what I did for a good reason. Or what I thought was a good reason," he says.

"Mom said you rustled cattle," I offer to get the ball rolling.

He nods and says, "I did. It would be more accurate to say that I rustled *back* some cattle."

That's new information to me. Once he was gone, the only version anyone was going to get was the one provided by the Texas Army, though I knew there had to be more to it. Maybe some part of me just wished there was more to it.

He gazes toward the shadows behind the house where the others are still sleeping inside. Then he asks me, "Are you and that boy Jovan an item or something?"

The look on my face must be answer enough because he laughs again and says, "Okay. I guess not. It just seems like there's something there. There's the whole "pretty eyes" comment, and the way you two look at each other is very telling."

"Huh...well, it's telling you a lie then," I answer, though that heat is back in my face again and I'm pretty sure I've turned as red as a sunset. I hate that I do that.

"It doesn't matter now, I suppose. He's in the same boat as the rest of us," he says, then cocks his head as if he's just had a thought. "Or maybe not. He's a Foley. They might be able to fix it."

He hops back up on the narrow wall and looks around again but keeps talking while he does. "I'd bet, now that I think about it, that those two soldiers have either met with unfortunate accidents, died of wounds we gave them or mysteriously disappeared." He suddenly squats next to me on the wall and adds, "And that those patrols are now looking for a *captured* Jovan rather than a criminal one."

My mouth drops open while he speaks and he taps it shut with a forefinger under my chin. All I can say to that is, "But we didn't hurt those soldiers."

"So naive, Karas."

"No," I insist.

"Yes," he says.

I don't want to think something like that could be true, but deep down I feel the ring of truth in his words. All citizens are theoretically equal, but the more land a person possesses, the more equal they seem to become. In Bailar, we have a handful of families who own most of the land and are, without question, living life under very different rules than the rest of us. Jovan is from one of those families.

That's fine to think this an unjust state of affairs, fine to wish it would change, but it doesn't answer my question about Jordan's strikes.

"What does that have to do with what we were talking about? The rustling?"

"Oh, a lot," he says and sighs again. It's a heavy sigh full of old burdens. "You know that my family used to own the parcel of land just east of Robin's waterway?"

I nod. I've never been there, but I have an old photo of a small house, a faded barn and the smiling child that was my father. "Your family lost it when I was a baby."

"No," he corrects. "My father lost it when Jovan's father decided he wanted to increase his acreage and the Robin waterway was closed. No water for our cattle."

That doesn't make sense. The smaller waterways are closed now and then when the river runs low or the lake isn't filling well, but no one is left without water. Right of way is never terminated. I shake my head.

"The details don't matter. What matters is that over time all the viable land came into the hands of just a few families and water was how they did it. Foley did it to my father. My father brought water from the canal using horses. I brought water, too, but it was never enough. We went down to just the breeding stock and tried to wait it out, but you can't pay your bills off breeding stock that can't be slaughtered or sent to market. When some of those cattle followed the dry waterway onto their property, they kept the calves. I went and got them back."

This is a very different story than the one I've heard. Not just different, but fundamentally so. It turns the young man who was branded a thief into someone trying to save his family's legacy. It sounds like a story from the creation of the Texas Republic, a hero's story. That makes it pretty hard to believe.

"So you say," I shoot back and even I can hear the challenge in my voice.

He purses his lips and his eyes grow distant. "Believe what you want," he says and I know there won't be any argument from him.

"Is that really what happened? Is that why your family left Bailar?"

"You're my family," he says, "but that's why my parents left, yes."

"And this?" I ask, holding up the pendants around my neck. They've been hanging there like hot coals the whole time. Every time they clink together against my skin I'm reminded all over again that he had one made for me. And I'm forced to wonder what that means.

His fingers are warm against mine when he lifts the pendants from them and turns them around to check their condition. He smiles and drops them so that they make a musical tinkling sound against each other.

"I haven't just been running around in the wild lands for all these years, you know," he says. "I got a message to your mother and waited, but I never got a response. Truth is, I never expected one."

He takes one more look around then sits next to me on the wall again. I've not looked once since we've been on watch, leaving all the real work for him. I'm not being a very good partner.

"At the time, I *thought* you'd be better off in town. I didn't know anything about what was out there in the world or what was possible beyond Texas. You were just a baby," he explains. The way he says it, the way his eyes light up when he says the words, makes me think that there's a lot more out there than the wild lands and wild people I've grown up hearing about.

"And when you did know?" I ask.

"By then it was just easier to think of you growing up happy, settled, with a family you loved. I always intended to figure out a way to come for you when you were eighteen and free to do what you wanted with your life. Or at least give you the option to come. I left word at the border that I'd pay for news from any Strikers coming out of Bailar. Over the years I've gotten just two bites since not many Strikers make it as far as the border between the Riverlands and the Southeast. One didn't know you, but you would have been just a little thing then. The other knew of you and told me you were doing well. Happy," he finishes and looks at me as if he'd like to know if that was ever true.

"Until Maddix came?"

He nods and I can tell it's a sad nod. I can only imagine what Maddix told him given how long he's known me. He's a year and change older than Connor and me, the same age as Cassi, but we all played together and he's seen marks on me plenty of times. It would be a hard thing for Jordan to hear, especially if he'd built up an idea of a happy daughter growing up safe in Bailar.

"So you came back to get me?" I ask finally. This is what I really want to hear from him. I want to hear that he couldn't sit still for one moment after knowing what my life was really like, that all he could do was hurry to rescue me.

"Basically, yes. There's more though," he says and picks up one of my hands to hold it between his two rough ones. He takes a deep breath and then looks me in the eye. "You have a little brother."

*****

By the time Cassi and Jovan come to relieve us on watch, the sun is at its mid-afternoon strongest in the hard blue sky and the wall has grown almost warm from soaking up its rays. It's still cool, but nice.

At my almost absent-minded turnover of the watch Jovan gives me a look of concern, then shoots a hard look at Jordan as if he might be the cause of my distracted demeanor. It's true, but not the way Jovan thinks. I wave his look away and give him a smile, though a somewhat weak and unconvincing one.

What I really need is time to go over all that I've learned and make sense of it. Though I know there's no way I'll be able to fall asleep, I'm looking forward to lying down and being alone with my thoughts. Maybe then I can process everything when there's no expectation of my interacting with others.

Maddix and Connor are lying near each other, both with an arm flung over their faces to shield them from the bright light leaking in through all of the broken windows and doors. With their straight hair and similar sleeping postures, there's no mistaking them for anything but brothers.

My little nest is waiting for me so I lie down without saying anything more to Jordan. He seems to understand because he doesn't press me for conversation and simply sends a whispered "Sleep well" my way. I don't respond to it other than to give him a quick nod.

Sleep seems miles away, though I know the night will be a long and hard one of walking on terrain I can barely see. I should at least try to drift off but it's not happening. The concept of a brother keeps rolling around in my head. Jordan told me he looks a bit like me and, like me, has a problem with smart talk when he's upset. The way he smiled while he talked about him, this ten-year-old named Quinton, brought a flush of feeling over me that I recognized as jealousy.

I think it's only natural to feel some resentment. Quinton has spent his whole life with a mother and a father, both of whom love him and provide him a safe home. What have I had?

That's not a good place to go so I shake it off, my deep exhalation blowing a little cloud of dust up in front of my face. As shocking as the idea of a little brother is, everything else he said is even more shocking.

Yes, there are wild lands to the north and there are people there to avoid, but to the east—not that far east if he's to be believed—the land is no longer dry. To the east of us is the rain line, past which the rain is more plentiful and water not hard to find. Texas has places like that too, south of Bailar, but I've never seen them. Those are places for people with more to offer than we cattle breeders and ranchers here in the north.

He says there are cities and normal life and opportunity. Other than the wild lands to the north, the land is divided into territories: the East, the Southeast, the Northeast, the Gulf Cooperative and Florida. Not all of them are friendly with each other but one thing they all share is enmity toward Texas. He told me that there's too much to explain until we get somewhere safe because I'll never believe him until I see it with my own eyes.

He ended our talk with the enigmatic words that all those lands were one huge nation long ago, that Texas was the cause of the breakup, and that the threat of loosing whatever weapon Texas used the first time—the one that made empty ruins of the cities—is what keeps the other lands at bay.

It's a lot to take in. Too much, really. Instead, I focus on what comes next. That's something I can understand and work toward. We're going past the rain line, past the flat lands and to Jordan's home far away near a forest. To a place called River Oaks where I will find a home and a brother waiting for me.

Chapter Seventeen

I'm starting to think that Jordan, who I'm still leery of calling Dad, is right about soldiers coming after Jovan to bring him home.

The night has been long and frightening. Even with the pace we've been keeping, we've not made it to the Benton outpost. Between hiding in brush while vehicles with searchlights go past and spending a breathless hour dug into the sandy soil so that only our noses and mouths were clear, we've fallen behind schedule.

It's near dawn and we're starting to run out of time. We need to find a place to lay low during the day because we have no chance of remaining hidden in this flat land without cover. There are a few old barns ahead but those are obvious and sure to be searched.

I'm so tired and thirsty that I've stopped being hungry. All I want to do is lie down, shake the sand out of my boots and sleep.

"I've got an idea, but I don't think you're going to like it," Jovan says quietly out of nowhere.

Jordan, who is far enough ahead of me that he's just a darker shadow, answers. "Anything is better than what we've got now."

"Let's just bury ourselves again. All day."

I stop in my tracks, about to tell him exactly how stupid that is when Cassi does it for me. "Uh, no. What if one of us rolls over in our sleep or has to pee or something? It's wide open here."

We trudge a few more steps in silence. I can't imagine trying to stay like that for the whole day. It's still cool but the sun is strong and I'll be fried crispy red by the end of the day. How could any of us stay still for that long?

I suck in a breath when I see Jordan turn on his flashlight again, his hand carefully cupping the lens so the light streams toward the ground. We've not been passed in about an hour, but we have no way of knowing if there might be a vehicle, dark and silent, lying in wait just down the road.

"There," he says, and I follow the thin line of light to a shallow depression. From here it just looks like a fold in the ground and not like something that would hide us, but at this point, my feet are hurting enough to make me believe anything will do. Even an anthill.

The noise level rises a little as we hurry across the loose ground toward it. While it isn't yet dawn, the pre-dawn twilight is almost upon us and we have very few choices left.

It's just as I thought. Some long-dry remnant of a streambed littered with old stones and a few scraggly short bushes drying out slowly between rains. It's perhaps four feet deep at its deepest and ragged along its length.

Jordan tosses his bags into it and scrambles down, a rain of pebbles and loose rock coming down behind him. He grabs a few loose handfuls of grit and grins up at us. "This will do."

"No!" Cassi exclaims. Even her sunny nature has been overcome by stress and exhaustion.

I feel the same way as she and I barely suppress a groan. There's no way this will work.

Jordan looks at our faces in the dim glow and then turns off the flashlight, turning us into shadows again. His words come out as a harsh whisper, meant to convince us as much as instruct us. "Come on, get down here. This whole area is loose and rocky. No one's going to bring a horse across here. They'll cross further down, where the ground is firmer. Come," he says, and motions for me to join him.

I slip off my pack at the bottom and he smiles encouragement. He digs out our last water carrier and holds it out to me. "Drink up, but not so much that you'll need to pee." To the others, he says, "If you think you might need to go, go now and then lie down. Break up your patterns with dirt and rocks. Get as comfortable as you can because once you're down, you need to stay still unless we're absolutely sure it's safe."

All of us disappear a little way away from the streambed for a moment of privacy and then drink again. When I upturn the carrier for one last drink, the temptation to wipe my face clean is almost unbearable, but in this case, the dirt will work for me and I resist. The feeling of grit in my teeth and on my tongue is at least relieved by that last drink and a sigh escapes me.

When I hand off the carrier to the next hands, I look up to see Jovan smiling down at me as he lifts the carrier to his own lips. The twilight has begun and his face is defined in shades of gray. His throat bobs when he drinks and for some reason I can't explain, it's a fascinating sight I can't seem to tear my eyes away from.

The moment is broken when Jordan grips my hand from below and urges me down into the shallow ravine. I settle, then shift and dig a sizable field of small stones from beneath me until it's bearably flat. The moment I nod, he tucks my pack near my arm as a brace and then piles sand and pebbles around and on top of me to break up the pattern of my body. It's a terrible feeling, like being buried alive, and I'm not sure how I'm supposed to bear this during the long day to come. My only hope is that we find it's clear often and long enough that we can get up and move now and again.

The first rosey hints of dawn are showing on the horizon when the last of us is covered and still. I can feel the press of Cassi's foot next to my calf. She's stretched out opposite me, her head somewhere beyond my feet.

A torn piece of burlap covers my face, the natural color blending into the surrounding soil enough so that I can open my eyes and breath through the rough weave. I'm not sure where everyone is specifically, except that Jordan is on the other side of the body next to me. I find it disturbing and a sudden need to sit up and catalog everything around me makes my breath come faster and my heart pound. I can hear it, harsh and rasping, but I don't seem to have any way to control it.

The sand shifts next to me and I feel the touch of warm fingers through the cool grains of sand. They aren't rough like Jordan's, but the hands are big, the fingers long as they coil around mine until we're palm to palm. It's Jovan, I realize, as the fingers squeeze my palm to his. In the space of a few minutes, as the light filtering through the burlap brightens with a new day, I feel calm seep into my body through our linked hands.

When I wake, it's to Jovan's hand squeezing mine with enough force to hurt and the sound of a quiet "shh." In the distance, I can hear loud voices exchanging shouted words and the harsh jangle of tack on many horses.

The shouts aren't the urgent ones of discovery but rather of people communicating over distance with no concern about being heard. It can only mean they haven't seen us yet.

At my leg, I feel Cassi's foot press into my calf but other than a brief patter of falling grains of sand and small pebbles, I hear no sounds of movement in our dry streambed.

"We checked every one of the barns and Bravo just radioed in that they've got 100% completion in Benton. They aren't here. Anywhere," a deep voice shouts.

There's a beat of quiet after that, then the sound of a horse being walked in a slow circle, the clop of shod feet against old asphalt and stone. It's the sound of someone on horseback thinking and looking. I can only hope he isn't looking as hard as he's thinking.

The same voice as before calls, "They could be long past here by now. We still haven't found the jumper they took. They're probably long gone."

"No," the other voice calls in a more thoughtful tone. I don't recognize the voice but Jovan must because his fingers twitch against mine. "The jumper would have died somewhere between Wicha and here. We just haven't found it. Unless they've been going without stopping at all, they should be no further than the north side of Benton."

"How do you know the jumper wouldn't make it to the border? It can go that far and more on a single charge," the first voice challenges.

"It was a half charge or so," the second voice says.

"How do you know? There were no witnesses."

Jovan tenses next to me and I think I know why. We left the two soldiers alive and well. I try to remember if Jovan was coherent enough when we made our exit to be sure of that fact, but all I keep coming up with is his unfocused eyes and daft smile. Does he think we killed them? Did Jordan tell him what he told me about them coming after him?

I can almost feel him thinking about getting up, announcing himself and sending us all to our deaths. Panic twists my stomach into knots. I breathe the words as softly as I can through the burlap. "Please. No."

"The time of death is how I know," the other voice answers. "Go put the sign up like I said, then get the rest of Alpha team back to Wicha. Search everything."

There's no more talk and the sound of hoof-beats speeding away in different directions is all we're left with. Eventually, they too, fade away. I can tell one of them is going north on the asphalt while the other goes west, toward the barns we'd barely dismissed as a good spot to rest.

The fingers tighten on mine again and it hurts. I can't just fling the hand off without giving away our position. The voices were too close for that, perhaps fifty feet away at best. I grit my teeth and tap his thumb with mine, loosening the hold my fingers have around his. It works because I hear Jovan exhale slowly, like he's trying to calm down. The feeling returns to my fingers as his grip loosens. Our hands still lay palm to palm but the touch feels accidental now.

I'm pretty sure I'll never be able to get back to sleep. My bladder feels uncomfortably full, my mouth is paining for a drink and the entire back side of me is one long ache. Through the burlap I can see the sun, small and hard and bright, just past its peak in the sky. It hurts to leave my eyes open with it staring down at me so I close them and wait for the afterimage to disappear.

We've got hours left here and I have no idea how I'm going to survive it without jumping up and screaming. It's contrary to reason, but I have to focus so hard on not jumping up that time passes more quickly, rather than more slowly like I think it should.

Whatever trance I've put myself into is broken by a small keening during the long afternoon. It's quiet but urgent and desperate. It's Cassi.

"I can't stand it anymore. I have to stand up. I have to!" she whines in a high, pained voice. It's not quiet enough. Anyone within twenty feet would hear the sound of a human over the low breeze and find us.

"Shh, Cassi. Just breathe," I whisper.

All I hear in return is the sound of her crying, but at least it's less noisy, if no less desperate. An hour or more passes before the last hitching cry dies away and doesn't return but we all lie there and listen to it without moving for that endless hour. It's a terrible thing to have to do and it makes the pain in my body more intense. I want so much to comfort her.

As the sun dips low and there are no more sounds of humans, vehicles or horses to break the hours, I begin to have hope. Then I shake that off, thinking that the quickest way to lose any good luck is to believe that I have it.

The dimming of the daylight feels like a blessing against my face, which I can tell is burned even through the burlap. I wonder if I'll have little dots of burn or if I've moved enough so that it will be red all over.

When Jordan stirs, I hold my breath, hoping he'll be happy enough with what he sees that we can all sit up. After a long moment, he clears his throat and croaks, "Okay. Sit up but stay low. We're clear for the moment."

I can't suppress the pained sound that comes out of me when I try unsuccessfully to sit up. My back won't bend and feels as stiff as a board. When I lever myself up using my arm as a brace, the burlap falls away from my face and the feeling of taking an unhindered breath is so delicious I groan again, this time in pleasure.

Next to me, Jovan is frowning, his eyes on his knees, which are folded up towards his chest. Cassi seems to be having trouble getting up, her little cries of pain rising toward whimpers as she rolls onto her side. I reach for her arm and give it a tug. We're almost face to face and close enough so that I can wrap my arms around her to some extent. The dust on her face is streaked with a fan of clear lines where tears have run down the sides of her face and her lips are puffy and cracked, a dark line of dried blood along the center of her lower lip where she worried at it during the day.

I let her cry and just hold her, murmuring whatever soothing thing I can think of into her ear while she does. My eyes meet Jordan's and the look on his face is both sorrowful and certain. I know he's thinking about what he told me. He was right. The two soldiers are dead and now there's no one to counter any claim that we're the killers and Jovan our hostage.

It also means that they will have to kill *us* to ensure the secret remains a secret.

There's just one more moment of panic before night settles in when we see a cluster of vehicles pass by going south, back toward Wicha from Benton. They don't pause, or even slow down, and we hunker down low in our stream-bed for the short time it takes for them to pass out of sight.

Jordan and Jovan huddle together, heads close as they talk. I can see the moment Jovan finds out what has really happened in the stiffening of his bent back. When he turns around to look at me, my heart breaks to see the defeat in his eyes. I know he believes what Jordan has told him about the soldiers and why it happened. It must be a terrible thing for him to know.

The water is finished before we head out and we can't spare any time for a fire to cook food. It's with a gnawing hunger in my belly that I set out with the others, heading north toward Benton and the border beyond.

Chapter Eighteen

We're hurrying and the night is filled with stumbles and the sounds of pain when the stumble produces yet another bump or bruise. Even so, we're making good time and the scattered lights of the Benton outpost draw near long before I had imagined they would.

Jordan leads us west of the outpost and the rough remains of the highway, urging us to be quiet when the first occupied dwellings are close enough to make out clearly. One light stands out among the indistinct blurs coming from behind drawn curtains and shades. It's bright and pointed into the sky against the backdrop of a building.

I can see the indecision in Jordan's face. He wants to see what it is but also fears it might be a trap. I know I feel that way. Finally, he turns to us and says, "Rest here and take a quick five minutes. I'm going to go see what that is."

Jovan squats but then springs back up and says, "I want to see, too."

We're all thinking the same thing. It's a message and it's meant for us. We all heard the riders talking about putting a message on one of the barns, but we didn't back track to see it. This might be another one. This one is almost on our path and it might be the last one. It's worth seeing, so long as it doesn't get us caught.

I've had no chance to talk to Jovan much during our walk, or even to thank him for his attempt to comfort me during the endless day. Whenever I look at him I feel the warmth of his fingers twining with mine and my mouth seems to lose the ability to speak. I've been able to see the difficult thoughts he's been dealing with in his drawn brows and the way his broad shoulders seem to bow under the weight of those thoughts. What can I possibly say to make that better? Nothing.

Jordan waves for Jovan to come as an answer. While the rest of us drop to the ground, reaching for tight calves or to empty our boots of sand, they disappear into the night with barely a sound.

I've just gotten my boots back on, now mercifully empty of irritating sand, when they reappear. Their expressions tell me the news isn't good.

"It says if we let the hostage go, they'll let us go," Jordan says without delay.

Out of the corner of my eye, I catch the quick look that passes between Maddix and Connor. I don't like that look. We can't let this devolve into anyone thinking Jovan is a threat.

"It's a lie," I say.

Everyone starts talking at once, their whispers rising one over the other as each tries to put forth their own idea.

Jovan silences them all when he says, "They'll have to kill you, no matter what happens to me. And if you do leave me here or something like that, I'll still run. I can't go back."

This works like cold water on us. The silence lasts for a long moment while everyone takes that in.

"You could go back, Jovan. You could live your life and just…just forget about all this," Cassi offers.

The laughs he gives is a bitter one and I feel even worse for getting him into this. "Right. Cassi, you know me. They killed those soldiers to hide my part in this. Seriously, do you think I could ever be okay with that?"

Jordan watches it all but the look on his face is cold when he says, "Like you don't know how your family operates. You didn't seem very surprised when I talked to you earlier."

Jovan's return look is just as icy. "I heard what they said while we were hiding. It's different to see it on a sign, to know for sure. Yes, I'm surprised. My dad isn't the nicest person, but I've never seen anything like this."

There's a tense moment between all of us. Cassi breaks it by slapping her hands onto her knees and saying, "Fine. Let's get moving then."

I can tell that Maddix, and perhaps Connor, aren't entirely satisfied so I say, "Listen. If we leave him tied up here for them to find, he could tell them where we are. If we kill him, they'll hunt us even harder. As it stands now, our safest course is to keep him with us."

I hate that it sounds so clinical, so without compassion, like I'm talking about whether we should keep a less-than-useful tool, but that's what will make it effective. Maddix has no reason to feel any attachment to Jovan and many reasons to want whatever advantage he can get. It can't get any plainer or clearer than my heartless words. He just nods and hoists his bags, walking fast into the night. I'll have to be happy with that as an answer.

We stay off the road and well away from Benton as the little town falls behind us. There are a few sightings of soldiers, once in their camp. A bright fire advertises their location from a long way away, so they're easy to avoid.

The others are all in vehicles, crawling slowly around Benton or near it. Why they aren't looking for us further out I have no idea, but it occurs to me that they simply won't risk their vehicles or horses. These are grunts, base soldiers without influence, and they wouldn't want the consequences of ruining either of those rare and valuable assets.

For the first time I'm actually grateful for the unfair differences between people, between those born with prominence and power and those who will never have any. For once, this is working in our favor. Those grunts are my people and we can't afford to do anything that might earn us a strike, like ruin Army equipment.

The word is passed along our ragged line that we're close to the Red River and we'll be able to stop for the day near a good crossing point that Jordan knows. I've never been to the river but I've heard about it from those who have. It's supposed to be wide and deep and lush along its borders. I hope I'll be able to see it for myself in the light rather than just this paltry moonlight. And best of all, the Red River marks the border between the Texas Republic and everywhere else.

I hear it first. It's a low whoosh of sound somewhere in the distance. After that, the smell of water reaches me and I breathe it in deeply, almost making myself sneeze by sucking in all the dust that's managed to stick to my nose and upper lip. Living where water is precious, where rainfall is never plentiful and where the canal seems like the oceans people talk about in other places, you discover that water has a smell. It's a welcome, beautiful smell that brightens the soul. My tired feet move faster toward it.

We veer off to the west a little as we near the river, the sound of it growing louder with every step. Jordan motions for us to follow him at a distance so that he's between us and the river—probably so we don't fall in. I'm worried we're heading in the wrong direction, but Jordan is jogging ahead and looking around intently, so I'm guessing he's looking for something specific. His voice is quiet but urgent when he calls out. "Over here. Watch your steps."

It's still dark, but the eastern sky is a lighter shade of black. The twilight will highlight our profiles to searchers when it comes but I can see the shadows of brush that can hide us all along the river.

Scrambling down a steep incline of loose soil and rock in the dark is an adventure the likes of which I hope never to experience again. Jovan's tight grip on my arm is all that keeps me from tumbling down and away. Jordan chances a quick flash of the light to show us the way and I see a small gap between a tumble of boulders and the bank. It looks far too small for all of us to fit into, but the others disappear, one after another, inside. I hang back because I'm not fond of small spaces. I've hidden in too many of them in my life, hoping my mother wouldn't find me, to find them comfortable ever again.

A pressure on my back returns me to the present and Jordan whispers, "Go on. It will be fine."

He has no idea why I'm reluctant, his expression curious and concerned, his fingers on the small of my back and pushing me forward. There's no time to tell him now and the light is growing with every passing minute. I take a deep breath and squeeze inside.

Behind me, Jordan's body sends us into deep darkness as it blocks the way out. It's just a flash of darkness, but it's enough to send my heart racing again. I rub my fingers against the rough stone and wait for it to pass. He slides past me and the gray light returns, taking my growing panic down a few notches.

It's roomier in here than it looked from outside. The boulders create a rough front wall, the brush above a sort of roof and the deeply dug out bank an irregularly shaped room. We can all sit, and even stretch out our legs if we don't mind being squeezed together a bit.

It's far more comfortable than the shallow streamed of yesterday, so I suppose I should be happy. I'm not though, I'm thirsty, terrified and on top of that, we all stink.

There's no time for a fire and Jordan tells us that we can't drink the river water without boiling it first so we'll have to just try to hold on until dark. The day lightens rapidly outside and a frightening amount of light seeps through. Above me, the border between the dug-out part of the bank and the brush clinging to the side seems far less dense than it did when it was dark. Shafts of light dance in the wind and rattle the silver-green leaves. The little breeze feels good on my upturned face.

Cassi and Jovan have their faces pressed to the gaps in the rocks, looking out at the river. Cassi's shoulders give a shake and I hear a smothered sob. I can only think that there must be soldiers and I reach out to pluck at her jacket for news.

She turns to me and there's no fear on her face, only a sort of wonder. Her eyes swim with tears she can ill afford without water, but there's a smile on her face when she says, "It's so beautiful."

Now I really want to see. The image I have in my mind is a sort of endlessly running version of the lake. I've been to the lake exactly twice, once with Cassi's family as a child and once more with Cassi and Connor last summer. It's a long walk, the passes are expensive and a trip means camping overnight as well, so a trip to the lake is generally out of the question for people like me.

When Cassi's family included me in their trip, I was too young to understand what going really meant. I'd imagined something like the canal but the lake was so much more. The music the trees made in the wind almost overwhelmed me because I'd never heard anything remotely like it before. I had put my hands over my ears against it and started crying.

Cassi's father had laughed and eased my hands down from my ears, his bright blue eyes and ginger hair making his whole face smile along with his lips. He'd tried to teach Cassi and me to swim that day in water shallow enough that we could stand if we needed to. The memory of the hot sun reddening my skin, the cool mud squishing between my toes and the victory of my inelegant dogpaddle is one of my most treasured and vivid. I fell in love with Cassi's family that day. She's the sister I always wished I had.

She urges me to take her place at the gap and we scramble up and around each other until I can see for myself. I open my eyes to disappointment. It's nothing like the lake. Instead of a body of water as large as a pasture, I see a muddy red stretch of languid liquid that I'm only sure is water because of its volume.

It's wide, yes. And it does stretch a good distance to the other side, but that is as far as it goes in conforming to my expectations. Sandbars break the surface in sculpted swoops and we are at the apex of a deep curve, the river bowing toward us and then away. Even though the mud prevents me from seeing through the water, I can tell from here it's very shallow, not even deep enough that it would require swimming to cross.

Behind me, Cassi asks, "Well?"

I like the lake better but I don't want to dampen her pleasure so I plaster a believable smile on my face—not too big or too small a smile—and say, "I never could have imagined it like this."

It's true, because I imagined something far grander, but she takes it like I hoped she would and beams at me through her chapped lips. Grand or not, I'm grateful Jordan knew of this place. Even I can see how good a place it is to hide and cross from. I turn to ask him but close my mouth when I see him with his head pillowed on crossed arms braced by his knees. It looks terribly uncomfortable but his face is slack with sleep.

Maddix and Connor are braced against the back wall, leaning against each other, their heads touching and fast asleep. Only Jovan, Cassi and I are wide awake.

"I'll take first watch," Jovan says. "You two sleep."

Cassi says, "Deal." She scoots back enough to lean on Connor and just like that, her eyes are closed while she waits for sleep. I know she can still hear us, but it gives the illusion of privacy between Jovan and me. It feels incredibly uncomfortable, like I've just discovered my pants are unbuttoned and I'm wearing old underwear. Very exposed. Mostly, because we still haven't even acknowledged that he spent hours holding my hand the day before. He saves me from finding some way to start the conversation.

"Karas," he says. His voice is rough in his dry throat. I wish I had water to give him. The sound of it makes me swallow but there's no spit to work up and my throat clicks loudly. His face is no cleaner than mine, but it takes nothing from his looks.

In the light through the crack where he's been looking at the river, his hair has strands of gold in the brown and his eyes remind me again of a bird of prey's. They are a nice, warm brown most of the time, but when the light strikes them just right, they are the precise amber color of the hawk that hunts my garden and stares at me from atop the safety of our fence.

"What?" I ask, avoiding his gaze by turning my face back to the crack. I stretch my cramped legs out into the space between us and give a sigh as the muscles stretch.

"I know you didn't sleep much yesterday. Go sleep. I'll watch," he says. Then he surprises me by leaning over the gap and touching my calf to get my attention. It does that and more. It stops my breath. Not because it hurts or anything, but because it's him and he's touching me in a place most people don't touch me. I find myself staring at his hand on my leg.

He takes it wrong, of course, and jerks his hand back like he's offended me. "I promise, if anything happens, I'll wake you first," he says, but the moment has passed and they're just words.

At least sleep will make the time go quickly and stop me from thinking about how much I want to stick my whole head in that muddy river and drink my fill.

Chapter Nineteen

The smell of smoke wakes me. Smoke is a two-edged sword so I wake confused as to whether I should be afraid or eager. Fire is always a danger in this part of Texas where the rain is fickle, but it is also a sign of fun, food and warmth. It might means camping, or it might mean my house is burning to the ground. Confusion is entirely understandable.

"Hey, hey," Cassi soothes. Her face looms before me, glowing white in the dark. "It's okay. Time to wake up." She darts out of the gap before I have a chance to do anything other than blink myopically at her. I hear a few harsh whispers and the clank of a pot, then she clambers back in with a broad smile on her face. Her clean face.

"You're clean," I say. I sound surprised and that's rude. "Uh, I mean…"

"Thirsty?" she asks, cutting me off with a wink. In her hand she holds one of the most beautiful things I've ever seen. A canteen. Water drips off her fingers and dots the outside and I swear I can smell the water inside.

The water is still hot and it burns the cracks in my lips as I drink. Cassi yanks the canteen down when I keep gulping and I groan as some of the precious water splashes into my lap.

"Hey! Slow down. I don't need you puking it up, too. We've had enough of that already."

"Who puked?" I ask, after I'm done gasping down the sheer bliss of that long drink.

"Oh, Connor," she says and ticks off the name by extending a finger. "Then Maddix and Jovan did a little harmonious puking," She demonstrates it for me until I'm laughing in my corner.

"Glad I missed that," I say when the laughter dies away. I hold out my hand for the canteen and she hands it to me with reluctance, so I reassure her. "I'll go slow."

"Come out when you can. If you hurry, you can get washed up," she says and then she's gone again, as quick as if she'd not been panting from thirst and whimpering in her sleep not too long ago. The sunshine in Cassi has returned, just like that. I wonder if she knows what a gift that is. I wonder if she knows how much I love that about her.

I'm sore yet again and I'm starting to wonder when I'll just stop recognizing it as something unusual and begin to accept that as my normal state of being. My feet feel like sausages stuffed into my boots and my leg muscles are as hard as old wood. I pull out the band holding my ponytail and run my fingers through my hair. It feels sticky at the crown, sweat, dirt and oil having made a mess of it. To say that I could use a wash is a mighty understatement.

In the shelter of the clustered rocks they've built a tiny fire and contained its light by stacking smaller rocks around it. The pot is already steaming with a new pot of water but this time I see chunks of beet floating around in it. That sight wakes up my stomach, or else the water did, because it grumbles loudly at the sight. No one else seems to hear it, for which I'm grateful.

"Why did you let me sleep so long?" I ask Jordan, who's carefully stirring the pot and poking at a beet to check for doneness.

It's Jovan who answers, poking his head over the ledge above us. "Because you needed it. I think you're the only one who didn't sleep enough in the ditch." His smile looks funny from this angle, all upside down, but it still brings out a return one from me. He ducks back over the ledge and out of sight.

"Go have a wash in the river. Just keep your clothes near in case we have to hurry. So far, we're clear," Jordan says and pokes at another piece of beet. "Oh, and drink another canteen."

We swap canteens, my empty one for his mostly full one, and I take off down the slope toward the sluggish river. The water has revived me in ways I find hard to believe simple water could. I feel alive down to the deepest parts of my body. And tingly. Of course, the tingles could just be the layers of grime shrinking on my skin. The jury's still out on that.

The moon is only just up and the night is incredibly dark. I should be more careful with my steps but I'm in a hurry to get clean. My flashlight needs a charge so I plop down and wind it while I look around as much as I can. There's not much to see, just darkness broken by darker shadows. The firelight behind me is well shielded, but the little bit of light that leaks out does wonders for showing the shape of the slope.

Once the light is charged enough to last the length of time it will take me to wash, I cup my hand around the lens and find the water. It's more than murky and not very inviting. If I weren't so dirty, I'd wonder if it could even get me clean. However, there's no time for daintiness and I'm not going to be the only one left wallowing in my stench.

It's takes mere seconds to strip down. Sinking into the mud and water feels like a special sort of bliss. I should be cold—the water certainly is, and the air definitely is—but I'm enjoying it too much. Scooting around in the shallow water to find a deeper spot, I get lucky and find one almost two feet deep.

I shove my flashlight into the sand and pile a bit of it against the lens so it's not so bright. The water may be shallow but who knows what might be living in it and making its hungry way toward me? Better to see bad stuff coming before it gets here, I always say. A few handfuls of the sand from the sandbar work perfectly for scrubbing and I start to feel a little more human as the layers of dead skin and grime come off.

I lean back and let the slow current sweep over me. My hair wants to stay in clumps next to my scalp at first. It just reinforces how disgusting it feels. But the water feels so good now that I'm not looking at it that I relax, spread my arms and let it do its thing. Tickles touch my skin as the dirt loosens its hold and my hair streams above my head with the current. It's glorious and I just want to enjoy this feeling forever.

The cold starts to get to me and my forever is apparently measured in short minutes. I hear the patter of falling pebbles and look up, thinking someone might be coming down, but there's no one there except the disappearing shape of Jovan at the top of the ledge.

That makes me lunge up, knees to my chest. Was he just looking at me? Could he even look at me? I put my arm in the water as a test. It disappears from view the moment it's covered and the tiny bit of light coming from my flashlight does nothing more than cause a shine to reflect back from the water. No, he couldn't have seen anything even if he was looking. He was probably just doing his duty, keeping the watch. Still, it's past time for me to get out.

Back at the fire, the beets are done and Jovan is with the group. I look at him, but it seems like he's avoiding my gaze. Wonderful. More awkwardness.

They've waited for me. My butt barely hits the spot they kept open for me around the fire before the spoon dips in. It's all I can do not to snatch the spoon when it's my turn or just stick my head into the pot and fish the beets out with my mouth.

I'm not a huge fan of beets as a general rule. I grow them because they do well in the early spring and by the time I can harvest them, we've usually been out of vegetables for a while. They grow fast and I can snip some of their greens even before the beets themselves are ready. So while they aren't my favorite, they are familiar.

Except that now they're not. How did I not know they were this sweet? That they felt this good to chew? How did I not recognize that when they hit my stomach they feel like I just ate a steak?

"Oh, this is so good," I moan. Laughter greets my pronouncement but it's a laugh of recognition and fellowship. When I look around me, I see the others feel the same way. "I guess I'm not the only one who's decided they love beets."

*****

We cross the river while it's still pitch dark, using just the cupped lights to aid with our footing. We take a quick stop afterward to put on our boots and we're off once more. Officially, we're out of Texas, in a place called Oklahoma, but that means almost nothing in the grand scheme of things. This is a sort of no-man's-land where no one lives and patrols wouldn't give a second thought to coming for us if they saw us here.

When the moon rises, I think it looks fatter than before, which is both good and bad. Good because we'll stumble less and bad because it means anyone out here will be able to see us better, too.

The pace Jordan sets is brutal, just short of a jog, and the night is broken by the sound of harsh breathing within an hour of our crossing the river. We're not paralleling the river but veering away from it toward the north, where a line of trees breaks up the flat profile of the plains. They look lush to me, new leaves shining in the moonlight. It's smart. We can take cover under them if we need to and have a ready place to spend the day.

I hear the tinkling of water a few times from within the trees, which explains why the trees are so lush. Eventually, we cross a stream that's clear and deep over the rocks in its bed. Its path meanders toward the river. I'd like to stop at it, but we have to keep moving so I just listen to the sound of it fading behind me.

There are plenty of patrols to keep things lively and send us running into the tree line. Their lights sweep over the bank but they hardly seem to be looking, more like making a show of having looked. Again, I'm grateful for their aversion to risk.

There are no bridges over the river that I know of. There are the remains of bridges, but the bridges themselves are long since destroyed. We have no trade north of the river, even if there were anyone to trade with, so a bridge would just offer an easier path for the smugglers or the wild people who decide to take a chance on raiding.

Dawn finds us snug and well concealed near an old deadfall grown all over with brush. It's a perfect spot. The loam beneath the trees is as soft as a bed. Once we settle down enough that the birds don't mind us, their songs let us know that no one is nearby. My heart feels lighter and the ever-present fear of being found has retreated for the moment, leaving me ready for sleep.

It isn't just the woods, a thing of beauty I've only seen surrounding the lake, or the cool moist earth that sticks together when I grab a fistful instead of crumbling to dust. It's everything. I've just spent hours walking with Jordan, hearing about River Oaks and the boy who is my brother. I've been listening to details of our trip to come and what lies beyond even the distant place he lives, further east where an ocean so vast it makes the Gulf look small stretches endlessly.

He spoke to me in such a familiar way, comfortable and glad to listen when I spoke in my turn. The way he looked at me, with such fondness, was enough to make me shy at times, but he smoothed over the awkwardness each time. And then, when we found this spot, he ran my dark ponytail through his hand—which seems to be his way, like another person might squeeze an arm or cup a cheek—and told me, "I always dreamed you'd be wonderful. I just didn't dream you as wonderful as you are."

I can feel the others all around me now that we're all settled in. I hear the scrape of Maddix's shoes on old leaf litter as he keeps watch and the small sound of Connor breathing through a half-clogged nose. I feel the presence of Jordan nearby, between me and any clear path so that I'll be safe against the trees. And I can feel Jovan, too. He gave me space last night, but I could tell he was keeping close and listening to Jordan talk, just as enthralled as I at what he heard. He's next to me now, a scant foot of space separating us.

It feels so good to drift and I can feel sleep approaching on little sleepy feet when Jovan whispers, "Sleep well, Karas."

I do.

Chapter Twenty

The next two days and nights pass much the same but we're out of fresh food by the time we wake up and get the fire going on the third night. My two tins of grain will only last so long and one of the metal lids on the dried fruit worked its way loose during one walk. All the fruit inside spilled out into my pack and is now covered in a liberal coating of dirt and general ickiness. We'll have to boil it before we can eat it so the dirt can settle out. That's what we're cooking tonight.

I feel much more comfortable with Jordan now. It surprises me how quickly it's become natural to be around him, to have a father close at hand. We've spent hours talking, which often consist of my endless questions and his patient answers.

We've also had the chance to really get to know each other. And when I look at him now, I can see myself in him. It's no longer strange or shocking, just familiar. I have the shape of his fingernails and the same toes. My dark brown hair came from him, but also the little cowlick at the crown of my head. In a hundred tiny ways, I have daily proof that I came from him and I'm growing fond of the reality of having a father, rather than just the idea of it.

As is becoming habit, Jordan smooths a bit of ground and starts drawing the route ahead in the dirt before we set out. He draws much farther than we could ever hope to go in one night, but it makes me feel more secure, more in control, to know what's ahead. The way everyone pays attention makes it clear that we all feel much the same.

"The river ahead has a pretty big lake that will add almost two days if we have to go around it to the north. Less if we go south, but that's not a good direction. It's an easy patrol route. It may be beyond the state line but it's a smuggling and trade route, so…"

"What do you mean 'trade'? We don't do trade that way. We're embargoed," Jovan breaks in.

Jordan smiles a knowing smile and says, "Officially, but that doesn't keep the Army from having a nice little side business using the patrols. Most smugglers aren't the gentlest sort anyway, but the ones that work with the patrols—well, they should be avoided."

He lets the statement hang and sink in. I didn't know this and clearly Jovan didn't either. He looks like someone just told him there is no Santa Claus. I have a hard time imagining Jovan being happy in the Army now that he's discovered the truth behind it. Maybe he would have become a Foley the likes of which my father describes, but I don't think so. This hurts him and I can see it. Disillusionment is practically rolling off him in waves.

Cassi eyes the drawing, then points a stick at the line Jordan's drawn across the lake. "What about this?"

"Ah, yes. There's a third option, but it's risky so it should be a group decision. There used to be a bridge here. It's long gone, but people still cross there. There are usually rafts tucked away and there's a guide-line strung along the pylons. But it's right through the middle, so we'd be seen by anyone who looks in the direction of the lake. The moon is waxing so it's going to get brighter every night," he finishes and leans back on his haunches to let us consider.

I have no idea what this trip is like, what the land looks like or anything that might help me contribute to a smart decision. We've passed the rain line—though we've not yet had any to prove it—and the land is lush with greenery. That makes it strange to me and I'm at a loss as to how to navigate it. Aside from Jordan, no one does except Maddix.

"Maddix, which way did you go on your way out? What route did you two take on the way back?" I ask.

Instead of answering me, he looks away. Jordan jumps in just a little too quickly for him to be doing anything other than covering for Maddix.

"Maddix went south but he made it through with some luck," Jordan says. He says it just a little too nonchalantly for me to buy it. "When we came back, we took the northern route."

"Then we should take that way," I say.

"Wait," Jovan says. "Why did you take the northern route?" He turns to me and adds, "We should know all the information before we make a decision."

I smile and motion for him to be my guest. I'm irritated he thought of it and I didn't.

"Easy answer. There were just two of us but there was a whole group of smugglers pacing us and we had to keep out of sight. They were motor mules. They aren't necessarily dangerous, but you never know," he says.

"So, if you hadn't seen these…what were they again?" Jovan asks.

"Motor mules. There's a strong market for motor parts, batteries, turbine parts…that sort of thing. But most of that stuff comes from Florida or the East, and they would never sell if they thought it was bound for Texas. Motor mules are just a link in a long chain. They make that trip often, the cargo is high value and they don't like to be seen. It's best to avoid them if you can," Jordan says.

I feel like he's telling me an adventure story. It's hard to imagine people smuggling for a living. It must pay a lot of money if that much risk is worth it.

Everyone is quiet. The sound of the pot of dried fruit and grain bubbling over the fire reminds me to stir it. The sweet smell wafts out and causes sniffs in that direction.

Finally, Cassi asks, "Will we get to swim?"

Jovan and I laugh. For one beautiful moment, all is right in the world.

*****

The lake is bigger than the one near Bailar town. Far bigger. As in a whole other species of bigness, bigger. I almost can't take it in. Luckily, it's also longer than it is wide or else I can't imagine how anyone could get across it.

Jordan shushed us into silence before we got close and he still seems hyper-alert, like he's expecting someone to jump out at us at any time. It's making me and everyone else nervous along with him. I have a weird twitchy feeling in my stomach that's normally reserved for bad nights at home with my mom.

There's a lot of leaf litter and endless old branches scattered on the forest floor. I'm starting to take this immersion in trees for granted, but that doesn't mean I've learned how to walk quietly in them. No one else has either except for Jordan. We're doing our best, but I know the sharp crackle of leaves and the snap of twigs is making it hard for him to hear anything except our footfalls.

We approach from an angle, well to the north of the old road that leads to the demolished bridge. At least this way, we have a good opportunity to watch the lake during the day while we rest. We'll also have a shot at finding out if anyone's hanging around.

It's already a bright, almost ideal, morning when we get to a suitable spot and make our cold camp. There's no fire for us this morning, given that it's already day, and we settle for passing around a water carrier and a few mouthfuls of cold leftover grains and fruit.

My mouth actually hurts when I take that first bite. It's like all the saliva saved up in my glands comes rushing out at once and strains them or something. It's a pain and a pleasure all at the same time. This cold mush is absolutely delicious.

Still, it's gone too soon and it's not nearly enough for my body. It can't be enough for anyone's body. We've been on the move for almost a week and I know my pants aren't just looser because I've been wearing them non-stop. I've never been rich enough to be fat, or even chunky, but I'm thinning out in ways that aren't healthy.

Everyone is. Cassi has always had great angles on her face, but her cheekbones are sticking out sharply and she looks especially pale behind her copper colored freckles. Even Jovan seems to be shrinking. He's a big guy with a lot of muscle, but it won't last unless we get more food. For the moment, this deprivation is actually making him look better, if that's possible. I saw him when he changed his shirt and had to be sure my mouth wasn't hanging open. The muscles in his back and torso stood out in stark relief, the lines no longer smoothed from being well fed. No matter how nice it appears at the moment, I know he must be feeling the effects of our lack of decent meals. Food, and a good long rest afterwards, are what we need to renew our bodies after what we've been through.

It's almost funny because we have the means to get food in plenty if what Jordan says about game in the forest is to be believed. We have three guns and three vests completely full of ammunition, plus a few boxes of ammunition scavenged from the Courthouse. More than enough to spare to shoot something edible. But we dare not use a gun and make noise. The irony of that isn't lost on me.

I'm not entirely sure I believe the whole plentiful game story, though. I've seen tiny birds all over the place, but nothing big enough to be more than a mouthful when plucked. What I would do for a chicken right now is not to be imagined in polite company.

From our vantage point we see a whole lot of nothing all day and I take my turn at watch with Cassi. No smugglers or anything dangerous is a lucky break and we're due for one of those.

I've missed Cassi even though we've been within a few feet of each other the whole trip. It's nice to just talk to her, quietly and honestly, as if we were sitting on her bed in her room with nothing better to do than that.

I'm surprised—and greatly relieved—to find out she really is doing okay. I can't say she's fine because none of us are fine, but she's doing far better than I would have expected. In truth, I've been expecting her to tear me a new one as soon as she found the opportunity. I did get her into this, after all, and I'd deserve whatever she might say.

But she doesn't. Instead, she gives me the full Cassi treatment. Smiles, happy words and lots of overall cheering up. By the time our watch ends and I settle down for a few hours' sleep, I'm more hopeful than I've been since those soldiers walked in and saw us at the Courthouse.

I wake when it's fully dark and there's still no fire for cooking or boiling water. Everyone seems antsy and anxious to go. Jordan says he spotted the little inlet where several rafts are drawn up and tied to the stumps of trees, so we know where we're going. I think he must be nervous since the rafts are tied up. Being stationary means they provide an excellent point to watch for activity. If we decide to cross, a watcher can be sure of seeing us there. It seems like a perfect location for a trap.

The water is placid, flat and shiny in the moonlight. The only ripples are caused by our raft. The lines strung between the pylons of the one-time bridge are right where Jordan said they would be and they work. Between pushing off from the shore with the poles and heaving on the lines once the water grows deeper, we make progress faster than I could have imagined. And best of all, there's no one to interfere, no shouts or sudden appearances of soldiers shooting at us.

At the far end, we tie up the raft and the poles with care for the next travelers who will need them, but we also take the time to minimize our own footprints just in case. Jordan takes one of the boxes of ammunition and weighs it in his hands, considering. We need to leave something of value—that's how this system works, the honor system—but we don't have much in the way of food. Everything else we have is something we desperately need. Except for maybe the couple of shirts I brought and I'm not giving those up.

The ammunition is in another category of value entirely. A full box would be worth more than I could make in the screen-weaving factory if I worked every day for a year. That box Jordan seems to be weighing as a trade seems excessive to me for the use of a wobbly raft and a few poles. Though he told me that ammunition is quite affordable everywhere except Texas—the embargo means that one ingredient is hard to come by there—it's still a full box that might be needed if worse comes to worst.

Before I can stop myself, I put my hand on top of the box and say, "Really? Why not just give them a gun to shoot us in the back with?"

He starts at my words, then sighs and drops the box back into his sack. "I would have only left one or two cartridges, but you're right. I hadn't thought of that. We should leave something that doesn't advertise who we are. But what? All the money I had is still locked up somewhere at the Courthouse."

Jovan digs into one of his many pockets and pulls out a coin. It's a little one, a silver tenth-ounce, what we call a teenth. It's enough to buy a used coat or a pair of boots with a copper or two in change, but he tosses it with a flick of his thumb toward Jordan, who snatches it out of the air with a grin.

"That's generous," he says. "You have anything smaller? Coppers maybe?"

He doesn't so Jordan leaves the coin in the basket hanging on a post for just that purpose. The lake still looks inviting but also like a huge trap, so we leave and I only look back at it a few times. Regretfully, given all that clean water, but only a little.

*****

Another abandoned town, more of a collection of rundown huts plus one larger building, looks ideal for a temporary hideout. Now that the woods are providing such great cover, we no longer have to hide during the day. We pushed on instead of bedding down and now the day is waning once more. We've gotten into a rhythm and for the first time, the mood is good, even though we're all very tired.

Cassi even jokes that she's going to hike out for a bath, as if she would really walk all those miles back to the lake. We all laugh but the real cracking up happens when Jovan tells her that's a good idea and we'd all appreciate it if she took a bath.

The buildings are very old, essentially tinder boxes of old wood, but our three water carriers are full of lake water that needs boiling. In the building we've chosen, there's a hearth of sorts that clearly sees use every so often. A ring of stones has been dug into the dirt under a gap in the roof. Piles of old ashes hint that it's safe to use.

133

We set up camp on the first floor, though there is an upper floor in this building. The floorboards on the second floor aren't very sturdy and there are holes all over our ceiling down below. Still, the walls are intact and the room with the hearth is snug. With the warmth of the fire added in, it's comfortable.

Jordan lights a small fire and digs out a pot, but tells the rest of us to sleep while we can. I know he won't be able to see much in the dark outside if he's near the fire, but he winks when I mention it and tells me he'll go outside as soon as he gets a pot going. When I settle down in the spot I've chosen—and I do notice that Jovan waits for me to sit before he picks his own spot, next to mine—I feel good. Safe.

Chapter Twenty-One

A gunshot is a terrible thing to wake to. It's sharp, harsh and always frightening. It's not a common thing to hear in Bailar, given the price of ammunition, but I know it and there's no question that's what jerks me from a sound sleep.

What else I wake to is utter chaos. Jordan is standing almost on top of the fire, a gun in his hand and his head jerking in every direction. Connor and Maddix are nowhere to be seen and Cassi is huddled in the spot where she went to sleep. She looks just as confused as I am.

"What?" I shout and Jordan's head swings in my direction, a finger to his lips. His eyes are wide and that frightens me more than the shot.

"We've got company. Get into the back room," he says. His voice is even but those fearful eyes give him away.

I scramble up, motioning for Cassi to come, but she just stares at my hands like she's never seen them before. My patience is never at a surplus and this situation calls for urgency, so I step over and yank her to her feet. She's like a wooden copy of herself and she practically falls on me when I force her to move so we can get to the partially collapsed rear room.

From outside—not near the door where Jordan stands, but behind me, where the opening of a long-gone back door leads out into the dark—I hear the cut-off cry of someone in sudden pain. It's like the startled sound of someone being hit when they're not ready for it. I know that sound well enough, given how often I've cried out myself before I got smarter about watching my back at home.

When I turn toward the opening, a very big man is holding Connor by the neck and squeezing inside, using my friend as a shield. He's also holding a very big knife to Connor's throat.

The sound I make draws Jordan's attention and I'm immediately sorry about that because a smaller man carrying what looks like one of our guns comes in the front door and points the barrel right at me.

"Drop it," he growls. He's looking at Jordan, the only one in the room holding a weapon.

Cassi drops to her haunches and buries her head in her arms. Perhaps she's hoping that if she ignores it all, it will go away. I'm not so hopeful. We have another weapon and a person who knows how to use it, assuming that is our gun the man is holding. Where is Jovan? Where is Maddix? Which one of them has lost their gun?

Jordan doesn't drop his weapon and directs his answer toward the incredibly ugly man holding the gun. "And then you'll shoot us, so I decline the offer. What do you want?"

The man grins a terrible grin. His front teeth are brown, dead a long time, and his eyes are full of that unthinking meanness of the truly bad. This is a dangerous person and the last thing I think we should do is drop any weapons we have.

"I'll make you a deal," he says.

Even Cassi looks up at the sound of those words because he says them in a way that makes my hair stand on end. I know what the deal is going to be before he says it when I see him lick his lips at the sight of Cassi.

"What deal?" I ask, my voice as cold as I can make it.

He flicks a single glance my way and then focuses on Jordan again. Which is smart because he's got the gun. "We leave you and your two boys alone, you give us the girls. We'll even leave you some of your silver…maybe." He flips something toward us and it lands at my feet. A silver tenth-ounce coin. Jovan's stupid coin.

I knew it was too much, but I never thought of this happening. We left too much so these creeps decided we must have more. And then they saw

Cassi and decided we have even more they'd like to take. It's all I can do to suppress a shudder at the thought.

The big guy's grip on Connor's throat is tight and his face is turning red, but the knife isn't quite pressed into the flesh. That seems to me like he isn't as eager to kill as the other one, though I have no doubt he would if he had to. There's still no sign of Jovan or Maddix, and that man got one of our guns somehow. I'm starting to feel a scream bubbling up inside me, an undeniable need to call out their names and find them.

The faint sound of someone moving tells me where one of the two is. It's just the tiniest shuffle of feet on old boards upstairs. The cautious movement lets me know he's aware of what's going on and the careful footsteps tells me it's someone with some training. Jovan. He's probably weighing his options. They aren't great options.

"You want me to give you my daughter," Jordan says, his voice flat and dangerously calm.

From outside, I hear the growl of another voice and an answering cry that can only belong to Maddix. So there are at least three of them, then.

The man's greedy eyes shift for the smallest second, taking in both Cassi and me, then dart back to Jordan. His grin grows, showing more of his brown teeth, and he says, "You've got a lot of kids."

"And you're not going to take any of them. Your friend better be careful with that knife. If he slips, you die first," Jordan assures him.

I've known a lot of tension and fear in my life. I've known the fear of a child too small and weak to run, the fear of someone who knows she can't fight back and the fear of the unknown now that I'm finally escaping. I've known the tinderbox tension of a house so filled with anger that it felt as if it might spontaneously catch fire. All of those things pale in comparison with what I feel around me now. The air is almost crackling with it.

There is nothing quite like a standoff with guns, a knife to a throat and men who want what these men want to create an atmosphere in a room. I'm still standing in a little crouch, ready to move, the tendons in my legs so tight I think they might spring out and unravel.

But it's everything else that unravels instead.

Cassi whimpers where she is on the floor, her eyes unable to stay focused on either of the invaders so that her head zips from side to side, looking at them in turns. The man with the gun takes a longer look at her—a mistake—and when he does, Jordan shoots him.

It isn't a clean shot and the man crumples to the floor to roll back and forth, his arms pressed to his belly. His gun skids across the floor so I grab it, snatching it up just as he reaches for it. I back away as quickly as I can, keeping him in view because I have no idea if he has another weapon. And also because he's certainly not dead, though the dirt floor around him is turning dark as his blood soaks into it.

More shots from upstairs ring out and I hear exclamations outside from more than one voice. Jovan is keeping them busy out there, but Maddix is still out there as well. Connor's eyes grow even wider and his hands are clamped around the arm of the man with the knife at his throat. The man no longer looks quite so secure and his eyes shift from person to person.

Jordan's gun is trained on him now. He seems to have dismissed the man on the floor, which I don't think is smart. He's in pain and the blood he's losing tells me he's dying, but that makes him no less dangerous. He'll be dangerous until the moment he closes his eyes and breathes his last. I'm inclined to help him along, but I don't think I could bear to get close enough to shoot and be sure I hit his head. I've never fired a real gun and my aim is a complete unknown to me. And that's not even counting this strange feeling I have that urges me not to fire. It's like some old mantra in my head that says, "It's wrong to kill, wrong to kill."

I wish it would shut up.

Two more quick shots ring out while Jordan and the knife-man stare each other down. At the second, a sort of horrible strangled cry answers from outside, followed by the dull thud of someone getting struck by something very heavy, interspersed with the labored grunts and curses of the one doing the striking. I can't tell, but I hope with every fiber of my being that it's Maddix who's doing the grunting and the hitting. Connor's eyes roll as if he might see what's going on behind him if he just tries hard enough.

A long moment passes like this, the crackling of the little fire punctuating our heavy breathing. My heart gives a jump in my chest when Maddix's frame fills the space where the door would have been. Up till now, his face had been healing, the bruises turning a sickly yellow-green and the swelling in his nose retreating until he looked more like himself. It's apparent he's going to be starting that process over again.

The whites of his eyes are the only thing on his face I can still clearly see. The rest is a swollen, bloody and battered mess. And he's limping, almost dragging one of his legs. In the wavering firelight, I can see a dark streak that must be blood on his thigh, reaching almost to his knee.

He growls a low, almost inhuman sound when he sees the man holding Connor, and Maddix's hand reaches out like a claw toward him. The man jerks Connor backward toward a corner where he can see both Jordan and Maddix. His eyes are fearful but he's still got the knife gripped tightly in his fist.

"There are more coming," Maddix says, his eyes never leaving Connor's. "These guys were sent ahead to scout to see if we were here and make camp if not."

"Shut up," the man says. His fingers flex rhythmically on the hilt of the knife. Whatever cool he may have had, he's losing it fast. We need to come to some sort of resolution and the best resolution I can think of is that this man die.

"Maddix, how many? How soon?" Jordan asks urgently.

He shakes his head and clamps a hand to the side of it when he does, his face a mask of pain. I see him pale under his blood and bruises, the few patches of bare skin turning sheet white.

Whatever move Jordan is planning on making must come soon if there are more men like this coming our way. I can see it in the way Jordan tenses and aims. Then his brows draw together—only the smallest bit, but I see it—and a look of confusion flashes across his face. I look in the direction of his gaze and see a gun slowly extending from a ragged hole in the ceiling. The hand and wrist attached to it, corded and strong, belong to Jovan. I'd recognize it anywhere.

When he fires, it is directly into the top of the man's head. We all jump at the sound and the man drops like a puppet whose strings have been cut. Perhaps even quicker than that. It's a terrible thing to see, someone boneless and utterly without life so instantaneously. Yet, I'm glad of it, inexpressibly glad.

Connor extricates himself from the tangle of the dead man's limbs, kicking his body away to get free. He's got a cut at the hollow of his throat but I'm relieved to see a trickle of blood rather than a stream or spurt. Above us, the sound of pounding boots rattles the boards, sending streams of dirt down between them as the steps cross the floor. It patters like rain onto our heads and makes the fire spit as Jovan passes over our heads.

Jordan lowers his gun and sweeps up my pack, tossing it to me. "Gear up. We need to go. Now!"

I snatch the pack out of the air and start stuffing the things I've taken out back into it. Cassi breaks from her stupor and starts pouring the last pot of water into a water carrier. Connor is tending to Maddix, and I feel like I should be helping him, but if we don't get out of here and more men like these really are coming, no one is going to be helping anyone.

"Can he walk?" I ask, nodding toward Maddix.

Connor looks up from the bloody streak on his brother's leg. He nods yes, but his face tells me he's not at all sure of it.

Jovan's boots pound down the stairs. "They're coming," he says, his voice harsh and urgent. "I see torchlight. We've got a few minutes, tops."

Jordan seems to come to a decision. "Connor, take your brother and go. We'll get the stuff. Just keep going as far and as fast as you can," he orders. Maddix tries to suppress his groans when Connor gets him moving. I can see very well the effort he's making, his jaw clenched and his free hand tightly fisted. But they do manage to stumble out of the back door and into the dark.

"If these guys are expecting a camp, I'm going to let them walk into a camp," Jordan says, tossing bags towards us as he speaks. He isn't looking at me and I know what he's saying. He's saying he is staying behind.

Jovan grabs up the bags and fishes around, pulling out clips for the gun. He checks that they are full and then hands them to Jordan. I see the look that passes between them.

"No. We just need to go. They aren't going to believe they're walking into a camp after all that shooting," I say. Leaving behind the father I just found to an unknown number of marauders is not an option I'm willing to entertain.

"Cassi, go. Catch up with Connor and help him with Maddix. Go," Jordan orders. Cassi just nods at him and gives me a beseeching look that begs me to come. She grabs two bags and runs.

"Dad. No. I'm not leaving you. You have to come," I plead and I can hear the waver in my voice.

He smiles at my calling him that but it's the sad smile of someone hearing it too late. He tucks the clips into his waistband and shoves his bag at Jovan.

"If anything happens, take care of her. Get her where she can be safe. Safe and free."

Something passes between them, a handing off of responsibility. It's as palpable as if they had just signed over custody papers. Jovan gives him one sharp nod and turns to me.

When Jovan grabs my arm I shriek at him, heedless of the noise, and he responds by clapping a hand over my mouth and pulling me out the back door. I see my father tossing wood onto the fire, too much for such an old structure built of old dry wood. Then he grabs a burning brand from it as he crosses to the stairs.

He pauses and looks at me for just a second, but it is the longest second of my life. Everything I have ever felt or imagined or dreamed about him runs through my mind at the speed of light. I think the same must have happened to him because his eyes are filled with more emotion than I can catalog.

"I love you," he mouths. Then I am gone and I fear he will be gone forever.

Chapter Twenty-Two

Jovan drops me on the trail after a few minutes of my kicking at him. He grabs my jacket, pulling my face close to his and hisses, "You want to make him die? Keep doing this and he will for sure. Right now, he has the advantage. He could make it."

We stand like that, both breathing hard and staring each other down, for a long moment. As much as I hate to admit it, he's right. The time for freaking out is not now.

By the time we spot the others, I'm moving under my own steam and running as fast as I can, given the undergrowth and the darkness.

Maddix isn't doing well and we catch up with them far too quickly, even with the delay I caused by fighting Jovan. Catching up with them, I take the few bags they salvaged so they can focus on Maddix. He's moving fairly fast considering his condition, but his leg is clearly hurting and his breath sounds like a bellows through this damaged nose and mouth. But we have no time to waste, so on we go.

We're well off the road, and the trail we're on must have been made by animals because it's irregular and too narrow even for my body. I'm being whipped by reaching branches and tendrils of thorny brush with every step. I can't imagine how bad it must be for the others, particularly Connor and Cassi, who have Maddix between them.

I have no real sense of time, only barely controlled panic, but it seems just a few seconds have passed when the first gunshots rip through the silence of the night. The woods play with sound, simultaneously muffling and accentuating the sharp reports so that they seem both far away and right next to my ear.

It makes me stop short, my feet skidding in the loam. The sound does something to me deep inside. It's as if every cell in my body is fighting a war with itself. The urge to run back, screaming in rage and tear at anyone in my way with my nails is exactly even with my desire to pull myself as tightly into a ball as I can and hide.

Jovan grabs my arm and growls, "Don't, Karas! We have to run."

He's nothing more than a dark shape in the forest and I can't see his face, but I can hear the determination in his voice.

The others are having trouble keeping up with us, a struggling Maddix between them. He's losing his battle to keep going and we'll need to stop soon or I think he might suffocate. His breathing sounds like someone blowing bubbles underwater, or in the grips of a bad summer cold. We need to find shelter and tend to him, make sure there's nothing life-threatening wrong with him.

We need to stop someplace safe and wait for Jordan.

The artificial shape of a tower outlined against the stars stands out ahead of us. We've seen plenty of those on our trip so far. Most of them are falling apart or falling down. Only one looked safe enough to climb up for a look around. Maybe this one will be sound enough. At least we might be able to see from there if there is some place to shelter once the moon rises.

I point to it and Jovan squints in that direction. I whisper, "Tower," when he doesn't see, and he nods his agreement. Cassi swaps places with him and we start out. Next to me Cassi smells of blood, a metallic scent that is both alarming and strong. If I can smell it, then Maddix leaked a lot of it onto her.

At the base of the tower, Maddix drops to the ground like a sack. Connor and Jovan follow, exhausted by bearing more and more of his weight as he weakened. The moon is only just brushing the tops of the trees. There isn't enough light for me to try to examine the tower and see if it's sturdy, let alone climb it.

"We need a fire," I say to Jovan. "Or at least the flashlights. Fire would be better." With fire I can boil water before using it to clean Maddix's wounds, decreasing the risk of infection.

Jovan's eyes are uncertain, but he can see the dark smear that is Maddix's face as well as I can and he knows what I mean. He starts digging through the bags until he comes up with the smallest of our flashlights and shines the light for me.

While Maddix's face is a mess, it's his leg that concerns me. The groan that escapes him when I pull his leg straight is weak and not entirely conscious. I'm glad because I'm about to hurt him.

There's just one small hole in his jeans, which isn't good because that means the bullet is still inside him. I don't think there's any question that the first shot we heard sent a bullet into Maddix's leg. When I slip the point of the small knife Jovan hands me into the hole in the fabric, Maddix stirs but doesn't fully wake. I wait a second, then slide it upward, parting the fabric as little as I can.

We have very few spare pieces of clothing and I know there are none for him aside from the uniforms, their personal goods having been taken and locked up. I'd like to save his jeans, or at least most of them, if I can. If there is one thing I can think of that can make getting shot in the leg worse than it already is, it's waking up afterwards to realize you have no pants.

The hole in his leg is so small it seems ridiculous, but I suppose any bullet hole is technically only the size of the bullet. Yet they are deadly. The smallest of things can end a human life. I have no earthly idea what I should do next. I'm no medic and I've never had any desire to be one. The very idea of dealing with the interior parts of any living thing makes me want to gag, to say nothing of when that interior becomes visible on the exterior. Even when Connor and I kill rats with our slingshots at the compost operation, he always cleans them before we cook them because I can't.

Jovan and I look at each other and I see my indecision mirrored there. He swallows loudly and says, "Okay. Basics of first aid. We march."

I wonder if maybe Jovan is in need of help himself because he's making no sense. March? We just stopped. At my baffled look, he takes a deep breath, holds up a finger and says, "March. M is for massive bleeding."

He nods for me to go on, pointing with his eyes toward Maddix's leg.

"No, it's just sort of welling up in the hole." I grab a piece of boiled cloth from the kit Jovan has open for me and dab at the wound, watching for a reaction from Maddix. His face scrunches up but that's all. I look at his pants leg, which is almost covered from thigh to ankle with a thick streak of blood, the material utterly soaked through. "But it must have been bleeding pretty good before."

Jovan reaches past me and presses a thumb into the flesh of Maddix's inner arm and then shines a light on it. It goes from bleached white to his normal tan color quickly, so Jovan nods and starts counting off, "A is for airway and that's clearly okay. Respiration, also good, though we're going to have to help him with that nose. Circulation, looks good to me. I mean, his color comes back after I press and I don't know how else to test for it."

He stops and drops his hand, clearly done, so I ask, "What's the H?"

"Oh, Hypo- or Hyperthermia but I don't think we have that problem here," he answers.

"That can't be it. I mean, he's got a freaking bullet in there. Do we just leave it?" I ask.

In the reflected light of the flashlight I see him pale and he says, "No. We have to take it out."

Connor and Cassi, who have been sitting there watching while supporting Maddix, both move back the smallest bit, like they want to be sure they aren't volunteered for that particular duty. Connor strokes Maddix's arm and tucks his brother's head more securely into the crook of his neck.

After we all look at each other for a minute, each waiting for the other to step up, I say, "Fine. I'll do it. But can it wait? We need to find some shelter where I can do this as cleanly as possible."

Jovan hands me another strip of boiled cloth and tells me I should bind it up to keep the bleeding down and the dirt out. By the time it's done, the moon has risen enough so that the world has turned to silver and black.

We've done as much for Maddix as we can for the moment, so I look up. The tower above us is standing firm. None of the more common telltales of structural failure are immediately evident. It's not leaning or sagging and there are very few pieces of it littering the ground around us. These are all good signs. I can't truly see how much rust might be on it, but the number of dark streaks along the lower parts of the tower is surprisingly small.

There's no good way to climb one of these towers from the ground. The ladder rails don't begin until a good forty feet or more up and it almost looks like they were designed to be difficult to climb. To me, that makes no sense.

Why construct a huge metal tower perfect for observing wide distances and then make it hard to climb? Jordan told me while we walked that they weren't meant to be watchtowers, but to function as communications relays. I couldn't, and still can't, see how that works but I'm grateful they've been left for me to use for a much more reasonable purpose.

Getting up to the ladder rungs is the hardest part and involves the careful climbing of a rope with loops tied in it to serve as footholds. We're in luck that our rope was still packed up and we grabbed it when we ran. Otherwise, I'm not sure how I'd get up there. Even with my rope, it's precarious and dangerous. Aside from some minor groaning from the metal and a few wild swings when I unbalance the rope by missing a loop, it's not too bad and I quickly transfer to the welded rungs. Each one requires testing with my weight, just to be sure it doesn't crack off and spill me to the ground, which is sure to be fatal at this height.

When I get high enough to see a good distance, I realize we got further than I thought. The collection of huts that made up the settlement isn't visible by itself, but I know the distance because the red light of an inferno is shining above the trees. I'm not even all the way to the top of the tower when the unmistakable glow draws my attention. If size is any indicator, at least a few of the other buildings have caught fire.

I think back to my last sight of my father, throwing far too much wood on the fire and then taking a flaming brand from it, and I know what he has done. This fire has been purposefully set, most likely to ensure that those who came after us became as trapped as he. Those flames tell me it is almost certain he will not be searching for us come daylight.

My eyes blur with tears, but at least I'm alone and there's no one to see them fall. I barely knew him, but he was my father. He was the father I had dreamed of, wondered about, hated and wanted to know in equal measure throughout my life. And then he came for me, just as I had wished for during those times when I hid outside in the cold or nursed my wounds. He was everything I'd hoped for and more. And now he is surely gone. But this time, he won't be coming to my rescue again.

My arms are aching so I wipe my eyes on my jacket and keep moving upward. Near the top I hear a noise I recognize from home. It's the soft "guh-runk" of a red-tailed hawk disturbed from its sleep in the nest.

Bracing myself with one arm, I take out my flashlight and aim it upward. Poking out of the complex web of metal braces and bars at the top is the huge and messy nest of the hawk. It's an old nest, used for many years, so the pair must be well matured and paired for a long time.

I can't bear the thought of disturbing them, so I settle for the lower platform. Balancing my butt between the bars, with my legs stretched out over the next few bars, provides a surprisingly comfortable perch. After a few minutes sitting still, the bird in the nest quiets.

The inferno to the west is burning bright, but there is no other light in view from any other direction. I'm especially watchful of any light moving away from the settlement. Not just because it might be Jordan—which I hope it is—but because it could be the men that came for us who have escaped. But there's nothing. It's dark beyond the ragged circle of flames.

There are also no lights to be seen anywhere else at any distance, and I can see for miles at this height. If there are any inhabited places around here, they're not producing power or not using it for lights. To the north I see an unnaturally regular gap in the trees that must be from human intervention, though whether it is just tilled fields or an occupied village or yet another ruin is beyond my ability to see. In the morning, if I'm willing to take the risk, I could climb back up, but that would mean staying within a few miles of the burning settlement—and any surviving members of the group that meant to take us. I'm not sure the risk is worth it.

I pull out the can and the roll of twine attached to it, scribble a note on a scrap of paper outlining what I see and then slowly lower the can with my note. A tug tells me Jovan has it and soon after, another tells me to pull up the can. Inside, the return note reads, "Stay up there? Maddix okay. All sleeping. I'm sorry about Jordan." A little sad face is the only other thing on the paper and I run my finger over the simple drawing that says so much.

I'm bone-tired but sleeping up here seems like it would be impossible. If I climb down, I can sleep, but then I'll need to wait until dawn before climbing up again. It will be too dark to try it once the moon sets. And from here I can keep watch for the others, let them sleep in safety.

I scribble my suggestion and lower it. Jovan returns with the words, "You are amazing. Drop this if you see anything." A small bag of wheat kernels accompanies the note and I smile at how easily he thinks of solutions that are just right. If I empty this bag of kernels, they will spread as they fall and patter all of them with the tiny seeds. It would wake them, but not harm them like pebbles would.

I settle in, trying to be quiet and not disturb the bird in her nest. Given the month—if they follow the same schedule as the hawks where I come from—she would have eggs or perhaps even young in her nest. Given how aggressive they can get, being quiet and unintrusive is a safer move for me as well.

*****

The fact that I fell asleep says more about my level of exhaustion than the comfort of the tower, but I did and I wake to the rosy glow of a coming dawn. It's breathtaking and I let it wash over me, along with a fresh round of grief when I think of Jordan. The purple and red turn to pink and then there is a moment of perfect balance, the sun poised to rise. Shafts of light pierce the clouds on the horizon in a way I have never seen before. I'm not sure how many of my tears are for Jordan and how many are for the heartbreaking beauty I see.

The moment is broken by the flap of wings and I look above me to see the hawk standing outside the nest and looking at me, his head cocked a little to the side as if bemused to find me there. I can hear rustling in the nest so I know there is a missus hawk at least. The rising sun breaks the horizon and he switches to look at me from the other eye. A flare of golden light shines when the sun catches his eyes and I see Jovan in that eye.

I'm familiar with this type of hawk, far more familiar than I should be, and I'm transported back home to the garden in my backyard for a dizzying moment. The red-tailed hawk from home has been my sort-of companion for a few years, though he's now old enough to want to find a partner and have chicks of his own.

As a fledgling, with his funny-colored feathers and less-than-graceful hunting skills, he stalked my garden from the fence, watching for the mice that raided it each and every night. Soon enough, I found a mouse and bashed it with my spade, as I did every time. But this time, he was still sunning himself on the fence and watching with wary eyes, so I tossed it toward him. The mouse hit the fence and fell to the ground, startling him, but they're smart birds and he discovered it was a fresh bit of meat much like what his mother and father fed him.

We developed a relationship of sorts that first spring and summer. Hawks are unique creatures and his species more than any other can form bonds with humans. I was no hawker, but it was nice to have my own hawk friend to keep my garden clear. When I killed a chicken, I gave him the entrails and the organs I didn't like after Connor cleaned it for me. And our garden, shed and house were almost entirely free of mice by the end of that first summer.

He won my loyalty without question late that first summer when I came out to gather produce one hot morning to find him agitated and pacing along the fence with his feathers ruffled and his head jerking, as if trying to draw my attention. I thought perhaps he had gotten a rabbit but lost it—he had done that before but I only found it when it began to stink—so I went to the garden, chatting to him and assuring him I would look for his rabbit.

When I drew near to the stacked stone that made up the borders of our raised bed gardens, he startled me by swooping down from the fence and crossing in front of me. His wings came so close I could smell the powdery scent of his feathers. It startled me enough that I dropped my harvest basket and heard a faint rattling in response.

The small rattlesnake had been coiled on the stones, where some of the warmth of the day remains trapped during the night. I backed away slowly and the hawk returned to the fence, watching me and the snake with equal interest. After retrieving my slingshot, I waited, talking calmly to the hawk, until the snake settled back into his tight coil. One sharp strike with a stone from my slingshot and the snake died.

I took off his head far enough back to ensure that no venom glands remained and then opened him up to make him more enticing. I'd never seen the hawk take a snake, but it was meat. It was one of the few times I ever gutted an animal myself, but I figured I owed the hawk this one.

He played with the chunks, a bit unsure of them, for a good long while but eventually settled down to eating. After that, I was never surprised by a snake and I shared whatever I had with the hawk. I like to think we were friends. Though he came less this last year and seemed more interested in other hawks he saw in the sky, he always returned. I wonder if he's noted my absence, perhaps wondered where I've gone. Or did he just fly away, finally free to find the mate he must surely yearn for by now?

The hawk above says, "Guh-runk."

"I agree," I respond and search the area as the day unfolds. The light leaves me exposed should anyone close enough look my way, so I find myself anxious to climb down. Below me, everyone is still lying down, all of them except Jovan curled on their sides to preserve heat. I can't see his eyes, but he's laying face up, his arms behind his head and I can feel him looking up at me.

The fire from the abandoned settlement has almost gone out, sporadic streams of smoke still rising above the trees. It doesn't look like the kind of orderly smoke that comes from a camp or cooking fire, but short of going down there and making a target of myself, I have no way of knowing who, if anyone, survived the night there.

Where I saw the gap in the trees, I can now see some sort of old industrial complex. There's a huge building and a large flat area surrounding it sort of like that parking lot we passed before. There are no cars—which is too bad, because I'd like to see that—but a few trees have broken through and grown there. Whatever type of building it is that lies in the center, it's vast. It seems as if there are acres of rooftop. It has the look of someplace left to rot.

There's nothing else to see except trees and a snaking gap in them where there's a road to the south and maybe another large stream or small river to the east.

I sigh and say to the hawk, "North it is, then".

Chapter Twenty-Three

Getting Maddix to the place I saw is a nightmare, especially now that we can see him and the pain he's enduring with each step in the clear light of day. The temptation to stop each time his groans reach a certain, unbearable level of agony is almost more than we can tolerate, but we have to keep moving.

Each one of us reaches that breaking point at different times, thankfully, and the others encourage the one faltering to move on. It works and we reach the open space before the morning is half over. It's a slow, dragging pace compared to the ground-eating one we've been keeping, but Maddix is so bad that I'm surprised he manages at all.

We're not so desperate that we'll march into the open without checking it out first. Connor and Cassi work to make Maddix comfortable on the ground within the cover of the trees, while Jovan and I walk the perimeter of the huge lot to see what we can see. There's nothing but the scurrying of animals disturbed by our presence and the lazy coils of a few snakes on the broken pavement.

The building is huge, bigger even than it appeared from the tower. It's in very poor shape, the roof sagging in folds against walls that appear to be made of metal. But not all of it is collapsed. It's simply too big to rely on any single element for support.

There are enormous bay doors that look like large versions of the garage doors at the Courthouse. I can't imagine how large the vehicles would be that would need such doors. And even more curious, they are elevated, with huge concrete platforms extending out from the bottom of the doors like the loading bay platform I hid under before going in to see my father.

"It looks like an old transport hub. I don't see any signs of people at all. You?" Jovan asks. In the dappled light, his eyes flash gold and I can't help but smile, which is ridiculous given that my father has likely just died and Maddix is in such bad shape that I have no idea if he'll recover.

He crinkles his face but gives me a tentative smile in return, and asks. "What?"

"Nothing. It's just that I saw a hawk. It reminded me of something good from home," I say.

He looks around for the hawk, but I nudge him and say, "It's gone now. Let's go check it out."

There are no surprises, for which I'm grateful. It's nothing more than a half-fallen building that hasn't been used in decades, if not longer. Rust coats much of the metal and Jovan draws back my hand when I reach out to touch it.

"Try not to touch much. Some of this could come down if we disturb it. But that's good in a way. If we keep our hands off, but anyone coming after us doesn't…" He lets the sentence trail off but I understand what he means. It could serve as a good warning system, like an alarm of sorts.

I nod and keep my hands to myself as we look. The safest part seems to be the corner of the building where the first of the big doors is. There are more braces and it has been better protected from the rain because the roof is intact.

Getting Maddix into the building is tough. He's feverish and anytime he closes his mouth he's utterly unable to breathe. When he chokes he opens his mouth again, but he's not responding properly to what we say to him. Connor is nearly frantic with worry and starts snapping at us with each bump and stumble when we are forced to start carrying his brother just to keep him moving. All Jovan and I can do is keep going and try to watch our steps over the uneven pavement.

Cassi runs around the border of the lot, collecting some of the ample dried wood that litters the ground. She passes us several times, dropping off armfuls at the partially opened bay door where we've decided to make camp.

Inside, Jovan starts a small fire and we discover only then how much we left behind at the settlement. We've got one pot, the smaller one, and only two of the canteens. One cup and two water carriers remain, but at least both of the carriers are full. It's a small thing, but I'm grateful for it. The greatest loss is two of my four tins of food. We have just two entirely inadequate quarts of food, one of grain and one of dried fruit.

Jovan's discovery of several of the military rations we stole from the Courthouse eases the panic I feel at losing so much food, but even with that, we have enough to stretch out only a few days. The way Maddix looks, we'll need longer than that. And from what Jordan mapped out for us on the dirt, we've got weeks left on the road, at least ten days till we hit the border to the Southeast and freedom.

As far as I know, none of us knows how to hunt larger game and I'm not familiar with the plants in this wooded land. It's simply too different here from the flat plains where I've lived my life. Maybe they'll have rats or something like that. Connor and I can get those with our slingshots if all else fails.

Once we've boiled the instruments and any of the boiled cloth that hasn't stayed sealed, there's no more delay, though I wish with all my heart there was. Connor and Cassi take off Maddix's pants and the flesh around the hole is red and angry-looking. The puffy flesh flares outward from the hole like a pair of ragged lips.

Jovan's hands begin to shake the minute he picks up the little forceps so I've got no choice but to hand him the flashlight and wash my hands. His look of relief when I take the forceps from him is almost laughable.

I can feel the little nub of metal on the side of his thigh, so I know it went in at an angle. He's been walking and his bones feel sound so this should be a simple matter of reaching in and pulling out the bullet along the path it went in. The real trick is to do it all without rupturing some vital artery or vein. None of us even knows where any of those might be except the one that runs along the inner thigh. Thankfully, his wound is on the outer side of his leg.

Jovan holds two freshly wound flashlights high and sits on Maddix's other leg so that he can't kick at me while I dig around in his flesh. Connor and Cassi each hold an arm and shoulder. He seems only vaguely aware of what we're doing but I tell him anyway, waiting until I think I see understanding in the form of fear in his eyes.

It's a terrible thing to have to force an instrument into the flesh of another human being. It's the worst kind of intimacy and I'm not sure I'll ever forget the way it feels to fish around in his leg trying to grab that bullet. It seems to move and slip around like it doesn't want to be caught. I let out an involuntary sound of victory when I feel the forceps click together around the small bit of metal.

It comes out with a fresh stream of blood and for a moment, I worry that I've done exactly what I feared and torn some vital artery. But the stream is more of a trickle and I let out the breath I've been holding when I don't see it pump along with his heartbeat. Maddix sags back to the floor the moment I withdraw the forceps, his face covered in a fresh sheen of sweat and his breathing ragged with pain.

"What do we do about the infection?" I ask Jovan.

He fishes around in the medical kit, curses and then digs around in the bag he took it from. With a little sound of victory, he withdraws a little pot, opens it and holds it out for me to dip a finger in.

"This is what we use in the field for cuts, even big ones that need stitches. It works."

It smells wonderful, a bit like herbs and flowers, but it looks like an ugly gray jelly. I wash the hole, making Maddix struggle with pain again, until it bleeds enough to wash out anything that might be inside, then I fill the hole with the goo as best I can.

Maddix actually sighs as the medicine starts to work and the lines in his brow smooth. Where my finger has touched the jelly, a faint sensation of numbness sets in. Inside the kit is a curved needle and special thread for use in sewing skin, but neither Jovan or I feel like we should close up the hole. I have no idea why I feel like that is the wrong thing to do, but when Jovan says he agrees, we bind the leg snugly and let Maddix rest. We'll deal with his face later. I don't think he can handle more right now.

I make it outside before the shakes hit me, but when they do, they are merciless. It feels like my entire body is going to come apart at the seams, leaving bits of me to rattle around on the ground like a spilled bag of beans. The sun feels warm, like spring should feel, and I walk around in tight circles and shake my hands as if I can fling the memory of the way the inside of his leg felt away from me.

A shadow falls on me after I spend a few minutes pacing, and I look up to the open door to see Jovan standing there. He looks helpless, like he wishes he could do something for me but has no clue what to do. I stand there and something comes over me. My mind feels as numb as my finger but I raise my arms a little to the side, an invitation to a hug.

He jumps down with the same smooth athletic grace with which he does everything and doesn't hesitate. His arms go around me completely and he presses my cheek into his chest. One hand strokes my hair while the other holds me tightly to him. It's so very comforting, and the tremors begin to subside after a minute or two. It's the best kind of hug, the kind that is patient and speaks far more eloquently than any soothing words every could.

When he feels me sigh and sag against him, he withdraws a little and looks at my face. His fingers push back the strands of hair that have escaped from my ponytail and are sticking to my face.

"Now it's your turn, Karas," he says, his voice so faint it's more like a breath.

My turn? My turn for what? The look in his eyes, the confusing mixture of wanting and pity I see there, doesn't help me discover that answer. For a moment, I think he means something far deeper than a hug.

I've heard many times that there are always babies born nine months after a death that brings a lot of grief. And the more grief that death causes, the more babies will be born. It's said that nothing brings out the desire to be close to another person, as close as two people can get, like loss. Is this what's happening here?

"Your face," he clarifies. "You're torn up pretty good."

His fingers stop pushing back the strands of my hair and pause against the skin near my temple. I feel a sharp sting where he touches and wince. The thorns and branches of the night before must have left their marks on me. I pull back from him, embarrassed by my previous thoughts, but he merely smiles, unaware of how close I came to throwing myself at him in a way I would surely regret later.

He turns and jogs a few quick steps back toward the platform and lifts something down I missed seeing before. His smile is genuine and a little shy when he returns, like he feels awkward at being the one tending to another's injuries. The lid of the medical kit is what he has. On it rests a small stack of the boiled cloth, its sun-bleached whiteness dulled from soaking in water, along with the little pot of ointment.

I sit right there on the warming pavement when he motions for me to. We're very exposed out here, but the light is good and we have a clear view around us. There are birds singing a loud chorus in the trees that surround us and that they are still singing and chattering with each other is the best sign we could have that we remain undiscovered. Silence would ripple outward from the trail of any encroaching human.

Jovan's fingers are gentle when he wipes at my face with the cloth. He shows it to me after he finishes my temple and I see the crust of dirt and blood that has transferred to it. It surprises me to see such a large amount of dark color there. I felt it while it was happening, but there was no time to think then, only to run.

He has his share of scratches, but they don't look too bad, certainly nothing like what my face must look like given the condition of the rapidly darkening cloth. The blood that had dried is now re-liquifying on the wet cloth and transforming into a fresh-looking red.

Still, I'm not the only one with marks. A few on his neck look angry and painful. I pick up one of the other folded squares and dab at his scratches, trying to remove the coating of dirt around them as gently as I can. We go on like this, exchanging winces now and again, but not talking. It's soothing to be touched like this. It's caring but comes without expectation, a simple tending of the body by another. It makes me want to cry.

I'm finished with Jovan's face long before he's done with mine, and there's not a single clean cloth left, or even a single square inch of cloth that remains clean. It's a little disturbing to see and I wonder how badly my face is marked. That may seem silly, but I can't help it.

The little pot of ointment sends out its peculiar scent again. The sting goes away like it never existed as he smooths it across the various scratches and gouges. I hadn't realized how uncomfortable I was until the discomfort was gone. I dab a little on his most serious scratch and he murmurs in relief.

"What's in this stuff?" I ask, sniffing at the ointment while I hold the pot for him. When I sniff it, it feels like my sinuses clear.

He shrugs, but answers. "Not sure of everything. I think there's lard in it, maybe eucalyptus, but I know for sure it has some plant that's actually poisonous."

I jerk my head back and stop inhaling it. "Poisonous?"

"Yep," he nods. "Supposedly, if you get the plant juice on you directly, it can numb you for days and if you eat it, it will make you stop breathing." At the look on my face, he chuckles and says, "It comes from someplace far to the south. What they put in this stuff is processed somehow. It's safe."

I'm dubious and it shows on my face. My finger is still numb and now my face is mostly numb as well, so there's no question it works.

Jovan leans close to me, so close I can see the flecks of gold in his eyes and the little scar on his lip that I once kissed when we were younger. He winks and says, "Just don't eat it. Or lick at your lips too much."

I stop rubbing my lips together right away. A little of the ointment he put near there has migrated to my lips and I was enjoying the numb sensation. He wipes my lips with his thumb and smears it on his pants. It's innocent enough, but the flush that creeps up my neck is entirely beyond my control.

Enough of this. I get to my feet, grab the medical kit lid with its now nasty contents, and stride quickly back to the building and the others.

Maddix appears to be sound asleep. Connor lies next to him with a hand protectively on his chest so he'll wake if Maddix stirs or just to reassure himself that his brother is still breathing. Cassi isn't asleep as she should be. Instead, she's peering out of the gap under the big bay door, her eyes keen on the woods beyond the pavement. Keeping watch.

Perhaps it's because of what happened in general, or more likely the specific nature of the attack, but it has created something new in Cassi. Her eyes are moving unnaturally quickly, every movement outside catching her attention and receiving a brief but sharp evaluation. Her whole frame is tense, her shoulders taut, and there is a gun within reach of her hand. It's even been laid on the floor with exacting precision so that it will take as little time as possible for her to palm it.

I'm pretty sure Cassi has no more idea how to fire it with accuracy than I do. She dry-fired just like I did, but neither of us has fired an actual round. This new Cassi concerns me even at first glance. No good can come from such over-vigilance, only exhaustion.

"Ready for some sleep?" I ask her as I approach with my dirty bandages and ointment-shiny face.

She acknowledges me only with another of those sharp glances, her eyes returning to the gap immediately. She frowns and says, "I'm not tired. They could be out there."

I drop to my haunches next to her and bump her with my dirty tray. She makes a face at it, then glances again at my face. I can almost figure out the pattern of my wounds by the way her eyes trace their paths. She shakes her head and says, "You're the one that needs rest. You were up in the tower all night. I slept like a baby down below."

"Now I know that's a lie. None of you are remotely like babies," I say and grin, hoping for some sort of Cassi-like smile.

I'm apparently hoping in vain because her mouth is stretched in a line that doesn't suit her face. Her freckles are like spots of pale copper against her skin, but what is normally pale is now white, strained and almost ill-looking. There are purplish-blue circles under her eyes and even her pursed lips are pale rather than their usual envy-inspiring pink. We've all been through a lot, but Cassi is perilously close to breaking. Men who wanted to capture her for what they no-doubt wanted may have been the last straw.

"Cassi, please. I slept in the tower and Jovan's going to go to the stream to get water and wash these. I have to stay sitting up so this stuff will soak in anyway. You know me, as soon as I fall asleep I'll be on my side and smearing it," I say.

She sighs and finally looks away from the bay door. "Are you sure?" she asks.

"I am. And the sooner you get to sleep, the better off we'll be. You'll need to take watch later," I say. I'd like to hug her the way Jovan hugged me. It did me so much good and acted like a calmative even as it revived me. But she seems so closed off.

When people are open to something, I can usually see it in them. I believe most people can. It's how we naturally behave, I think. But there's not even the remotest hint of invitation in her. She might as well be behind a wall. Before I can think more about it, I lay down my tray and lean in, wrapping one arm around her.

She stiffens at first, then sinks into my shoulder as her tears come. It seems terrible to think like this, but her tears, her simple sadness, are what she needs. As long as she can cry, she's still her and nothing is so broken that it can't be repaired.

We stay like that a while. Jovan comes in to grab the containers and the bandages I was supposed to bag up with anything else that needed washing, but he quietly holds up a hand to let me know he's got it. Then he's gone, shining with his own coating of ointment and his endless energy. He must have found a stream, which is good. We'll need a lot of water for boiling to keep Maddix clean and cared for. And our need for freshly boiled bandages isn't likely to decrease for the time being.

When her sobs subside, she sits back up and looks at me, her expression a bit sheepish but also more herself. The tender Cassi, the one who sees the good in the world and would like to see only that, the one who can find the smile inside me no matter how much anger and hurt I have stuffed down, is back.

"I'm so sorry about your Dad," she says, her voice still shaky and rough from her tears. "I was glad to strike with you all and so happy to see you get to know him. I could tell how much he loved you just by how he always looked at you. This is just so unfair."

I nod because I don't want to start crying too. I have a feeling that if I let it start again, it might never stop and right now, I need to be strong. They need to understand that I don't blame anyone here for what happened and that I can go on.

And I know why Cassi was glad to strike with us. I don't want her to doubt her decision now that it's too late for her to change her mind. Her inability to read or do math properly has cut off all but the most menial labor when it comes time for her to get a job. Except that Cassi has something very few have and that's her almost unbearable beauty.

I've never seen anyone like her and neither have most others if the reaction she inspires is any indication. And the moment she turned sixteen and it became legal for recruiters to contact her, she's been under a near constant barrage of offers from the owners of Pleasure Houses all over north Texas. Some have even come from much further south. One claimed to be from Houston.

Her offers grew from standard to outrageous as she turned each down. As it stands now, she could make more than I'd make in a lifetime in a single year. And lately the offers have gone right into territory unheard of before, such as the right to turn down any customer, no matter who they might be, if she finds them disagreeable.

But Cassi isn't just a pretty girl with freckles from the roots of her red-gold hair to the tips of her toes. She is more than a doll-like face with eyes that seem almost too large for it. She's a gentle soul. And though her parents have tried to respect her decision to turn down various recruiters, they have grown more insistent that she at least consider the offers. The change that her taking any offer could make for her family is more than they can afford to ignore. It's not that it's a bad profession, but Cassi isn't the right kind of girl to want to do that. Neither am I.

Yes, I know she is very glad to be a Striker now that the deed is done and I understand why. I don't want her to regret that decision for even a moment. I soothe her as best I can until I can finally talk her into resting.

She's asleep by the time Jovan gets back with the two water carriers, both full and sloshing with clear water. I had feared the water might be brownish like what comes from the canal, but it is as perfect as the guy carrying it.

I stoke the fire a little and put up the little tripod we use to hold the pot. The first pot fills both canteens and provides Jovan with a long, warm drink. I hate the idea of using the same pot for sanitizing the blood-stained, but relatively clean, bandages. It feels wrong.

Jovan sees me hesitate, dangling my handful of bandages above the merrily boiling pot, and he plucks them from my fingers. They drop into the pot and he laughs at the look of distaste on my face.

"It will be fine. We'll finish with the bandages, dump it, boil more water and let that get anything out. Then it's good. Trust me. You don't even want to know what all we do with the same pot out in the field," he says. Another rueful laugh and a shake of his head let me know I probably really don't want to know.

The morning turns into afternoon and the air smells of a coming rain. For people like us, rain is a welcome thing whenever it comes and I'm anxious for it to arrive. When it finally does, Jovan and I run outside with our pot and try to catch some of it. In less than a minute, the pot lays abandoned and we head to opposite sides of the building to strip down and wash off in the downpour. The ointment has long since soaked in, doing its work but leaving my face feeling as dirty as the rest of me.

It comes down in sheets, heavy and cold, but it feels delightful to me. At first the water runs off of my body in brown dribbles, but the drops are so sharp and hard that they scour me clean. I let my ponytail out and try to wash my hair, but it's going to need more than just water to get truly clean. Still, just having the dust and a little of the sweaty grease out is delightful.

Once I start shivering in earnest, I put on my soaked clothes and make a dash for the bay doors around the corner. Jovan is watching for me and we grin at each other as we build up the fire and shiver next to it until our cold, wet clothes become warm, wet ones. We probably shouldn't be having fun with all that's going on, but in truth, I feel remarkably refreshed by it. It doesn't change anything about our circumstances or what we've lost, but it let me be free of them for a few precious minutes.

Connor wakes at all the activity and immediately checks on Maddix. He, in his turn, stirs at all the movement and groans. He's been breathing through his mouth, but when he asks what's going on, he tries to suck in air through his nose. The sound almost makes me want to put my hands over my ears. It's an impossible combination of wheeze, whistle and popping that sounds incredibly painful.

When we took off his shirt, we found a spreading bruise bigger than my head on his ribs where he'd been kicked at least once. I didn't know if he had broken ribs or, even worse, a punctured lung. Jovan had settled the matter by working his hands over the ribs, a flinch ready on his face. But they had felt solid, though no less painful. Now, Maddix's hand reaches for his side and he presses on them himself before letting his hand fall back to the floor.

"They aren't broken," I tell him, leaning over his head so that he won't have to turn to see me. "Your face is far less pretty and your nose will be interesting, but it's your leg we need to worry about. I'm going to have to unbandage it and take a look before we lose the daylight."

I look him in the eyes—or rather in the eye that isn't swollen shut—until he gives me a small nod of assent. His hand finds Connor's and I see the knuckles whiten as he squeezes. Jovan and I unwrap the bandages as carefully as we can, but they are stuck near the wound and fresh blood seeps out even after I loosen it with some of the warm water.

When the wound is revealed, both Jovan and I suck in our breaths simultaneously and smile. The flesh is far less red, though still a little puffy around the hole. It is a good sign and I'll take it.

Once he's again covered in ointment and bandaged, he settles back and the rigidity leaves him. In our pot is a disgusting mix of blood and dirt and I have no desire to eat out of it ever again. Jovan laughs and takes the pot to do what must be done while I clean up the rest of the mess. We're all hungry, starving really, so I have no doubt that my squeamishness over the pot will be gone once I smell some cooking grains with jerky in it.

As night falls, I'm delighted to find out that I'm right.

Chapter Twenty-Four

We decide to camp in the big building while Maddix heals. None of us feels very comfortable staying put, especially without knowing who might be left to look for us, but we really don't have much choice. Maddix is a mess and even if he tried to walk on his wounded leg, his ribs and face would stop him from going. All we can do is just wait it out and try to remain vigilant for any signs of pursuit.

For almost the entirety of the first day I do nothing but sleep, take my turn on watch and then promptly go back to sleep. Everyone does, except for caring for Maddix when he wakes.

On the second morning, I wake feeling well rested and immediately think of Jordan. I really want to find him, or find whatever of him that I can. While we eat, I suggest going back to the tower and seeing what I can see. Jovan and Cassi both insist that I should go no further, and really, neither of them is keen on the idea of me climbing the tower alone. But what good will it do to have someone else there should I fall? Will they catch me? Though I do give in and agree not to go back and search for Jordan at the settlement, I don't agree not to look for some sign of him.

Jovan gives me a dirty look as I leave like he knows I'm up to something, but I just wave as I head across the lot toward the trees. I walk perhaps a mile back down our old path but there are no new signs of people passing. No cooling campfire, no scuffs or tracks other than the ones I think we left. Best of all, no smell of decay that might signal Jordan made it out only to die on the trail without finding us. I think that would have been the worst thing to find.

Despite what I said, I head to the settlement. There, I find nothing I can definitely say is my father. The buildings are nothing more than blackened piles of wood and gray ash. The body of the man Maddix tangled with is where we left it, but in a condition so awful I have to walk away. There's a horse, too, and I feel terrible when I see it, knowing it must have been terribly afraid and completely at the mercy of the humans fighting around it. It's hopeless to try to find anyone inside the piles of debris. I still try, but I find nothing.

Back at the tower, I climb and sit, completely alone except for my hawk friend and the chicks as the day progresses. There's nothing to be seen for miles. No smoke from any source is a good thing. Either Jordan was able to take out however many came after us or the survivors went a different direction.

The hawk "guh-runks" at me a few times and spreads his wings, making sure I know that the top of the tower belongs to his family. When he hops out and struts along the metal braces of the tower, I hear the piping "klee-uk" of the chicks. Once in a while, I hear the occasional sound from the mother hawk.

He flies off during that day and when he returns bearing a torn-up rabbit for his family, I asked him if he might want to feed me as well since I like rabbit. He hands the rabbit off to his mate with some speed when I say that, perhaps thinking I mean it.

When I laugh, he hops closer, peering at me from each side and then straight on, just like my hawk friend at home used to do. It always seemed to me that our laughs fascinate them for some reason. Perhaps they're just trying to figure out our calls.

A pang goes through me at that. I miss seeing the hawk in the mornings in my garden.

"Will you tell him where I'm at?" I ask the bird. His only reply is to cock his head at me again. After that, he flies away and I make my way back to the camp.

*****

On our third day at camp, it's Jovan's turn to scout around, but this time ahead of us. With Maddix on the mend but still weak, the last thing we need is to find more people. People weren't bringing us a lot of luck up to that point.

He comes back almost at dusk, just as the point where my worry for him has grown so great that I'm actually considering going up on the roof to light a signal fire. That is a stupid idea if ever there was one, but it shows how worried I am. Appearing at the edge of the tree line, he looks none the worse for wear but he's clearly tired, his head hanging and his hair dark with sweat. It's not exactly warm, though it was briefly for a little while in the afternoon, so I can only guess that he ran a long way.

I grab the full canteen and jog out to meet him. The way he smiles when he sees me lights a little fire inside me. Though I do my best to restrain it, I know there's more warmth in my return smile than I might wish. When I extend the canteen, he almost empties it in one long drink.

"Well, anything?" I ask, rather too abruptly. The look he gives me is one I earned. "Sorry. You've been gone so long. I got worried."

Instead of apologizing, he gives me a wolfish grin and says, "You were worried? Hmm."

"Oh, for Pete's sake. Did you find anything worth telling?" I ask, and snatch the canteen back, motioning for him to come back to the shelter with me.

His grin doesn't falter as he falls into step beside me and I'd swear on a giant T-bone steak that he's actually swaggering a little. How do we go from him all but ignoring my existence for two years to this? I give him a sour look and clamber up the platform to our camp.

Maddix is awake and sitting up near the fire, his back braced against the wall. The swelling in his face has gone down considerably and his eye is open, though very bruised. Jovan set his broken nose with a sharp tug the first morning once we knew he was out of the woods with his leg. It's huge but less painful, he claims, and he sounds hilarious when he talks. Still, it's an improvement and the ointment takes away much of his pain.

He and the others are playing some weird game they made up using tiny bits of broken pavement, a circle drawn using charcoal from our fire and an assortment of debris we've found while prowling around the huge building. I can't understand it and the rules get more complicated every time I turn around.

"Ha! That's a chicken scratch, a pie and two mice. My longhorn and two windmills beat that!" Cassi crows after looking at the assorted scattered mess on the floor.

Maddix scowls and grabs up the pieces, but stops when we blot out the lowering light at the door. "Howdy, stranger. What's up out there?" he asks Jovan.

I've saved a little of our meager supper for Jovan. I hand him the cup with his few spoonfuls of grains, fruit and jerky cooked up into a mush. He digs in with a finger and scoops clumps of it into his mouth, making satisfied noises with each bite. It pains me to see him so eager for food since I know he's used more energy than any of us today. Plus he's bigger than we are, even Maddix. But our stores are running low and we'll be out of food completely in another day, two at most.

It's while he's wiping out the last remaining bits that I see the smears of blood on his arm and I jerk it up to see where it came from. There's a matching smear on the bottom of his shirt. "You're hurt!" I say, plucking at his shirt.

He looks for some injury, confused, then his face clears. He flashes me another of those grins and says, "Nope. That doesn't belong to me. I've got a surprise." He shrugs out of my pack, the only real pack we have now, and takes out one of the burlap bags. There's something lumpy and, if the red spots soaking through the fabric are any indicator, bloody inside.

When he pulls out what's inside, my first thought is that he's caught rats. But they aren't exactly rats. More like their much cuter cousins with enormous bushy tails.

"What on earth are those?" I ask.

Jovan shrugs and rolls one of them over in his hands. "I think it might be a squirrel. I've never seen one, but I've heard of them." His fingers brush the tail and he adds, "The tail is just like what I've heard described. I've heard other soldiers say they are really common down south, where there are trees. They're supposed to be good eating."

This last has my attention. I'm all in favor of anything that could be even remotely classified as tolerable eating, so good eating sounds very fine indeed. I note the blood has come from each of their small heads. "You used my slingshot?"

He nods and produces it, handing it off to me along with my small bag of steel balls. Jovan was always the best at using the slingshot when we were kids, so I shouldn't be surprised he was able to bring back food using it once he was alone and could control his noise.

Aside from the slingshot, all I have is an old sling. With a sling, I'm hopeless, but Cassi is amazing. She has an eye for it. But slings need space to use and one of the downsides of finally getting to a place with trees is that there's hardly any place to swing one.

"I even found all the balls," he adds when he sees me fingering the bag to count how many remain inside.

Connor and I take up the animals and one of the belt knives and go outside to skin and gut them. Animal parts aren't something I want to leave near where we sleep, so we use a flashlight and go far enough away from our camp to do our bloody business. By the time we get back with the small—yet wonderfully meaty—carcasses, the fire has been built up and three sticks have been scraped clean and soaked in water.

"They look like skinny rabbits," Cassi says, then cocks her head and adds, "Or rats."

Connor and I sneak a quick look at each other but no one seems to notice. Cassi doesn't know, and I don't necessarily want the others to know, that Connor and I are very familiar with the way a rat looks without his fur suit on. It's not that I'm embarrassed, because that not's completely true. What I really don't want is pity and, at least in this case, I don't think pity would be necessary.

When we turned thirteen and could legally find work, we joined up to work the compost operation as Turners. Compost is incredibly important in the dry lands. No one would be able to grow enough to eat without that nutrient-rich, black soil. I have my own little pile, fed by my garden prunings, the parts of vegetables I trim away and bundles of dried grass I stockpile to let brown and turn crispy each year. But that wouldn't be enough, so I, like everyone else, buy it from the composter.

Working there is a great way to balance the cost with earnings. Turners are almost always kids. We're lighter and more nimble, yet still strong enough to wield a pitchfork. Each of the huge piles has to be turned regularly so that the heat distributes and "cooks" the entire pile.

For Connor and me, as well as a few others, there was the additional income from the rat bounties. After work, we'd station ourselves someplace where we might watch for rats that came to inspect the new piles of compost material. One shot with a steel ball from a slingshot and a rat would inspect no more.

Rats are a problem at the compost station. The amount of fresh material draws them like, well, like rats. And they spread disease as well as breed rapidly. So we earned a small bounty for each one we brought to the supervisor's shack for inspection. It seemed a shame to let them go to waste. There were many nights that Connor and I improved our protein intake and there's no shame in that for people who can't afford to buy the cattle our territory is known for raising.

The smell that comes off the roasting meat draws us all closer to the fire and we pluck the still-sizzling flesh from the bones the moment it's done, snatching back fingers from the hot meat but not slowing down. There's almost no fat on them, but that's fine by me and for the first time since we ran, I go to sleep content and with a full belly.

The morning means checking bandages, my most un-favorite duty of each day. Maddix's leg is healing and no longer angry-looking, but there is no question he has a substantial hole in it and could use a couple of weeks of peace and rest. After we use up the last of our boiled water to clean up his leg, change bandages and wash the used ones, Jovan heads off to the stream for the daily water run.

It's a beautiful morning, bright and clear, with skies so blue they're heartbreaking. The hundreds of birds who've made nests on the ragged and uneven roof above us seem to have gotten used to our noise and movements, because they pause for only the briefest moment in their activity when we come out. A line of them, eyes dark and avid, give me the once-over when I step out to enjoy the mild weather and stretch my legs. I give them a little salute and they go back to their business. Something in their posture makes me laugh. It's as if they're dismissing me with lots of attitude.

Jovan comes through the undergrowth just like yesterday, but I can tell something is wrong right away. Like the birds, it's in his posture and the hurried way he shrugs off the greenery.

When he looks up and sees me, his pace increases and I feel like our time here has just come to an end. The idea panics me a little, like I'm losing my home or something, which is stupid because this has been nothing more than a place to rest. A place to let Maddix heal and figure out our next move. But that doesn't change the way I feel.

"Pack up," I call up to the others before taking off to meet Jovan.

He hands me one of the containers as soon as I get to him. His face is tense so there's no question the news is bad.

"Is it the same guys?" I ask. For me, and especially for Cassi, that would be the worst-case scenario.

With a shake of his head, Jovan catches his breath. He's sweaty and his dark hair is plastered to his forehead, the golden glints buried by the wetness. Wide streaks of sweat mark the front and back of his t-shirt, and he's got new scratches from brush and vines covering his arms. It's clear he ran the whole way back.

"Worse," he gasps, then hands me the other heavy container and leans over, bracing his hands on his knees. After a few loud swallows and rasping breaths, he looks up at me. "It's my Dad's foreman, Creedy. He's got one guy with him I don't know but he's rough-looking, like those guys at the settlement."

I'm not entirely sure what to make of that other than the obvious, that those men may have been tracking us for this Creedy person. But Jovan's face when he said that name displayed more than just recognition. It was fear and loathing, maybe even hatred. It's the way I might feel about some of the soldiers, the ones who don't think much of those like me and are a little too eager to show it with their nightsticks.

"So, your father sent someone to get you back. The sign we saw didn't leave any doubt he wanted you back," I say, hefting the heavy containers and walking toward the building.

Jovan catches up with me and takes one of the containers back, trying to meet my eyes. When I don't bite, he places a restraining hand on my arm to stop me. He glances quickly at the partially open bay door and says, "Wait."

He wants only me to hear this, which means it's for sure going to be bad. I nod for him to talk.

"Creedy is *not* a good guy." The way he says it communicates many things. The way his eyes move over me tells me what kind of bad he means.

"Oh," I say.

"Yeah, exactly. There's a reason my father sent Creedy and not one of the others. He can take care of business my father needs taken care of and doesn't mind how dirty that business is. I'm sure you and Cassi would be a part of that deal, especially if Jordan was right and they are planning on killing everyone except me to keep my secret."

"Oh," I breathe, understanding now what he means and why his face is so pale underneath the red of exertion.

"I heard metal banging so I just went a little way down the stream. They're north of the old road but still close to it. Creedy was mad because one of the horses had gone lame from a stone in its shoe or maybe thrown a shoe. I know his voice, so I went closer to be sure. There's no mistake who it is. The other guy was hammering on a shoe over a rock and I got a look at him. Scruffy, like those others. I listened for a few minutes and it looks like they're going to make camp there and do their searching on foot so the horse can recover."

"How many horses do they have?" I ask.

"Four, but one of them looks like it got burned here," he says and waves a hand down the back of his head, like he's describing the mane of a horse.

"So, definitely the same guys," I say.

He nods and we stand there for a moment, both of us thinking hard. Cassi interrupts us by coming to the bay door. She eyes us, purses her lips in understanding and asks, "How long do we have?"

I shake my head and she lets her hands fall to slap the side of her legs, as if she were already tired. "I'll get everyone ready. I can try to cover up our signs, but the smell is going to give us away."

She's right and I could kick myself for letting us get so comfortable. The smell of a fire is unmistakable, even after several days. Scattering the evidence won't help us much, but it might at least confuse them as to how long we stayed.

"Gather up all the ash and such and scatter it in the brush," I say, then think twice. "Better yet, scatter a little bit in a lot of places."

She disappears back inside and I turn back to Jovan. His color has returned but he looks like he's ready to bolt. Like he just wants us to take off running as fast as we can. That scares me more than what he said.

"We need to go," he urges.

"We need to make sure we don't give them information if they find this place after we're gone. Like the fact that Maddix is wounded and will need rest and might slow us down. That kind of information."

He closes his eyes and sucks in a deep breath, calming himself. Then he gives me a pained smile, "You're right. But let's do it fast."

There will be no boiling this water now, but we might be able to later. And I'm not about to risk being unable to find some nearby when the time comes when we can safely stop. We need at least one container's worth plus the canteens we've already filled with safe water. I have an idea about how to use what we can't bring.

Inside the building, everyone is busy, even Maddix. He packs what pitiful belongings we still have, even shaking out the burlap bags stuffed with dead grass we've been using for pillows. Connor has a bundle of brush I tied together and used as a broom to keep dirt away from Maddix's leg. Now he's using it to methodically sweep away our footprints from deeper inside the building, where we'd explored for anything useful. Cassi is nowhere to be seen and there are only a few dark chunks to show where our fire has burned.

I dribble out the water over the areas where the fire was and where we've been sleeping and use the broom to smooth it so that it looks like just another place where the rain came in. It's not entirely convincing, but sprinkling the dried grass from our erstwhile pillows helps.

It's the best we can do and when we jump down, carefully helping Maddix so that his wound doesn't re-open, we all stand in front of the opening for a long moment. Even though I'm looking to see if there is anything to give evidence of our few days in residence, I'm also saying goodbye. When will I sleep so comfortably and safely again? When will I wake up to the sweet and somehow joyous sound of birdsong above my head again?

Jovan is fidgeting, leaning from one leg to the other and looming behind me like a big nervous ball of energy. Even Maddix, our least capable member at the moment, seems antsy. He keeps testing his leg and I can see from the corner of my eye how he sets his face against the discomfort, his blackened eyes making him look a bit like a raccoon.

"Which way, Jovan?" I ask.

He looks like he's going to uncoil like a spring. He points northeast and says, "We've got to get well north of them and then go straight east. As fast as we can."

I'm sure that no one meant to make Maddix feel uncomfortable, but I notice that all of us send a glance his way. He sees it and says, "I'm good. I'll keep up. I just need to warm up the muscles."

We start out, but we're not making good time. It's a rougher start than it should be. It isn't Maddix slowing us down, it's us slowing down to make sure Maddix doesn't have a problem. Between Connor, Cassi and I pulling brush to the side, pointing out roots that might trip him up and asking if he's okay, we barely get a mile away in that first hour.

Jovan runs out of patience about the same time one of us asks Maddix if his leg is bleeding for the dozenth time. He stops so abruptly that Cassi smacks into his back and yelps. "He won't be fine if Creedy catches up with us. He's fine now, though, so let's keep moving."

His tone is harsh and makes the hairs on the back of my neck stand up. He's really afraid. Our eyes meet and his are pleading, asking for me to help him out. It won't help any of the others to know what sort of person this Creedy is. Too much fear can paralyze.

"Come on, let's go. The sooner we go, the sooner we'll get where we're going," I say, and move into the green world around us.

Chapter Twenty-Five

It's so late it's early again and we've found no place to hole up. We've walked at a hard pace through the whole day and into the night, trying to get some distance between us and the place where we were. Maddix is dragging, his breath coming in hard wheezes, and his nose started trickling blood an hour ago. Jovan took off a few times during the day, snaking his way south to check our progress while we rested, but so far he's got nothing specific to report.

We took a short rest of just a couple of hours in the afternoon, but pressed on even though Maddix really needed more time. The forest here is thick and hard to get through and our pace has slowed over the past hours. We're all tripping over the roots and branches that litter the ground and I finally have to force the issue.

"We have to stop! Maddix can't keep on. And there's no reason to keep trying to go through the night in this forest. There's not enough light!" My whisper is harsh and probably a little too loud, but the trees dampen sound and I have to get through to Jovan.

In this land of endless forests, there's no longer any need to travel at night. You'd have to be relatively close to someone to see them. In a way, that makes me feel better, but on the other side of that coin, it means that I won't see anyone coming after me until they're close either.

Jovan's jaw clenches in the little bit of moonlight that leaks through the trees, but he acquiesces when I make it clear I'm not going another step by helping Maddix to the ground and settling him against a tree.

He draws the line at lighting a fire, even though we need one for boiling the water. Even if we decided to risk drinking it without boiling it first, it would be foolish to use it on Maddix's leg, which needs tending.

The night is a restless one, punctuated by one or another of us jerking up from our sleep at every noise, half expecting to be pounced on by pursuers. It's not a really reasonable expectation and I think most of us realize that. At least I do. We didn't have a fire because Jovan said—and I believed him because it's what I would do—that he thought they would try to gain a vantage point to look for the light of a fire.

Other than that, the night is not a time to worry about them tracking us. They have horses and horses need rest. Horses also make noise and don't do well in heavy brush like the kind we've made a point of traveling through. And this wilderness is far larger than anything I could ever have imagined.

I know, or at least my mind knows, that far south of Bailar the lands of Texas are green and lush, but it's one thing to know it or see a photo and another thing entirely to be immersed in it. The perspective changes when you're pushing away reaching branches and dealing with thorny vines that seem intent on snagging clothing and skin with every step you take.

Creedy will be no different from us in that regard if what Jovan says is true. He's from the flat and open lands we call home, so that's what he'll be used to. Plus, he works as a foreman for a rich rancher and is used to seeing the world from the top of a horse.

The wild-card is the man he's with. When he was able to, Jovan pulled up next to me for a quiet talk while we walked. He told me that he thought the men who had found us, and the one remaining with Creedy, were local "talent," probably motor mules, hired specifically because they are familiar with this territory.

It was true that the ones who found us spoke in a strange accent and the man speaking with Creedy spoke the same way according to Jovan. That's bad, but now he's just as encumbered with horses as Creedy is. In the end, what does it matter who Creedy is with so long as we stay well off their path and do nothing to draw them to us?

I wake up for watch confused and in a foul mood from my poor sleep, but Jovan raises my spirits immediately by presenting an unlit, but perfectly constructed, fire pit. Somehow he's managed to find enough big stones in this wild area to create a tall enough light break. When I look up, I see the moon is gone and the sky is deep black. A flashlight buried under a burlap sack gives out a weak light.

It's enough light to see my grin, apparently. His white teeth flash right back at me and he hands me a flint so I can do the honors. Without the waxing moon to highlight the rising smoke and a tall ring of rock to block the light, we have a small window of relative safety.

"We call this the dead time," he says as we watch the small fire take hold, our eyes drawn to the glow.

"Why?" I ask. It's sort of a ghoulish name and I shiver, not entirely from the chill in the air.

"Because in the couple of hours before dawn, even animals go to sleep. It's the quietest time of the night. Creedy knows that, too," he says quietly.

"So he won't be looking for us?"

He breathes a quiet laugh and sets our pot on the tripod, his face turning a golden color by the small light of the fire. "I didn't say that, but he's more likely to sleep now thinking this is about the time of night we'd let a fire go out. It's a risk, but a lesser one."

The fire feels so good on my night chilled skin that I'd like to curl up against the rocks surrounding it and just absorb what I can, but I'm awake because I'm supposed to be on watch and the firelight, even as small as it is, is ruining my night vision. Jovan has a good handle on the water situation, so I empty the canteen closest to me in a few loud gulps. When I toss it to him, he gives me a look and says, "Greedy." The smile lets me know he doesn't mean it.

"I'm going to head out a little, get up one of those trees if I can," I say and stand up. Even just standing up and putting those few feet of distance between my hands and the fire lets the chill back in.

Jovan turns a little to the side, showing me scuffs and dirt-darkened pant legs. "Be careful. They aren't easy to climb."

I can't tell Jovan it's because he's just too tall, but it's true. Cassi, Connor and I practiced on them while at the building and found it easier than climbing fences or the sides of buildings. On those we've got only chipped concrete and windowsills for hand and foot holds. The trees offer more paths up.

"I'll be careful," I say. He hands me the flashlight and I make my way a little south of our resting place. Creedy is still southwest of us if we're estimating correctly, but we have no way of knowing how much of the night they may use to try to catch up with us, horses or no horses.

Personally, I doubt they've stirred if they've got a lame horse. And there's no way they would give up their horses and be stuck walking. Still, better safe than sorry.

The trees are huge and getting even bigger the further east we go. And they get more wild looking, too. Branches spread so far out that I'm amazed the trees can hold them up. A good many of them bend low as they stretch further from the trunk. They make handy climbing points for those of us light or nimble enough to take advantage of them.

One of the trees looms out of the darkness. It's so high it blots out the stars along a ragged section of sky. I don't dare shine my light up there—it would be like a beacon—but I see enough through the finger-covered lens to know it's a live tree with excellent footholds.

I'm not confident in this so I go slow, using more caution than I need, until I have a nice view around us. A rustling in the leaves tells me I'm not the only inhabitant of this tree. The shine of reflected eyes and the chittering from some animal puts me in my place.

It seems like mere moments before purple begins to stain the horizon and a hiss greets me from below. It's just light enough for me to see something of the world around me and what I see is Cassi, grinning up at me.

"Your turn already?" I ask in a loud whisper.

She nods and motions for me to come down. Getting down is harder than getting up, even with the improving light, and I earn myself a few scrapes before I hop down. The thud is a faint one, but I feel exposed now that dawn is breaking and can't stop the wince.

Cassi looks up at the tree and asks, "Comfy up there?"

"Yeah, but there's something living up there, so don't go much higher than I went."

"Maybe it's a squirrel," she muses. "I could go for some more of them."

"I could too, if truth be told, but we're about to move on and we'll have no way to cook it for a while. And it sounded heavier than that when it moved. I think it might be a raccoon," I say.

Raccoons aren't common where we live, but no one seems to be able to get rid of them entirely. There are too many empty houses in the allotment area where we live and they always seem to find a way inside them. And they're a menace at the composting station, but never when anyone is there to do anything about it. But one thing *everyone* in Bailar knows is that raccoons carry rabies and other diseases we can do nothing to cure, so we keep clear.

I take my leave once she's up the tree and in a good perch, dragging my weary self back to the camp. The fire is long out but the stones are warm so I lay down next to them to nap for as long as I'm able. Everyone's asleep and their quiet breathing sounds nice. The sky is going from purple to pink and I feel like maybe this time, I'll be able to sleep without dreams.

Chapter Twenty-Six

Days and nights pass in ceaseless, but never monotonous, travel east. Ever on edge, ears perked for the sound of horses, we stay inside the forest even though it's far slower than the road. So far, we remain undiscovered as far as we can tell. With each day that passes, I feel that much safer. That worries me because that's usually when something bad happens.

Twice we saw inhabited places, both times because water stood in our way. The first was a permanent settlement clearly built around a ferry system going across a river. Sizable flat barges were lined up neatly along a pier with a matching set on the other side of the river.

We came upon it at night, having seen the many columns of smoke from fires during the day, and merely watched. The smells of food wafted out even as far as the tree line where we hid and I think all of us were tempted to go knock on a door and work out some sort of trade—or just beg—for a bowl and a warm place to sleep. Temptation or no, we didn't. Jovan dashed cold water on my dreams of a belly full of whatever I was smelling by reminding me that Creedy had almost certainly promised rewards for us. On top of that, he'd probably spread the word far and wide using motor mules.

And now we're seeing our second group. This time we purposefully observe them during the day, when they're active. A darkened village and a bit of firelight brightening a window doesn't say much about what sort of people might be living there. And we need to know as much as we can about what kind of people are in these new territories.

According to Maddix, we're in the Riverlands territory. Lying between the Southeast Territory and the Texas Republic, the Riverlands stretch over a wide swath but are further sandwiched between the Valley Lands to the north and the Gulf Cooperative to the south. He says it used to be called Arkansas and still is by the people who live there.

A small territory it may be, but they control passage over the big rivers, both for people and supplies, and are supposedly fierce when threatened. That gives them power. I, along with everyone else, want to see them. More importantly, we want to see them when they don't know they are being watched.

A large lake spreads out from the river. The borders of it are so regular it seems almost artificial. Ruins are visible on the far shore but from our lookout on a small rise covered in brush and trees, we can see the neatly tended huts on the near shore. The huts—because they're certainly not houses as I understand them—could contain no more than one large room or perhaps two very small ones. There are a couple of dozen of them, and a circle of small conical structures stands in a clearing at their center. Little streams of smoke waft up from the conical structures and dissipate almost immediately in the breeze.

All of the structures seem to be most accessible from the water, where at least a dozen strange boats are being paddled about. Long poles equipped with round paddles at either end are being dipped into the water by those inside the boats. The people look incredibly agile and at ease inside the boats, like the paddles are extensions of their bodies.

They're fascinating boats. Long and curved up at either end, they are also quite narrow—not much wider than the people seated inside them—but wider near the middle where some of the people are dumping what can only be fish.

They don't seem to be catching them so much as harvesting them, dipping a basket on a pole into the water and pulling it back out full of wriggling silver forms. For all the people we see, what strikes me most is that they're harvesting far more fish than they need.

"Fish!" Cassi hisses. "I haven't had fish since I was little!"

Connor and I look at each other and roll our eyes. Neither one of us has ever had fish, and it has been a topic of conversation more than once when we've heard others speak of the experience. To my surprise, both Maddix and Jovan nod, eyes on the boats with a certain greed. I might have expected Jovan to have eaten fish, given the wealth of his family, but Maddix?

At our collective stares, he flushes and says, "They eat it a lot in the Riverlands. It's not like where we live. Here, getting beef is what's hard. No matter how much money you have, you'd be lucky to get any jerky, let alone fresh beef. Fish is almost the cheapest thing to eat."

Now I know I want some fish. And those people seem to have a lot of it.

Strains of laughter reach us from below, the sound of it light, carefree and genuine. When one of the skinny boats scuffs ashore, a few children dash out with empty baskets and fill them from the catch inside. I can't see where they take them, because the view is blocked by the huts. When the breeze shifts, I get a whiff of something rotten, something like meat, but also different.

After a while, Jovan motions us back and we wriggle on our knees and elbows until we're below the rise and well out of sight. Once we're all seated in a hollow in the underbrush, he says, "That's a farm of some sort, I think."

He looks to Maddix for confirmation and he nods absently while he pokes at the flesh around his healing wound. His pants are still ripped there, making access easy, and he doesn't seem to be able to stop messing with it whenever we stop. We're all waiting for him to go on and he looks up when the silence continues. He stuffs his hands underneath his legs at my look.

"I don't know about this place specifically, but we passed a few others closer to the Mighty Miss and it looks the same. If it is, then they live there during the harvest season and then just have a few people to tend the fish the rest of the time," he explains. His forehead wrinkles in uncertainty and he adds, "But I'm no expert."

"Mighty Miss?" asks Jovan.

"Oh, yeah, that's the big river Jordan was talking about, the one that has the border to the Southeast on the other side of it," he explains. Mighty Miss sounds like it might be a big girl rather than a river, but I'm more concerned with the water in front of us.

We consider our options. We have to get past that water. So far, we've had to go further north than we wanted to because we've seen no decent crossings along the river, not even a broken bridge. North of the lake is our best bet.

"I vote we move back further, maybe try to work our way north a bit, and then go past at night. There are just too many of them about," Jovan suggests.

I agree with him. There are too many of them for comfort and they're all moving around too much. There's no telling if one or more of them might not come our way.

Connor stays to keep watch while we move back deeper into the woods. The break is nice. While I lazily doze, the low murmur of Jovan and Maddix talking while they sketch out something in the dirt is a distant background hum. I'm starving, as we all are, but I got three squirrels while on my last watch and Cassi got two more on hers. Just knowing they are there and waiting for our next fire makes it easier to forget the gnawing of my empty belly.

I'm actually a little regretful at taking the squirrels now that I've had a chance to watch them while alive. They have such energy and seem so playful. And then I come along with a stone or steel ball and end their fun for good. I can't bear to clean them now that I've seen them alive and Connor has to do the dirty work for me.

*****

Connor rushes back through the undergrowth like a confused calf. His frantic motion jars me from my lethargy in an instant. He's in a panic and gulps down some air as he smacks Maddix awake and the rest of us gather.

"Two men, four horses. They just rode right up the river and into that fishing camp or whatever. All very friendly," he gasps in short bursts of speech.

Jovan hits the ground with his fist, anger sketched across his features. "We just can't get a stinking break," he growls, punctuating his words with another punch into the ground.

"Wait," I say. "Who took the lead going into the camp? Which man?"

That gets Jovan's attention. Connor's face screws up in thought for a moment then he says, "The scraggly one. He's younger. The older one with short hair followed behind."

Jovan and I look at each other in mutual understanding. Those mules may have worked—and one still is working—for Creedy, but this isn't his world or his territory. He'll have to tread lightly.

"Well, what happened?" Cassi asks impatiently.

"I don't know," Connor shrugs. "They all greeted each other, shook hands and stuff. Normal, friendly stuff."

I'm enormously relieved that we haven't given into the temptation to reveal ourselves and very glad the sight of laughing fishermen didn't lure me down. This bit of information also tells me a lot about how Creedy is looking for us. We've been on the move for days, barely stopping and moving quickly. They have horses, but even with horses they can't be spending much time actually looking.

It seems to me they are going settlement to settlement, relying on us eventually needing something or simply getting careless and being seen. They are relying on the less interested eyes of strangers rather than their own.

That's good to know. We won't get careless and no matter what we need, we won't contact people. It seems relatively simple, yet simple is generally something I mistrust. There's nothing more to do for the moment. We can't risk a daylight trek into the open with the number of people out and about. We'd need to melt far back into the forest before turning north again to be sure we don't get seen, and that would take just as much time as waiting here for dark. So we settle in and try to rest.

I'm not much in the mood for resting anymore. Maybe I slept more deeply than I thought during the day and I'm just no longer tired, but I think it's more likely agitation. The sighing of the trees annoys instead of lulls me because it might cover the noise of someone approaching. The sound of the birds is equally loud and abrasive, their numbers such that even if one area quieted because of a person walking this way, the rest are simply too loud for me to notice. After a while, I kick off the sack I'm using to keep the bugs off my skin and go join Jovan on watch.

He starts when he hears my footsteps, his hand going for the gun far too quickly for my liking. He motions me down when I get close. Crawling quietly on all the old leaves is difficult. It seems to take forever to reach the place where he's lying prone and peering over the rise through some obscuring plants.

When I get near, he points at something down below and I don't need to look hard to know what he's worried about. The two men are there with their four horses. One of the horses has a red streak along its neck and its mane is nothing more than a line of bristly fuzz.

Two women are packing something that looks like gray or white jerky into sacks while the men watch. Two of the horses, the burned one and another, have sacks tied to them. There are so many tied into stacks on either side of the horses, I can't believe they can carry the weight. But then one of the women tosses a filled sack toward the scruffy young man with one hand and he catches it without registering any weight at all.

"Dried fish?" I ask in a whisper.

Jovan nods and puts a finger to his lips to forestall any more speech.

When she gives the man the last bag, he counts out coins. I can't see them, but I can hear the clink of them dropping into her palm from here. It sounds like a lot of money, more than I've ever had. If it's true that fish are the cheapest thing to eat out here, he just got robbed. It makes me smile.

The older man, the one Jovan called Creedy with such fear in his voice, doesn't look like much from here. He's older, his hair a short buzz. He's tall and even with a visible paunch, he looks fit enough as he returns to his horse. Creedy has that loose-limbed walk of someone entirely confident of his place in the world and I don't like it one bit. It makes me want to punch him in his paunch.

They mount up and Creedy puts on his cowboy hat which he then doffs toward the women. He must cut a fine figure because I see them put their hands to their mouths and turn to the side like girls flirting. Some things are apparently the same everywhere.

The sound of their hooves is loud as they ride back down the riverbank, going south and away from us. We stay silent for a moment, listening to their retreat until they're gone and the women hurry back around the huts, out of view.

"They went south. That's good," I say.

Jovan gives me a quizzical look so I add, "That means there probably isn't another settlement we might run into north of here. So, it's safe."

His expression clears and he nods, "Yeah, I guess it does."

He eyes me speculatively for a minute, an amused curl at the edge of his lips, until I get uncomfortable and ask, "What? Why are you staring at me?"

The little smile turns into a grin and I swear the birds stop singing to watch him. Being this close to him when he smiles is more than uncomfortable. It's delightful and at the same time makes me feel like I just ate something that didn't agree with me. I can feel the flush creeping across my face, but what surprises me is that I can see pink in his cheeks, too. He reaches out and plucks a leaf from my hair, catching a few of the dark strands in the process, and blows it from his fingers.

Instead of doing what I'd like to do, which is kiss those smiling lips, I smack his hand and repeat, "What?"

The smile falters a little and he seems to search my face for something. He must not find whatever he's looking for because the smile drops entirely and he says, "Nothing. You're smart, is all I was thinking. You think of things sort of backwards, which is what we need." He finishes with a little shrug and returns his gaze to the fishing settlement. Whatever that moment was, it's clearly over.

There are fewer boats on the water. Our vantage point allows us to watch a group of people gathering at a long line of tables by the water where they're processing the fish. Every few minutes, a couple of children pass with a long pole, fish split and hanging over the pole like laundry on a clothesline, then disappear into one of the conical huts. That must be where they smoke the fish. I'd like to get into one of those.

It strikes me finally that what Jovan said was a bit of an insult if I decide to take it the wrong way. Backwards? That's how a thief thinks when trying to be sure they aren't caught. "Are you saying I'm sneaky?" I demand.

My expression must be telling because he flounders for words. "Uh, no. Not at all," he says and then pauses. "Not sneaky, strategic. Those are very different things."

I purse my lips at him, making it obvious that the only difference I see between those two labels are the actual words, but I don't call him on it. Sometimes words aren't needed to call bull on someone. This is one of those times.

"We've got another hour or so before sunset. I'll keep watch, you make sure everyone is ready and erase any signs of us being there," I say and turn my face away to watch the people below.

He hesitates, probably trying to decide if he should speak. In the end, he just sighs and scoots backward. Before he's out of reach, he squeezes my ankle and I look back just in time to catch his wink before he turns to crawl away. I swallow hard, my mouth suddenly dry, and watch the people. Still, I can't help the smile that creeps onto my face.

Chapter Twenty-Seven

The people of the settlement close up for the evening with the remarkable speed of those who live by habit. Before dusk has fallen deeply enough to give me trouble seeing my way back, they are in their huts. The merry light of lanterns creates squares of gold on the ground outside their windows and lines the rims of their doors.

Back at camp, there is no sign that we were ever there. Old brush and leaves cover the hollows made by our bodies and everything is neatly packed. The moon is already up, fat and almost full, so the silver light replaces the warm yellow of the sun almost seamlessly, though it does wash the color out of everything.

Jovan hands me my pack and we set out. The village hugs the shore of the lake in a fairly tight cluster. The buildings peek out between the trees as we make our way past. We're far closer than I'd like. Even walking with care, the noise of our footsteps on the old leaves is loud to my ears. If anyone came outside and was quiet enough, they would hear it too.

The faint sound of singing reaches us from one of the huts. It's a nice voice, young and sweet, but I can't make out the words. It fades behind us as the sound of night insects swells. The smell of the fish offal grows very strong—strong enough that Cassi and I put our sleeves to our noses—and Connor points out a line of baskets along the shore. The drone of flies is loud enough to tell us what's in them. I can't help but wonder what they do with all of it. I hope they don't feed it back to the fish. Even the idea of that is enough to make me reconsider my desire to try fish.

There's a solitary hut on stilts at the edge of the village that we have to get past, but just when I think we're home free, Jovan darts off into the darkness toward it. His long legs take him out of range of any whispered calls, and the rest of us freeze. My first thought is that he's changed his mind and he's going to turn himself in. He'd be welcomed. The reward those people would get would ensure it. The four of us stare at each other in shock.

Connor breaks our silence by hissing, "Run."

We do, crashing through the underbrush along the lake, heading north as fast as we can. I didn't think Jovan would turn us in after everything that's happened, but I didn't think he would take off toward the village either. I honestly thought he was with us, so I have no idea what I'm supposed to think of this. More than once I've felt the closeness we shared as children coming back, but in a new and different way. A more grown-up way.

I was clearly wrong and if I wasn't running for all I was worth while trying not to get my eye put out by greenery, I'd be a lot more angry about it. At the moment, I'm just terrified.

Connor stops short, his feet skidding on the ground so that he falls backward on his rear with a whump. Cassi and Maddix each grab an arm to help him up but he shakes them off and points. I'm expecting a pack of angry villagers, but what I see is Jovan. He's carrying a good-sized sack on his back. He's running in a crazy full-on sprint like the hounds of hell are after him. All I can do is put my hand over my mouth to muffle a laugh.

He went after fish. And I know he didn't do it for himself.

Connor waves him over with a little flash of the light. That's a dangerous move but he won't find us otherwise because of our panicked run, and he shifts his aim for us.

I almost can't believe he makes it when he gets to us, out of breath, his face shiny with sweat, but smiling like there's no tomorrow.

"That was stupid!" Cassi whispers and shoves his arm. "We thought you were turning yourself in. Maybe us, too."

He looks hurt by that, the smile gone. "You think I would do that?" he asks, hefting the sack more securely on his back. He shifts his gaze toward me and asks, "You think I would?"

"What were we supposed to think? Anyway, it doesn't matter. It was stupid. We need to get out of here. Someone might have heard," Maddix says and walks on like he's not even remotely interested in any further conversation on the subject.

I agree with him and shoot a dark look Jovan's way before I follow. I'm glad it's dark and the moon makes all our faces look like gray and black imitations of themselves. I don't want to see the hurt on Jovan's face anymore and I don't want him to see the shame on mine. But really, what *were* we supposed to think? He may think it's cute and nice, but not giving us a warning was thoughtless. Still. He's given up a perfect life to go with us and he doesn't deserve for us to assume the worst of him whenever he does something that isn't planned.

I have a feeling this night's walk is going to be a long one and there won't be any friendly chatting to pass the time.

*****

I discover during our next stop that fish is indescribably nasty. What Jovan picked up was a bag full of the dried stuff, basically fish jerky. We halt for the night when we're a few miles out and safely away from the fishing village. I drop a few pieces of the stiff jerky into a pot of water, thinking it will work like beef jerky and turn the water into a nice broth. The result is not tasty and if we all weren't so thirsty, I'm pretty sure we would toss it.

But we are thirsty and we drink it, making faces over the shared cup. It's actually pretty hilarious when it's not my turn to drink. Then it's suddenly not at all hilarious. I pinch my nose when it's my turn to drink and soon, everyone is. The whole thing is ridiculous.

The squirrels, on the other hand, are mouthwatering and we each get a whole one, which makes up for the fish nicely. I pass the cup to Cassi and she dips out another serving of broth, her face steeled against what she knows is coming and I almost laugh.

"So, this is fish," I say, tossing the words out to the group to see what they toss back.

Jovan nods, his face absolutely expressionless and giving nothing away. Connor isn't so shy and says, "And it's gross."

Maddix laughs and says, "This is *not* what fish tastes like. Trust me on that. This is what dried fish that probably isn't good when it's fresh tastes like."

Cassi makes a gagging sound and passes the cup to Maddix, who dips some out then adds, "Just do me a favor. If we get someplace where you can really taste fish—and if I say it will be worth trying—reserve judgment until you taste it then."

I'm leery of making a promise like this. We need water in our bodies for tomorrow, and we passed no decent streams to replenish our containers so we're making do, but I have no intention of ever subjecting myself to this particular flavor again.

Suddenly, Jovan lets out a laugh and slaps his knee. He gives me an evil little grin and says, "Just wait till Creedy finds out what he paid for."

We all crack up at that, but we keep it a little quieter so the sound doesn't carry. The mood is good and everyone seems to be forgiven. Jovan is forgiven for taking off like he did and scaring us and we for immediately assuming the worst of him.

"Here's to the fish, then," Maddix says and raises his cup.

Chapter Twenty-Eight

The last of our luck is well and truly behind us. At the moment, I'm questioning whether or not we'll ever catch up to it again. I truly cannot understand why there are so many people living out in this region, but there are. More settlements seem to be popping up almost as soon as we put one behind us.

And they aren't just settlements where people do whatever it is they do and stick close to home. That would be too convenient. No, these are all industrious, purposeful places where there's apparently much to be done and people are all over the place. Inquisitive eyes would certainly seek out the source of any uncharacteristic sound, like the sound of five fugitives blundering past in the woods.

The number of streams and rivers increases with each passing mile, and trade seems to be flowing down each of them, making our situation even worse. Crossing takes far longer than any of us have patience for and we're snapping at each other before each day is halfway done.

We find a little hollow where the bushes are thick enough to hide us, so we stop to rest. There's been no opportunity for a fire for the last two nights, so we've been rationing our two gallons of water far more stringently than is comfortable.

My throat feels like it's been scoured and I resent every drop of sweat that comes out of me. Each of us has complained of a headache from our increasing dehydration at least once. These ill effects just sour the general mood even further.

Squatting in the little hollow that night is miserable. I'm not the only one having a hard time dealing with the changing environment. It's grown humid, the air so moist it leaves a film of dew on exposed skin while we sleep. When we wake, our clothes are damp and heavy. It's uncomfortable for people like us who've lived our entire lives in air so dry that it can crack the skin. It's not truly hot, but it's much warmer during the day than it has been. Darkness brings a chill made worse by the damp.

"This is nothing," Maddix says. "The border we need is over the Mighty Miss and those bridges were purposefully destroyed a long time ago. And you better believe this Creedy guy would have put the word out along this side of the river."

I can't imagine a river much worse than the ones we've been crossing lately. Every crossing is a gamble. At some rivers, the water is so fast and turbulent it's frightening just to look at. At others, it's deceptively calm and it's only when you sink in thick mud that the danger becomes clear.

"How much bigger can the Mighty Miss be?" I ask.

I'm not sure how to take the look he gives me, but I know it doesn't mean anything good. "It makes all the rest look like the canal back home," he answers in a flat voice.

"Then how did you get across it?" Cassi asks.

"A decent handful of beef jerky will get you passage on one of the boats if you're willing to pitch in and work. I'm telling you, beef is a luxury out here. But, no one was looking for me, not like they are for us now."

"Then how do you suggest *we* get across?" Jovan asks.

Maddix shakes his head, unsure. He says, "I suggest we get to a place upstream and see what we can see. Maybe we can steal one of the little tender boats. We don't need to get it straight across, just across in general. We can always walk back to the nearest border gate once we're on the other side of the river."

I'm about to ask what a tender boat is but Jovan beats me to it. Maddix says, "They're just small boats used to tend the barges or take small deliveries from the big grain barges."

I'm completely out of my element. I have nothing more to offer on the subject and the truth is, I'm so tired that I'm not sure I'd give any reasonable input anyway. It all sounds good to me because it means an end to being chased.

In the morning, I just try to focus on the fact that our journey is coming to an end instead of how disgusting I feel. My clothes have been damp for so long that I'm pretty sure I'm going to start growing mold. Our breakfast of a few sips of water is a joke, but it's what we have. All of us still refuse to eat any of the fish jerky. We're not that hungry yet.

I smell the river before I hear it, and I hear it long before I see it. It reminds me of the way the Red River advertised its location but far more intense. I doubt something as small as the Red would even attract any notice now that I've seen so much more. It's amazing how quickly I've become adapted to so much water, even after a lifetime without any to spare.

The smell is wild and a little fetid. The sound is a low rush, a second bloodstream I can feel through the soles of my feet, deep and thrumming and very powerful. The river is clearly bigger than my imagination allowed for, and I find myself thinking back to the way Maddix looked at me when I questioned how big it could be. I'm starting to understand that look for what it was. It was a "you'll see" look without the slightest hint of doubt in it.

The city lying between us and the river is abandoned, so we decide to go through rather than around it. The river has either flooded many times in the past or changed course more than once.

There are flows of old mud, dried as hard as concrete, piled in what used to be streets and up against the sides of ragged buildings. In some places, the flows stand as tall as my hips against glass that remains mysteriously unbroken, while doors are forever braced open by knee-deep flows that came in sometime in the past.

Inside those open doors, where the rain can't reach, the dried mud has maintained all the marks of its flow, waves and rivulets clearly showing on the surface. It's beautiful in a terrible and destructive way.

I've seen cars many times during our journey, but nothing like what I see here. They absolutely litter the streets, either pushed up against buildings or in jumbled piles. They're big and roomy-looking, some even larger than the prairie jumper, and I can't help but look inside a few with open doors. Rodents have made nests in the seats and I hear the cry of a bird of prey from somewhere high in the buildings. This may have once been a place inhabited by people, but it has been re-made since to suit a whole different web of life.

Near the edge of the city the buildings grow squat and wide, with fewer windows and more old fences. Eventually, we reach a vast wall that is more collapsed than upright. Whole sections of it lie in piles while short expanses remain defiantly upright.

As we reach one of those standing sections and squat in its shade for a rest, I tap the concrete and ask, "Is this the border?"

Maddix swigs some water, a loud sigh following as his thirst is quenched. He shakes his head and wipes his mouth with the back of his hand, leaving a smear of dirt across the faint yellow bruises on his face.

"No, Jordan told me this was put up to try to keep the river out a long time ago, but it didn't work. That's why there's no one here. We still have to get across the river to reach the border wall." He waves at the top far above our heads. "This is nothing. Wait till you see."

He seems to have a thought, shoving the water carrier at me and walking down the wall toward the nearest pile of rubble. That one apparently doesn't suit him, because he rushes past us going the other way and I hear him give a satisfied grunt at the next pile. His leg has healed up well, but it's not a good idea for him to climb, yet that's exactly what he does.

It looks like he's climbing the wall itself, so we hustle over to join him.

"Be careful!" Jovan says harshly. "Someone will see you, and then what will we do?"

Maddix looks down and grins. "No one's going to see through the trees. Just a minute."

Then he's off again. Where the wall has crumbled, there are gaps in the concrete that make for handy footholds. Thin white plastic pipes run along the interior of the wall and leave almost perfect circles of empty space for the entire height. I can also see that the wall is tapered at the top. They must have tried to use less concrete in building the wall, either to do it faster or to decrease the weight at the top. I look at the piles of rubble that were once wall and decide that probably wasn't the right decision.

We see the seat of Maddix's filthy jeans as he settles himself onto the top of the wall. He scoots further down, making room, then looks down at us with a wide grin and waves us up. Cassi and Connor go next. There are low exclamations as they see whatever it is Maddix wants to show us, but Cassi's face shows trepidation in it when she peers over the side at me.

Jovan motions for me to go next and gives me a boost to get me started. The rusty rebar sticking out of the concrete makes for great hand and footholds, but touching anything rusty makes me nervous. I wipe my hands on my jeans before touching the first one. I'm so concerned with not letting any part of me get cut by the rebar—I have a fear of tetanus that is far beyond normal for such an uncommon disease—that I don't see what they are looking at until my butt makes safe contact with the top of the wall.

But then I do see it and I am amazed. There are enough trees between us and the river so that we don't stand out, but not so many that we can't see through to what lies beyond. It's almost beyond description. The slope toward the river is mild and the banks of it are wide and red-brown with silt and mud.

It's incredibly wide, the far bank perhaps a quarter of a mile from the near bank. The waters seem placid enough on its gray surface until I spot a floating branch racing along. The current must be immensely strong.

I don't know much about rivers, but I know I won't be swimming across that. Or using a pole to guide a raft, for that matter. If we're going to get across it, we'll need a bridge or a sturdy boat. Better yet, a boat with someone who knows what they are doing at the helm.

Jovan scrambles up next to me but there's little room left, so he squeezes in. We're pressed so tightly together that we can't even put our arms to our sides, so we awkwardly rest our hands on our knees. I try not to turn my head toward him because we're so close, but it seems rude, so I do it anyway.

He's smiling at me, of course. He looks like a kid just told he's getting a bonus day off school or something. He's close enough that I can see the grime ground into his skin and the clean spot on his upper lip where he's been licking them. His eyes are that hypnotizing golden color they take on when he's in sunlight.

Basically, he takes my breath away and I'd like nothing more than to move that hand on his knee over to mine, but I don't and I won't. Whatever it is between us, I won't know if it's real until there's no pressure on us and we have time. Time for what specifically, I don't know.

I just hope that time eventually comes and we get the chance to figure it out.

I look away, back toward the river, and finally see what Maddix really meant to show us. Across the river, behind an obscuring screen of trees, there's a gap where the trees have been cleared, though I can only see that by the absence of their green crowns.

Beyond that is a wall unlike anything I've ever seen. It makes this one look like a neighborhood fence. While the trees are shorter here close to the river, they are still a good thirty or forty feet high. Yet, I can see the top of the wall above the tops.

I think it's concrete, like this one, but not consistently so. There are notches and holes in it at staggered points along its length. From here they look small, almost like little mouse holes in baseboards, but it's an illusion made by the distance.

"How do we get across that?" I ask.

Maddix leans forward enough that it makes me nervous. He looks up and down the river, uncertainty stamped on his features. He shrugs a little and says, "When I went across, I asked at places along the way and wound up at a crossing. When I came back with Jordan, we took an elevated crossing, a sort of carriage that goes across one of the broken bridges. It's hard to explain. But I don't think we're anywhere close to that."

We all peer both ways down the river, hoping against hope to see something that might save the day. There's nothing and I really didn't expect there to be. Jovan leans forward and then finally scares me half to death by getting up to stand on the wall, exposing his full profile to anyone who might be looking. His eyes shielded by his hand, he looks downstream for a long moment.

"What?" Maddix asks finally.

"You said a bridge? Was it a huge bridge, like really tall? Tall like those buildings in the city?" he asks without taking his eyes from whatever it is he's looking at.

Maddix gets to his feet as well and looks in that direction. He bursts out laughing and says, "It's a bridge alright! I can't be sure it's the same one, but it's big enough that it must have good crossings. Which means boats. Lots and lots of boats."

I wish I could see it, but I'm not about to stand up like they are. Twenty feet is a long way to fall and this wall has to be at least that, given the slope of the ground below. Maddix teeters a little and sits down in a hurry, so I tug on Jovan's pant leg—which I notice is just as filthy as mine—to get him to do the same.

He does, practically landing in my lap, but he apologizes at my grunt and slides off onto the wall again.

"What about people over there?" I ask, nodding toward the wall. I've figured out that the holes and dark smudges are probably sentry posts, which means sentries.

"Don't worry about them. They aren't interested in people here unless they try to bring their problems to the border. That's the place people are trying to get *to*. Once you show them your pendant and tell them who you are, they'll let you through. I'm already registered so Connor and I are good, too."

He doesn't seem to register the looks on Cassi and Jovan's faces or the fact that he's left them out of the equation.

"What about me? Or Jovan?" Cassi asks before I get a chance to.

Maddix starts at that and then looks at me. "Aren't you going to sponsor them? You're a land-owner," he says. The way he says it makes it seem like I should know this and that irritates me.

"And how exactly am I that?" I ask sharply.

He nods toward the pendant and then his face clears as he realizes I have no idea what he's talking about.

"Dang. I thought Jordan would have had a chance to tell you, to explain," he says.

"Explain?"

"You're his daughter. That makes you and his other kid land-owners along with him. Now, well, you're his heirs. That makes you a land-owner in your own right. Or, it will until you figure out how things will go with you and the kid," he says.

It's all very matter of fact, like there's no missing father and no boy who will never see his father again in the equation. It hurts to hear it said like that. I've been doing my best not to think about Jordan because all that will do is slow me down. But when it comes up, like right now when I can't avoid it, it feels like my chest hollows out just a little. Like my heart is shrinking.

Everyone looks uncomfortable. While that's almost as effective as sympathy at making me want to cry, we've got no time for it.

"So, you're saying that I can sponsor them in? How?" I ask.

"Well, it isn't quite that easy. They kept me hanging around for days while they waited for an answer from Jordan when I told them where I was from. But you've got the pendant and I was with him when he left. He left a message before we went through the border," Maddix says.

"And this is that border crossing? You're sure?" Jovan asks. He looks as confused as I am. I clearly didn't ask the right questions when I had the chance.

Cassi breaks in with a frustrated sigh and says, "Can we get down first before someone falls and breaks something? I'm just about over this view."

Getting down turns out to be considerably more difficult than getting up, but no one breaks anything so I figure we're good. There's no possibility of a fire or anything like that so we get as comfortable as we can leaning against the cool concrete wall. The shade on this side makes it even cooler, but we've sweated enough during today's trek to make it feel nice.

"Maddix, just tell me everything you know. We'll go from there," I say.

He looks uncomfortable for a moment, perhaps because he knows more about my father than I do. It's not like we didn't talk, because we did. But when we spoke it wasn't about official things. He wanted to know things about me, mundane things, like how I liked rosemary the best of all the plants in the garden and how it made me feel like I could fly when I ran across the rooftops in my neighborhood.

And when I asked him things, I asked about Quinton and what it was like where he lived and what he did with his days. The questions I had for him were the ones that helped me form pictures of his life in my mind.

The things we didn't say were almost as important as the things we did. I thought I would have time with him, time to get comfortable with each other and talk about all the things we wanted to. I'd built up a future with him in my mind and now, there will be none. Now I have to find out what I need to know from someone else.

I prompt him with a wave of my hand and a smile that feels false on my face, but it seems to work.

"As to your question, Jovan, no. I have no idea if that's the same one. I wouldn't know till I got close since the stations are numbered. But it doesn't matter. What one station knows, they can all find out. They have phones," he says.

I've never used a phone but I know what they are. We have them in the Courthouse, the school and any other place where officials talk to each other. I've seen one used while I waited to have my strike tattooed onto my neck.

I've heard they have them down south in the cities, but I have a hard time imagining that much wire being used for something like that. What could people have to talk about on a phone? The very idea of not seeing a person's face when you talk to them seems odd. But in the case of a long border, I guess it makes perfect sense. They'd need to be in touch.

"And as for them knowing, when Jordan left the territory he signed out and made sure the border knew he was coming to get you, his daughter. He made sure it was logged. And I'm logged as a resident so I can get back in," he explains.

"How does that help these two? You said I can sponsor them?" I ask, still not sure how they'll take my word for anything. I could be anybody. I could have stolen the pendants and killed Jordan. I can't see why any territory cautious enough to have that huge wall and all those manned stations would believe me, with my marked neck and dirty clothes.

Maddix shrugs and says, "Truth be told, I'm not sure how they do it, but they can find out if you're the person who is keyed to that pendant. And they have a policy about Strikers anyway. Takes longer, but they usually let them in. Or so I'm told."

He must mean my DNA. They must have a way of checking that. I can only hope it actually does key to me and everything works out. Otherwise, I have no idea what I'll do.

Connor's been quiet and thinking this whole time, turning to watch each of us as we speak. He breaks in while we're all trying to sort out the information and asks, "Yeah. That's all fine and dandy, but how do we get across the dang river in the first place?"

Chapter Twenty-Nine

Our plan is shaky, at best. That would be the optimistic assessment.

Jovan takes a trip to scout in the afternoon and reports back that the bridge is not a bridge, per se. It's an old railroad bridge and it's missing a big chunk in the middle. The disappointment is almost crushing when he breaks the news. The wall, the border and something that might be safety are just on the other side of that water. How many times will we have to take yet another turn, wake up in fear or fight for our lives before we get there?

On the upside, there is a thriving settlement of at least a few hundred people near the bridge and a whole slew of barges and boats of all sizes tied up there. He saw horses, but not Creedy's horses, in the paddock. He thinks we might be able to steal one of those boats if we're careful.

As night falls and the moon rises, we take once more to the trees. With that first step I commit to myself that I will not do this again. Even if I have to swim, I will get across that river and through that border and I won't look back.

My confidence lasts right up until we hear the whinny of horses ahead of us. I freeze, holding out a hand for the others behind me in case they didn't hear. They must have because the small sounds of our footsteps on the leaf litter stop abruptly and a single hiss of a frightened indrawn breath escapes behind me.

The moon is full and I can see Jovan's face sketched in the silver light. His brow is furrowed and I know he's thinking the same thing I am. That was the whinny of a horse in pain—like one with a burn in need of tending that isn't because she's still being used too hard.

Two careful steps is all I need to get next to Jovan. I pull his head down so that my lips almost touch his ear and breathe, "You said the horses were down below, by the village."

He pulls back enough to see my face and nods, his eyes wide, the whites gleaming in the moonlight.

I mouth, "Creedy?"

He nods and shrugs at the same time, but motions us backward just the same. The minutes it takes to retrace back far enough to get out of earshot are eternal ones, fraught with the convincing notion that someone is going to hear us and that will be the end of us.

"The people at the river had their horses in a paddock near their village, not in the woods. There's a road somewhere around there, though. I saw a sort of main street ending at the banks of the river. Either those are travelers waiting out the night, or it's Creedy," Jovan says.

"How would he know to come here?" I hiss, fear making me angry. It's hard to believe that he found this spot right when we arrived at it. It makes no sense unless we've been seen somewhere recently. Given that crossing spots aren't exactly common along the river, maybe this was the closest one.

"The fish!" Maddix whispers harshly.

Of course. The fish that Jovan stole. They probably reported it and maybe got word to Creedy. He would have gone to the nearest spot along our very stupidly direct path east. Why bother searching for us fruitlessly in an endless wood when he can stop us at the nearest crossing?

There's dead silence in the group, each of us processing that possibility in our own way. I'm angry. The theft was an impulsive act that may wind up trapping us on this side of the river or force us to sneak further north before we can cross. My anger is dampened only by reminding myself that his impulsive act was borne out of a genuine desire to help us and provide Connor and me with something we'd never been able to experience. He meant it to be kind.

With that thought, I pull in a deep breath and think about how we can get past this. Maddix is healing well, but he can't run for long, or quickly, before his breathing sounds like a bull in rut. Cassi is quick and agile, but she's not aggressive and can't force herself to be. Connor can be aggressive, but he might be of more use in getting those two to safety. That leaves Jovan and me.

If there were any proof needed regarding Jovan's ability to get his hands dirty, it's been amply provided already. He didn't hesitate to reach down through the hole in the ceiling and shoot someone in the head. In truth, he has more cause to doubt my ability to do the same. I have no such qualms. I don't have to sit down for a heart-to-heart with Creedy to understand what our situation is. I know it's a grim one.

If he, as the trusted and ruthless right hand of Jovan's father, is supposed to bring Jovan back into the family fold, there is only one way to do it safety. There's exactly one way to be sure there's no other story except the one they choose to tell, and that's to be sure there's no one left to tell a different one. If there is a confrontation with Creedy, I know he won't hesitate to end my life.

That makes the situation rather easy for me. I have no choice. And left with no choice, I'm left with no qualms either. I know I won't hesitate. This isn't like the Courthouse. There, it was us who brought the danger into the Courthouse and the soldiers merely doing their jobs. Taking their lives would have been wrong. Creedy isn't giving us options so there's nothing to feel bad or guilty about.

Even so, I'd rather simply get away from him. He's a ranch foreman with lots of experience with firearms. The only person here that even knows how to properly use a gun is Jovan, and he's only had a little practice as a Cadet. Unless we catch him sleeping I can't be sure we would win against him.

The glow of lights from windows in the few buildings at this end of town is visible from our little rise. The hum of a water generator makes a low noise that would be enough to cover the careful footsteps of people passing, but the moonlight will make it easier to see us.

We could sneak down there as a group and try to make our way through the town to the piers. On the downside, any alarm will also alert Creedy, who is surely watching and waiting. He may have even put the people below on notice that we might come. I would have if I were him.

Given that those boats are their livelihood, I would have made sure the people thought we were dangerous thieves. We're going to need a two-pronged approach if we want to increase our chances of making it.

"I have an idea," I say. I roll the details around in my head while the others stop their whispering. Maddix is leaning heavily on his uninjured leg and the yellow-green of his bruises and swollen nose stand out even in this colorless light. That's all I need to see to know this is the right approach.

"Maddix, Connor and Cassi. You three can head through the trees and make your way to the boats. Keep quiet and don't get caught." As I expected, sounds of disagreement come from four throats so I hold up my hands and say, "Please. Just hear me out first."

I don't get anything as positive as agreement, but at least everyone goes quiet and seems ready to listen. I press on, knowing this next part is what is really going to get them going. "Jovan and I are going to track around and find out who's really camped out there. If it's Creedy, we'll make sure he can't come after you if you're seen. Once you're there, do what you have to and get across the river. Jovan and I will follow and meet you on the other side."

The silence that greets my less-than-brilliant plan is telling.

Maddix lets me have it first. "Uh, Karas. That's just stupid. If we get separated, how will we find each other again? What will you do to Creedy? What if he's already got a whole crew again like before?" he asks, ticking off points on his fingers to the agreeing nods of the others.

What follows is more like an intense haggling session at the market than making a plan our lives might depend on. In the end, no one gets the exact plan they want, which is probably as good as it gets. At least the most idiotic elements of our various plans have been weeded out.

Jovan and I are going to watch until enough time has passed that the others should be clear and out on the water. If anything happens, we'll do what we have to. We aren't specifically going to kill Creedy unless we have to, but secretly I'm hoping there's a good opportunity to do just that.

With Connor's slingshot now firmly tucked into Jovan's pocket and a gun with extra magazines in his utility belt, and my slingshot and all of my good steel balls in my pocket, we're ready. I don't bring a gun because I'm completely unproven with one and that makes it more dangerous to me than any other person. Instead, I've got one of the big knives from the utility belts tucked into my waistband. Up close and personal, if I need to defend myself, I'm more confident with that.

Maddix and Connor have the other gun but know that they should avoid using it at almost any cost. The silver coins Jovan gives them should be enough to buy passage if they are caught, or the possibility presents itself. None of us are happy about the idea of stealing, but we rationalize it by saying we'll really only be borrowing it to get to the other side, where it can be recovered.

Jovan and I move closer to where we heard the horses, listening for any sounds that indicate our friends moving toward town have been noted. There's no change and that's good, but it's going to take some time to get through the town if they use caution, so we're not home-free yet.

The trees are thick here and only broken where the small road runs through it. The branches almost meet in the center, creating a canopy that's probably beautiful during the day, but just looks ominous now. At least they break up the moonlight and offer us some concealment if we're forced to cross.

Two huge trees with low spreading branches appear out of the gloom about twenty feet from the edge of the woods and I stop and point to them. Jovan leans his head back and then turns to look in the direction from which we're hearing the sounds of restless hooves, perhaps figuring out the angles I've already decided are good. The road is close, and the thinning of trees ahead of us tell me there is a widening in the road—like those we have in Bailar so that one wagon can pull aside when two meet on a narrow road—and there's the low orange glow of a fire.

He nods and climbs, his long legs making it look easy after all the practice he's been getting. Now it's me that has the harder time of it. For this kind of tree, his height is an advantage. By the time I get up through four levels of branches, I've circled the tree. When I look down, the ground is nothing more than a dark blot thirty feet below. It makes me almost dizzy to look, so I swallow and resolve not to do it again.

The higher perspective does what I had hoped and makes the group visible. There are still only four horses so it's unlikely Creedy found a new crew. A huge pile of bags that must be the fish look like sleeping forms at first, but they are far from the small fire. No one would willingly sleep like that. On the ground like that, I'm surprised they haven't been under a near constant sneak assault by raccoons or other animals drawn to the smell of the dried fish.

That gives me an idea. The proximity of the horses to the bags means they will startle if there is such a visitation. Perhaps Creedy is using the natural skittishness of horses as a sort of early warning system.

Near the fire, the light flickers on a single person lying on a blanket, but I can't tell who it is. There's no sign of the other for long minutes, then I hear the crunch of boots on gravel. Creedy's form resolves out of the darkness as he approaches the fire and pours a cup of something from a pot. Then he walks slowly and calmly across the road and blends into the shadows.

It's smart. He can keep watch in both directions, all the way to the main thoroughfare into town, while allowing all the attention to be drawn to the fire and the sleeping man. Had we come upon him while traveling that road or beside it, we might have crossed and tried to pass on his side in the dark, leaving him to intercept us at his leisure.

Jovan is too far from me to allow us to converse, but when Creedy is fully dissolved into the shadows on the other side of the road, I risk a small hiss to get his attention. I see the pale moon of his face turn toward me so I pull up my sleeves so he'll see my arms. I wave closer and start edging my way around the trunk toward the branch that extends in his direction. When I lower myself to crawl along it in his direction, he seems to understand, hopping with enviable grace to a lower branch and moving to meet me.

We can't get as close as I would like, but it's close enough that we can speak in whispers. He's only a few feet below me but it strikes me that the only time I've ever seen him from above, at least up close, was when I was about to harm him back in the Courthouse. A shiver of foreboding runs down my back.

"I think I can hit one of the horses from here with a slingshot. Maybe more than one of them. Get them to bolt," I say.

I see him look toward the horses, evaluating, and then he nods in agreement. "They're tired and probably ready to go home. They might not come back," he says and I can tell by the tone of his voice that he likes the idea.

"He'll go after them," I say, adding something to tempt him.

"The other one will wake up," he adds to counter my temptation.

"And he'll go after them, too," I say with certainty.

He considers for a long moment. We'll have one chance to do this right, one chance to make the way clear for our friends and ourselves. We have one chance to achieve freedom beyond the border.

Chapter Thirty

Jovan pulls out Connor's slingshot and a few of the tumbled stones that Connor and I spent countless hours turning in a tumbler while we talked and laughed. It seems like another lifetime, when I had time for such things. When Jovan lets those stones fly, another small piece of that life will be gone, never to be retrieved.

He nods at me and I turn to regain my vantage point in the tree. By the time I get there, he's already well out on his tree limb, face forward and tension in every line of his shadowed form. I feel as tense as he looks when I pull out my slingshot and palm a few of the steel balls.

The horses are well within range and I hate to hurt them, but this will only sting. It should do no lasting harm so long as they don't trip or otherwise hurt themselves in their fright. But they are his most significant advantage and any advantage I can take from Creedy I must. Plus, the slingshot is almost silent. Even if he does figure out it isn't a raccoon, he'll have no way to know where it's coming from.

A quick exchange of nods and then it's time. Slingshots are crude weapons but they can be used with subtlety and to excellent advantage, whether it's a head shot on a rat so that the meat is undamaged or on the rump of a horse to create a maximum fear reaction.

Two of the horses offer tempting targets and I take aim at the further of the two, leaving Jovan with the one closest to him. The slight thump and whistle of his shot follows mine so closely they are almost in unison. The alarmed whinnies of the horses, shrill and sudden, tell me that we have made contact.

There's no time to have second thoughts, no time to feel bad about those pained sounds. I fight back the almost overwhelming urge to soothe them, to go and help them, and instead load another ball into the leather patch of my slingshot. They're in motion, yanking at whatever their leads are wrapped around, probably an old log or branch. Whatever it is, it's moving under their frenzied movements.

The balls and stones fly, each strike less precise than the one before as the horses try to flee. Creedy's yells are joined by those of the no-longer-sleeping man and they shout conflicting instructions to each other. It's clear they think there is an animal amongst the horses but that won't last.

I send three balls in a row into the flank of one of the rearing horses. There's the distinct sound of breaking wood and the horses run headlong away from us and back down the road.

Creedy shouts for the man to get the horses and I see him run down the road as well, profanities spilling from his mouth as he curses bears, cougars, raccoons and every other thing that might live in these woods. It's almost enough to make me smile.

This is diversion enough, so Jovan and I waste no time. We both scramble down our respective trees, not nearly as cautious as we should be about making noise. It's only unnoticed because there's so much other noise to compete with it. At the bottom, we meet up and make our way through the trees just off the road toward town.

Suddenly, our feet freeze as a shout rings out. "Jovan! I know that's you!"

It's Creedy. I don't recognize his voice and don't know him, but it can be no one else. The cool certainty and anger in the voice chills me to the bone. A shot rings out and there is no question now that we won't be able to sneak through to town. The sound of a shot carries with it the imperative of alarm. It stirs an instinct in humans to be ready for anything. The people in that town will protect themselves first and ask questions later, not caring to risk the time to find out who is posing the danger and who is running from it.

I have one brief moment to wish with all my might that the others have secured passage already. If they haven't, they aren't likely to after this. Jovan and I stand perfectly still, hoping we're still hidden, only our heads moving as we search the road to see where Creedy might be and if he has located us.

Jovan's touch on my shoulder draws my gaze back. His eyes gleam in the moonlight and shadows hide the rest of his features, but I can read the desperation there all the same. He leans in close and breathes into my ear, "Trust me."

Another shot rings out and I jump at the sound. This one was closer, not toward us, but directed into the trees as if he knows we're out here and wants to herd us, panic us into making noise. It takes all my willpower not to shriek and take off running, which is exactly what Creedy wants me to do. Jovan tightens his grip on my shoulder to give me strength.

His eyes are on me again and he whispers once more, "Trust me."

I give an almost imperceptible nod of my head but it's enough. He takes off, running lightly away from me to disappear into the woods.

Strangely, I don't need any explanation to know what he's doing because it's what I would do if our positions were reversed. He's going to draw Creedy back, leaving me to run for the river. I have no idea how he intends to stop Creedy, but he has a gun and that seems a likely—and permanent—solution.

I go, trying to keep my footsteps light but the crunching of leaves seems incredibly loud in my ears. There's another shot but I can tell it's not aimed in my direction, but far behind me.

Jovan's shout is loud in the night and I almost freeze right then, fearful he's been hit for a second. He's the one person Creedy doesn't want to see harmed. Jovan is smart and after that first fearful second, I realize what he's doing. He was probably just waiting for that shot.

"It's me, Jovan! Stop shooting! I'm on my own! They left me and I'm hurt!"

There's a beat before Creedy answers, so I know he's suspicious. I place my feet carefully, slowing my steps to a crawling walk so as to not waste this chance.

"Come out, Jovan," Creedy yells somewhere far behind me.

"I am! Give me a minute."

I keep going, not risking a look back, but ahead of me I can hear the distant shouts of an awakened town and my heart sinks. We aren't going to get across here unless Creedy is permanently removed from the equation.

The sound of an alarmed shout and a shot is followed by Jovan's yell, "Run!"

I do. I can't see if I'm staying on course, weaving around the trees and brush that seem to appear directly in front of me out of the darkness. Behind me, I hear the pounding of Jovan's feet on the gravel road and then him crashing through the trees.

I risk a yell. "Here!" I can only gamble that it's safe and hope that last shot took out Creedy.

It's not. I hear Creedy's angry shout from somewhere further behind me. The edge of the forest is ahead, evidenced by a distinct lifting of the darkness as moonlight reaches the ground unimpeded. Rather than burst out of the trees, which is sure to attract attention if anyone is out and looking, I slow and ease my way out.

I'm standing at the small rise before the town proper. It's not much of a rise, maybe ten or so feet, but going down means coming into full view of those gathering in the town by the main thoroughfare. Lights are coming on and flashlight beams cross each other as people search both the water and the trees. I sense they are uncertain, not knowing what might be going on, but are ready to react to anything. That would include me. With the river and the border beyond so close, they are likely always ready for almost any conflict.

The bridge we'd originally had such high hopes for is ahead of me, almost directly so. The rails that lead to it lie half-buried in the forest floor, and the bridge arches above the river like a beacon of hope.

I have few choices. I can go back into the trees, which is probably my smartest course, or I can risk that bridge and hope it goes far enough across that I can swim the rest of the way. I can't even think about the height right now. Going down to the town, which is now crowded with people and lights is out of the question.

I huff a few quick breaths to draw up my courage and sprint the short distance to the bridge. The clang of metal against my boots draws at least a dozen lights toward the bridge, each one hitting somewhere along the length of it. A beam of light bounces along until it touches me. It's only the distance that prevents it from blinding me and sending me tumbling down to the rapidly receding ground below.

Running on this railroad bridge is much harder than it first appeared it would be. The grate that makes up the base of it is rusted and entirely untrustworthy. With each step I hear pieces of it break and fall away. My only real way to the top is using the old wooden crossbeams, the ties, and many of those feel soft under my feet. I dare not let my feet linger and the trip up the long shallow incline makes me feel like my heart will burst from the sheer terror of it.

I see the gap, but it looks impossibly far away. It's well past the peak of the arc, which is good, but I'm not at all confident that the bridge won't dump me long before that point. I'm barely over the water yet. The bridge was built to be much wider than the river, either because the river rises and falls, or because it once did.

A sudden shifting vibration comes through the soles of my boots and I look behind me in time to see Jovan jerk upright after putting a foot through the grate. I can't see any details but I hear a groan of pain even above all the shouts and noises below. Some of the flashlight beams move away from me and find him, perversely making it easier for me to keep moving without so many confusing, moving beams of light changing the way the bridge looks.

When I stop to look back, I see Creedy burst out of the trees and I hear a shot. There's no question this one is aimed at me because I hear the whine of it even though it misses me by a wide margin. The shifting lights and distance are doing nothing for his aim.

I take a risk and shout down to the people below, "He's a kidnapper! We escaped! Don't let him get us!"

Whether it's because the lights show the people below that I'm clearly young or the simple fact that I'm running and Creedy is shooting at an unarmed girl, there is a change in the tenor of their voices and more of the beams leave me. I risk one more look back and see Creedy framed by the beams a few flashlights, one arm thrown across his eyes to block the light. Jovan has the hang of the rails now, and he's rapidly catching up to me.

I turn and run and all that I have left inside me is required for me to place each foot firmly onto a tie. The river is finally below and the sound of those waters is strong, it's voice a roar that says I'm no match for it. It says I'm not going to make it to the other side alive.

The gap is there before me and it's far worse than I thought. I have to stop so suddenly that I lose my tentative footing and drop to my knees, one hand barely catching the last tie to stop my headlong fall into the water. A single beam of the old rail reaches out into the gap, ragged grating clinging to the support structure, and I know from the terrible groan when I scramble forward that it won't hold my weight. This is the end of the line.

The water below me is an unending ribbon of deeper black. The flashlight beams attenuate at this distance and create just enough glow that it's impossible to use the moonlight to see details. Is it shallow or deep? Are there rocks or is it a soft muddy bottom? There are several hundred feet between me and the shore and I'm more than halfway over the river. No good options are on offer at the moment.

I rise to my feet and Jovan sees me standing there, arms akimbo to keep my balance, and he stops, too. He turns, holding his arms out as a barrier between Creedy and me. Creedy is fit, but far older than we are, and he hasn't made it very far running along the rails. We stand there for a breathless moment, each of us knowing our choices have narrowed to exactly nothing.

"I'll let her go if you come with me," Creedy shouts.

Jovan shakes his head, almost sadly, steps backward onto the next tie toward me, and answers, "You won't."

I can't see much of Creedy with Jovan between us, but I can see the gun lift, the barrel glinting in the moonlight. He says, "I'll shoot her now unless you come."

Jovan takes another step backward, risking a fall by not looking, but his step is sure and firm. He's just three ties from me, almost close enough to touch. I have the terrible feeling I will never touch him again, and a sharp pang of regret for all that I will never experience pierces me. If this is the end of my life, at least I can have the final moments of it with Jovan, who I have loved since I was too young to understand what love was.

"If you shoot, you'll hit me and all those people down there will know it. You might be able to spin a tale for my father for a while, but he'll find out the truth and you'll be a dead man. You and I both know it," Jovan assures him and takes another step backward. "Stop coming forward or I'll jump. I'll be just as dead."

I can only see bits of Creedy now. Jovan is covering me as best he can, but I can see Creedy's feet as they stop short. I can almost feel the wheels turning in his head from where I stand. Jovan takes ones more step and I put my hand on his back, feeling the sweat-dampened fabric and the heaving of his breath. He's frightened but also determined.

The words I need to tell him before I die are forming in my mouth when he looks over his shoulder and whispers, "I'll get you. Trust me."

He knows how poor my swimming skills are. We discussed it when we crossed that first lake. Braving water of unknown depth on an open-sided raft made me visibly nervous. He knows I won't survive the river even if I survive the fall. He's asking me to risk it all based on trust.

But really, what choice do I have at this point? I can see that Jovan's holster is empty so there's nothing else that we can reasonably do.

Seeing my indecision, he smiles and whispers, "You need a bath anyway."

That's it. It's all I need. His smile, the certainty in his eyes and the way those eyes move over my face is more than enough. He turns back toward

Creedy, who has lifted a foot slightly, like he's about to step forward. The lifted foot comes back down and the stalemate resumes. I take a long breath, then another, and jump.

*****

It seems I'll fall forever and I hold my breath, only dimly aware of the shouts from the shore as I do. I try to stay straight, my legs together and arms at my sides. My pack is on my back but there's nothing I can do about it now except hope that it doesn't drown me.

The impact is bone-rattling and I have no sense of how far I sink, only that I'm turned and tumbled in the water, entirely lacking control. My pack slams into the back of my head and jerks my arms painfully. Stunned and confused, all I can think of is the breath that just whooshed out of me and that I have no way of knowing which way is up, no way of finding the precious air I need.

Opening my eyes is almost no help at all. The moonlight makes the river around me a confusion of bubbles and brown water. I can feel the current like a cold embrace, pushing me with shocking speed away from the bubbles. My lungs are burning and the temptation to simply breathe in anything, even water, is an instinct I have to fight with every fiber of my being.

Instead, I do the thing that is exactly opposite to my instincts and simply go still. The confusion of bubbles resolves into a receding curtain that is moving past my feet. I'm upside down. I flail my arms and feet, turn and then kick until my head breaks the surface.

Air has never tasted so sweet or felt so good before. I suck in great gasps and let the stars in my vision clear. The bridge has fallen behind me and I have no control over my direction of travel. Coughing, I try to dog paddle, to stay afloat, but the cold current below wants to tug me downward and it's all I can do to keep my lips and nose free of the water.

I'm exhausted almost immediately and my frantic looks around don't show me anything that might be Jovan. It's getting harder to keep my head above water and it seems every few seconds a branch or something else comes looming out of the night to smack into me. My pack has filled with water, the clothes inside weighing it down. With a pang I realize I will have to let it go.

Everything except what I have tucked into my pockets is in that pack. Not just the few spare clothes that I have, but also the food, which will likely be useless now anyway. My flint, the medical kit and even our pot is in that pack. The loss of those things is far more crucial.

Most hurtful is my little box, the few reminders of my life tucked within it. Except for the single photo in my pocket, which is no doubt getting ruined, all the photos of my father and mother are in that pack.

I shrug out of it and it falls immediately away, taking with it my past. It's like I've shed a body's worth of weight and the relief is immense. Keeping my chin out of the water seems almost possible now.

I gather what little energy I have left and shout, "Jovan."

It comes out sounding more like a croak than a yell, but I hear my name in response. It's not close and I can't tell where it's coming from, but I hold up my arm, hoping he can see it. I'm paddling with my legs as fast as I can, but my head dips lower in the water again and I have to lower my arm again.

After doing this a few times, holding up my arm till I can't anymore, then gathering my strength for another round, I feel him grab me and hear him say, "I've got you."

Chapter Thirty-One

His hand grips mine, our thumbs locked and his fingers tight around my palm as he pulls me to him, chest to chest. He spins us around in the water until it is his back pointing downstream where all the debris appears from. I can feel his legs scissoring underneath us with strong strokes very unlike my pathetic dog paddle.

His free arm wraps around my back and I feel the sharp points of his knuckles digging into my chest where our clasped hands are squeezed between us. He gasps, "Put your arm around my neck. Hang on."

I do, wrapping my arm almost too tightly around him, loosening my grip when he winces though my instinct is to hold on even tighter. His arm releases my back when I have a good hold, but he doesn't release the lock he has on my hand. I feel a change in his kicks as his one free arm guides us with more purpose in the river that still carries us swiftly along.

We aren't in the middle of the river, but close enough so that either bank looks impossibly far away. He's guiding us toward the opposite bank from where we began but I can't even imagine how far down the river we'll be before we're able to reach that bank. He seems tireless to me. Little grunts punctuating his effort are the only indicator he gives as to how hard he's working.

It seems like hours have passed, though I know it can't be more than minutes in reality, when I hear the sounds of arguing over the roar of the river. Jovan stops his work for a moment, just keeping us afloat while he looks around, so I know he heard it, too. All the muscles in my body clench until the voices resolve and then I laugh.

"You're such a jerk-off! If we want to get across we have to use the paddles to help it push us, we can't fight it!" Cassi's voice is clear and high and very angry.

I can't see them, but I shout out her name before we move past them entirely.

"Karas! Where are you?"

The beam of a flashlight is joined by another a moment later and it plays over the water far behind us. Any hope I had of being able to climb up into a handy boat are dashed when I see that they are still on the other side of the river. We've actually made more progress than they have.

I shout out, "We're past you already. Get across and look for us south of you. We'll wait!"

Her voice is fainter, less clear, when it comes back to me but I can understand that she's acknowledging me and that's enough.

Jovan resumes his work with a grunt, his efforts redoubled, and I do my best to help him without tangling our legs. I can't help but wonder why we are moving faster than the debris floating on the surface and the boat—or whatever it is they are paddling. I feel that cold current on my legs and how hard I have to work to keep my body fairly upright and realize the water moves faster under the surface than on top of it.

That gives me an idea so I tighten my grip on Jovan and push my body to the side. It puts me facing the faster current at an angle, allowing me to act almost as a rudder for Jovan to work with. It seems to help and Jovan looks at me with a sudden smile.

His face is inches from mine and I feel a perverse desire to kiss him, remembering what I almost said before I jumped from the bridge. Life is entirely too short for fear to be a factor in how we live it. Before I can think again, I dart my head forward and press my cold lips to his.

Like mine, his lips are cold, but they are also soft. They feel exactly how they look like they should. I press our lips together, my hand around his neck, until I feel his surprise melt into something different. I can feel our motion become less controlled, his kicks less strong, so I pull away and kick my legs back out to the side.

His smile returns but it's different, meant just for me. I think I will forever love the way the light of the moon makes the world look because of this moment. His smile warms me all the way to my toes.

Jovan goes back to work and the addition of my makeshift rudder changes our path dramatically. A new danger looms out of the night in the form of deadfall along the banks of the river. We're still moving too fast to want to risk plunging into range of it and take our chances, though we've begun to slow a little as the bank nears.

"Pull your legs up," I say through chattering teeth.

That slows us even more and I see another huge deadfall looming ahead, so tall that I think it is an old ruined building at first. It's a tangle of branches and trees that must have piled up after something large enough to provide a good base caught hold.

Behind it, there will be a lee, a small pool of calmer water free of debris because everything is already caught up in the deadfall. It will break the flow of the river, but it will be a small window of opportunity that we must not miss.

"Now. There. Now!" I exclaim as we draw even. I kick for all I'm worth, as does Jovan, and the sudden loss of current sends us those last feet toward the bank. I'm still kicking when Jovan gains his feet so all I accomplish is to knock him over again. He gets his feet back under him and I can feel the firm hold of the earth in the way he holds me.

"Oh!" I say as my boots touch the mud.

He laughs, but it is a tired laugh, weary all the way through to the bone. The mud is sticky and sucks at my boots, so he hauls me closer to shore with an arm around my waist. It reminds me of how he picked me up when I first saw my father, the day all of this started.

Once on the bank and out of the mud, we collapse into a heap. My limbs feel boneless and weak, trembling with fatigue. I fall onto my back and decide that I love solid ground. Jovan flops down next to me and I can't help but grin at him as we pant out the exhaustion.

He lifts an arm and then lets it fall again. "I feel like my bones fell out," he says.

"Me, too," I answer. It's pretty much all I've got the energy for right now.

I'd like to just lie there a while, but the air is too cool to stay in the open with soaked clothes and there is nothing save dark trees for as far as I can see. The border should be behind me somewhere, but there's no evidence of that from where I am. And we have three friends in the water to watch for, possibly still having problems steering their boat.

"The others," I say and brace myself on an elbow.

Jovan stands, groaning at the effort, but he holds out a hand and I'm not ashamed to use it to stand up. There's nothing obvious, but with the moon there's only so far we can see. When I listen, the sounds of the water flowing past the tangle of deadfall is almost all I can hear aside from our still ragged breathing.

We look at each other and decide without having to say a word. I cup my hands around my mouth and yell, "We're here!"

It's shockingly loud and it goes against all my instincts. We've had to be so careful, so quiet, since we left that it seems wrong to be anything but quiet. I hear a faint answer that I think came from upstream. I see Jovan has begun to collect wood further up the bank where it's dry. I hate to tell him that I have no way to start it.

"Jovan, I had to dump my pack. I've got no flint," I confess. I cross my arms in front my chest to hold in what little heat I have and contain my shivers. He just keeps collecting wood and tossing it into the cleared space between us.

"Are you listening? I don't have a flint, so unless you've got some secret superpower I don't know about for making fire, collecting wood isn't going to help us," I say, the cold making me sound sharp and short-tempered when all I really want is for him to come and hold me so we can share some warmth.

In response, he stands and pats his pocket, his white teeth flashing in a grin. "I've got one."

If I weren't so happy to hear that, I'd probably be angry he left me guessing. Then another thought strikes me.

"Wait, maybe we shouldn't light a fire," I say.

He stomps over to me, tossing another armload onto the ground as he does, and says, "We need a fire. We're both freezing and we need to signal the others."

That's a reasonable and true statement, but it's only half of what we need to consider. "And it will signal anyone else who comes down the river looking for us, too," I counter.

He stops and shakes his head, like he can't believe he didn't think of that. Then he looks back up the river, perhaps expecting to see a boat, its searchlights seeking us. There's nothing, of course, but that doesn't mean it will remain true for long.

As cold and wet as we are, as eager as we are to see our friends, we need to remain calm and keep thinking. Given that they didn't seem to know what they were doing with the boat, it's unlikely they obtained it legitimately. It's a distinct possibility the owners of the boat will come looking if Creedy doesn't.

It may feel like we've left Creedy behind, and if we're lucky, the people who just saw him drive us over the edge of a bridge will detain him, or at least not allow him access to a boat. But we simply can't count on that so we have to use our heads.

We hunker down next to our useless pile of wood and after a moment of solitary shivering, Jovan scoots closer and pulls me tightly to his side, his arm draped over my shoulder. It doesn't feel the same as when we were in the water. This is less intimate, without that sensation of being entirely together like before. It's more functional than emotional. That's a disappointment, though I feel bad for thinking that way.

Functional or otherwise, there's comfort in it and the warmth we share is welcome. I curl into him and we watch the river together, hoping for our friends.

Their arguing reaches our ears long before their small boat comes into view. We yell out, unwisely given how long Creedy has had to come after us if he did manage to find a crew and a boat, and they pass us with assurances that they are alright and getting the hang of the boat.

They look relatively close, maybe fifty feet out from the shore. It's almost close enough to tempt me to suggest they jump in and swim, until I remember that Connor can't swim at all and Cassi is only slightly better than I. I have no idea if Maddix can, but I do know he's been shot recently and that usually doesn't mix well with dirty river water.

After their still-arguing voices fade and we sit there for a while, absorbing the fact that they are safe, Jovan bursts out laughing. I stare at him for a moment, not at all understanding what might be funny about any of this. That seems to just set him off even more. He's laughing so hard he falls over, making noises that sound more like choking than laughter. I start to get worried so I poke him in the side, hard.

"What?" I ask, pulling a face, when he keeps laughing. "Are you alright?"

He waves a hand at me, telling me to wait, while he chokes on his laughs and then quiets a little. When he looks at me, he starts laughing again and we go through the entire cycle once more.

Right about the time I lose my last bit of patience, which doesn't take long, he says between laughs, "The arguing! They've been arguing the whole time. While we were…"

He trails off with more laughter but I don't see what's funny. And then I do. While we were jumping off a bridge, possibly to our deaths, and fighting the river, they were arguing and making incredibly slow process. And they did it all while remaining entirely unaware of our circumstances. It's sad, yes, but also hilarious in a very twisted sort of way. I chuckle too and soon we're both laughing so hard it hurts.

When the fit is done and our amusement has tapered off, we look at each other a little awkwardly. Jovan coughs and says, "That probably wasn't that funny."

I nod, because it wasn't, and answer, "No. But I sure do feel better."

And it's true. Beautifully and wonderfully true. The fear and tension that has bound me like ropes, the dread I felt when I looked down at the dark river so far below me, the sadness of losing a father I'd only just begun to know; they are all gone. Loosened and fallen away, I feel free. It might not last. Tomorrow I may be just as frightened, just as sad, but for now, this moment, I feel unfettered.

He grins at me. It's open and warm, everything a girl could ever hope to see in the face of the boy she loves. And it's all for me. Rather than do what I'd like to do, which is jump on him and kiss that grin from one corner of his mouth to the other with a hundred tiny kisses, I look away and slap my hands on the ground to break the moment.

"We should go. Meet them downstream when they finally get their act together," I say.

He looks disappointed for a moment, and not about us needing to start walking. It makes me perversely happy to see that, the possibility that he was thinking something along the same lines as I was. But he stands, offers me a hand up, and we go.

It turns out that it is far more than merely uncomfortable to walk in wet jeans. They're cold and heavy from the thighs down and warm in a way that makes me think of someone peeing their pants above the thigh. And they are chafing and pulling at my skin, guaranteed to leave me raw and red if we keep it up.

A quick glance at Jovan confirms he's uncomfortable about something too, and the wet rubbing sounds he makes with each step tell me we're probably in the same boat. When I stop, I put an arresting hand on his arm and say, "My pants feel like they're made of wet sandpaper. I can't walk like this."

"I'm so glad you said that. I thought you'd think I was being a wimp if I said something," he says, relief clear in his voice.

This is about to become one of the most embarrassing situations I could imagine. It almost rivals that dream I have once in a while where I wind up realizing I have no clothes on in the middle of school.

I start to untie the line that I use for a belt and try to sound casual when I say, "The pants have to go until they dry."

He gapes at me until my expression makes it clear he should not be looking at me quite so closely. He turns around and, after a great deal of hopping around trying to get wet denim off, we are both pantsless.

It's just as horrifying as my dreams indicated it would be. I'm just glad it's dark and my underwear are relatively new and a plain dark blue color. Jovan isn't so lucky. His look like they might be some sort of tan color very similar to the color of the Texas Army uniform, so they stand out like a beacon under his brown shirt.

We both hang our jeans over our shoulders so that the cool night air will dry them, and head downstream without further conversation. The chill quickly overtakes any sense of embarrassment and we're shivering within minutes. The sound of the river is loud beside us, but our frequent calls to check on the location of the others go unanswered.

Right about the time I start to worry that they've overturned their boat or had some other calamity befall them, I hear a response from ahead of us. Jovan and I share a look and then dash toward the sound as one. They should—at least I hope they do—still have their packs and while that won't help us with dry clothes, they at least have the empty burlap sacks we can use to wrap around us. And they have water. After drinking half the river during my plunge, I'm surprised to find that I'm incredibly thirsty.

We arrive to find them on the shore, dry and waiting for us, the little boat they used pulled up on the bank and secure. With the moon almost down, there is less light, but there's still enough for them to see that we're half-naked and soaked to the bone.

"Uh, why aren't you wearing pants?" Cassi asks rather loudly after she gives me a hug in greeting. She turns to hug Jovan as well but stops, eyes his legs and steps back. The way Connor keeps looking at me, his eyes mostly on my face but dipping down and away like he can't stop himself, makes me laugh.

"We sort of fell in the river. It made for an interesting swim," I answer, preferring to leave the details for a time when I'm not shivering and wet.

All three of them turn as one and look back out at the river, perhaps remembering how much trouble they had steering their boat in the swift current. Then Connor digs a couple of the burlap sacks out and tosses us each one. Maddix flicks on a flashlight, leaving it on the low setting, so we can see each other better while we talk. I'm not entirely sure seeing each other clearly is what I'd like at the moment.

"Maybe a fire?" Connor suggests after seeing the way we grab at the rough sacks and wrap them around us.

I shake my head and explain, "We got away from Creedy, but we don't know if he might have talked his way out of things by now. If he did, he could be coming down this river right now to see if we survived." I glance over at Jovan and add, "He's quite committed."

"What happened to taking him out if necessary?" Maddix asks, exasperation clear in his tone.

"We managed to drive off their horses and the other guy ran after them. I doubt those horses will stop for him. The horses weren't in great shape and probably just want to go home. Um..." I trail off there, not sure how to explain the loss of Jovan's gun because I don't even know.

Jovan, a big bag wrapped around his middle like a skirt, looks abashed but he answers. "I tried to tackle him—because I'm an idiot—and lost my gun. But, I managed to whack him a good one and we got away. Sort of."

Maddix scrubs a hand across his cheek, clearly containing his frustration only with effort. "So, the bottom line is that we still have him to worry about. Have I got that right?"

There's no weaseling out of confessing this unpleasant truth so I nod. Mostly, I get frowns in return. Except for Cassi, of course.

She claps her hands to break the mood and says, "Well, the border is somewhere back there and we just have to get that far and we'll be safe." She shoos us toward the woods and grabs a sack. "So, let's get moving."

Chapter Thirty-Two

Dawn is still an hour or two away and the woods are dark, a maze of thick undergrowth and no paths that I can see. We've got only two flashlights left so I find myself stumbling along behind the beam trying to remember what obstacles it illuminated a few seconds before. Given the number of times I trip, I'm not doing so well. Given how many curses and exclamations of pain I hear from the others as they do the same, I'm not the only one who's having trouble.

By the time the wall appears through the trees, I'm covered in what will soon be rising bumps, scrapes that sting with every step and tender spots that will surely blossom into an unattractive array of bruises come the day.

Before we leave the protection of the trees, Maddix stops us and says, "Listen, when we get to a gate, or meet anyone from the other side of that wall, we'll need to be careful. Strikers from Texas can come to the Southeast, but not if they're considered a danger to society."

"Uh," I say, "strikes equal crimes, so how does that work?"

Maddix waves away my concern and says, "It's not the same. They have all this stuff about human rights and stuff—I don't understand it—so they don't look at strikes the same way, especially if you're under eighteen. Anyway, be careful what you say. Also, they take this border seriously. No one, and I mean *no one*, gets past without the proper and official checks."

It seems a little weird to me, but I suppose I have no idea what to expect from any other place aside from Texas. I'll just go with what seems right at the time. There are nods of agreement all around.

We stumble out of the trees into a cleared space in front of the wall at least fifty feet wide. We get only a few moments of peace to catch our collective breath and stumble a half-dozen paces into the clearing when a floodlight from above blinds us.

As one, our hands come up to cover our eyes as the darkness is torn apart. An amplified voice comes from the wall. "Stop where you are. Keep your hands in sight. State your purpose."

I'm not sure what I expected at the wall, but an emotionless and authoritative command from some unseen person behind a blinding light is not it. This doesn't feel welcoming, or even like a passage we're allowed to try to travel. It feels exclusive, like I'm not on the list.

Maddix seems to collect himself first. He holds his free hand out and calls, "I'm Maddix Blake. I'm a registered citizen. We're being pursued."

There's a beat before we get an answer, but it comes. "And the others with you?"

Maddix points to each of us in turn and yells, "Connor Blake, my brother. I pre-registered him before I crossed the border. Karas Quick, a pre-registered citizen and daughter of Jordan Quick, a citizen. She's a land-owner and these two—Cassidy Langfer and Jovan Foley—are being sponsored by her as workers."

It all sounds very official and formal. I'd be convinced if someone told me all of that with such certainty. It hurts to look up at the light, but I can't help it. I can't see past it to the person doing the talking but that doesn't stop me from trying.

There's a much longer pause this time before the tinny, amplified voice comes back and tells us to hold on. I hear the crackle of someone talking on a radio behind the voice so I imagine that they are communicating with whoever it is that holds records to verify what they can.

While we stand around in the cold, Jovan and I put on our pants, which is doubly embarrassing with that giant bright light illuminating every bit of us. My heart is warmed, if not the rest of me, when Jovan holds up his burlap bag to shield me from any eyes above.

A gray dawn is lightening the sky by the time we hear more from the wall. The searchlight doesn't bother me as much now that the sky isn't quite so pitch black. It's either that or I've gotten used to it. My attention is drawn back to it when it moves slightly away from us, as if to keep us easily viewable, but not blind us. I take it for a good sign.

"The names Maddix and Connor Blake and Karas Quick check out, but you're about eighty miles from the crossing you left through. And the log lists Jordan Quick, but he's not with you. He's your primary. Where is he?" the voice asks. The tone has changed slightly, become more conversational, but still wary and cautious.

Maddix glances quickly my way and at my nod, answers, "He was killed during our trip back by the same people still chasing us. Texas wasn't too happy with us bringing out the others."

It's an incomplete answer, but still honest enough that I can justify it for the moment as the right one to give. Once we're over the border and safe, I'll be happy to tell them all that they might want to know.

"Are you guys the ones involved in the fuss at Logan's Crossing?" asks the voice.

The other three don't know much about that fuss, only that Jovan and I wound up in the water somehow and that gunshots echoed along the river, which they had assumed were the result of their theft of the boat. Maddix looks like he's about to ask what fuss the voice is asking about, so I touch his arm and motion that I've got it.

"Yes," I yell up toward the light. "That was Jovan and me. We barely got away, as you probably already know if you're asking about it."

To my surprise, a laugh comes down at us from the speaker above, harsh but friendly. "Yeah, we heard. If you're wondering about the guy chasing you, they kept him for a while, but let him go for some reason. He must have some pull. They usually aren't so accommodating there. Someone from the Crossing will come and sell us the news later this morning and we'll get the whole story then."

There's a warning in those words that I take to heart. It means that our story had better match, or at least mesh, with the story they'll get from the town. I decide to take up the gauntlet the voice just tossed down.

"Good! Then you'll have no reason to doubt us. Just to be clear, I'll tell you what I can," I say and give Jovan a look. His lips press into a line, but he gives me a tiny nod so I continue. "The man chasing us is named Creedy and he works for Jovan's father. He's telling people we kidnapped him, but that isn't so. Jovan is standing right here and he can confirm what I say."

I motion for Jovan to speak up and he yells, "I'm here willingly. I'm a Striker."

He looks a little pale at those words, like it's just now hit him that he is, in fact, a real Striker. Not a young cadet out on a lark, or a student on a camping trip or even a friend helping another friend. A Striker. Even without a single tattoo on his neck for any crime, he's officially an escapee. A defector.

I touch his shoulder, wanting to comfort him if I can, because he needs it even if he doesn't know it. He tilts his head down, like he's about to brush my hand with his cheek, but stops himself and just gives me a sad smile instead.

"I'm okay," he whispers.

The others are watching us from a few steps away. Cassi's the only one who seems to grasp what Jovan's going through and it almost looks like she might cry. I nudge Jovan and he gives her a wink and a smile that brings the brightness back to her face.

"That's it?" asks the voice.

"Oh, no. Sorry. But if he's been released and he's coming this way, won't your loudspeaker simply advertise where we are?" asks Jovan.

There's no response aside from a faint rhythmic pattern of clinging metal somewhere behind the wall I take for footsteps on metal stairs. I look around but see no door or opening in the wall. I'd be surprised to find such, considering this is a wall meant to keep people out and a door would just be an invitation.

There's the sound of sliding metal and an ear-piercing squeal, then a small square opens up in the wall above us, maybe twenty feet from the ground. The metal of the square is ridiculously thick and there must be something mechanical taking the weight of it. No person, no matter how strong, could possibly dislodge it.

Once it swings away, a bearded man pokes his head out of the opening and smiles at us, looking from one to the next. He puts a radio to his mouth and says something I can't hear but the searchlight goes out above us. I hadn't realized how much strain it was to look up with that light shining down, but with it gone it suddenly seems dark again. The dawn is well underway and there's plenty of light; it merely seems dark in comparison.

"Hey," the man says. "I'm Rev. To answer your question, my partner just called in to the Logan's Crossing gate again, and they say he appears to have walked out of town the way he came. Doesn't mean he won't come back. We'll know in a few hours."

Jovan looks each way, sighting along the wall now that the light is improving, then frowns. "Where's the closest gate?"

We all look up hopefully at that. I want him to say it's close by and not the one we just passed, the one in the direction of Creedy.

Rev grimaces a little, so I know the answer before he speaks. "You passed it about five miles back; Logan's Crossing. The next one is about fifteen miles south, at the next major crossing. I don't suppose you want to go back to Logan's, do you?"

Maddix laughs bitterly and says, "That would be a big no."

Rev nods toward the trees and the river beyond and asks, "I don't suppose that boat was bought, either."

Maddix looks down and away like he's embarrassed. But he answers honestly. "No. We didn't have a lot of choices."

"Can you give us a second?" I ask, breaking in.

Rev waves an invitation, a knowing grin on his face at our discomfort.

"I know we can get to the next gate much more quickly in the boat. I know that also decreases the chances of Creedy catching up with us. I get that," I say, prepared to need to do some convincing.

"But if we have a stolen boat, probably one someone relies on for their living or getting food, then what does that say about us," Jovan finishes for me.

"Exactly," I confirm.

We're all silent a moment, either thinking it over or waiting for the others to think it over. I'm not sure which. I know what my vote will be. I don't want to take any chances they won't let us in. I have a half-brother to meet and a life to begin.

"I say we don't take the boat," Cassi declares.

"We've already stolen it. I say we keep it until the gate. Then we can turn it over," Maddix says. This surprises me because he was the one urging caution before. Has he decided that getting into the gate with Connor— now that he's confirmed with this sentry that he's still a citizen—is more important than ruining the chances of those who don't have such a confirmation?

Connor seems torn, chewing his lip. He probably doesn't want to disagree with the brother he just got back but I know him. He's genuinely honest and probably felt bad about stealing the boat in the first place. He meets my eyes for a moment and I do my best to convey that he should vote no.

Jovan doesn't wait for his answer and says, "I vote we figure out a way to return it." At the understandably alarmed looks he gets from all of us, he holds up his hands and says, "If we can figure out how to do it, that is."

That settles everyone down. Maddix nudges Connor and he gives his answer, carefully avoiding any eye contact with me or Cassi, when he says, "I say we keep it. We have the right to go through already. We need to get through before anything else can happen."

To say I'm disappointed would be an understatement. Jovan and Cassi have no guarantees. And this leaves us in the precarious position of needing to distance ourselves from Maddix and Connor if they won't accept the way the majority vote goes. Especially since I'm the final vote and they must know what I'll choose.

"I vote we don't keep it. In fact, I think we can earn some points here. Maddix, you still have the silver that Jovan gave you, right?"

He nods, but looks like he'd rather I not remember that.

"Well, I think we should bring the boat up more safely on the bank and give some silver to this guy to be passed to whoever comes to get it and ask if they'll contact Logan's Crossing so the owner can come and get it. It doesn't erase the theft, but it does ameliorate it some."

I know I'm trying to sell this idea a little too hard, but I really don't want to have to separate from Connor. Or Maddix for that matter.

When we were little, he teased us for being pests and generally behaved as any other annoying older brother of a friend, but he was also kind. And he came back for Connor. Even knowing what might happen, he came back and he brought my father with him. I owe him for that.

After a long, tense moment during which I half expect Maddix to take off for the woods and the boat beyond, he lets out a sigh and says, "Fine. I still say it's a risk but if that's what we're doing, let's do it and get moving." He digs in his pocket a moment and holds out a handful of coins toward Jovan.

Rev has been watching us from above, that same smirk on his face the whole time. I can only guess that he knows exactly what we're doing and why. His eyes shift at the clinking of the silver and the smirk turns into a smile. It's a genuine one so I know we made the right decision.

"We did take the boat and we didn't pay for it," Jovan says.

His cheeks are a little flushed and I could swear I see shame there, even though he had nothing to do with the theft. That he's using the inclusive "we" as he speaks gives me a warm feeling. Before I even have a chance to think about it, I reach out the few inches between us and give his hand a squeeze, then let it go just as quickly.

He clears his throat and gives me a sidelong glance before continuing. "We felt we were in a bad position and that seemed like the only option at the time, but it was still wrong and we'd like to return it."

I hear Maddix whisper something about laying it on thick but ignore him.

Rev scrubs a hand across his beard and says, "But you figure it probably isn't safe to go bring it back if it isn't safe enough to go to the gate back there. Am I close?"

Looking up at him, I wonder exactly how many times Rev has had conversations like this. Perhaps not exactly, but at least in general. How many Strikers made it this far? How many people from the Riverlands or wild lands have come here, wanting a better life beyond the wall?

"Sir...Rev, we have silver and would like to ask if you'd let the gate, and the town, know that the boat is here and perhaps pass the silver to them for us?" Jovan asks, holding out the silver in his palm.

Perhaps Jovan is laying it on just a little thick, but I can't think of a better way to ask the favor, and he sounds sincere. He is sincere. I'm not sure Rev believes him, though, because his smile has taken on a decidedly skeptical look and his eyebrows have crept up.

"We're serious. Jovan is just *really* polite," I call out.

That makes him laugh and he says, "Well, then, I suggest someone else do the talking until that wears off of him a little. Too much politeness just makes folks suspicious." His hand goes across his beard again, considering us, then he holds up a finger for us to wait and disappears.

He's only gone for a few seconds and when he comes back, he lowers a basket. Inside is a little cloth bag that Jovan takes out without hesitation, slipping his little pile of coins inside. It seems too much. It's Jovan's, but realistically, it's all we have. What if there are bribes later on at the next gate or worse, suppose Rev doesn't pass it anywhere except into his own pocket.

I hold my hand over Jovan's to stop him and ask Rev, "How much is the right amount?"

He grins that knowing grin again. This guy reads me too well. "Getting a ride across costs a tenth. You took it a whole lot farther, and without permission. There's a lost catch to consider as well. All told, you could get away with a quarter but if you want a whole lot fewer hard feelings, I'd leave a half ounce. It seems you have more than enough for that," he says, nodding at the shiny pile.

We do have that and more. Actually, Jovan has as much as I've seen in my entire life just hanging around in his pockets. Still, it's such a precious amount that it hurts. A quick look at the others tells me I'm not alone. Except Jovan, who is still standing there, ready to keep pouring.

Once the basket is back up and we're a whole lot poorer, Rev says, "The owner will get it along with their boat."

He directs his words to me and gives me a solemn nod, sensing, I suppose, my inherent skepticism. But I believe him and I'm glad the boat will be returned.

"You best get going if you're going to make it today. I'll pass word that you'll be coming and that you're walking on this side, near the wall. Typically, we discourage that but you look harmless enough."

The crossbow I can clearly see now that the light is good, plus the rifle in the hands of the man still peering at us from the top of the wall, give me a clue as to how they discourage people. I'm glad we won't get that kind of discouragement.

There's not much more to say but it feels awkward to just turn and leave. Rev makes it easy by saying, "If we hear anything about that fellow following you, I'll pass it along the sentries along the wall. You just keep moving."

Then Rev and the little opening are gone, the thick metal slamming home with a loud bang you could probably hear for a mile. That sets us in motion quick enough. I've got no pack and there are just the few bags from the boat to carry, so I'm left without a burden. I wish I had something to carry to keep my hands busy. Before, I could hook my hands into the straps of my backpack and feel occupied, but now they hang free and I'm keenly aware that Jovan's hands are swinging right next to mine.

It would be a simple matter to occupy at least one of my hands by holding one of his while we walked. That would be good. But I can't seem to bring myself to test and see what he would do if I did just grab his hand. In front of the others, I feel exposed for just thinking it.

Instead, I speed up and tap Cassi's shoulder so she'll walk with me. As we chat and walk, talking about what it might be like on the other side and whether or not they'll really let me sponsor her, I'm constantly aware that Jovan is right behind me. For most of the time, I'm convinced he's looking at me, his eyes burning along my back.

Eventually, I feel a tug on my hair and turn to glare at him. He just smiles and holds up a little twig. It must have been in there since the river and that was what was drawing his attention. I'm a little disappointed but I turn around and keep walking.

Cassi digs into her pocket and hands me a wide-toothed comb, the only kind she can use on her curly hair. With my hands free for the first time in ages, I feel a strong desire to keep them busy. I find some relief over the next hour by patiently combing out the tangles while we walk.

But I can't just comb my hair forever while I'm trying to escape with my life. Eventually, it's once again a smooth curtain down my back and I can't find a single knot to mess with. And as a bonus, it's no longer quite so greasy after my long swim in the river.

After I hand Cassi back her comb, she reaches out and runs some of my hair through her fingers. She sighs and says, "I always wanted long hair like yours. Straight."

I laugh because it's such a ridiculous thing to say. Cassi is as close to perfect as a human can be. But we always want something different than we're born with, even if what we're born with is perfect the way it is.

Whether it's because we're on the final leg of our journey and safety is mere miles ahead of us or because the weather is fine, I feel hopeful. That free feeling from before is creeping up on me again and I wonder what it's like on the other side of this giant wall we walk along. The sentries above seem to be spaced fairly widely, because it's late morning before we see the next ones popping their heads over the top and whistling to get our attention.

"Any news?" Jovan calls up. There's hope in his voice, too.

"Nothing good. We just got a call about an hour ago that the man you described came back out of the woods and into town. They wouldn't rent him a boat or take him as passenger so he's walking south, downstream."

"Did he have a horse?" I ask.

The man shakes his head and says, "No. One of the ferry guys came over to give us the news and he said someone took off with his horses."

"Well, it isn't all bad news, then," Cassi calls up, a brilliant smile on her face.

The man was already looking her way with interest. Now he looks like someone whacked him on the head hard enough that he lost some of his sense. It's almost comical, but I've seen it enough in the past. She doesn't seem to notice it at all and just keeps smiling, not understanding that some smiles aren't just smiles.

"Anything else?" Jovan asks, his expression just a little less open and a little harder. He feels protective of Cassi and this is putting up his hackles. I give his arm a little squeeze and he pulls in a tight breath, pushing it out like I do when I want to get rid of stress or irritation.

His words seem to shake the sentry out of whatever Cassi-induced fog he was in and he gives us a rueful smile, perhaps aware how we might take his stares. He says, "He's walking and you've got hours on him, but he is walking. You're still about nine miles and change from the gate so I'd get a move on."

With one last wave, he backs out of sight and we move on. It's not a leisurely stroll and hasn't been, but we haven't been pushing it like we should have. That changes and I hear Maddix give a little groan as the strain of the uneven ground takes its toll on his still damaged thigh muscle. He's a fighter though and he gets through it, using the balls of his thumbs to dig in and loosen the muscles.

I'm not particularly worried that he'll be able to catch up with us on his own. Creedy is a lot older than we are and I saw his paunchy belly and the cowboy boots on his feet. He was dressed for the comfort of horseback, not the rigors of walking.

But that doesn't mean he won't find a way to get a ride on a boat or barge. He must have plenty of silver. He may have angered the town in the dead of night, and they may have turned him away in the presence of others, but once away from judging eyes, his silver might be too much to resist. That thought spurs me to move a little faster and the others do as well. It's not a huge leap to consider that happening, so I'm guessing everyone else had the same thought.

The hours pass quietly enough, nothing but the sound of the river and the occasional quick exchange of words from another sentry to break the constant rhythm of our footsteps. By late afternoon, we risk a trip past the trees to the riverbank to see what we can see. The last sentry told us we were just a few miles from the gate, and we've seen the billowing sails of boats peeking through the foliage more often over the last few hours.

At the far edge of our vision is one of the most awe-inspiring sights I have ever seen. I can't even imagine how huge the bridge that must have once stood there was. On each side of the river the supports for the bridge rise so high that even the wall we've been walking along seems dwarfed. In the center, another support stands even taller in the water like a giant, intent on guarding the river from all comers. Whatever small parts of the bridge remain attached poke out from the sides like short arms.

There's no real indication of a town at this distance, but small dots in the water must be boats with their sails up to catch the ever-present breeze along the river. It's a walk of less than two hours to get there. We exchange smiles and a few breathless words but that's all any of us wants to waste time on. I can see it in the eager lines of their bodies, the way they're half-turned toward the trees. They're ready to go and get this last bit of distance behind us.

By the time I can just make out the dark swath that marks a gated section of wall, a sentry peers over the side and whistles for us. He drops a coil of tightly rolled paper weighted with a pebble down to us. We gather to unroll it and find a short note, neatly printed in well-schooled handwriting, letting us know that the coast is clear to the gate.

It's like the best present I've ever received and I can't help but reach out and grab Connor and Cassi, the two next to me, around the shoulders in an exuberant hug. It's catching because soon we're all doing it, grinning like loons and slapping each other on the backs. The laugh of the sentry above us breaks us up, but he gives us a thumbs-up and that makes it alright.

Chapter Thirty-Three

At the gate we don't waste time gawping at the amazing town sprawled across the river, though it's tempting. Instead, we follow the posted directions and push a button and then back up behind the yellow line painted on the pavement.

A whir of noise draws my attention to a little box with a tiny red light on it that moves across the line of us like it's watching us. The glass lens on the front does remind me of the camera we rented once a long time ago, so I assume that must be what it is.

After an endless moment, a small door opens and I see from the edge of it that it is thicker even than the metal hatch the sentry opened for us this morning. Several inches thick and made of dark metal, it's inset into a human-sized door, which is further inset into a gate big enough to pass a prairie jumper through. The interior side of it, from the quick look I get, seems banded with yet more metal. These people are very serious about their wall.

I had hoped, perhaps stupidly, that one of the sentries we talked to might be the one that met us at the gate. It's completely unreasonable, given that they have stations that they man and the gate is miles away from most of them, but I can't help feeling fearful of having to explain again.

The man who looks us over with a guarded expression is older than the sentries, his dark hair graying at the sides, but he's clean-shaven and his hair is combed with precision. It all screams "official" to me. That's probably a good thing.

He stays inside the gate, his head framed by the two-foot-square opening, and takes in our dirty clothes and weary faces. He's probably seen it plenty of times.

"You're the kids from Logan's Crossing," he says and it isn't a question, but I nod and so do the others.

He purses his lips as he looks us over once more, like he smells something bad emanating from us—which is entirely possible—then glances down to something I can't see and studies it a moment.

When his attention returns to us, he looks directly at Maddix, then shifts between Jovan and Connor, finally settling on Connor. He says, "Maddix Blake. And that's the minor brother you want to sponsor?"

"Yes," Maddix says, and the relief is palpable coming off him. "He's seventeen."

"Scooting under the wire then. You come forward first and then we'll get him," he instructs and holds up a small, odd-shaped box out of the opening.

Maddix walks forward and doesn't seem at all nervous. In fact, he looks like he's familiar with what's going on. When the man turns the box, I see a curved protrusion on it and Maddix presses his face to it without any prompting. It beeps after a few seconds and the man takes it down, peeks at the back of it and then smiles at Maddix, like he passed some sort of test.

"Yep, you're you. Welcome back to the Southeast and Mississippi Territory," he says with a smile. I guess he did pass a test, though I can't imagine what test requires a person to put their face up to a box.

He holds out another flat and shiny black surface, no thicker than a roof shingle, and it lights up. I can't see what it's doing other than emitting a vague blue light, but Maddix sticks his hand on it, fingers splayed just so, and it beeps as well.

That seems to settle the matter for the man, because he opens the larger, man-sized door and pushes out a cart, the top of it covered with neatly arranged objects. He's dressed rather oddly, in a way I imagined wealthy people dressed only inside their homes. His bright green shirt has something embroidered above the left breast pocket and his khaki pants are very neatly pressed. There's not a stain anywhere and even his shoes are clean and new-looking.

He's slender, too, but very fit. It's odd, how new and perfect he looks to be so old. People tend to look worn with age in Texas, but this guy looks like he's spent his whole life indoors or something. Kind of unused looking. It's a bit unsettling and it makes me aware of how dirty I am, even after my long dip in the river.

"Let's get your brother first, shall we?" he asks, his tone friendly but officious, sort of like the school administrator when I go register each year.

The man hands Maddix another of those shiny black shingle-looking things and he studies it, tapping the surface every now and then while he does. Connor gets the box to his face, then his hand on a shingle, but it doesn't stop there. The man scrubs the inside of Connor's cheek with a small brush, pricks his finger and all sorts of other things that look altogether frightening.

I try to move closer, so I can hear the quiet instructions the man gives to Connor, but he gives me a look and waves me backward. "No cross-contamination," he says by way of explanation.

When Maddix is done with his part, he puts the shingle on the cart and jogs over to talk to us. There's no way he can miss the confusion on our faces.

"Okay, I know this looks weird, but remember how we talked about your pendant being coded to you, your DNA only?" he asks, pointing to my necklace.

I nod, no wiser.

"They get your DNA from your cheek and a second sample from your blood. That thing they held up to my eyes? That's a retina scanner and it's a quick way of confirming who you are if they have it on record. Same with the fingerprints on that tablet," he explains.

Since Maddix got sponsored by my father and is a citizen, I assume that is why he's on record. And that would mean that Connor is getting his record done right now. Which means we're next.

When Connor gets finished and he sucks on the finger the man jabbed, he looks a little stunned. All those gadgets and all that touching by a stranger must have been unsettling, but he smiles so I guess he's alright.

The man puts all that he used for Connor into a clear bag and seals it carefully, then drops it into a red box on the lower shelf of the cart. He waves us over and performs the same series of tests for Jovan, Cassi and me. It tickles when he rubs the little bristled brush on the inside of my cheek and I can't help but wrinkle my nose. He gives me a little smile when I do and I feel better.

When he's done he directs his next words only to Maddix. "You're clear, but you know the drill. You have to go directly to the clinic in town and get checked. Your brother will need the same two days as the others to have his identity verified, so he'll have to come back once that's done."

The alarm in Maddix's face is real and his voice is a little higher when he asks, "How can he be verified if he's never been here? I didn't have to be verified before Jordan brought me in."

"That was different. You were a Striker seeking sanctuary, and you had a sponsor who would vouch for you. A sponsor who had the means to cover a vouching should you run amok inside the wall. You're sponsoring this boy as a brother. His DNA needs to be tested against yours to confirm a familial relationship," the man answers, quite reasonably.

Now that I'm closer, I can read the letters stitched into his shirt. They read Immigration Enforcement and below is his name, Gary Walder. I may not know much about the Southeast, but I know what the words immigration and enforcement mean and they don't mean that he belongs to the welcoming committee.

"Do you mean that the four of us will need to wait two days to go in?" Jovan asks, trying to clarify the situation because he's just as confused as I am.

"I thought we were going to be good to go. I mean, I have this," I say, holding up the pendant.

Gary's face clears as he realizes our situation. He says, "You are registered, but I have no way of knowing that you are you. Your sample will be tested against the one registered to you and if it matches, you're welcome to come right in. We've got your retina scans and your fingerprints now, so in two days, when the results of your DNA test show up in my system, you'll be able to come in just the same way I cleared your friend here."

"Two days," I whisper. I'm not alone in my unhappiness with this new situation. The idea of having to run, hide and then somehow get back to this gate, or another gate, after two days staying ahead of Creedy is enough to make me nauseous. It's like my organs shift inside me and I wasn't prepared for it.

I've been able to ignore my hunger because I thought it would soon be over, that food was just a wall away. Likewise, I've been able to push back the soreness of my body, the tenderness of my many bruises and the nagging sting of chafed and reddened skin. All of it was tolerable only because I could feel an end to it just around the corner. With that hope gone, my body suddenly feels like a loosely filled bag of bones incorrectly assembled.

Pushing that aside, I force myself to think. Perhaps there is a way to make this less painful for at least one of us.

"Can't Maddix just sponsor Connor the same way that my father sponsored him?" I ask.

"He could," he says and addresses Maddix. "If you have the funds to commit to it. But you'll need to sign a bond and set aside the right amount of funds. Do you have that?"

"I have no idea," Maddix answers wearily.

"What about sanctuary? You said you have that?" Connor asks.

"We do. Minors with three strikes or in imminent danger are automatically granted sanctuary inside while we do all the rest. Just to keep them from harm, you see."

Holding out his hands to the side, Maddix says, "We've got those conditions up to our necks."

Gary looks sympathetic, but professionally so, like he's heard this story a hundred times. He probably *has* heard it a hundred times, if not more. "The rules are very clear and I see no imminent danger coming up on us."

At our expressions, which are pretty lost and hopeless if how I feel is at all reflected on my face, he softens a little and says, "Try to think about it from our perspective. Things look peaceful, but it wasn't always that way. People have come to claim sanctuary who have been deliberately infected with contagious diseases. Others were dangerous criminals—and I'm not talking about the petty stuff you get strikes for—who hurt or killed our people after claiming sanctuary. Our rules are there for a reason and learned through hard experience."

When he finishes speaking, he meets the eyes of each of us in turn, his sincerity evident and believable. As much as I would like to be able to punch a few holes in what he said, I can't. If it were me, I'd do the same.

Whatever there might be on the other side of that wall, it's clearly worth protecting. Even from us. I can see the near future unfolding before me right now and it isn't the safety of walking through that gate.

My immediate future is two more days of keeping my head down and my feet moving and then hoping I do get confirmed as the person my father registered to this pendant. But I can help Maddix and Connor.

"I have funds. How much is a bond?" I ask.

Gary eyes me like I've surprised him but answers. "If they stay in the Gate Town at the quarantine facility and agree to curfew and restrictions on their movement, then it will be a hundred silver ounces. You'll get it back if they stay out of trouble till he's medically cleared."

My face falls and my mouth drops open at the amount. That's more money than I can imagine. It's enough to buy a stake in a salvage run, several head of prime cattle or even a windmill capable of powering enough lights to keep a bulb in every room. There's no way so much is on my pendant. Even Jovan looks shocked and he was carrying more than I've ever seen in his pockets. Maddix looks like he just got gut-punched, hard.

"I've got maybe twenty on my chip," he says in a hoarse voice.

I hold out my pendant and say, "Can you check to see if I have that?"

I place my necklace in his hand, trying not to look reluctant, and he eyes my pendant as well as Jordan's. "My condolences on your loss," he says softly. I guess he heard our story when the sentries passed on our information, but it feels strange to hear him say it. He's a stranger to me and, I assume, to my father.

He picks up yet another mysterious implement from the cart and waves the pendants across the surface, eyeing the readout after each pass. When he turns back to me, he places the jewelry with extra care into my palm, folding my fingers around them securely.

He glances to the side and then leads me a few steps away from the others. He leans uncomfortably close to my ear and whispers, "You have over nine thousand, nine hundred ounces on yours and your father has a little over two hundred."

All I can think is that I've heard him wrong. Almost ten thousand ounces? That's enough to buy ninety acres of prime grazing land, the kind that has water on it year-round from a sweet water spring deep in the earth. It's a fortune. And it's on a necklace?

"That's not possible," I gasp.

"It would have to be verified, but the last date on there is pretty recent. The bank it's attached to, GeneBank, has an office here. You'll be able to get it verified pretty easily," he says and pats my shoulder in a kindly way.

I'm guessing that this is rather the opposite situation than they usually have. I imagine most people get here destitute and without anything of value to their name. And here I am with an unimaginable fortune.

He lets me catch my breath and just try to absorb it for a moment while the others look on, worried looks shooting my way. They must think I don't have enough. Rather than let them worry further, I tug my shirt down and straighten my shoulders. Smoothing the shock off my face is a little harder, but I think I do a passable job of it.

"Maddix, I can put up the bond for Connor if you like," I say.

They both smile and thank me and the business is over with another swipe of the pendant and a quick press of my thumb to the tablet. They're dirty and tired, but life comes back to them at the thought of getting inside. Connor almost glows with excitement and it makes the dark circles under his eyes and the gauntness under his cheeks less noticeable.

They take only one of the empty bags with them aside from what they're wearing. Maddix has a gun and one of the utility belts but he doesn't take any of the boxes of ammunition, leaving it for us.

And then they are gone, through the door and out of sight. It feels strange to be separated. We've been together for weeks, constantly so, and that forges bonds even closer than family in some ways. Nursing someone through a bullet wound, running for your lives step for step and huddling together for warmth creates something different from friendship, different from family. It creates something essential between people.

I wave at the doorway, but they don't see it. Neither of them turns back. Gary is ordering his mysterious devices on his cart in preparation to follow them through. Jovan and Cassi aren't doing anything except looking at me, at Gary and at the door in a sort of helpless shock. They look like I feel.

Gary finishes and puts his hands to the cart's push bar, ready to wheel it inside but he doesn't. Instead, he sighs and looks down with a little shake of his head. He extracts a small pad of paper from his pocket, scribbles something on a page, then whips the page off the pad and holds it out for one of us to take.

Jovan steps up to take it, glances at it and asks, "Where?"

"Listen, I've read the sentry reports and if it were up to me, I'd put you in a sanctuary cell right now. But it's not up to me. That doesn't mean I can't help you as much as I'm able to without doing that. Go to the ferry landing, go across to Willton, hire a barge or boat or whatever else you can and keep going south," he says.

When I open my mouth to ask questions, he holds up a hand to stop me and says, "I need to get back inside, so just listen. Give the note to whoever you decide to hire and it will help convince them. I'll send a warning across about this Creedy fellow and that'll keep him from easily getting a ride. He'll get one eventually, but it won't be easy. Your best bet is a barge going down the Mississippi to the port at the Gulf. They go quickly, making stops to load and unload and there are far too many of them to keep track of. Another hundred miles or so and the gates get more common, every five miles or so, and almost everyone has a trade town across from it. Every gate will have your data the moment it is ready."

He starts to push the cart toward the gate, then stops and looks back over his shoulder. He seems to think for a second, then waves me over and asks, "Do you have any money left?"

Without thinking, I clasp the pendant around my neck, confused.

"No, I mean spending money. For the trip?"

I think back to the few coppers and the tiny tenths of silver and wonder how much boat rides for fugitives cost. "I don't think enough, if you want the truth," I confess.

He holds up a finger, dashes back in the gate and then appears once again, holding yet another unfathomable gizmo and a small metal box. He motions for me to lean forward with the pendant and dangles it near the glossy black surface. It lights up with words and images like I've never seen before, beautiful and crisp, yet artful. I want to touch it so I curl my fingers at my sides to stop myself.

Gary seems to be counting, his head leaning just a little to one side and then shifting to the other, his eyes blinking like he's added something with each movement. When he seems satisfied, he pushes the screen and then holds it for my inspection. "I think four should be enough, even if you're delayed. Do you agree?" he asks.

I have no idea how much he's even talking about, let alone what all this is going to cost, but I nod like that makes perfect sense to me and press my thumb to the spot he indicates. It beeps and glows green and that's apparently a good thing, because he sets it down and opens the box, plucking up small bundles with quick hands.

"We aren't a bank branch, but we do small transactions all the time. Don't worry," he says, dropping the paper-wrapped rolls of coins into my palm. "But if you turn out not to be you, best watch out if you show up at another gate."

He finishes by dropping two half-ounce coins with the rolls. They make a delightful sound when they clink together and I can't help but smile.

With that, he pushes his cart inside the door. While I'm still trying to sort out what he said, Jovan starts gathering the few remaining bags we have and hands one off to Cassi. As they pass, he tugs my arm and says, "Let's go, Karas."

Once we hit the trail, I stop him to divide up the coins. I don't feel comfortable carrying them all, given that I've already lost everything I own once. I'd rather not have all our eggs in one basket, so to speak. But I do feel better about not being the one who has to rely on everyone else to pay my way anymore. It's a good feeling and I think of Jordan, thanking him in my thoughts yet again.

The moment we start walking again, the mood reverts right back to serious. Jovan's brow is furrowed and his lips set, but not like he's worried, more like intent on getting a job done. It's a relief because I'm still a little shell-shocked from the combination of finding out I have a fortune and realizing that we're still going to be on the run for another couple of days. My hands are empty and fidgety as I follow along, so I jam them into my pockets.

When I catch up to the others, Jovan says, "There are plenty of barges going past. I saw three while we were at the gate, but they might be on some kind of schedule, so we want to get there and get one. The last thing we need is to wait for hours or have to walk again."

His eyes are in constant motion, scanning the banks as they come into view, looking at and for boats, I suppose. There's a flat-topped barge berthed at a wide set of piers, a group of people unloading bags, boxes and baskets from it in quick, practiced moves, tossing each container from one hand to the next till each reaches the end of the pier and the piles there. It looks almost fully unloaded and we head in that direction, following Jovan.

Wary at first, probably because of our dirty clothes and overall ragged appearance, they grow friendly enough when Jovan starts haggling for the cost of passage across to Willton. For the price of a silver tenth ounce—plus our assistance loading up the return cargo—he secures us a ride.

As soon as the barge bumps up against the pier on the other side of the river, Jovan is off the deck and heading toward the larger piers the barge workers suggested. After an offer to help unload, which the barge workers politely decline, Cassi and I head the other direction, toward the smaller vessels often let for hire.

The entire area is a confusing mass of colors, sounds and scents. Talking, bickering and haggling rises above the clanking of the boats and gear. Boats of every shape and size are clustered up to three deep at the piers, the outer ones tied to the inner boats. Awnings are spread or draped everywhere. It makes the colors even more riotous and I can barely tell where one boat ends and another begins. I feel like my eyes don't know where to stop and I'm almost dizzy from the experience.

A deep breath brings no relief. The smells of food cooking over smoky braziers and grills fight with the dank and fertile smell of the river bank. Over it all, the smell of decades of fish catches have soaked into the worn boards of the piers, leaving the smell of spoiled fish.

I suspect that Jovan thought sending us to the small boats would be the easier task, but a few vessels, no matter how large and intimidating, can be nothing compared to this. I think I love it, though I know it terrifies me.

Cassi smiles at everyone as we pass, garnering appreciative looks. I hope she can keep it up long enough for us to find a boat and then charm whoever owns it. It's a mercenary thought, but she has the magic. Who am I to turn down the help, no matter how it comes about? She's charming and that's a good thing at the moment, since I'm not and never have been. For my part, I have to work just to keep a scowl off my face around strangers.

The piers extend from a long walkway made of boards weathered to gray. It's wide enough for carts and people to cross easily and bordered by a row of equally weathered shops, tightly packed together on the other side. The only gaps between them are too narrow to navigate save by a child, except where the street leading into town joins it at the head of the pier. That street is backed up with wagons, people pushing carts and bicycles loaded down with goods meant for the boats. People on foot, either workers or passengers, weave through the fray and join the crowds here on the piers.

Cassi takes the lead, looking at the people like she'll see some clue as to who the right person to ask is in their smile or the cast of their eye when they see her. At the third of the piers jutting out into the water, she stops short and her lips part as she stares down the length of the pier. I catch up and look in the direction she's staring.

At the end of the pier is a boat that doesn't look any different to me from the dozens of others with one exception, and I think it is that exception that has drawn her eye. High on the mast is a young man. With just one arm and the pressure of his legs around the beam, he's pointing at something below. Then he uses his free arm to give one of the many lines dangling from the mast a hard yank.

As we watch, he deftly untangles himself from the mast and grabs one of the lines, hooking a foot into it and lowering himself back to the deck. Cassi grabs my hand and I see from the corner of my eye that she's mesmerized.

He's definitely something to see. Shirtless, his skin tanned from the sun and hard from work, he's got the additional draw of a head of dark curls. And the way he moves so lithely down the rope *is* pretty spectacular.

"Pirates," Cassi breathes.

I can't help but laugh. "More like fishermen," I say and nudge her with my elbow.

She shakes her head and smiles, a little embarrassed. "Sure, but still. He looks like a pirate, doesn't he?"

Since I have no idea what a pirate looks like and doubt very much that anyone who steals for a living could just park his boat around everyone else, I have my doubts. But Cassi is who she is and she's the girl who has listened to Connor read her far too many books with pirates in them.

I give her a wink and ask, "So, I guess that means we ask him, then?"

Chapter Thirty-Four

His name is Marcus Flint and I will, at some point, have to admit that Cassi has excellent taste. That will have to wait until after she and Marcus have stopped staring at each other for more than a minute, and I don't see that happening anytime soon.

I'm actually relieved that Connor and Maddix aren't with us now. It would hurt Connor to see them. This, or something like it, was bound to happen at some point, but that wouldn't make it any less hard. Jovan doesn't look pleased either. The way he keeps eyeing Marcus with a sour look on his face reminds me of an older brother not very keen on a little sister's choice of boyfriend.

I have to say, there's a certain something about the way Marcus moves, so sure and efficient, or maybe it's the way his body seems to obey him in a way I've never seen before, that draws the eye. He also looks different.

In Bailar, the classification of good-looking is fairly straightforward. A straight nose with a bridge that isn't too deep or too protruding, nice teeth and a good smile are the traits that will get such a label. Pretty eyes help, too. Basically, guys like Jovan.

Marcus is almost the opposite but in a really good way. His hair is almost black and flops about in loose curls, but not in a girlish way. His nose swoops down deeply underneath a strong brow, but once again, it's perfect. His eyes are large and deep brown, the lashes so thick I'm envious. But his smile is what seals the bargain. His lips are wide and his teeth brilliant. He's everything that shouldn't be good-looking put together in such a way that it's almost too handsome.

That might explain some of Jovan's displeasure and why he sat so close to me on the bench attached to the side of the boat when we first came aboard. Or maybe it's the fallout from that stupid kiss.

Whatever is going on between us, I feel like it's starting to come out into the open. Like one of us is going to say or do something that will make it hard to pretend it's not happening.

He'll just have to get over his protective feelings, or else Marcus and Cassi will get over their mutual admiration. Either way will work, but somehow, I don't think they will be the ones who do the adjusting.

Marcus's boat is big and it makes me feel secure. Below decks are two cabins with a larger one between them. The big room is sort of like a kitchen and living room, but much more compact. Underneath the rear part of the boat, which Marcus informs me is the fantail but is also just called the deck in general, is a hold where he puts fish. It smells of years of fish, but it looks perfectly clean and I've seen how careful Marcus is with his boat.

For over a day we've been sailing, allowing the current of the big river, which is slowly and steadily growing wider, to add to our speed. It's liberating to be away from land, to glide past it and see it fall away behind us. I can't help but feel a small sense of victory when we sail effortlessly past areas we would have struggled to cross on foot, if it had even been possible to cross at all.

The banks of the river are changing, becoming flatter and wetter. Marcus tell us those are marshes and that soon enough, there will be more marsh than dry land and towns will be connected to the river by long piers or platforms on tall pylons. On the other side of the river, the wall has been a constant and comforting companion, the gates coming more frequently just as Gary told us they would.

But the wall is retreating further from the banks under the pressure of these watery areas and I feel a pang every time I see it curve away. There are piers, places where we could tie up and dash toward a gate in a run if we needed to, but it's not the same as knowing the gate is close enough to see.

So far, there's no sight of Creedy, but we wouldn't know where he is anyway now that we're on a boat unless he came very close. In my thoughts, he's never far behind. And I know I'm not alone in that because Jovan looks behind us, examining every sail, almost as much as I do. I have this nagging feeling that he's still chasing us.

The boat itself is a marvel and I can't help but enjoy it, thoughts of Creedy aside. I felt sick when I laid down to sleep for a little while yesterday, but by the time I woke, the feeling was gone and I was hungrier than I'd been in a long time. That evening, Marcus fed us freshly grilled fish and cold porridge.

I was wary of it after our fish jerky experience, but it was a surprisingly delightful combination. It turns out Maddix was right about the taste of fresh fish versus fish jerky. I wish I could tell him that and I keep my gloomy thoughts away by convincing myself we'll find each other.

It turns out that Marcus is more than just a fisherman working a boat. This is his boat, or rather, his family's. And they have more of them. This one is meant for some fishing, but also for bringing trade goods, including fish from the Gulf, up the river where they fetch a higher price.

When he said that they traded inside the Gulf, out on the actual ocean, I didn't really believe him. Everyone knows Texas can't access the sea because of the mines and that sea is the Gulf. Marcus pulled out a map and showed me my world in a way I've not seen before. A thin red line is drawn at a distance from the Texas coast and inside that line is where Marcus says the mines are. Beyond it is a vast ocean perfectly safe for travel. It hardly seems fair, but I'm not feeling particularly generous toward Texas at this moment.

Aside from a nagging feeling that Creedy is going to show up behind our boat at any second, this trip worries me for another reason. We are making too good a time, traveling too far. Maddix and Connor are far behind us and the distance grows each passing minute. Marcus only laughed when I asked about it, telling us with utter conviction that distances aren't the same inside the wall. We can travel by many means once inside and finding people who want to be found is as simple as placing a call.

I'm not entirely convinced of his assertions, but he shrugged it off, shaking his head at the backwardness of Texans. I'll confess that rankled a bit, being thought of as somehow more primitive. Yet, I have to admit that just what I've seen at the gate—Gary's cart of magical equipment—tells me he's right about us. We were living without a lot in Texas and I can't wrap my head around any possible reason for it.

*****

When I wake from my post-breakfast nap, I see the splayed form of Cassi on the deck, a smile on her face and her skin exposed to the sun. She's wearing nothing but a pair of shorts that she borrowed from Marcus and an undershirt. She's even hiked the legs of the shorts up so that they show her entire thighs. It makes me nervous, her showing that much skin with a near-stranger in plain view.

"You're going to burn," I say. She's too fair and too freckled for sunbathing and she knows it.

"Maybe," she says, a dreamy tone in her voice. Her words comes slow and lazy when she says, "But this feels too good not to enjoy. Can't you feel that breeze? It's like nothing I've ever felt before."

She sighs with pleasure and turns over, her cheek to the deck and her hair lifting all around her. I do feel it. It reminds me a little of the way it felt when I dangled my feet over the edge of the swimming platform at the lake. Moist but somehow light and difficult to explain or put into words. It's glorious.

Marcus is at the wheel, his eyes quick as he keeps everything moving together under the power of the wind and the current. He gives me a smile and I return it. His expressions are infectious and it would take a sterner person than I not to respond. His dark curls are tossing in the wind, but at least he's got a shirt on.

"Where's Jovan?" I ask, looking from Cassi to Marcus. Cassi shrugs but doesn't open her eyes. Marcus jerks his head behind him, so I carefully make my way along the short rail attached to the side of the boat—I'm still not that confident so close to the moving water—until I get to the open deck space behind the wheel.

Jovan is sitting on the deck, his arms wrapped loosely around his knees, gazing out at the wake behind us and into the river beyond. He's relaxed but still focused, like the worry we share over Creedy isn't enough to entirely overcome the lulling effects of sailing.

His hair has grown out a bit from its former cadet-worthy shortness, and that strange combination of gold shining out from the darker brown is on full display in the breeze and sunny day. It turns my throat dry and a flush crawls uncomfortably up my neck. Uncomfortable, but nice.

He turns to look my way, apparently sensing my presence, and gives me one of his amazing smiles. That's my cue to come forward, an invitation, but I feel hesitant. Since coming aboard, we've been dancing around each other, looking away when we pass each other in the tight confines of the cabins or on the deck, talking freely only when others are also talking.

There's something hanging over us and it wants to come out and be recognized. Maybe it's that impulsive kiss I pressed on him while we were in the water. Maybe it's just that the weeks of being together, relying so entirely on each other for safety and comfort, have brought back what we had before his father put an end to it.

Whatever it is, I can feel it coming and I think he does to.

The smile fades a little when I don't join him and he sighs, looking back at the water once more for a moment, checking for sails. He pats the deck next to him and says, "Help me keep watch so I don't fall asleep. This rocking wants to knock me out."

The way he says it, very casual and without any double meanings, smooths over the momentary weirdness. I'm grateful for it and sink to the deck next to him. I can't sit like him and keep any sense of modesty. Instead, I stretch my legs out in front of me so the sun will keep me warm.

I'm wearing a huge shirt, one meant for a very big man, and it comes halfway to my knees. My freshly washed jeans, along with everyone else's, are flapping on a line strung below the sails. Marcus has a veritable shop full of spare clothes below decks, but none of it is meant for girls so I had to make do with what I could find. It's not any shorter than a pair of shorts, but it feels like it is, especially with the wind licking at the hem.

I think it's worse because I'm not wearing my boots. Why having bare feet should make me feel naked is beyond me, but it does. Marcus says the boots are bad for his decks so they're off limits unless we see danger.

For a moment we don't say anything, just watch the water behind us. It is rather hypnotic, I have to admit. That initial awkwardness that settled between us like a physical thing fades under the calming spell of it. We both sort of relax, his arms going loose on his knees and mine moving behind my back to brace against the deck.

"One more day," I say. It's a safe topic for us to start on and I hope it leads to us being comfortable with each other again. Safe topics and no kissing is my current strategy.

He glances at me out of the corner of his eye very quickly, then looks back at the water. He seems worried, or perhaps just thoughtful about something, but I don't push. That would take me well off my safe topic agenda. Finally, he asks, "What will I do over there?"

Then he looks at me and I see that he is more than worried. If I had to guess, I would say that he's frightened, or at least intimidated. But I understand that. His life was laid out before him and it would have been a comfortable one.

A short career in the Army, then sharing in the responsibilities of his family's ranch, learning the ropes before eventually taking over. Marriage to a nice girl with a good pedigree, more than likely a daughter of one of the few other wealthy families. Possibly a marriage to someone from down south, a younger daughter from a city family with contacts that would increase the wealth of both families. Children would follow and the cycle would begin again.

That is what *was* waiting for him. Now, unless he lets himself be found by Creedy, he has nothing. No prospects. No money. Nothing to distinguish him from any other relatively bright and eager young man looking to make his mark.

"Do you want to go back with Creedy?" I ask.

He sighs and plucks at the edge of the thin drawstring pants he's wearing where the hems are frayed. A string unravels at his touch and he sighs again but stops worrying at it. "No, Karas. That's the hard part."

With one quick swivel, he turns to face me and crosses his legs, his hands tucking his feet tightly to him so that we can sit closer together. He leans forward a little, his eyes so earnest I feel my heart go out to him a little more. He says, "I know I should. There's nothing for me out here. I don't know how to fish or boat or farm or anything. Look at all this green!"

He waves a hand at the thick trees that border the river and the marshes where the trees pull back. I understand what he means, though. This is a world very different from our own, where knowing how to pluck water from the air with a few simple tools and salvaged parts is a skill worth knowing and cattle are the currency we trade in. I have no idea what I'll do here either. Maybe he needs to know that, to know he's not alone with that worry.

"None of us do," I say, but he cuts me off by holding up a hand.

"I'll figure out something—maybe I can use the little I learned in the military. No, I'm worried that it will never end. If I don't go back, will my family just keep sending people? Will they bribe their way past the wall and just ask till they find me? I wasn't worried until Marcus started talking about how easy it would be to find Connor and Maddix. Will I someday get tired of being the poor guy with no real skills, give in and come back?"

I hadn't actually considered that possibility. The idea of never knowing when some agent of the Foleys might come across us or show up at one of our doors is a disturbing one. And I also think he could be right. How long before there is a bounty too large to ignore for the return of Jovan to his family, before someone just takes him? Or, given his easy upbringing, how long until he lets himself be found just to end the struggle?

"Oh," I say, because there isn't much more to say.

"Yeah, my thoughts exactly."

"We've got one more day," I say, trying to sound upbeat and confident. "We'll think of something."

"We'd better think of something good. Otherwise, I don't know how I'm going to make it. Not with you guys close, anyway. I couldn't stand it if you got hurt in the process," he says and lays his hand on top of mine where it rests on the deck.

He must feel me tense at his touch, because he pulls away and that wall of awkward starts rebuilding itself between us. I wish I had the guts to just spill my feelings for him, tell him all that I want. But I don't. Instead I just say, "We will."

Chapter Thirty-Five

We while away our afternoon and evening learning about the world from Marcus. I'm surprised, even disbelieving, of a lot of it. I'm skeptical even though I'm aware that it's likely true. Or at least, I'm aware that what he says is probably true-ish.

I know about trains and trucks and vehicles. We have oil in Texas, but everyone knows that our inability to pull enough of it from the ground and then refine it limits what we can use. Still, there are plenty of gas-powered trucks where such are needed. Not in Bailar, but the kind that travel come there often enough.

The small truck where people sell their hair shows up twice a year. Likewise the bigger Commutation Day truck comes each year to remove strikes from the necks of those who have earned off their crimes through years of good citizenship. A dozen others make their rounds of Texas and they all use petroleum of one sort or another. Trains for cattle come during selling season and the tracks are kept in excellent repair by the soldiers.

But Marcus is telling us another story. Trains supposedly run on lines all over the Southeast and East lands, carrying passengers and all sorts of goods. Trucks and buses are as common as anything, he claims. And no one is disconnected from everything unless they choose it.

There's more, but I can only take in so much. It all seems like so much babble after a while, full of words I don't understand and concepts that seem impossible. Eventually, I'm reduced to nodding every once in a while and smiling when that seems the right thing to do.

Settling into bed in the tiny room Marcus assigned to us, Cassi gushes on for a bit about the world beyond the wall. The way she breathes the word "Southeast" is almost a sigh. A dreamy one full of wishes.

Our bed is tucked almost into the bow of the boat and narrower at the head than the foot. It puts us close to each other, our heads almost touching, and provides some extra warmth in the cool little room. It also means I must listen to Cassi blather on until she unspools enough to be quiet and maybe, just maybe, fall asleep.

She finally seems to notice that I'm quiet because she rolls over toward me, her face nothing more than a pale spot in the darkness. She asks, "You're not excited. Why not?"

I feel her finger touch my chin, and then she pinches it between her thumb and forefinger, just like her mother used to do to all the children, including me. It brings a lump to my throat, knowing that she's not likely to see them again, yet she's bringing a part of her mother along with her in that tiny habitual gesture.

I swallow it down and say, "I am. Just a little worried, too." I reach for my pendant and clasp it in one hand. I still haven't told either of them about the amount on my pendant. It's partly because it doesn't feel real and I don't trust that it isn't some sort of mistake, but also because it feels wrong to have it. I didn't earn it. How is getting this any different than people like the Foleys, who inherit not just money, but the power and influence to keep getting more until there is no hope for anyone else to earn a better place in life?

"Don't worry," she says and I can hear the smile in her voice.

"Go to sleep," I say, pulling the covers up a little higher, like she's a child that I need to tuck in instead of a full-grown woman.

She's quiet for a moment, her breathing steady and slow but definitely awake. Then out of the darkness, she whispers, "He's like a pirate, only better."

I laugh and roll over, leaving her to her dreams.

In the morning I find the world outside has changed yet again. The river has grown to a preposterous width and there are marshes on either side, wide and flat, covered by a carpet of hip high greenery and reeds. The wall has receded from those marshes and is reduced to a smudge in the distance. The air is warmer, almost languid feeling, and the sails waft in the half-hearted breeze, making flapping noises when the wind dies and then returns again.

Marcus is already long awake and Jovan is cooking a delicious-smelling breakfast on the little stove on deck. I stretch in the delightful air and moan at how good I feel. I'm still bruised and battered but my cuts are scabbed over and the aches in my muscles have drained away after another good night of sleep. There's one thing I can say about sailing. The quality of sleep on a gently rocking boat is the best I've ever had.

When I stroll over to the stove, drawn by the smells, Jovan hands me a cup and says, "Tea. With sugar."

I breathe it in and feel the tingle almost immediately. Sugar is a rarity I've had very few times in my life, but I remember it well. The taste of the tea is divine and I smile my thanks.

The look he gives me is affectionate and a little amused. He waves a hand in the general direction of my head and I reach up to feel it. I've got bed head of the worst kind. Since I braid my hair into three braids before I sleep to keep the knots to a minimum, I can imagine the lumps of loose hair he's seeing. I shrug and sip my tea again, which makes him laugh.

Marcus whistles and then nods in front of us when we look his way. We're coming up on a pair of towns, or trading stations at least. They're still too far away to see much, but the number of masts is impressive and the piers look extensive. Small buildings seem clustered very close to the water, so they must be on the piers themselves.

I hand Jovan my tea and say, "I'll be back for that. I'd best get dressed."

He smirks at my long shirt and answers, "Probably a good idea. And maybe do something about that hair?"

I shoot him a rude gesture as I walk away, but all he does is laugh.

When I return to the deck, we're much closer. Boats are launching in a steady stream, the river populated with sails and the hum of distant machinery floats across the water. I can't make out individual people with any detail, but their movement and mass is obvious. This must be a popular port with a large population coming from somewhere nearby.

Marcus is looking through his binoculars at the pier on the opposite side of the wall's pier, his lips tight. When he takes them from his eyes, he gives us a concerned look.

"Something's up," he says. At our alarmed faces, he adds, "I don't know what. It probably has nothing to do with us. There's a flag up at the tower."

He told us about the towers. They aren't usually real purpose-built towers, but rather good vantage points to keep watch from. In most places they are just higher rooms with plenty of windows, but big ports have actual watch towers. From there port workers watch for fire—a hazard feared with so many boats in such close proximity each other—or trouble on the water.

Signal flags tell boats coming near of troubles like disease, infestations which might impact them if they tie up or any other sort of difficulty. The color combination of the flags indicates what specific problem or bit of news there is to share.

"I do need to pick up my boat," he says uncertainly. "It's hard to come back around when it's this crowded if we pass it. What do you think?"

Our only stop is supposed to be to pick up a newly refurbished boat for Marcus's family, so he can tow it to the port where he lives. But stopping if there is trouble is something I'd rather avoid. Still, this is Marcus's boat. I try to read Jovan's answer, but I think he's just as undecided as I am. Cassi is still sleeping below, and I'm almost glad because she's not good with caution, even now when she should have learned to be.

Finally, with a shrug in my direction, Jovan asks, "Can you get out fast if it is about us?"

Marcus tilts his head, considering, then turns the wheel just enough to guide us out of the center of the river. "I'll come up to the area where people go who can't pay for a berth. Be ready to work the sails."

He's showed us how to do basic things to help him around the boat. Normally he does it on his own or has a second hand aboard. The deckhand he had on the way upriver disembarked with the trade goods due to an injured foot that needed attention sooner rather than later. That's part of the reason he so willingly took us on, though I think Cassi had more to do with it if I'm honest.

By now, we can work the sails with only a modicum of yelling required on Marcus's part. A quick holler down to let Cassi know she should stay below, mostly so that her looks, which would certainly have been included in a description of us, would not tip anyone off immediately.

Jovan and I lower the two sets of propellers attached to the back of the boat. The breeze running through the small turbines at the top of the masts and on the bow of the boat power the batteries he uses for these propellers. They don't move the boat quickly, but they do allow for precise control, or so he says.

A man is standing next to a rough hut on the bank of the river. It's on a small area between marshes that looks as if it were built up to provide a dry, elevated walkway of dirt. There's nothing special about the way he's looking at us, nothing that would tell me he's been alerted about us. In this place, we've actually committed no crime, unless the stealing of the fish counts, but that doesn't mean people won't be swayed by what is, no doubt, a sizable reward for Jovan's safe return.

The man clearly recognizes Marcus's boat, which is no surprise, and once we begin edging up to the cluster of ragged boats anchored there, the man begins making rapid hand signals with his fingers in the air. It reminds me a bit of the signals used by the deaf, but I don't understand those either so it means nothing to me. Marcus sends back a rapid series of his own signals and then yells at us to man the towing rope.

He increases power to the little propellers and we slow almost immediately, then start backing up. I turn to see his face tight with concentration and his hands quick on the wheel. I glance at the man and find him running towards the piers. He's not yelling or drawing attention, and his run is the calm one of a person who needs to get somewhere instead of the kind that telegraphs alarm. Even so, it feels urgent to me and my heart kicks up the pace a little.

The towing rope is a thick one, heavy and hard to manage, but we've been schooled in this as well and I'm as ready as I'll ever be.

The boat veers back out into the flow of the river, the current taking over to move us neatly and slowly toward the cluster of crowded piers. I've lost sight of the man, but Marcus looks confident about where he's steering the boat.

At last, I see the man from the shore again, heaving along with a few other men on ropes. They're pulling a boat with a battered looking topside but a strangely pristine hull. It's an odd juxtaposition, the gray and weathered wood on the top against the gleaming blue and white of the bottom. I'm guessing this must be Marcus's newly refurbished boat.

They move the boat in the water between the piers, two men on each pier with ropes, tugging it toward the end of the pier just about where I think Marcus has our boat aimed.

"Bumpers! Toss them over!" Marcus yells without taking his eyes off his task.

We toss over the huge tires attached by ropes, almost just like the tire swing in the school playground, so that they line the back of the boat. Just as we start to come even, I see that the smaller boat has picked up momentum and is moving with some force toward us. Simultaneously, Marcus changes the power to the engines and spins the wheels so that our stern begins swinging toward the oncoming boat. I'm pretty sure it's going to smash into us, which isn't how Marcus explained this procedure, but I grit my teeth and get ready to do whatever needs doing.

It's surprisingly elegant and graceful in the end and my appreciation for Marcus's skills on the water expands tenfold. He shimmies the boat, nudging first one way and then another, calling out short and precise directions as needed. Before I have time to get really worried, we slip the end of the towing rope over the fitting and Jovan hops over to secure the remaining lines. Just like that, it's over.

At least, our part is. When my attention is no longer completely monopolized by this new adventure in boating, I find Marcus exchanging more hand signals with the man, who now stands at the end of the pier.

He's so close I can see the deep, worried furrow between his brows and the curls in his hair are the exact same shade of almost-black as Marcus's. They are more than close enough to speak, but they don't. And I notice that others are giving us sidelong glances from various boats along the edge of the piers, too.

Marcus clicks his tongue to get my attention and gives a sharp jerk of his head downward, his glance encompassing Jovan as well. We scamper below and wait. It can't be good news, not at all. All I can do is wait to find out how bad it is.

Chapter Thirty-Six

Creedy is far more resourceful, and far more determined, than I gave him credit for. Jovan tells me there's more than his job at stake. He's not at all surprised at the news Marcus has relayed to us from the man—Marcus's cousin—at the port. And that information is that he's offering a piece of gold for Jovan's return, and a matching piece for the detention of the four people traveling with him. Gold is a hard thing for anyone to refuse. Such a lure would be enough to make friends turn against friends, never mind total strangers, no matter how poorly they view the Texas Republic.

But winning Jovan is not just some personal need of Creedy's. Not only does Creedy work at the ranch, he lives there. His failure might well result in the loss of the only home he's got. And there's more. The information that Jovan has been reluctant to share is finally revealed now that we're in trouble once more.

This bit of information would have changed much in how I dealt with Creedy, how I approached my decisions on whether or not to run from him or just shoot him. Before, he was just a man—though by all accounts not a nice one—and we had our suspicions that he would want to eliminate us to prevent any word that Jovan had joined us from getting out. But those were just suspicions, speculations we had no way to confirm. Even the deaths of the two soldiers we couldn't lay at his door in any sure way.

Jovan is leaving me alone for a while. My anger at his leaving out information I consider vital is obvious. I can almost feel him at the other end of the boat, out of sight on the deck behind Marcus, while I fume silently here at the bow. The jumpy way he reacted to Creedy is now explained in full.

Though Jovan doesn't know exactly how old he was, he knows that he once heard the unmistakable sound of pain coming from Creedy's house on their property. Curious, he ventured closer and was rewarded with the sound of Creedy's harsh voice coming from inside, along with a woman's scream. It made Jovan yelp and Creedy came out, shooing him away with an explanation of a hurt dog.

At the time, as a small child, he hadn't understood. Jovan's father had merely punished him for encroaching on the foreman's area and confirmed it was a dog. Only later, much later, when rumors swirled about female Strikers caught but never returned to Bailar and female Climbers from the south found buried in the desiccating sands to the west, did he remember that long-ago day.

And once he remembered, other things made themselves plain as well. The way the female hands avoided Creedy's gaze or traveled to and from the barns and fields in pairs all said something to Jovan. But his father once again brushed it aside as imagination. Except that this time, Jovan didn't believe him. Instead, he felt—and still does—that it was something his father not only knew about and ignored, but used as a tool of control over the foreman.

And now I'm left with the regret of having not killed Creedy, which just feels wrong in every way. I also fear him finding us and perhaps doing what he must have done to those other women. The sigh I let out is loud enough to hear over the breeze and Cassi sinks to the deck next to me, tucking one arm around mine. "Don't be mad," she says, brightly.

"I'm not mad," I say. When she gives me a skeptical look, I correct myself, "Okay, I'm mad, but I'll get over it. It's just that Jovan has known, or at least suspected, that this Creedy is the worst kind of creep and not shared that? I wouldn't have hesitated to kill him had I known that. Just think of what would happen if he got hold of you, Cassi. Or me for that matter, if what he says is true."

Cassi squints in the sun but doesn't look away from me. She's always been good that way, at listening. Maybe it's because someone has always had to read everything to her, giving her practice, but I don't think so. I think it is just that she has a much kinder and more patient nature than anyone else I know.

She gives a little hum as she thinks, then says, "And what would have happened had you or I known that it wasn't just a chase?"

I shake my head, thinking of that day in the dry streambed, "We did know that. We knew they were probably going to kill us if they caught us. That's more than a chase, Cassi."

"True, but we—as girls—weren't the targets of anything in specific. We always knew we could ask Jovan to go back and that would be the end of it."

At my look, she adds, "Okay. It would probably be the end of it if we kept going fast."

I nod.

"I don't know about you, but if I had time to dwell on what Jovan just told us, then I wouldn't have been able to sleep. I would have been even more frightened. I might have done something I would regret. Maddix," she says, giving me a significant look.

"Oh," I say. I know what she's saying. If I try to put myself in that frame of mind, one that fears what a man like Creedy might do if he catches me, I can see how I might make mistakes. I can see how waiting for Maddix to heal up in that old building might have seemed too much to ask.

And yes, I would have regretted leaving Maddix behind or not giving him time to heal. And if we had pushed, would Maddix have lived through his injury? Would he have been strong enough for all that we had to do when we left that building? Possibly not. Did Jovan somehow understand this about me, or perhaps understand it of Cassi? It would be just like him and that thought makes my anger drain away.

Cassi nudges me and says, "You should go talk to him. I dunno, maybe apologize for calling him yellow-livered?"

I roll my eyes, because I distinctly recall my mismatched insult. In my defense, I was too angry to think straight. Marcus says that the news of the reward will travel fast and that the guards at the wall gates are not all immune to such a bribe. He's offered to bring us further south, almost to the mouth of the river itself, where he's from. The wall retreats but the gates are trustworthy there and the people known to him.

I can't fault his logic, though I know having hands on board to help him and keep watch is part of his thinking. That, and Cassi. At night, he takes the wheel but during the middle part of the day, he allows Jovan or me, or both of us, to guide the boat in the wide river with only a small sail and the current to push us on. We won't be able to slow down now and Jovan and I will need to work together. Which means I do need to go make up with him, even if only so that we can work together in harmony.

Cassi hops back up, her bare feet red on top from going without shoes in the bright sun, and almost bounces her way over to stand by Marcus. They fall into quiet talking, their heads close together in a way that tells me they're getting along just fine. The way they talk and look at each other makes it seem like they are mere seconds away from kissing most of the time.

I sigh again and grudgingly get up to go make my apologies. I'm no good at that. Having to apologize and be sorry about things means I did something I regret and that means I lost control of my thoughts, my words or my actions. I don't like that idea at all. I've always felt like there was so little in my life I could control that what I *chose* to do was all that I truly possessed. Losing my temper just shows me that I didn't keep the control that was mine.

I tap his shoulder, even though I'm quite sure he heard my hard footsteps on the deck. I don't seem to be able to keep my heels from striking the deck with the same firmness they do when I wear boots. It hurts, but it's also quite satisfying.

He looks up at me, his eyes flashing that golden, bird-of-prey color in the sun. His face is a study in conflicting emotions and he looks miserable. "I'm sorry," he blurts.

"No. I'm sorry," I counter and sit next to him. The deck is warm on my behind through the shorts. I finally found some that fit while digging in a pile inside the storage pit under the bed. It feels good to be dressed. We sit there, both of us with our knees pulled up and arms braced on them for a long while. I can't delay forever. Marcus will need to sleep soon and our hard feelings should be resolved before we take over the boat. Otherwise, our watch will be interminable.

"Jovan, I shouldn't have called you names. It was wrong," I begin tentatively, but get no further. It seems my opening was all he was waiting for.

"I should have told you, but I just...I don't know...I couldn't stand the idea of saying that to you. Or to Cassi. It's so," he pauses while he searches for a word, then adds, "dirty. Filthy. I figured that if it came down to it, I'd kill him and no one would need to worry."

I remember the gunshots when Jovan rushed out of the woods and ask, "Is that what you were going to do before we went to the bridge?"

He nods, his face grim. "I screwed that up, too."

He looks so forlorn that I reach for his hand. It's a strain because we've both got our arms crossed on our knees and I wind up holding his far hand with mine. When I grip his hand in mine, it turns our knees just enough for them to touch. When he entwines his fingers with mine, our thighs press together and it's almost like an electric shock to my system. We sit like that for a moment, an expression I don't quite understand in his eyes as he stares at me.

"Do you remember the grasshopper?" he asks softly.

I laugh because I do remember. It wasn't the first kiss we'd shared, because he'd kissed my cheek and I his since we were nine or ten, but it was the first time he'd kissed my lips. I was fourteen and he must have just turned fifteen. And just as he did, under that hot summer sun behind the school, a grasshopper disturbed by us had jumped right onto his face. We'd both leapt back, surprised, and the moment was gone as fast as the grasshopper who decided his new perch wasn't to his liking.

"I remember it," I say and squeeze his hand.

ANN CHRISTY

"I wish no one had seen us," he says and I can hear the regret in his voice. The regret is because it wasn't just our first real kiss, it had been our last as well.

"Me, too," I say.

I'm pretty sure that this would be the perfect time for him to try again. We aren't drowning, there are no teachers to run and tell his father, no Army ready to send him to do his duty. And best of all, I think I'm ready for him to kiss me.

He doesn't.

Instead, he kisses my hand and lets it go. He smiles at me, guileless and quite clearly unaware that he has missed the perfect moment, then runs a lock of my hair through his hand, letting it fall to the deck with the rest.

"We need to get Marcus to go below and get some sleep. The wind is coming up, so you should get ready, braid your hair, or put it up in one of those cute buns or something. We might need the money from selling it soon, so you should take care of it."

He grins and winks to give lie to his mercenary words, so I smile back and go.

Our watch is smooth sailing, which is a new term for me but one I like immensely. The river is free of obstacles and there isn't a single port to go past. A vast marsh, the likes of which I could never have imagined, stretches to the west as far as I can see and beyond. Skeletal trees, their branches almost absurdly crooked, reach up out of the marsh at intervals while others crowd in patches with great knobby knees poking up out of the water all around them. It's beautiful, but creepy.

There are other vessels on the water, barges and wider sailing vessels loaded with goods, but most of those we pass quickly. I keep my braid tucked up under a cap and wear a baggy shirt, which gives the impression that I'm a boy. It works, from a distance. So far, Marcus assures us that no one knows we're on his boat. Even his cousin at the port wasn't sure until he saw how carefully we approached the port. I'd like to be sure any suspicion stays far from us.

Once full night falls, Marcus returns, eager to get back at the wheel. He's pleased with our work and that makes me happier than I might have expected. There something very satisfying about doing a job you're completely unprepared for relatively well.

Cassi comes up a few minutes after Marcus, which I'm sure she thinks is discreet, but she's not fooling anyone and Jovan gives Marcus a hard look when he sees her mussed hair. She see it and says, "No, Jovan. You can settle down right now. It's not like that."

It takes Marcus a few seconds to catch on but he bristles when he understands and says, "I'm not that guy."

"Alright, now that we've got *that* out of the way," I say, sarcasm fully engaged.

Cassi snorts and starts some food going on the deck stove, shaking her head as she goes. "I'm keeping watch tonight," she asserts, lighting the stove and handing Jovan the coffee pot so he can fill it with water. She raises an eyebrow and adds, "So I was sleeping."

Chapter Thirty-Seven

Despite everything, the days pass in such peace that it seems a long time ago we were stumbling through the dark woods in abject fear. It's given me time to think, which is both good and bad. I've had time to think of my father and the half-brother who must surely have heard the news by now if the gate-keepers or Maddix passed it on as promised. It gives me time to think of my mother, to worry whether or not she's eating and wonder if she's at all worried about me in turn. Or is she simply angry that my Striking brought people with questions to our home and interrupted her nightly bottle? I'll probably never know.

Other thoughts crowd in, demanding their turn at the forefront. I'm not immune to a little self-pity now and then, and the uncertainty of our future probably adds to that. I push those fearful thoughts away as soon as I realize it because they won't help me right this minute. Surviving now is the best road to having any future at all when it comes right down to it.

Cassi seems content to stay on the boat forever, and I confess that I've grown rather fond of it as well. Jovan seems to be taking to the work of manning a boat like he was born to it. At least, Marcus claims that is the case. Now that we're so far from where we left Maddix and Connor, it seems silly to worry over a little more distance, and I'm not the only one that can smell the change in the air. Marcus tells us that it is the scent of the Gulf. The ocean. While Cassi is almost beside herself with excitement over the prospect, I'm anxious to see it, too.

Weslyn, the town that Marcus is from, rolls into view one early morning while the sky still has hints of pink dawn in it. A radio I didn't even know Marcus had squawks suddenly and the smile on his face after he answers calms my immediate panic. It must be a family member, given the way they interact on the radio, but he is discreet where we're concerned, only saying that he's brought home some friends.

The port isn't a large one. It isn't even really a port, but rather a community of people whose living is made on the water and who therefore, need extensive pier facilities. There's a larger pier, now empty, at the far end that looks big enough for trade or passenger vessels. It must be if the signs posted all over it are a reliable indicator.

Like every other port we've seen, this one is a mix of old and new. Gray boards are interspersed with newer brown ones, the smell of fish is pervasive, and the tiny shops that border the piers are so close together they're almost piled atop one another.

The marsh in this area is absent save for small patches to the sides of the piers, which is handy for more than just building a town on firm ground. It keeps boat traffic from approaching except at the piers and no one in their right mind would try to walk across it. The mud is deep enough that it can suck down a full grown man, Marcus claims.

Jovan and Marcus do the docking and tying up, Cassi and I remaining unseen below until the situation can be figured out. We busy ourselves by creating disguises, sticking with the standard boy disguises since it's been working well up to now. For Cassi it's a more difficult problem because she is so obviously a girl in every way. Clever binding, a bit of padding around her middle and a cap hiding her hair transform her into a rather pudgy fresh-faced boy. I'm skinny and wiry enough that it's almost too easy to turn me into a boy, but my hair comes past my butt and I do look like my head is just a little too big with it all wrapped up under a hat.

The wait is interminable and by the time Jovan pokes his head down, the entire main area of the boat is as clean as it's probably ever been. Even Marcus's unusually large clothes stash is neatly folded and separated by type in the storage areas.

"Wow, we should trap you two down here more often," Jovan says and whistles in appreciation.

My scowl wipes the grin off his face and he clears his throat. "Uh, yeah. We're good but you guys are going to need to just go straight to where we're staying. It's pretty clear of people right now, but you know the drill."

A last check of our disguises, mostly to tuck stray curls back into Cassi's cap, and we go. When I step onto the pier, I feel almost immediately unsure of my feet. It feels like I'm wobbling, or rather, that the ground is wobbling beneath me. The dizziness only lasts for a few seconds, but the disturbing sensation lingers in the background while we follow Jovan.

Just off the piers, a town almost immediately begins. There are no outskirts, no gradual increase in the number of buildings. It just begins, full and crowded. Houses with tiny yards crowd around narrow streets.

The streets are laid out in imprecise lines, following the contours of the land rather than barreling through it, but I can see the distinct lines of a typical town center at the end of the street we're hurrying down.

My inclination is to hug the sides and try to remain out of sight, but Jovan whispers that we should be casual and walk like we're just another group of sailors with a destination in mind. It's a surprisingly difficult task, but I think we do a passing job.

The house we come to is a little larger than the others, but not so much that it stands out. Green shutters, tall windows and a fresh-looking coat of paint give it a friendly air, but it's still just a regular house. For some reason, the notion that Marcus was wealthy because his family owns boats had taken root in my head. Compared to the citizen housing in Bailar, it does seem that way, but most of the houses we've passed are in the same neat and well-tended state.

We've no chance to knock. The door swings open even as we come up the walkway. A small woman, plump in every way, smiles out at us and welcomes us inside. Marcus stands behind her and his grin widens when he sees Cassi in her chubby boy disguise.

"Well, this is going to be interesting," I say, smiling.

Jovan must realize I'm talking about Cassi meeting Marcus's family because he grins back and says, "Oh yeah, and I'm going to enjoy watching it."

After showering and changing into clothes provided by Marcus' mother, Susanna, we look more ourselves again. Or, perhaps I should say, Cassi looks more herself. I don't look anything like my regular self in the dress Susanna left hanging for me on the back of the door.

There's a full-length mirror in the room and I almost cringe to see myself. I've lost weight, which I couldn't afford to do in the first place, but seeing myself like this really makes it hard to ignore. Cassi sees my discomfort and gives me a swift peck on the cheek before leaving me alone to finish dressing.

I've never had a great deal of extra weight on my body, but I've done well enough gardening to avoid looking scrawny. And no matter the source, Connor and I have always managed to provide ourselves with enough protein to grow straight and decently muscled. That is not the case now. I've descended past scrawny into skinny territory and I look malnourished, with hollows under my eyes and cheeks. My ribs stand out as do my hip and collar bones. When I put on the dress, much of that fades away and I wonder if she chose the color to counter my pallor on purpose.

The dress is simple and pretty, made of cotton in a pattern of tiny white flowers against a pale blue background. Hints of yellow in the flowers brighten the fabric even further. I've had very few dresses in my life, mostly when I was small and my mother was still making an effort. I've not seen myself in one since, and the difference is striking. I look almost pretty.

I take some effort with my hair, combing out each tangle until it gleams then braiding two small sections away from my face to keep it neat. Aside from my boots, I have no shoes. I guess it would be too much to hope for that anyone else in the family is my size and wouldn't mind me wearing theirs, but Susanna left me a strange pair of slippers. They almost look like they are made of rubber, with two thin straps that come to a point. It takes me a few tries to figure out the joined strap is meant to go between my toes and the loud slapping noise they make against my heels brings out a laugh.

I hesitate when I near the bottom of the stairs and the noise of laughter and conversation grows. I feel a bit naked with my legs showing, especially given their current thin and scarred up state. There's no help for it and I'd prefer not to look timid and give a bad first impression. I lift my chin and make sure there's just the right curve on my lips when I enter the main room where everyone is gathered.

The smell of cooking food is almost overwhelming. I've been smelling a hint of it—meat, something sauce-like and more—since Cassi opened the door to walk out, but now it's almost like a fog enveloping me. My stomach makes such a loud noise it sounds like my guts are twisting around on themselves. For all I know they might be doing just that. Either way, it's loud enough for Susanna to hear as I pass into the room and near her chair.

"Well, if that isn't a call for dinner, I don't know what is," she says brightly.

Her words come out sounding as round as her cheeks look. The vowels are drawn out and the words almost luxurious in the way she speaks them. Marcus has the same sort of accent, but his is less pronounced. As the others—several of Marcus's brothers, their wives and two small girls—file past me into the dining room, I hear more of the same. Most were introduced to us before we went up to shower, but I'm pretty sure more have arrived and I can't remember anyone's name anyway.

Their kitchen is large and inviting, full of homey touches. A long table crowded with chairs and benches beckons. Mismatched cloth napkins lay across equally mis-matched plates. A waft of cool air kisses my bare legs from behind and I turn to see Susanna in front of a huge metal cabinet taller than I am. Tendrils of frost curl out and I realize it's like the giant cool-room in the school, except smaller. I don't remember what those are called, but I've never seen anything like it.

Before I can think twice, I step in front of it and reach in, feeling the cold air and touching a pitcher so cold there's ice bobbing in the liquid.

Susanna gives me a curious look and asks, "Have you not seen a refrigerator before, child?"

Of course, that's the name of it. I feel like a fool when I answer, "Only one that's like a room. They have one at our school."

Her brows draw together and I can see the pity in her expression, but she says, "Well, I imagine not everyone really needs one, but it gets so hot and humid here that milk sours coming out of the udder! Go on and take a seat. Marcus, get out of that chair. Let the ladies have the padded ones." She ends by tsking and muttering about bad manners as she shuttles hot food and cold pitchers to the table.

After much shuffling of chairs and re-introductions, and my immediate forgetting of names yet again, we set to. The dinner is remarkable and nothing like I have ever eaten before. Spaghetti with sausage made of alligator and pork—an alligator sounds awful and I hope I never meet one—salad, fresh hot bread dripping with butter and spices and endless glasses of iced tea are devoured with equal fervor by all. I'm confused by the pasta until Susanna demonstrates how to twirl it onto my fork and tells me not to worry about the stragglers. Marcus then demonstrates by sucking up a long noodle, spattering sauce in the doing.

Conversation is easy and they are kind enough to avoid the topic of our flight while we eat. I can see everyone, not just Susanna, evaluating Cassi. But like everything else they've done so far, they do it kindly.

It's quite clear that Marcus has no intention of hiding his interest in her, and equally clear that the family is interested in this choice of his. But it's not the kind of judging that I would expect in Bailar, where individual considerations are the least important ones. There, family worth and earning potential are the more prominent issues. Families care if two people get along, of course, but love is rarely the primary motive in a match where one or both have anything worth owning. I suppose in that way, at least, the poor have it better than the wealthy.

I feel nothing like that at this table and the interest is on her as a person. She doesn't disappoint. Her bright and bubbly personality is perfectly suited to this place. By the time we're all stuffed and plates are being pushed back with satiated groans, she is perfectly comfortable hopping up to help clear the plates with Susanna. It seems entirely natural and in no way forced.

Once cups of rich black coffee are served, the mood shifts and I don't need anyone to tell me what's coming. We're going to turn to the topic these welcoming people must have been intensely curious about since we appeared. Susanna studies her cup for a moment and the children are shooed off to play in another room. It feels strange to tell our story to a room full of people, but they are offering us aid instead of taking the gold for turning us in, so it only seems fair.

Jovan tells our story, with Cassi and me adding bits as needed. The people around the table are rapt, coffee forgotten and cold in their cups or else absently sipped. It's so strong that I feel jittery and switch to water, also cold and sweet-tasting, after politely emptying my cup.

He's kind enough to leave out the conditions under which I lived and I don't offer those details up, but Cassi is quite frank about her own prospects had she stayed in Bailar, and the reasons she welcomed escape with us when the opportunity arose.

There is utter silence around the table when we're done. Not so much as a breath can be heard. For one unreasonable moment, I think we made a mistake by telling them about the fish Jovan stole and then Susanna breaks the spell.

Her voice is full of compassion when she says, "You poor children."

My defenses go up immediately. We didn't tell them our story to gain pity or so that anyone would feel sorry for us. The way she says it, like we're small and defenseless, just doesn't sit well with me.

She notices me stiffen and waves her hands as if to retract her words. "I didn't mean it like that. You were very brave to do what you did and I don't think I could have managed any of it. Please don't misunderstand me, dears."

For a moment she searches for words, the others watching her and waiting for her to take the lead as their mother, the woman of the house. She meets my eyes and I see the strength there, the grit that it took to raise all her children with a husband who leaves for weeks at a time for his work in a world inherently hostile to the survival of the young.

"I suppose I'm thinking more of life in Texas. One hears things, secondhand stories that pass along the river, but few Strikers come this way so who knows what's true and what isn't? Now, hearing from you, I have to believe that much of what I've heard over the years is true. Or true enough," she says.

She looks at Cassi, reaches out to clasp her hand and says, "Such a life for a young girl to have to contemplate isn't right. Not right at all."

I can only assume she means the Pleasure Houses, but I'm not entirely sure. There were enough scantily clad women hanging out of windows and walking the piers we passed for me to know they must have them here. Perhaps it isn't viewed as an acceptable profession is all I can figure.

With a final pat, she releases Cassi's hand and nods to one of her sons, Mario. He looks like the oldest to me, but I'm not a fit judge of that.

He's all business and gets right to the important stuff. He says, "There is a bounty out for you, Jovan. An endangered minor bounty. That's a small, but important, distinction in terms of bounties. Those are usually laid on girls who get lured away, kidnapped kids or the like. It was a smart thing for this Creedy fellow to do. People don't feel bad about collecting those. And gold is gold."

I'm about to interrupt with questions, but he holds up a hand to forestall me and I clap my mouth shut, twisting my fingers in my lap to force some semblance of patience.

Mario taps his fingers on the table as if counting out his various points, "So, people have got the excuse of doing something good while really going after gold. That will work against you. Going for you is that no one knows where you are or who you're with, though rumors are swirling that a boat like ours picked you up. Also, there are only three of you now, not five. That won't last, though. Soon enough someone will figure out that the other two passed the gate. All it takes is a small bribe to a gate where someone is smart enough to check." Finished, he slaps his palm onto the broad surface of the table as if everything were settled.

I'm not sure what to make of the information. It's no more than I could have guessed but to hear it from someone else makes it real and far more difficult to figure a way out of. Jovan's downcast expression needs addressing, and that I do know how to do.

"Jovan, snap out of it right this minute," I say, my voice a little sharper than I intended. "Giving yourself up or whatever you're thinking of doing isn't an option."

He purses his lips but says nothing. He doesn't need to because I can read that stubborn look and it says he'll either go on his own or do something else stupid.

"Wait, Jovan, hear me out," I say and wave my hand in the direction of the river and the wall beyond. "We are just this close to the wall. All we have to do is get to it when someone trustworthy is there and we're free. Running off or going back is like throwing all that we've done, all that we had to go through, away."

Susanna clears her throat and says, "Getting past the wall won't solve your problem entirely. It won't solve it at all, really. Not here, not right now."

My heart drops in my chest like someone just tied a stone to it.

"There are other options," suggests Mario after another assenting nod from his mother.

"Why isn't it finished if we get across the wall? What other options?" I ask.

I feel like running, escaping. I can feel my toes curling against the flimsy rubber of those strange sandals and I want my boots, my safe and sturdy boots. And then I want to run straight for the wall, even if I have to run over the water to do it.

I don't feel any danger coming from these people. I genuinely think they want to help us but that just makes it worse, because I can tell they hate having to break this to us. That means they're probably minimizing the issue, trying to make it not sound as bad as it probably is. What more will I have to do? How much further will I have to go?

"You might as well just tell us. Get it over with," Jovan says, sensing my anxiety.

"The wall is just a border and all borders are permeable to some extent. Some traders have regular access, and at times passage to the East is allowed because they have rails that go straight through to the East Coast. There are more reasons people come and go through, but you get the idea," explains Mario.

I nod, urging him on with an impatient wave of my hand he very kindly overlooks.

"Well, that means that people on the lookout for Jovan, and his companions, will get through without a doubt. Southeast has a firm policy about accepting Strikers under their political asylum rules, but that doesn't mean they'll put you under guard or anything. And once you get beyond a crowded city, or even just in a spot not visible, you're fair game for bounty hunters."

"We're screwed," I say.

Susanna leans forward and forces me to meet her eyes with her earnest gaze. "No, you're not. You just have to be smart. And watch your language, if you please."

Suitably chastised, I take a deep breath to calm my nerves and ask, "Then please tell us how we can be smart about this, because I'm at a loss."

"That's where the options come in," Mario says and pulls out a big green log book. He flips it open, thumbs past bent and well-worn pages, to check something. "We've got a trade with Florida scheduled for the coming week. That will take you as far as you can get in the Southeast and still be in the Southeast. Or at least, you will be once you get past the Gulf lands and that's an easy trip on good roads. We can land you in just the right spot."

"How does that actually help us? Won't a bounty hunter just find us anyway?" I ask.

He inclines his head, admitting the possibility, but says, "Or you can just wait it out. Eventually, the clock will run out because he'll turn eighteen so any bounty will be an illegal one with a lot fewer takers. Or, even better, they'll think you died."

Died? I hadn't actually considered that as a viable option while I was worrying about whether or not I would actually die. But now that he's brought it up, it's a good idea. Carrying it off successfully means not being seen though, giving no one any reason to believe we're still alive. And that I have no idea how to do.

Jovan pushes his freshly washed hair back, though all that does it make it stick up in a way that begs me to smooth it for him. He seems to be waiting for me, or perhaps Cassi, to either decide or ask another question.

"Okay, we're listening," I say.

Chapter Thirty-Eight

We're going to owe the Flint family a boat. Specifically, we're going to owe them a replacement for the blue-bottomed boat Marcus just paid to make seaworthy. That, plus an engine that burns gasoline and can push a boat very fast. Right now, I don't think they're too worried about any actual repayment. Marcus says that he's gained something much better than a boat. Then he looks with such moon-sick eyes at Cassi it makes me laugh. She's got it just as bad for him. Even Jovan approves.

We're leaving tonight, but for three days we've been resting and recovering here inside the Flint house, taking care not to be seen. Jovan is like a different guy. I've never had the opportunity to see him at home—his home—before, so I've never seen what kind of person he is around the house. He's like some kind of weird new form of domestic dynamo. It's not just that he's neat, since I've always known that about him—it's that he seems to like tidying things.

It's a strange juxtaposition, fitting the Jovan I know in with this interesting new form of him. Washing dishes is a good example of how he's different. Connor, Cassi—everyone I've ever had occasion to wash dishes with—would rather dry dishes than wash them. Even I would prefer that. Not Jovan.

We volunteered that first evening to wash dishes in an effort to be good guests. While Cassi and Marcus went off to whisper and stare at each other without a boat in their way, Jovan and I tackled the mountain of dishes that a dozen people can leave after a big meal. When I stationed myself at the washing side, Jovan neatly tapped my waist to move me to the other side of the sink and took my place.

As he set to work, I realized he wasn't just putting on a facade as a guest. The way he worked, so efficiently washing the dishes and then dipping them into the rinse water just so, made it clear that he's done this a lot. I couldn't help but give him a look, which just made him laugh. It was a full laugh, the kind that tilts the head back and brings a smile all the way up to a person's eyes, and my heart nearly stood still in my chest. I also nearly dropped a plate.

"Whatever," I said, turning back to my chore.

He shrugged and picked up a handful of suds, letting them drop back into the water with a soft plop. "I used to do this with my Mom. I just like the way the soap feels. It's no big deal."

It is a big deal. It's a connection with people he loved. I patted his arm and kept drying. Ever since, he's been helping out Susanna with the extra load our staying has made. He's even good at laundry.

The three peaceful days we've had since have provided a much needed rest and some comfort. I've got clean clothes, hand me down's from members of this huge family, and my skin is truly clean. Even my bruises and scrapes are fading and healing up. I'm still skinny, weeks of inadequate food can't be made up for in a few days, but I feel better. Stronger.

Mario has enlisted the aid of family and friends in our endeavor. It seems there are benefits to being a member of the biggest family I have ever personally heard of. That is especially true when that family has fished and traded along the Gulf and the river for generations. Everyone is related to them, it seems, if only by marriage.

A cousin of some sort, who is also possibly an in-law as well as some other relation I can't determine, is bringing Creedy via a slow ferry downriver. I think it's foolhardy, but they assure me that it's better to know where he is than not and I can't argue with that logic.

According to radio traffic, he's adjusted his offer and increased the bounty with no requirement that Jovan be untouched, only that he be alive. As for those of us with him, he still wants Cassi and me alive, which is chilling, but his offer for Connor and Maddix requires only a proof of death as a minimum to collect the reward. And he's been actively polling everyone for information about us.

This is a bad turn and broadcasts that he's not satisfied with leaving an open bounty and moving on to wait for someone to come claim it. And it's not just a case of not giving up easily. It's a clear signal that he's not giving up at all. Whatever hold Jovan's father has on Creedy, it must be a strong one.

Susanna calls me in to her bedroom on this final day of rest and I leave the small sunny room that must have once belonged to a pair of young girls. It's filled with frills and pink things. I feel out of place in it, much too big in every way, but I like the soft bed piled with warm quilts and the clean scent of freshly washed linens. And I like sharing with Cassi, hearing her breathing and knowing there's someone I can trust and care for an arm's reach away.

On Susanna's big bed she has laid out a startling array of things, all lined up neatly with a pair of bags to contain it all nearby.

"Okay, this is where we're at," she says as soon as she sees me in the doorway. She waves a hand over the items on one side of the bed and says, "This is for you and this is for Cassi. Check to see if I've forgotten anything."

I have absolutely no idea what half of the things on the bed are aside from the clothes, so I'm equally clueless if she's forgotten anything or not. There are tiny bags and boxes and plastic bottles that I'm almost afraid to touch. She gives me a sympathetic look and explains it all.

There are bottles of hair dye to use after we are finally safe, which she says we'll have to reapply every couple of weeks, more often if we spend a lot of time in the water. Scissors for cutting hair, which makes me cringe a little. Shampoos that smell like flowers, soaps that smell like herbs and all sorts of stuff. It's a lovely, generous gesture.

I help her pack and I can plainly see the worry on her face. "It's going to be alright," I say, though I'm trying to convince myself even more than her.

She shakes her head and answers, "I hope so. But you're all so young. It's not right for all this...this thing you're planning." She stops and turns to me, strokes my cheek in the tender way I've always wanted my mother to, and then gives me a motherly peck on the cheek. It's such a warm gesture that I instantly feel pressure behind my eyes, like I might cry. All I can do is push it back and give her a shaky smile.

"Don't worry," I say. "He didn't give us much choice in the matter. We're just doing what we have to. None of us, not even Cassi, will be safe if we don't."

When her lips purse, I'm pretty sure that she's thinking of her grandchildren, the ones living and the ones she'll have from Marcus and Cassi if things keep going like they are. She gives a sharp nod, hands me the bags and says, "Then don't miss."

When darkness falls, I see that the moon is rising in that same slender sliver it did when we first escaped from Bailar. It's hard to believe that we've been gone a month. It's been both the longest and the shortest month of my life, though it would be hard to explain that to someone else. Each night of walking in unfamiliar territory and hiding in fear was endless when taken individually, yet they all blend together into one long night and day when I think of them together.

We slip out in groups of two, Marcus and Cassi, Mario and Jovan and finally, another brother named Georgio and I take to the streets. It's quiet at night here in the place they call the suburbs, but not empty. People stroll along in pairs, jog with dogs on leashes—which surprises me because only the very rich keep dogs as pets in Bailar—or sit out on porches and fan the damp air as they talk.

We don't dally, but we also don't make a show of hurrying. We just go straight to the docks as casually as possible. The night watch is taken care of, yet another cousin of some sort. There is little business there during the night hours so we aren't observed.

Georgio isn't coming with us, but he tends the lines for us on the pier. Mario takes the smaller boat, still ragged-looking on top but now sporting a powerful engine, and roars away to do his part. We launch next, the four of us once more on Marcus's boat. The sails are rather limp in the early night air, but he assures us that the winds will pick up. The little engines and the current do most of the work getting us into the flow of the river and moving south again.

A quick radio check between Marcus and Mario is the last open communication we will have. Once he gets near the slow ferry and the port where it will land, we'll use only clicks and codes to be sure our plans are going as they should. That makes me nervous but Marcus says it's normal and he doesn't seem in the least bit worried.

We've got two days, maybe three, before our plan comes to fruition and I'm wound up so tightly I doubt I'll sleep between now and then, but I have to try. Jovan and I have our shift steering the boat in the morning so he interrupts my pacing on deck to urge me below and to bed. I don't feel like I could sleep or even stop moving, but he's right that I should try. In the same cabin I shared with Cassi before, I feel like the snug space has grown smaller and tighter. I feel like I can't breathe.

After tossing and turning for what may have been an hour but feels like days, I throw back the covers in frustration and pad into the main cabin to wait out the night. I'm not the only one who's had trouble dropping off. Jovan is sitting on the long built-in couch, his legs stretched out in front of him, his eyes on the small windows that line the upper parts of the cabin. The gun remaining to us is laid out neatly on the couch, the cleaning kit nearby. The oily rags he used release their sweet, but somehow dangerous, scent into the cabin.

I clear my throat to let him know I'm there, to give me a chance to gauge how welcome I might be from his reaction.

"Can't sleep either?" he asks.

He seems relieved to see me, or at least, relieved to see someone. I take that as encouragement and sit down next to him on the side that doesn't have the gun.

"No," I say with a sigh. "I'd really like to but it just isn't happening. I just keep thinking about all the things that can go wrong. And about what happens if it goes right, too."

Jovan hands me a pillow from a stack at the end of the couch and I stuff it against my middle. How he knew I needed it, I don't know, but I suppose we've been together long enough for him to know I'm a hugger of random things. My pack, one of the bags we carried, whatever else may be at hand. When I sit and am worried, I clutch one to my middle. It comforts me.

"Thank you," I say, patting the pillow.

"Sure," he says, and goes back to staring out the narrow windows that show nothing but stars. We're silent a while, just looking at the bright points of light as they bob back and forth with the motion of the boat. I hear a soft laugh from above, Cassi's, and am glad that she and Marcus have each other on this beautiful night.

"I'm afraid I won't be able to do it," he says, suddenly.

I look at him, the stars no longer of the slightest interest. "If it comes to it, I'll do it. Unless it's just the idea of killing him in general that you're having second thoughts about," I say.

He shakes his head but it isn't a convincing shake at all. That worries me. This plan we've cooked up with the help of the Flints—or rather, the Flints have cooked up with many enthusiastic nods from us—is complicated but clean. Creedy will only wind up dead because he continued the pursuit. And he will meet that end out on the water, where there is no law and his body won't be found. It's perfect.

I feel weird about it as well, but really, what choices do we have? With the bounty, this never-ending chase and Jovan's status as the only son—and heir—to one of the richest landowners of Bailar, we have to cut the ties and do it permanently. The simple and stark truth is that none of us will ever be safe to go and live our lives unless we do this terrible thing. Jovan knows this as well as I.

"I can tell you why it's hard for me to think about killing Creedy, even though I know as well as you that he deserves it," Jovan says.

When he doesn't speak further, I motion for him to continue. It's an impatient move that says very eloquently that he's wasting his time.

"When I was too little to sit a horse, Creedy used to sit me up in front of him and take me with him through the pastures. He'd give me milk right from the cows, still warm, even though my father didn't like it," he says quietly. "You don't understand."

He turns to me, his eyes pleading for me to see whatever it is he sees in Creedy, but I don't and it shows.

"It was just different when I was young. I didn't understand about people working for other people or anything like that. All I knew is that my father was never around and when he was, he was stiff and had time only for business. And I knew that when I went outside, Creedy would call me "Pardner" in a funny voice and lift me up for a ride on the horse. I remember *that* guy," he says to his feet.

"And then that same guy was dragging Strikers or Climbers or whoever else wouldn't be missed back into his house and doing who knows what to them," I add in a bitter voice.

His head sinks a little further at that and he nods. "I know," he says. It's an admission, a sad one, and it's filled with grief.

In my heart, the feeling part of me, I can understand a little. I have memories of my mom when she was younger, before drinking became something she did every day. I remember bright sunshine and the smell of cookies and her laughing. But the part of me that thinks, the cold and logical brain, is well aware that the woman who did those things is as dead as if she had truly died. That part of me is aware that she is dangerous and I stay clear of her.

Creedy is far worse than my mother. In this matter, my heart and my head both say the world is better off without him. And for certain, we will be better off.

"I'll do it," I say. "It's just pushing a button."

In the end analysis, that's all it is. On Mario's boat is a bundle of explosives. It's a small thing, no bigger than a bagged lunch, but it will blow the boat to pieces. As well as anything on it. The trigger is on this boat, though Mario has one as well in case the opportunity arises—along with a gun and who knows what else—but the intention is for us to take care of it.

This is our responsibility so the guilt must be ours, too. That's the way they do things out here in the Gulf lands. Though, generally speaking, they don't take the law into their own hands to this extent. Our situation is too different for comfort, too nebulous for clarity and too filled with influential and moneyed backers for us to be sure justice will prevail.

The plan is for Mario to pick up Creedy at a pre-arranged location. He's been vouched for and it's all arranged under the promise of a fast boat and knowledge of where we might be. Once he enters the Gulf and the open water beyond, the problem belongs to Jovan, Cassi and me. We just have to make sure Mario is off the boat and away before we do anything.

It would be better if we could shoot him—and if we can and spare the boat, we will—but the explosives are a safety measure we need. There's the added incentive that this boat is newly refurbished, so accidents do happen during their first voyages. If we blow it up with a nice big explosion, providing smoke that can be seen on land, then the story that we died as well is much more believable. Besides, Creedy is a much better shot than any of us and from a moving boat, I doubt we could hit him except by accident.

Jovan jerks me out of my dark thoughts by taking my hand and holding it tightly in his. His fingers are cold and I can smell the gun oil on them. He says, "I'll do it, but I had to tell someone—you—that it's not easy or simple. It's important that you know there's more to me, more to Creedy."

I squeeze his cold fingers in mine. Then on impulse, I lift his hand and press the cold back of it to my cheek. He smiles a little and says, "Warm."

Nodding, I say, "That's the point." I can only do that so long before it gets weird, so I pull his hand down and hold it between both of mine against the pillow. It's a good compromise and I get to keep holding his hand without the weirdness.

"I'll be okay," he says, then yawns.

"I'm guessing you could sleep now," I say and feel a yawn tickling at the back of my throat as well. I let his hand go—so much for the hand holding—and make to get up from the couch and go back to my sleepless bed.

"Stay," he says. At my look, he clarifies, "Just for sleeping. The couch is big enough for both of us. I don't want to be alone."

Since I know with absolute certainty that I don't want to go back into that room and stare at the curving wall till it's time for watch, I'm happy to take him up on the offer. We settle in after an initial period of uneasiness at touching each other with so many parts of our bodies.

The couch really isn't big enough for two, though it is meant to serve as a bed, and it just fits the two of us if we nestle in close. At first, Jovan puts his arm up on the back of the sofa, which can't be comfortable, but finally gives up and lays it over the top of me, careful to let his hand rest over the edge of the couch rather than on me. It's so solicitous that I smile in the darkness.

With a blanket over us, his icy feet warm up quickly. I hadn't expected to feel like I could sleep, or even get any decent rest despite the exhaustion I feel, but the sound of his soft breathing behind my ear and the warm, safe feeling I get from feeling his body close behind mine makes me drowsy almost immediately. I think it does for him, too, because his breathing slows and becomes deeper, his arm heavier. Even as I wonder at this, the first time I've slept next to a boy, I fall asleep.

Cassi wakes us with good natured teasing and a few ribald jokes that I don't take very well in my freshly woken state. It's full daylight, which means they've let us sleep in. I appreciate it, but jokes really should wait till after I've brushed my teeth and had some coffee. Jovan won't meet my eyes and his face is flushed due to Cassi's teases, but by the time we're both well awake and on deck, whatever embarrassment he felt seems to have passed. When I pass him a cup of hot brew, he smiles and thanks me just like any other morning.

Marcus tells us that Mario is slated to pick up Creedy late in the afternoon, but he is far behind us and anticipates we'll be entering the Gulf by the time they get close. This is good, because being out to sea is what we need. And that will be tomorrow, late in the morning by Marcus's best estimate of our speed.

Our day is quite pleasant, all things considered. We're not stopping anywhere and I'm wearing my standard boy disguise to alleviate suspicion from boats passing by or observers along the distant river banks. The wind is fresh and the sails snap, a sound I find liberating for some reason. We cook pork kabobs over the little stove, chunks of fresh vegetables I wouldn't be able to harvest for months back in Texas interspersed with the seasoned chunks of meat. One of the most interesting things about sailing, I have found, is that everything tastes and smells far better than it does on land. Whether it is the freshness of the air or the simple act of sailing, it is universally true of everything I have tasted or smelled so far. Even the lingering scent of fish has changed into something pleasant.

I know Jovan is feeling it, too. His brow has cleared of worry lines and his feet move lightly over the deck as he tends the lines and adjusts sails. He really is a natural at it. The way he swoops past a boom, one arm on a line to keep him from flying over the side, is a study in grace. It's strange because Jovan is tall and muscular, even with the lack of food during our escape, but I never think of him as graceful. I think of him as strong, sure and confident, but never graceful. Yet, that is exactly what he is and I can't tear my eyes off him.

The sun is hanging large and low in the sky when I hear stirring below decks. I almost wish they'd go back to sleep and leave Jovan and I up here alone to enjoy the sunset. We've not spoken in several hours now, but it isn't uncomfortable. It's like we're both trying hard to take in every single moment we have because tomorrow at this time, our lives will be different. Win or lose, we will be forever changed.

He smiles a secret sort of smile at me when the little hatch opens and our two friends make their way up on deck. It warms me from my toes up. He gives me a hand up from our spot and for just a second, we are very close. Then the envelope bursts and the evening is filled with cooking, changing the watch and catching up with Cassi.

She is aglow. There's simply no other word for what I see in her bright eyes and utterly content smiles. Everything about her radiates satisfaction and I wonder for a moment what's been going on down below. In truth, I probably don't want to know. How two people can fall so completely for each other in such a short span of time is beyond me, but there's no question it has happened. And I don't think it is merely a physical attraction gone out of control because they are far too compatible in every other way. They hand each other things before the other has a chance to ask for it and do all the other things that people who have been together for a long time do. His family clearly fell in love with Cassi from almost the moment they met her, which just supports my theory that it is with the Flints that she belongs.

It gives me a pang to think of it, but I smile through it and hold up my end of the conversation as we eat under the glow of a perfect sunset. There's even a cake that Susanna packed for us. Chocolate is a rarity in Texas, but here it is quite common and this cake is all chocolate and then some. There are even curls of chocolate poked into the frosting and I shamelessly snitch them off of Jovan's piece before he can even reach for a fork.

When night falls, the wind picks up and we stay to adjust the sails once more before going below. My mouth still tastes of chocolate and as Jovan closes the hatch behind me, I feel heat move up my neck when the thought comes to me that he probably tastes of chocolate as well. He must read something in my eyes because he brushes his fingers across my cheek and I see his face flush even beyond the color that the wind and sun have given him. Though I actually try not to, I lick my lips and could just about sink into the deck knowing what he must think. It's just that my mouth has gone dry, my throat tight and I have an almost overwhelming urge to touch him. Instead, I turn around and clench my fingers into fists, leaving his hand in the air and my cheek missing his touch.

This time I stay in my room. Tonight it seems to have shrunk even further and every few seconds the blood rushes to my head until I have a crashing headache. Eventually, I resort to counting cows like I did when I was little. Surprisingly, it works.

*****

"It's time for all hands on deck," Cassi says into my ear. I wake so suddenly that I bang my head on the shelf above the bed, then fall back to the pillow with a groan and an unpleasant word.

Cassi only laughs and hands me a steaming cup of coffee. When I take it, she wrinkles her nose and leans forward, sniffing at me. Then she waves her hand in front of her face and says, "You smell like you've been running for hours. Rough night?"

I'm not sure how I feel about being woken after a few restless hours of sleep, striking my head hard enough that I need to probe for a wound and then being told I stink. I sip the hot coffee and glower at her while she waits for an answer. One of her eyebrows creeps up so I finally put the cup down and say, "Come closer for a second."

She gives me a questioning look, but does it. As soon as she is in range, I pull her down on the bed and rub my stink all over her hair. She gags dramatically and laughs, but when I let her go, I feel better. I take my cup, sip my coffee and say, "Want to take a dip?"

Even as I open the hatch, I can tell there's been a change. The air smells different, almost spicy, and the wind is cool and stronger. Cassi motions me onward with a grin on her face and I step up into a whole new world. During the night, we've left the river and entered the Gulf. The ocean. It's almost heartbreakingly beautiful. Puffy white clouds dot the sky and the water is brilliant with a million glints of reflected sunlight. I want to jump in immediately.

Marcus stops us from doing anything so rash, informing us in teacher-like tones that the ocean is not a river and not a forgiving body of water. We nod obligingly until he gives up, hands us two floatation vests and tosses the ladder over the back of the boat so we can get up and down conveniently.

I'm eager until the moment I'm standing over the water, my feet on the top step of the ladder and the choppy waves licking at my feet. I decide there's nothing to do but go for it, so I step down into the blissfully perfect water before I can lose my nerve. There's no possible way to drown in the huge vest. I can barely dip back far enough into the water to wet my head. Cassi splashes in and paddles around, shooting arcs of water out of her mouth at me and making noises of delight that are almost indecent.

Marcus has struck the sails and is using the little engines to keep close. Jovan stays on deck to help him until we come back and he can take a turn. He and Marcus keep looking back toward shore and I know they'd both feel better if we kept moving, even though we have hours of time left. I cut my adventure short since I still feel less confident in the water, especially since I can feel how endless the depth is beneath my feet.

I hand off my vest to Jovan and he wastes no time getting in the water. He fills some pails that I hand down to him so Marcus can wash in the salty water up on deck. Then he swims around like a fish, which is very interesting to watch, and not just because he's beautiful.

Cassi's nose gets red from the sun quickly so she comes back too, wiping a streak of thick white ointment onto her cheeks and nose and cramming a wide-brimmed hat onto her head. Marcus doesn't seem to mind her ridiculous appearance because he kisses her soundly and then taps the tip of her nose with a finger affectionately.

She spends the next hour telling me every detail of a sunken city called Nola that we passed during the night. Half underwater and half not, the tops of taller buildings leaning over the shorter ones and boats tied to anything that stuck up out of the water. I almost regret missing seeing the ghostly ruins as she describes them, but then again, everything fills her with wonder.

Soon enough, fun time is over. We're all a little sticky from the salt but far cleaner. At least I don't smell like the sweat that bathed me in my nightmares anymore. Jovan looks better, too. No one wants to think about what we're going to do, but that doesn't stop us from hanging on every crackle and pop of the radio.

The latest transmission said that Mario was at the final port before they entered the Gulf and that he was refueling. He's not in danger, which is good, and his passenger is behaving, but seems determined. Creedy's also got a serious grudge going against us and isn't shy about sharing it. In a way, this is good news, too. It means that we have no cause to second guess what we're doing.

In a way, I wish Creedy would make a move so that Mario would have to take care of the problem, but that's a cowardly thought and I know it. On the river, there are too many people and sound carries from bank to bank. And Mario shouldn't have to deal with the problem and carry the guilt. Still, if Creedy would just be more himself and do something aggressive, all our problems could be readily solved with no lingering doubts.

Marcus and Jovan get us underway, the sails full and tight in the wind. The strange little turbines on his mast and at the bow whir so quickly they whine even over the sound of the water on the hull. The batteries will charge quickly with that much wind and I'm glad for it. I want every tool we have at our disposal ready when we need it.

With nothing left to do but wait and watch, I decide we might as well eat. I've also decided that I love the idea of refrigerators and already, I miss the delight of cold water and tea straight from inside one. We don't have that aboard the boat, but there is a large ice box, much like a smaller version of the hold where they put their catches, and it's lined in metal and blocks of ice. Marcus says it will last for over a week but even now, there's a small pool of water under the grate near the bottom.

From its depths, I gather all that we'll need for a meal big enough to keep us, but not so much that it will slow us down or make us need naps. There's no fish, which seemed odd until Marcus explained that once they start netting their catches, they eat fish for every meal. His mother likes to start them off with something other than that to keep them happy. It also serves to keep them eager for home when it runs out. That information just makes me like the Flints more.

Jovan helps me, turning the food with quick, meticulous flips of his knife. We're enjoying the meal until the crackle of the radio brings Marcus to his feet, his plate forgotten. There are no words, only pops and squeals, but Marcus takes notes on a slate tied to the console. When it's done, he presses a button in a quick sequence on the radio and then turns back to us with a grim smile.

"They're in the Gulf, past the gate. We've got to slow down and circle back a little or they won't catch us. The waves are a little much out here for Mario to take a long swim," he says and dips the last bits of food from his plate without sitting back down.

We travel back toward land, which is nothing more than a smear of green on the horizon, for about an hour then strike the big sails, leaving only the smaller ones up to keep us steady. The small boat that Mario is in starts as just the smallest dot of white, the blue hull lost against the water. It's easily mistaken for a wave top for a long while, but the steady approach makes it grow until there's no mistaking it for a random wave.

I'm pretty sure it takes a million years for the boat to go from a smear of white to a recognizable boat, but when it does, I want it to go away again. Cassi crouches in front of the wheel, the platform hiding her from view. Marcus steers but keeps looking behind us, gauging the distances and adjusting our course in ways and for reasons I don't fully understand. He looks confident enough, so I ignore that and focus on Jovan.

He's got the detonator clutched tightly in his hand but the safety cap is firmly in place. It's a rather large thing, with a big red case and a handle molded to the shape of gripping fingers. The cap is bright yellow and is perfectly placed so that a thumb can flick it upward to press the button inside. It doesn't need wires, but it has to be close enough that the signal will travel through the air—yet another strange mysterious object from the East.

The roar of Mario's engine changes pitch and the boat lowers in the water as it slows, still a couple of hundred yards from our boat. He turns it sideways to us and I see a figure lurch to the side with the sudden motion. Though he's just a tiny thing from this distance, I can tell it's Creedy when he rights himself. There's an almost tangible chill coming off the water from his direction.

"Are you ready?" I ask Jovan, keeping my eyes on the boat.

He doesn't answer for a moment, just flexes his fingers on the detonator a few times like he can somehow make it more comfortable to hold. "Ready as I'll ever be," he says.

The boat is creeping closer, but slowly. Creedy gesticulates for Mario to hurry, but the boat doesn't speed up at all, which is good. I judge the boat to be about a hundred yards away, perhaps less, when Mario executes a neat dive over the side and into the water. He doesn't delay, and I can see the regular strokes of his arms as he swims away from the boat.

Creedy seems at a loss for a moment, shifting from one side of the boat to the other. He grabs at the wheel and the boat jerks as he clumsily steers. Then he points toward the water where Mario swims away and the report of a gun sounds out. I can hardly believe my ears. He's actually shooting at Mario. I don't think about my actions—or how inexpert I am with a gun—when I reach down and grab the gun from Jovan's belt.

Even if I had actually ever practiced and done more than dry fire a gun, there's no way I would have been able to hit anything at this distance. Even Jovan told me that these types of guns are only good for shooting at a few dozen paces, so they certainly aren't for a target at seventy-five yards and closing. But before all this can do more than flash through my mind, I raise the gun, click off the safety and fire.

The reaction from the other boat is immediate. Creedy ducks down and I see him peek over the console. I have no hope that it hit him and the fact that he doesn't fire back tells me that he knows accuracy at this distance isn't possible and he'd just be wasting ammunition. But that doesn't matter, because he stops firing into the water at Mario and that's all I wanted.

Jovan's looking at me like I just grew another head, but I ignore it and pull him down to make him less of a target. For all I know, Creedy has a better gun than we do and I certainly don't underestimate his ability with a firearm.

"Sorry. But he was shooting at Mario," I say while peeking over the back of the boat. The boat is aimed toward us again and moving slowly our way. He seems to have figured out steering but not speed, because it's still a slow approach only a little faster than ours. The little green light we should see on the top of the detonator is still stubbornly unlit, so we can't just push the button and get it over with. It has to be in range and the detonator's parts must be communicating with each other for it to work.

His eyes keep flicking back from Creedy to the detonator and his jaw is so tight I think he might shatter his teeth. When I peek back up, the boat is closer. It's close enough for me to see the details of the boat and the gray in his hair. A short gasp behind me makes me turn, only to see a slowly blinking light on the detonator. That green flash means it is trying to connect with its twin on the other boat. Jovan looks frozen, his knuckles white around the handle and the cords in his arms standing out like he's carrying an unbearable weight.

I don't need to ask him if he's okay to do this thing. I can see that he's not. He delayed not a second when it came to a stranger in that old building where I lost my father, but this is different and far more personal. I stand so that I'm in full view of Creedy. He's within fifty yards of us now and we can see each other plainly. I hear a shout from his boat and then his hand comes up. It takes all my will not to flatten myself on the ground, but I'm counting on his anger, the motion of two boats and the distance to keep me safe. It's a foolish thing to do but I can't just take the detonator with it gripped so tightly in Jovan's fist and his thumb clamped over the cap. "Down," I say behind me.

Just as I knew it would, a shot rings out and it's close enough to make me cringe, but a quick inventory tells me I'm not hit and the shot went wide. Jovan's free hand tugs at my arm, but I pull right back and say, "Give it to me, Jovan. I'm not going to spend the rest of my life running from him or others like him."

It seems like a short eternity that we stare at each other and when a second shot rings out, I flinch and hear the round thunk into the water ladder, now lifted up and no more than two feet from my legs. Jovan flinches too but stands.

Creedy is perhaps thirty yards from us and the steady green light on the detonator signals its readiness. And now, I think Jovan is ready as well. For a long moment, they look at each other and I see from the corner of my eye as Creedy lowers the gun. Then Jovan flicks the cap and presses the trigger.

Chapter Thirty-Nine

I'm just another girl enjoying the sunshine with pixie short hair and tan lines on my feet. I couldn't be happier about it. Everything else aside, there is something wonderfully liberating about being on the water with no land anywhere in sight. Also a little scary, but I think that's part of the fun of it, too.

Cassi's bright red-gold hair is no more and the dull shade of brown that covers her unique shade somehow makes her look more grown-up. The curls are still there, now hidden by the two tight braids that rest on her shoulders and swing like fat tails when she moves. She's coiling ropes on the deck, excited about the day to come, while I'm doing little to help and just enjoying the way the early sun feels on my skin. It's nice and with the salty breeze, it's like I've grown more nerve endings with which to feel it.

It was hard to cut my hair off, to see it flutter away in the wind and fall into the sea, but I have to admit that I like it now. I don't even need to comb it with anything other than my fingers and the knots that plagued my daily life are a thing of the past. Jovan and Marcus still start now and again when they see me, even though it's been two weeks since I cut it.

Two weeks since the day after our final confrontation with Creedy. By now, the news that Creedy and his boat-load of prisoners were lost at sea has traveled up the river. Given that we radioed that Mario was the only survivor and the family is well known, I'm pretty sure it will be believed by those who need to believe it. I feel bad for our families, but I'm confident our choice was the right one.

Only Mario and Cassi seem to really like my new look and Mario's taste simply can't be trusted. He's long married and has four little girls, so he says everything is pretty as a self-preservation instinct.

Today is our first trade, the first we'll need to make in order to pay back the rather nebulous cost of the boat and engine. I really don't think they actually care much about it and I could probably pay it many times over with what's on my pendant, but it's an excuse for us all to stay together for a while. It gives me the time—and Cassi the time—to decide on the future. I have a feeling that when we move on, Cassi will be staying behind. That's a hard thought and I'm more than willing to put it off.

When we pulled into a huge port called Pensacola, supposedly once a part of Florida but now belonging to the Gulf Cooperative, a quick visit to the wall confirmed my message had reached my father's wife and a return message awaited me. And my approval as a citizen awaited me as well.

My first experience with a computer followed and I was amazed at it. Afraid to touch it, the gate-keeper had operated it for me and I read the glowing letters with trepidation, fearing the words would be accusatory and angry. They weren't though. Instead, the message was simple and direct and very understanding. So much so that I found tears stinging my eyes. She ended by telling me to come when I could, that I was and always would be welcome.

Her words freed me in so many ways. I'm not ready to face them yet. I'm not ready to start a life that I'll continue forever. Right now, I'm just happy to wallow in the pause between lives, relishing the moment.

Not wanting her to think me dead if the news ever made it that far, I wrote back to let her know I was traveling for a while but would see her when I was done. I hope she understands. I hope Quinton, my as yet un-met brother, understands.

On the upside, we were able to get a message to Maddix and Connor. These computers are amazing. All I had to do was give their name and a border worker looked him right up for me. They are fine, though missing us, and making their way to Pensacola to meet up with us. I'll be so happy to see them again, whenever that may be.

Today, we're about twenty miles off the coast of Florida. I can't see it with my eyes, but it's on the chart kept flat and weighed down by old stones. Our trading mission isn't exactly legal or illegal, but lies in the vast gray space between.

Florida doesn't get along with the East or Northeast, but has a relatively benign relationship with the Southeast and the Gulf Cooperative. Yet theirs is the land of the best technology, highly sought after yet traded only under the most stringent circumstances. Hence our little trading deal. Off the books and no one the wiser is how these things are done.

"There they are," Marcus says from the bow, pointing to a spot in the water.

I look out but see nothing for a moment. There's something, a small white spot, far too small to be a boat. After I've got that one resolved, I realize there are two and they are speeding toward us. The ball Marcus dropped over the side on a line will tell their trading partners where we are. I didn't believe it then, but there's no denying the two small white objects coming toward us at a decent clip.

"Okay," Marcus hollers back at Mario, who is tending the wheel. He includes us by saying, "Let's lower the sails and get ready. You three are okay with doing the trade? You're sure?"

I know I am, and the way Cassi is bouncing on her toes says she is as well. Jovan already has the big orange floating buoy and the line attaching it to the boat in hand, ready to toss it over the side at Marcus's sign. I'm guessing that means he's ready to.

"Let's go!" Cassi squeals, tugging on her life vest.

Luckily, these life vests are smaller, the kind meant for people who can swim. Instead of feeling like I'm stuck inside a much too large bubble, it feels like a little orange hug around my middle. As a bonus, they make me feel less self-conscious wearing these so-called bathing suits. Purchased in Pensacola, it clings to my body and makes me feel more than naked. Still, it's better than swimming in my heavy clothes.

The two white-topped buoys come close, but not too close. Both of them have plastic bundles strapped to the top. We'll swap those with our own bundles.

"Looks good. In you go," Marcus says, flipping the ladder over for us. We all clamber down into the choppy water, but it no longer feels strange to have such a yawning depth below me. The water is so blue it's almost magical from far away, but clear as air once you're down in it.

The buoy is attached to a line, which is in turn attached to a winch on the boat. The clicking of the line paying out as Jovan pulls the buoy is loud in the quiet air.

Cassi reaches the nearest buoy first and circles it in delight. We've been told about them, but they are something else up close. Florida is the most advanced of all the territories and zealous about remaining so. No one can even land there save at specified ports, and access beyond is strictly prohibited.

They apparently live very differently than the rest of us. The Flint brothers have told us stories of tall towers where thousands live and work, never leaving the building at all and technology so advanced they can control machines with other machines implanted in their bodies. It sounds rather horrible to me, but who am I to judge?

The buoys seem to give weight to those assertions. Small screens and glossy lenses rise from the surface and I can see more moving around under the water behind thick glass. Marcus says there are people who look through those lenses from back on land, so Cassi does just what I would expect her to do. She ducks under the water and waves into one of the lenses, pressing a kiss to the glass and grinning.

Jovan and I don't dawdle, but unhook the first parcel and replace it with our own. It's heavy, so I'm glad for the buoy. Inside should be advanced engine parts and difficult-to-find computer components. Inside our parcels are things banned in Florida: alcohol of several types, cocoa powder, butter and all sorts of decadent foods. I can't imagine living life without those rich additions now that I've had them. Minus the alcohol, which I won't have anything to do with, of course.

When we move to the second buoy, one of the camera lenses rises from the top inside its protective glass and the little lens darts around until it focuses on me, where it stays fixed. I smile down into the lenses and see the aperture widen and narrow in response, which makes me laugh. I wrap my legs around one of the protrusions off the body of the buoy to remain steady and I can feel the hum inside it as whatever propels and guides it keeps it in position.

Our parcels neatly tied to our buoy, Jovan and I prepare for our swim back. Cassi is already halfway there, swimming with sure strokes. Jovan gives the high sign to Marcus that he can pull in the buoy.

At the last second, he grabs my hand and then grips the handle on the buoy with the other. The buoy shoots forward and Jovan pulls me up until I can wrap my arms around his neck. It's an amazing sensation, zipping through the water so quickly I can feel both of us rise a little. I let one arm go from around his neck and hold it up behind me so that we move more smoothly on the water. Those few seconds feel almost like flight, or like we've become some sort of boat ourselves, the water lifting us like those fish that fly above the water sometimes out here.

It's over quickly and I climb the ladder, bringing my dripping self up on deck. Cassi tosses me a towel on her way to the stern for her hat and I move out of the way so Jovan and Marcus can bring up the laden buoy and inspect their treasures.

It is in that moment that I feel it and freeze, my towel forgotten in my hand. I am free.

I. Am. Free.

My life is my own. I control not just what I do now and in the future, but how I will feel about the past. I get to control how I will let it shape me. And in that liberated moment, I decide that it doesn't matter. I decide that I am grateful for it all. That all my past pain, the fear and everything else in my life was a gift that left me the person I am now. The free, strong girl who stands here with the entire world before her.

Jovan comes up on deck, dripping and golden in the sun. His eyes shine like that hawk's and his smile is tentative for a moment. Whatever he sees must be the answer he's been looking for. I know it's mine.

Just two steps each and we meet in the middle. There are no words, no hesitation. He cups my face in his hands and kisses me. Not the fumbling press of icy lips like in the river, not the uncertain and unskilled kiss behind the school of years before, but a real kiss. My first real kiss. And it is everything I have ever wanted and more. My toes curl into the deck and my arms tighten around his neck until he has to shift his hands from my face to around my back.

The kiss seems to go on for a lifetime and there is nothing else in the world except us. He seems to feel as if he doesn't have enough arms as he holds me, his hands shifting to press me to him, his fingers hot against the knobs of my spine between my shoulders.

Some eternity later, a voice intrudes and Mario says, "Aw, get a room!"

We part then, suddenly aware of the three people looking at us, two with mouths agape and Cassi with a smile from ear to ear.

"About time!" she shouts at us and then disappears into the hatch.

There's no awkwardness, no embarrassment, just the feeling that we've done the right thing at the right time. In front of us the sails snap into place and the boom shivers as the force of the wind tightens it into position. Jovan slips his arm around my waist and it's perfect there, like his arm was designed to fit me and no one else.

For just a flash, I think of the pendant and the life it can provide. But it's just a flash and I push it away. It's a tool meant for me to use, not meant to control my future. I understand that. It was given without obligation. A gift from the father I thought didn't love me. In the end, he gave it all for me, even his life. Someday, I'll venture into the interior of the territories. I'll see the East, the Southeast and maybe even Florida. Those are thoughts for some other tomorrow.

Right now the water ahead of me is so blue it almost rivals the sky. The sun is yellow and warm. Salty water is pooling at my feet and I feel the wind like a beckoning kiss across my skin. And Jovan's arm is around me, finally. Right now, I'm right where I want to be.

Dear Reader

Thank you for reading! I genuinely hope that you liked what you read.

This is a self-published book. I turned down traditional publishing contracts for a few very simple reasons. I want to write what I think will make people happy and do it at the pace that works for readers—and for me. I just can't stand the idea of waiting two years after a book is done to get it out to the readers. So, I take my chances with self-publishing and hope the readers and I can connect somewhere in the vast world of books.

You can help me with that. Self-published books—and self-published authors—rise or fall under the weight of their reviews and the enthusiasm of their readers. If you liked *Strikers*, please take a moment and review it on the site you purchased it from. You'll be doing me a huge favor and allowing me to continue to write quality work without constantly worrying about marketing. And if you really liked it, share the news with fellow readers or on your social network.

You can connect with me on almost every social network and get signed up on my mailing list at http://www.annchristy.com. I send updates and do giveaways of cool swag only for newsletter subscribers. Even free stories now and again!

About the Author

Ann Christy is a career naval officer and secret writer. She lives by the sea under the benevolent rule of her canine overlords and assorted unruly family members. She's been known to call writing fiction a form of mental zombie-ism in reverse. She gets to put a little piece of her brain into yours and stay there with you—safely tucked away inside your gray matter—for as long as you remember the story. She hopes you enjoyed the meal.

36896006R00187

Made in the USA
Lexington, KY
09 November 2014